T0326269

**Her body straightened. She looked him in the eyes.
"If I heal you, then I want something in return."**

He dropped his hand. Surprise shot through him. "You wanna make a deal?" What would a witch leader want from a shifter who lived across the ocean from her?

She nodded, her shoulders going back. "Yes."

To live, he'd do almost anything. "What do you want?"

She met his gaze, her eyes deadly serious. "If I heal you, then we mate. For life."

Wicked Bite

Realm Enforcers, Book 5

REBECCA ZANETTI

LYRICAL PRESS

Kensington Publishing Corp.

www.kensingtonbooks.com

LYRICAL PRESS BOOKS are published by

Kensington Publishing Corp.
119 West 40th Street
New York, NY 10018

All Kensington titles, imprints, and distributed lines are available at special quantity discounts for bulk purchases for sales promotions, premiums, fund-raising, educational, or institutional use.

Special book excerpts or customized printings can also be created to fit specific needs. For details, write or phone the office of the Kensington sales manager: Kensington Publishing Corp., 119 West 40th Street, New York, NY 10018, attn: Sales Department; phone 1-800-221-2647.

LYRICAL PRESS and the Lyrical logo are Reg. U.S. Pat. & TM Off.

First electronic edition: August 2017

ISBN-13: 978-1-60183-868-1
ISBN-10: 1-60183-868-9

First print edition: August 2017

ISBN-13: 978-1-60183-869-8
ISBN-10: 1-60183-869-7

This one's for Karlina Zanetti,
my daughter who inspires me every day.
You're so talented in every area from sports to school,
and the fact that you also work hard to reach
even higher levels of success makes me so very proud.
Your insights and kindness with people are true gifts
for somebody so young. Someday, in the far future
when you're old enough to read my books,
I hope you remember that this one is for you.

I love you, Beans.

ACKNOWLEDGMENTS

I have many people to thank for help in getting this final Realm Enforcer book to readers, and I sincerely apologize to anyone I've forgotten.

Thank you to Big Tone for giving me tons to write about and for being supportive from the very first time I sat down to write. Thanks also to Gabe and Karlina for being such awesome kids and for making life so much fun.

Thank you to Augustina Van Hoven, who came up with the idea of using *Wicked* in the title of the Realm Enforcer books. Thank you for being my friend from the very beginning of this wild publishing journey;

Thank you to my hardworking editor, Alicia Condon, who is talented, creative, and insightful;

Thank you to the Kensington gang: Steven Zacharius, Adam Zacharius, Lynn Cully, Alexandra Nicolajsen, Vida Engstrand, Michelle Forde, Lauren Jernigan, Kimberly Richardson, Fiona Jayde, Allison Gentile, and Arthur Maisel;

Thank you to my wonderful agents, Caitlin Blasdell and Liza Dawson, who work so very hard for me.

Thank you to Jillian Stein for the absolutely fantastic work and for taking such good care of me.

Thanks to my fantastic street team, Rebecca's Rebels, and their fearless leader, Minga Portillo.

And thanks also to my constant support system: Gail and Jim English, Debbie and Travis Smith, Stephanie and Don West, Brandie and Mike Chapman, Jessica and Jonah Namson, and Kathy and Herb Zanetti.

Chapter 1

Somebody was in his cabin. Beauregard McDunphy lumbered around the side of the modest wood structure, his fur rippling in the wind, his big paws leaving tracks in the wet dirt. At one point, not too long ago, he'd been bigger than any bear in the area—shifter or animal. Now he was merely normal size. Yet he could still take a human trespasser without much effort. He lifted his snout, and the fur rose down his broad back.

He was a loner, and he liked his privacy, so anybody who even remotely knew him understood to stay the hell out of his space. What was that smell?

Irish roses and something . . . female. The scent of woman.

He growled, the sound hollow.

Who the hell was in his cabin? He stalked toward the front door, which remained open. Oh, he was going to scare this interloper. He sucked in air to snarl, rolling his neck so he could fully flash his canines.

A woman came into view, turning around, skirt rustling. "There you are."

He paused and studied her. Thick black hair piled on her head, violet-blue eyes, smooth features. Delicate. Something stirred inside him, and he shook his head, trying to focus. Why wasn't she screaming? Most people freaked out when faced with a grizzly bear. Wait a minute. He knew her. Didn't he know her?

She pressed her hands to her hips. Her green houndstooth designer suit looked like something out of the fifties. Somehow, it worked on her. "Do you mind shifting back to human form? We need ta talk."

The brogue. Irish brogue. Pretty eyes. Small stature. Sparks of power all around her.

It hit him then. A witch. There was a witch in his home. He growled again and set his bones to transforming into his human shape. The process took longer than it should have, considering he'd *mainly* been in bear form for nearly three months. Three useless months that hadn't changed a damn thing about his failing health.

Pain lanced down his spine and through his arms. His bones broke and reformed, hurting much more than they should. The fur receded on his arms and then the rest of his body. Agony flared through his face, reshaping it, nearly making him black out. Finally, he straightened, his body elongating. He kept his expression stoic and tried to banish the ache.

"That looked painful," she whispered, her gaze soft on his face.

"It was," he responded before he could think. Then reality crashed back. "Why is there a Coven Nine *witch* in my fucking cabin?" His safe cabin in the Seattle wilderness where witches and the Coven Nine couldn't get to him. What was her name? He couldn't place it. Everything was cloudy. Yet he remembered seeing her in Ireland at witch headquarters—she was a council member. When was that? Months ago.

She hummed and looked around, her gaze high and a light pink dusting her cheekbones.

He settled his stance. His human brain kicked back in. "As a member of the Coven Nine, what are you doing here?" She was on the ruling council of witches, and she should have security all around her. His back stiffened, and he turned to scan for threats.

"I'm alone," she said.

That was impossible. Yet even with his senses returning, he couldn't find any other people near, much less any witches. "Why?" he barked. His voice was rough and hoarse from disuse.

She blew out air, her pretty lips pursing. Her gaze rose nearly to the rough wooden ceiling. If she craned her neck up any more, she might fall backward.

Bear frowned. "What the hell?"

She cleared her throat. "Do you, ah, do you mind?" Her hand swept out, even the small movement graceful.

"Mind what?" he snapped, glancing over his shoulder again. Trees and silence met his gaze. Thunder ripped above, and an angry autumn rain began to slap the ground. Summer had given up the fight, and the oncoming winter scented the breeze. He stepped inside the cabin.

She backed up so quickly her butt hit the ancient stove, and she gave a startled *eep*. "Please, Mr. McDunphy."

What in the world was wrong with the woman? "Please, what?" Was this some kind of trap?

"Put some clothes on," she said through pearly-white teeth.

He started and looked down at his naked body. "Oh." Clothes were such a damn annoyance. "Uh, okay." A small dresser sat by the bed, on the north wall. He moved past the raggedy sofa and modest fireplace to yank out a pair of faded jeans. He struggled into them, wincing as he engaged the zipper.

Life was so much easier as a bear.

He glanced down. The jeans hung low on his hips—nearly too low. How much weight had he lost, anyway? He stretched his arm, noting the reduction in muscle mass. He'd get his ass kicked in a good fight.

The rain increased in force and blew water inside the door. He strode over and shut it. Silence descended. The smell of Irish roses filled the space, and he breathed deep before turning around to face her. He leaned back against the door and crossed his arms. With the dim light sliding in through the windows, shadows cascaded around the woman. But she was all light. What would she look like with that dark hair tumbling free around her shoulders? His groin tightened.

"Mr. McDunphy?" she asked.

"Nobody calls me that. You know my name is Bear." The Coven Nine no doubt had extensive dossiers on him. They probably knew his shoe size, favorite color, and how many freckles he had on his back. He rubbed a hand through his shaggy hair. It reached his shoulders now. While his people weren't enemies of the witch nation any longer, he still didn't like witches. At all. Except for one, and that was because she was his sister.

His memories flooded all the way back in. Ah ha—the trespasser's name. "Why are you here, *Nessa*?"

"You do remember my name." Her focus landed on his chest and moved to his left arm. She gave a slight shake of her head as if to concentrate. "That's, ah, a very nice tattoo."

He glanced down at the talons over his left bicep and shoulder that led to a black dragon across his back. "Thank you." He pushed himself off the door, noting her eyes instantly widening.

So she was afraid of him. At least a little bit. Good.

She cleared her throat. "A dragon. How apropos," she murmured, her focus remaining on the tat.

He lifted his head, staring at her through heavy lids. His chest heated. "Don't even think of going there, little girl. Ever."

She shivered but met his gaze directly. "That's why I'm here."

He blinked. Once. "Then it's time you left." He moved to open the door.

"I can help you," she said.

He paused, looking over his shoulder. "I don't need help."

Her snort was unladylike and somehow adorable. "Sure you don't. Look at you. You've lost substantial weight since I saw you in Ireland."

He turned quickly, gratified when she took a step back, putting her flush against the stove again. There were yards between them, but they both knew he could get there, and fast. Yet as a witch, she had powers, too. So why was she afraid? "I've been on a diet," he lied. His neck started to pound, and his bare feet swelled. His lungs hurt. Hell. Everything hurt. Yet he refused to wince.

She rolled her stunning eyes. "You screwed up, Bear."

"Did I now?" he asked softly.

She swallowed. "Aye. You know as well as I that species, immortal species, can take one form and one form only." She wiped her small hands down her slim skirt.

"Time to leave, Nessa," he said, reaching for the doorknob behind his back. Not in a million years was he going to talk about his health or his lineage with a witch. Even one as pretty and intriguing as the one staring at him . . . and not moving. When he told people to move, they usually moved. "Don't make me kick your pretty ass out."

"You're dying." Her head lifted. "Period."

Yeah, he was. If three months spent mostly in bear form hadn't healed him, then it wasn't gonna happen. "Leave me to it, then." Patience had never been in his arsenal, and he was done. The door opened easily, and then he turned to head straight at her, windy rain in his wake, his bare feet slapping the cold floor.

She held up both hands, her eyes widening as she pressed back against the porcelain stove. "Wait a minute. Just wait. Let me explain."

He stopped two feet from her. What was up with the damsel-in-distress act? In his current state, she could probably take him. "Why aren't you throwing fire?" Witches could alter physics and create plasma fire out of air, and the stuff really burned.

She rolled her eyes and reached behind her to clasp the edge of the cooktop. "We're not in a fight, for goodness' sake. I just want to engage in conversation like civilized people."

He leaned toward her, scenting both fear and awareness. "I'm neither civilized nor part of *people*." He was a bear shifter, for Christ's sake. One who had to get his affairs in order rather quickly. While he'd like to mess around with the witch, and he'd love to get her out of her head and that dignified suit, he didn't have time. "There's nothing to talk about."

She looked up at least a foot to meet his gaze. "You tore yourself apart on a metaphysical level when you shifted into dragon form so many times three months ago."

The hair rose at the base of his neck. His temper stretched awake. "Tell me something I don't know." His father had been a dragon shifter, and his mother a bear shifter. Shifters could only have one true form, and his was as a bear. Shifting into dragon form had been suicide. "But it was worth it."

Nessa's breath panted out. "It was?"

"Yes." He took another step toward her. Shifting into dragon form had been necessary to save his half sister, and he'd known the risk. The cost. But Simone was safe now, so he didn't regret a moment. "Tell me you're not here to study me." As part dragon who'd been actually able to shift into the form, he was an anomaly.

"No," she burst out. "Not at all."

"Nessa," he warned, reaching for her shoulders. Man, he'd love to mess her up. She was just so proper and put together. Damn witch.

She swallowed and went still beneath his touch. "I, ah—"

"Am trespassing," he finished for her. "Now you're leaving." Her bones felt fragile, but warmth came from her body. Witches were hotter than most, weren't they? A tug centered low in his belly. One he ignored. "Thanks for dropping by."

Faster than he would've expected, she slammed the toe of her shoe down on the flat of his foot.

Pain ricocheted up his shin, and he bit back a howl. "What the fuck?" He tightened his hold.

She leaned up into his face, her blue eyes glittering. "Next time, it's the heel."

Not good. That thing was at least four inches long and kind of spiky. He growled and lifted her up on her toes to prevent any further injury.

She gasped, her breath brushing his chin. "Bear."

For good measure, he lifted more, taking her completely off the ground. He didn't have the strength to hold her aloft for long, but a lesson needed to be taught. The second her temper arose, he saw it. "Kick me and you'll regret it. A lot." He leaned down into her face, his nose almost touching hers.

Thoughts crossed her expressive face so quickly he had trouble keeping up. She stared into his eyes. "This is *not* going as planned."

His arms protested, so he lowered her back to her feet as if he were in complete control. Yeah, right. Why hadn't she burned his hands completely off? "What plan?" he rumbled.

She drew air into her pert nose. "That's what I've been trying to explain to you. Do you know how witch powers work?"

He released her, and his palms instantly felt empty. And cold. "Something about quantum physics and altering matter," he said. Truth be told, he didn't give a shit. Witches created fire and threw it, so he got out of the way. It didn't seem to matter *how* they did it. "You're all firebugs."

She sighed. "We use applications of quantum physics, string theory, Brunt's theory, and—" Her gaze narrowed. "Don't look bored."

"I'm not," he said quickly. Then he frowned. "Forget that. I am bored. Get to it."

"Fine. We can alter physics. When you shifted into dragon form, you hurt yourself. I can heal you by the application of physics. I can heal you internally, on a subatomic level."

Hope burst in him, and that just pissed him off. "Bullshit." He shoved his hands in his pockets to keep from grabbing and shaking her. While he wanted her aware of his strength, he didn't want to put bruises on that delicate skin. "If a witch could heal me, my sister would've already done it. What are you playing at, lady?" Simone was half witch, and she could throw fire with the best of them.

Nessa shook her head, and a couple of dark tendrils fell down. "Simone can't heal you. I can."

He lifted his chin. "Explain."

Her mouth tightened. "The vast majority of witches can create fire out of air. A small minority, very small, canna' do that."

He frowned. "You can't create fire?" At her sad shake of the head, he added, "Why not?"

She lifted a shoulder. "It's most likely a genetic mutation, just like anything else. But those few of us who can't create fire can do something else."

"Alter physics on a subatomic level," he whispered.

She sighed. "In ancient times, we were called healers."

He'd thought healers were myths. "You can cure diseases?"

"No." She rubbed her hands together as if chilled. "We can't cure naturally occurring diseases. We can help to heal the types of injuries you created deep down by doing something in such violation of the physics of our world."

He'd violated physics by shifting into a dragon instead of a bear? The entire process had felt terrible. "So you're here to help me. My sister sent you?"

"Aye," Nessa said, looking pointedly at the talons on his bicep.

Warning ticked down his spine. "Nessa?"

"Aye?"

"What aren't you saying?" His body went on full alert.

She didn't so much as twitch. "There's a cost."

"Money?" How disappointing.

"No," she whispered.

He reached out and lifted her chin with one knuckle. Her skin was the softest thing he'd ever felt. "All right. What are you saying?" He wasn't sure he could believe anything she said.

Her body straightened. She looked him in the eyes. "If I heal you, then I want something in return."

He dropped his hand. What would a witch leader want from a

shifter who lived across the ocean from her? "You wanna make a deal?"

She nodded, her shoulders going back. "Yes."

To live, he'd do almost anything. "What do you want?"

She met his gaze, her eyes deadly serious. "If I heal you, then we mate. For life."

Chapter 2

Nessa stared up at the tall male, her voice barely shaking as she made her demand.

He didn't move.

She blinked.

Then he threw back his head and laughed, long and hard. His entire body, his bare chest, even the sharp dragon talons on his arm danced. His laugh was deep and somehow sexy—yet oh so very insulting.

How dare he. She lifted her foot.

He stopped abruptly, and his chin lowered. "I don't give a warning twice."

Her mouth went dry. Even ill, Bear McDunphy was all predator. He looked like a bear, and she had to wonder how humans failed to notice that he wasn't one of them. Not even close. Shaggy brown hair fell to his shoulders with a defiant curl. He stood many inches over six feet tall, and his chest was wide. A promise of danger poured from him. For the briefest of moments, right after he'd laughed, his honey-warm chocolate eyes had softened. A little.

Now they'd returned to the solid hardness of flint.

She slowly lowered her foot back to the floor. "You're correct. Violence doesn't solve anything."

"I disagree." His voice was a low rumble that somehow wound all over her sensitive skin.

She frowned. "What do you mean?"

"Violence can solve a whole lot of situations." He took a step back from her, staring down from his unfair height advantage.

"Figures," she returned, relaxing as he gave her space. "Shifters employ violence when thought and reason would do."

His eyes darkened, and he moved right back into her personal bubble. His knuckles brushed beneath her jaw and caressed down to tug her jacket away from her pounding jugular. "And you want to fuck one until his fangs connect in your flesh."

The image shot into her mind, and tension uncoiled in her abdomen. His touch was warm and oddly determined. Mating a bear shifter, a leader of his nation, would be animalistic. Probably outside the scope of her imagination, such as it was. She was way beyond her comfort zone, so she withdrew into etiquette. "There's no need for such language," she said, her voice going hoarse.

His upper lip quirked. "Baby, you definitely picked the wrong shifter."

No. He was the absolute right shifter—for more than one reason. At the reminder of his species, she relaxed. She could handle this. She smiled.

His eyes narrowed.

She smiled wider.

"What are you up to?" he asked.

More than he could ever know. "You need to be healed. I'd like to be mated. It's a simple transaction."

"Simple?" He snorted. "Right. Matings are never simple."

"This would be." She had it planned. Well, most of it. If she ended up having to kill him, that would be unfortunate. "I heal you, we mate, and then I go on my way." Maybe. Probably not. Evidence showed that Bear was probably a bad guy doing bad things, and she'd have to stop him. *After* they mated.

He rubbed the scruff already appearing on his jaw. "Most witches believe shifters to be a lower class of immortal."

Aye, they did. Shifters were animals, for goodness' sake. "That's not true."

He tugged on a tendril of her hair—none too gently. "One rule. No lying. Got it?"

Her mouth opened and then closed. "Of course." It wasn't a lie to completely leave out most of the truth, was it? Maybe. But she had a job to do. Several, really.

"Why, Nessa?"

The way he said her name, in a way that drew out every sound. Like he was rolling all the letters around and settling on the soft ending. "I'm a century old, and I'm tired of following all the rules— being on the Council and creating laws," she whispered.

His eyebrows rose. "So mating a shifter is your rebellious stage?"

She sighed. "Kind of. It gets me freedom."

He studied her, the hard planes of his face sharp in the dim light. "Bullshit."

She jerked back. Nobody spoke to her in such a manner. "Excuse me?"

"I'm calling bullshit." He crossed his arms. Even weakened by his illness, sinewed muscle flexed. "Let's see. You didn't choose any old shifter. You chose me."

"You require my assistance," she gritted out, her breath heating. Thunder rolled outside, and she jumped.

His eyes glittered in the small cabin. Even just standing and talking, he was all predator. "I'm a bear shifter who has turned into a dragon before." His voice grew thoughtful. "Dragons employ fire . . . like witches."

She couldn't back up any more. Oh, she'd underestimated Bear McDunphy. He was much smarter than she'd thought. "Yes."

"Mating me might give you the ability to create fire," he said slowly. "Interesting. Why don't you just mate another witch and get his powers?"

She sighed. Revealing secrets of any kind went against her very DNA, and pretty much everything having to do with witches that the rest of the world didn't know—was a secret. Yet there was no doubt Bear wouldn't cooperate with her until she gave him a truthful answer. Aye, she had to respect him for that. "When a witch healer mates a fire-throwing witch, both powers are subdued. They both get weaker instead of stronger."

"You sure?" He lifted both eyebrows.

She nodded. "Aye. It has happened twice that we've tracked." She definitely wanted the ability to throw fire and fight, to not be such an oddity. Especially in her line of work. "You've figured out my motivation." One of them, anyway.

"Have I?" he asked silkily, his hard stare going right through her.

Bollocks. He was beyond smart. So much for the good-ole-boy act. Just who was Bear? "Aye," she murmured.

"How many witch healers are there?" he asked.

"Not even ten that I know of," she said.

He lifted his chin. "That is rare, then. Your parents?"

"Were both healers," she said. "Lost them before I remember." She didn't have time to really get to know him. "My offer?"

"What happened to your parents?" he asked, completely ignoring her words, his eyes mellowing to the color of an expensive bourbon catching candlelight.

She shook her head, and more of her hair escaped the pin. "We don't need to bond."

He pulled on another tendril, and the pin dropped to the floor. Her hair cascaded down. He exhaled sharply.

"Uh," she murmured, pressing back.

"Pretty." He tangled one broad hand in her hair, his voice roughening even more. He leaned in and sniffed. "Roses."

She held perfectly still. Her body flared alive, and lava heated through her abdomen. "Bear? This is unnecessary. No bonding. Let's reach an agreement." Her voice remained level only through supreme effort.

He straightened, and his smile was almost lazy. "Baby? You wanna fuck, bite, brand, and mate . . . but not bond. Do I have it right?" His hold tightened.

Erotic tingles rippled along her scalp, and she couldn't help a small gasp. "That isn't quite how I'd put it, but close enough," she said primly. Her clothes suddenly felt too restrictive. The shifter was overwhelming her, and she needed to regain control. "Would you please step back?"

His grin widened. "We're gonna have to get a lot closer than this for your plan to work."

Bear. Naked. Over her. The images slammed through her brain so fast she could barely breathe. Her nipples peaked against her thin cotton bra. Maybe this had been a bad idea. "Perhaps we should re-think this."

He leaned in, his lips barely brushing her temple.

Her knees wobbled.

"What happened to your parents, Nessa?" he asked softly, his breath heating her skin.

She swallowed over a lump in her throat. "Ah, they were, ah, killed in a skirmish with a demon squad." Now witches and demons were allies. Life was weird. "I was raised by my Uncle Boondock— a witch who taught me to sew and shoot arrows by the time I was five."

Bear remained way too close. "Sounds like a character."

That was the understatement of the millennium. "Aye. He's a healer, too." She slapped both hands against Bear's naked chest and shoved. Hard.

He didn't move a centimeter.

Hard and smooth, his chest warmed her palms. What would he be like at full strength? Healthy and complete? She spread her fingers out and slid healing heat inside, seeking the damage he'd caused by defying physics and her laws.

Bear jolted.

"Let me show you," she murmured, stepping closer to him and resting the side of her face against his upper chest. Her hands moved lower, toward his solar plexus. She closed her eyes to concentrate and settled in, her body starting as she brushed against an obvious erection. Her knees almost gave this time. "Well then." She moved slightly to the side, her hands moving with her.

He sucked in air. "What are you doing?"

"Showing you." She concentrated harder, going beyond muscle, bone, and tissue. The need to heal lived within her, so she went deep looking for the damage. Beyond the physical. Somewhere else. A place fundamental to shifters, one below and behind Bear's heart. The damage there, the rips and gouges, made tears fill her eyes. In him, trying to help him, she shared his pain.

She heated her energy, slowly and methodically picturing the essence of Bear healing.

His growl was a low roll of pleasure.

She shivered. The damage was extensive, so she concentrated on one small area, soothing it over and putting the pieces back together, much like restructuring a bone. But this was more fundamental than a mere bone. All sounds and sights of the world around her disappeared. Nothing else existed. She lost herself in repairing that small part of the damage. Her hands began to shake, and her strength ebbed. She swayed.

"Hey." Bear grabbed her shoulders and held her upright.

She jerked back into the present. Drawing a deep breath, she slowly tried to move away from him. There was no way he'd been in bear form for three solid months, or there'd be at least a little more evidence of healing. He had definitely shifted from bear to man more than a couple times during the summer. What had he been doing?

He held her in place until her legs regained enough strength for her to stand on her own. She looked up at him.

He studied her, his eyes unreadable, his entire body one long solid line. Gone was the dangerously teasing cranky Bear. This was the real Bear, and he was way too primitive.

This was too much. *He* was way too much. She'd overestimated her power and strength, and she'd underestimated his.

"That felt good," he said softly.

She nodded. "You have a lot of damage." Could she completely heal him? She wasn't even certain any longer. "I've never seen anything like it. Ever."

"I'm sure," he murmured. "Mating a witch would help me, right?"

She stilled, and the walls felt like they were getting closer. "Probably."

"Mating a witch with healing abilities would probably really, really help," he mused.

She couldn't see past him to the door. "I, ah—"

"You wanna back out, Councilwoman?" he asked, not moving an inch.

The use of her former, temporary, title reminded her of all she had to lose. All she had to gain. Yet her plan, her glorious plan of mating him and remaining in perfect control of the situation, seemed silly now. The situation was beyond her. The male was way beyond her, and she'd only gotten a glimpse of who he really was. What had she been thinking? "I'm not certain I fully thought this out," she admitted.

The corners of his eyes crinkled. "No shit."

She cleared her throat.

"I'm thinkin' it's too late to back out," he said.

Her chin lifted. "That is not your decision."

"Isn't it?"

Oh, she'd give anything for the ability to throw fire. To burn him a little. "No."

He released her and traced one finger—just one finger—across her cheekbone, nose, and down her jaw. "I've never had anybody that was just mine. All mine."

His touch ignited her skin, heating all the way down her body. A pulse set up between her legs. She kept perfectly still. "I have no intention of being all yours. If this happens, after a lot of negotiation, then we'll go our separate ways."

His hand caressed down, easily enclosing her entire neck. "You really think that's how a mating happens with a shifter? Any shifter? Much less with me?" His hold was infinitely gentle, but the strength in those fingers, in that broad palm, couldn't be denied. "You chose an alpha, baby. Head of the entire grizzly nation."

"Aye," she whispered, her trachea moving against his hold.

His head lowered slowly, deliberately, his molten gaze trapping hers. "Do you honestly think I'd let my mate go? Ever?"

She couldn't shake her head, so she didn't. "A mating of convenience doesn't carry possession with it." While she wanted to sound determined, her tone had gone breathy. Soft.

"There ain't nothin' convenient about a mating." He leaned in, his lips barely brushing hers. "Possession is too tame of a word to describe what mating me would *carry with it.*" His emphasis on her words held a clear warning.

Yet if she was correct about him, very soon he'd have a lot more to worry about than an absent mate. "I need ta think about this." The more nervous she became, the stronger her brogue emerged. She cleared her throat. "If we're going to discuss this rationally, then we both need to sit down and introduce our terms."

"Terms?" Amusement lightened his eyes to a honeyed warmness. "Seriously?"

She began to nod just as he straightened and stood back. His head lifted, and he scanned the area, his body going tense.

Witch signatures and power slammed into her a second later. She sucked in air. They were close. She'd been distracted by Bear and hadn't been paying attention.

He kept perfectly still, his gaze slashing to her. "There are witches on my property."

"Aye," she said weakly, looking for the door. How had they found her so quickly in Seattle? She'd left no trace.

"Friends of yours?" he asked.

"No." Just as she said the word, the door burst open. "Run!" she screamed.

Chapter 3

Bear rolled over Nessa, tucking her into his chest and dropping to the ground. "Stay. Cover your head when I shift." He moved into a crouch.

She gasped and curled, slapping her hands over her ears and shutting her eyes.

He leaped over the crappy sofa, shifting in midair and sending out a wave of power strong enough to cause concussions. The air vibrated and shimmered behind him. Excruciating pain flared through his head, blurring his vision for a second as he turned back into a bear. His eyesight cleared just as he reached the door and crashed into two men, throwing them both out into the pounding rain. Animalistic rage consumed him, along with the smell of Irish roses.

The first guy flashed fire down his arms and burned Bear's right paw. Agony burst through him. Bear snarled and struck out, slicing his razor-sharp claws through the witch's neck. The witch fought hard, struggling, flaring more fire down his arms. Flames burned into Bear's chest, and he roared. Fury raked him, so he dug through cartilage and bone to reach the mud beneath his enemy—severing the head from the body. He batted the head toward the forest.

He turned for the other threat, rain matting his pelt. His hindquarters went numb. Where was the other guy?

"Bear?" Nessa whispered from the porch.

Ah, shit. He spun to see the other witch, a tall blond man dressed in black combat gear, holding a knife to her throat. She'd gone pale, and her eyes glowed a frightened blue in her classically beautiful face.

"Shift back to human," the man ordered.

Bear growled. His shredded jeans had sunk into the mud. Sucking deep, he rose on his injured hind legs and forced his unwilling body to change shape again. The air popped around him, and even he could smell his pain on the wind. His arms changed first, and all the fur receded. Then his face broke and reshaped with loud cracks. Tears filled Nessa's eyes. Even the guy holding her swallowed, his lip twisting. "Whoa," the guy muttered.

Bear forced his legs to turn back to human form, each broken bone an agonizing snap. Finally, he stood in the rain, buckass naked, his hair falling into his face. He smoothed it back. "Who are you?"

The guy shook his head. "What is wrong with you?"

Bear edged toward them, trying to concentrate on the threat and not on Nessa's fear. "We don't have that kind of time."

"I don't have a problem with you," the guy said. "Let us leave, and then you can just deal with whatever you have going on."

"Why?" Bear wiped rain off his face, even as it poured harder from the sky. While he had no intention of mating a witch, ever, he didn't like trespassers. Nessa was on his land, on his property . . . and nobody took from him. "Why do you want her?"

Nessa struggled, and the guy pressed the knife into her neck, causing a small cut. She stilled.

Her blood scented the air, and everything in Bear settled. He stopped feeling the pain in his arms and chest. His legs held fast. "Not gonna ask you again."

"Lark Redmond," the guy said. "My name."

"The bounty hunter?" Bear took another step forward, each movement spiking pain up his calves. He'd heard about the guy but they'd never met.

"That's me." Redmond smiled, full of confidence. Since he'd been collecting bounties for two centuries, the confidence was probably earned.

Why was a bounty hunter after Nessa? When Bear had gone under for the summer, he'd made sure the Coven Nine Council was back in working order, complete with the protection of Enforcers and the Guard—all of whom worked in Ireland. It was necessary for his sister's sake. None of this was making sense, and an odd ringing set up throughout his head to pound in his ears. "I'm wondering why you're holding my guest, and I'm really not liking it. I've already taken one head today and wouldn't mind taking another."

"Your guest? That's rich," Redmond scoffed. "You can barely stand." He held out his free hand, and a ball of lightning-blue fire morphed into a weapon. "I can smell your burned flesh from here. Do you really want to do this?"

"I asked you a question," Bear said evenly, his senses finally tuning in to the area. His clubhouse, garage, and shop were only half a mile away, and there should be shifters ready and able to help fight. They should've already caught wind of the witches. But as he reached out, he couldn't sense anybody. Damn it. "Why Nessa?"

"She's just the bounty, buddy. I don't know anything about it." Redmond drew her closer. "Now get out of the way. I have a car waiting on the road."

Where were his people? Bear eyed the plasma ball. If it hit him square on, it'd knock him out. He wasn't strong enough to fight Redmond while remaining in human form, but he wasn't sure he'd survive another shift. His illness was progressing way too quickly. "Who wants her?"

"Ah, man. You know I can't divulge that kind of information and then let you live." Redmond pulled Nessa to the right of the porch.

She kept her head up so the knife didn't cut her. "What's the price?" she hissed.

"One billion. Human dollars." Redmond lost the smile. "I'm not the only one after you."

She swallowed. "Wonderful."

Bear stepped over the corpse on the ground. "You're just gonna leave your dead friend?"

"Wasn't a friend. Local muscle who got me to your cabin." Redmond didn't even shrug. "You going to get out of the way?" He lifted the fire.

Nessa shot an elbow into his gut, jerked away from the knife, and then executed a perfect roundhouse kick to the rib cage.

Redmond stumbled back, righting himself on the cabin wall. "Bitch."

"That's not nice." She threw a hook punch to Redmond's jaw and then kneed him in the groin. He doubled over with a squeal of panicked pain.

"You can fight?" Bear said, moving closer in case she needed backup, his limbs barely following his brain's instruction. He stumbled. His vision went gray.

"I'm a hundred years old," she gasped, punching Redmond repeatedly in the lower abdomen, looking like a lady from the previous century in her pretty skirt and proper blouse. One who could kick some ass if necessary. "Of course I can fight."

Redmond reared up, screaming. He lifted his arm with the fire.

"Nessa," Bear yelled, moving toward her just as Redmond smashed the fire across Nessa's upper chest. Bear rushed for them and grabbed Redmond, throwing him face-first into the log siding. Blood sprayed. He smashed Redmond's head back and forth twice, as hard as he could, before shoving the asshole to the ground. Bear moved toward Nessa. Could he get her to the river fast enough?

She watched him, the blue fire playing across her upper chest and neck. Then she smiled, and the fire was snuffed out.

He stumbled. His head went numb. "What the hell?"

"Fire doesn't harm me. Part of the curse, I guess. Did I not mention that fact?" She moved closer, her face wavering before him. "Bear? Are you all right?"

Redmond shoved to his feet, his face a bloody mess. He fell off the porch and turned, running toward the forest.

Everything in Bear screamed to hunt and kill. He turned and bunched his muscles. His legs gave, and he dropped to one knee. Damn it. He swayed. The last thing he felt as darkness tried to take him was Nessa's soft hands catching his head before it smacked onto the rough boards of the porch.

Nessa stoked the fire she'd created hours ago and turned back to the silent male on the worn cabin floor. She'd been able to drag him inside, but there was no way she could lift him to the bed. So she'd covered him with a blanket and set a pillow beneath his head, trying very hard to ignore his nudity.

Her hands ached, and she shook them out, moving back to her perch next to him. The rain had lightened outside but the wind had increased in force, scattering pine needles against the cabin. A wolf howled in the far distance followed by a mournful train whistle echoing over the mountains.

It had taken an hour to heal most of the burns over Bear's chest and arms. Then she'd set to work on a deeper level, trying to repair the damage. For the first time in her life, she wasn't sure she could heal an immortal injury. It was too massive. Even injuries from a demon mind attack didn't cut so deeply or permanently. Could she save Bear?

She brushed his now dry hair away from his rugged face. The firelight flickered across his features, highlighting his prominent brow, straight nose, and stubborn chin. Her fingers traced along his scruffy jaw and down the strong cords of his neck to his collarbone. Even that was masculine.

The dragon talons on his bicep looked deadly sharp and somehow glowed in the firelight. She caressed each one, impressed with the play of muscle beneath the ink. Even injured to this degree, his body was all male. She swept her hands across his chest and down, counting the ridges of his abdomen. So many.

"Keep going," he whispered, his voice gruff and growly.

She started and looked up to see his gaze on her. Honey and chocolate. Bear's eyes. "How are you feeling?" she murmured.

"Better." He reached up and tucked a tendril of her hair behind her ear before looking at his healed arm. "The burn is almost gone. Did you do that?"

"Aye." She sat back on her haunches.

He traced beneath her eye. "It tires you. Healing people."

She nodded. "The energy needed to heal is much like that needed to make fire. It's all a workout."

"Does it hurt?" He stretched his other arm above his head, gingerly at first and then with more strength.

"Yes."

He stilled and focused back on her. "It hurts?"

"It can." How could she explain to him? "The burns didn't hurt, and stitching a broken bone doesn't take much. But the fissures you've put in your energy are deep."

"If it hurts you, we're not doin' it."

She rolled her eyes. "Healing you won't kill me. After about an hour, it feels like a rubber band snapping against my skin." It was the closest she could come to describing the sensation, though she'd underplayed the pain involved.

His focus narrowed as he sat up fully. "Healing others doesn't hurt for the first hour?"

"No." That was mostly true. The blanket fell to his waist, barely covering him. She tried to keep her breathing normal and her expression mildly interested, but it cost her.

His lips twitched. "What else did you do to my poor naked body while I was out cold?"

Her cheeks heated. Thank goodness it was dark in the cabin. "You're hilarious." Not that she hadn't noticed, well, him. She had had to drag him inside before covering him with a blanket. The guy was gifted. "I'm afraid all I did was heal you."

He swallowed and slid one hand beneath her hair to cup her nape. "Thank you, Nessa." His gaze dropped to her lips.

Her breath caught and held. "You're welcome."

"I'm feeling a lot better," he mused, drawing her toward him.

She should stop. But she allowed him to move her until she was in his space, his mouth so close. He was such a mystery to her. His hand tightened on her nape, holding her in place.

Her lungs stopped working.

He leaned in, his lips brushing hers.

Electrical shocks zipped through her body.

He hummed and moved in again, his focus absolute. His lips were warm and firm, and they settled against hers as if they belonged right there. His tongue ran along her bottom lip.

She sucked in air, mini-explosions rocketing through her.

He settled over her again, this time kissing her. Her eyelids fluttered shut, and she leaned into him. The lazy kiss was all relaxed Bear as he explored her, his tongue moving inside her mouth, his movements gentle and deliberate. He took his time, slowly deepening the kiss and pulling her toward him until she was in his lap.

She pressed a hand against his chest, leaning into him, her mind blanking.

There was only pleasure. Hot, smooth, nearly drugged pleasure from his kiss. She'd never in her one hundred years been kissed like that, with complete focus and leisure. Need swept through her with a painful edge. It was too much. She needed to concentrate—to think. So she pushed against his chest and tried to lever her head back.

She didn't move.

Her eyelids opened.

So did his.

Those eyes studied her, his mouth on hers, his body bracketing her.

She couldn't speak. Even if his mouth hadn't remained right on hers, she couldn't think of any words.

Then he growled.

The sound rumbled up from his chest and into her mouth. The sound, the vibration, ran right through her with the sense of a claim. She trembled.

He held her there for a moment longer and then slowly lifted his head.

She gulped in air, her mind still blank. Her body rioted with conflicting impulses. To run or to push closer to him? She blinked. This was way out of her control. Slowly, she came back to reality. The fire crackled and the wind burst wildly outside. Only a threadbare blanket was between her and his hard erection. Really hard. Was there steel in shifters? A hysterical giggle tried to push its way out of her.

She forced it down. "Um."

"Yeah." He kneaded the back of her neck.

She wanted to snuggle against him. No. Enough of that. "We, ah, we need to talk."

"You think?" he asked dryly.

The door burst open—again—and he jumped to his feet between her and the intruder. Her rear hit the floor, and she winced from the pain, turning to face the newest threat.

"Hold still, or I'll blow your head off," yelled a harsh male voice as a man pointed a gun inside.

Chapter 4

Bear kicked the blanket out of his way. He knew the voice. "Lucas?"

Lucas stepped farther inside, his shoulders barely clearing the door. "Bear. What the fuck?"

Bear grinned and moved toward his second-in-command. He clasped Luke's arm. "It's so good to see you." He'd missed his friends as he'd roamed the forest, trying to mend. Being in bear form had been his only chance. Now Nessa was.

Lucas lowered his gun and then tucked it in the back of his dark jeans. "Dude. Put on some pants."

Oh yeah. Bear snorted and yanked Lucas inside before shutting the door against the wind. "Lucas, this is Nessa. Nessa, this is Lucas. He's been running the Grizzlies since I, ah, took a sabbatical." Lucas was also his best friend and had been for three decades. They'd both been alone, orphaned years before they'd met. They'd instantly bonded and created the Grizzly Motorcycle Club. Bear strode over to the dresser in the corner and yanked out a pair of jeans. There were a couple of holes down the legs, but they covered everything.

Lucas stepped from one foot to the other, his gaze roaming the room. Finally, he moved to Nessa and held out a hand. "Hi."

Tension rippled down Bear's back. Geez. Lucas was his best friend, and here Bear was, turning possessive. Anyway, no way in hell was Bear mating a witch. Ever. They were full of secrets and intrigue. So why care if Lucas touched the woman? Bear reached for a dark T-shirt to tug over his head.

"Hi." Nessa shook hands and then stood. She edged toward the door. "You gentlemen most likely have much to discuss."

"You're not going anywhere," Bear said evenly. They needed to talk about a few things, including why bounty hunters were on her ass. He had the terrible feeling that if he let her go he might never see her again. Why that mattered, he'd figure out later. He could still taste her—sweetness and woman.

She turned, a fight in her eyes.

Lucas cleared his throat. "When did you get back, what's going on, and why is there a dead witch out front?"

Bear frowned. "Oh yeah. We might want to get rid of him."

"I'll have it taken care of," Lucas said, his brow furrowing. "Um. Wanna catch me up? I thought you'd be gone a few more months."

"I'm feeling better." Bear stretched his neck. Whoa. He really did feel better. A lot better. Tingles of the healing kind spread throughout his body. His natural healing abilities had kicked in again. They had been useless just last week. Excellent. Nessa was amazing. He smiled at her.

She frowned back. "You can't keep me here."

He lost his grin. "Wanna bet?"

The sound of Metallica echoed on the wind. Bear lifted an eyebrow.

Lucas shrugged. "It's Friday night—not even midnight yet. We all just got back from a ride, and now we're having a party."

"Well then." Nessa smoothed her skirt down and turned to leave, prim and proper once again. "I'll leave you to your celebration."

Bear moved to intercept, easily putting his back to the door. "I'm not messing around, Nessa. You're staying here until I know all the facts." And until he kissed her again. Yeah. One more kiss. The first one would've knocked him on his ass had he not already been sitting, but it had to be a fluke, an effect caused by his illness and returning strength. That made sense. Plus, he liked the way she tasted. And he wanted to hear the little sounds she made deep in her throat again.

"Bear?" Lucas asked.

Bear shook his head. He'd totally forgotten his friend. "Sorry. Still getting used to human form. My brain is on one track and hasn't begun multitasking again."

"Uh-huh," Lucas said, looking from him to Nessa and back again. He shuffled his feet. "Are you better?"

"Yeah," Bear said. "I'm back."

"Thank God." Lucas ran a hand through his long hair. His gray shirt stretched tight across his chest. "I hate being in charge. It's been a disaster."

Bear frowned. Had Lucas gotten bigger? "Why?"

Lucas popped his knuckles. "I'll get you all caught up tomorrow. For now, how about we party? Nessa is right. We should celebrate." His grin was infectious.

Bear wanted to know what he was walking into. Especially if Nessa was with him. "First give me a heads up."

Lucas sighed. "All right. When Titans of Fire was blown up and disbanded, the DEA got pissed. They'd had some sort of undercover op going on, and it was lost. Mainly."

"Wait a minute." Bear lowered his tone. "Fire got blown up?" What had his friends done?

"Titans of Fire?" Nessa asked.

"Rival motorcycle club," Bear said. "Human. They were trafficking Apollo." Shouldn't she know that, considering Apollo was a drug that killed both humans and witches? She was on the Council and must know all about Apollo and Titans of Fire—especially since three of the witch Coven Enforcers had gone undercover with the club.

"That's right. I'd forgotten their name," she said.

Uh-huh. Like she forgot stuff. What was she playing at? Bear scrutinized her.

Lucas settled his feet. "The DEA looked at us—tried to take us apart. We're good, but they froze our accounts for a while, and we've had to make do."

"Are the accounts still frozen?" Bear asked.

"Yep," Lucas said.

That was unfortunate. Who did they know who could take care of the DEA problem? There had to be somebody with clout. Yet he hated owing favors. "Are the Coven Nine Enforcers still in town?" Bear asked.

Lucas looked toward Nessa.

"She's okay. No secrets," Bear said easily. He turned toward her. "I can just ask you. Are your Coven Nine Enforcers still in Seattle?" The enforcers worked only for the Council of the Coven Nine and weren't attached to the Irish Guard, the witch main police force. The enforcers had been undercover as members of the Titan's MC, trying to find the manufacturer of Apollo.

She cleared her throat. "No. They're in Dublin helping the Council to rebuild. One of the enforcers actually blew up your rival MC."

Bear blinked. He'd wanted to blow up Titans of Fire for a decade. His mouth turned down. He'd missed the fun. "It was Daire."

"Nay. Adam." Nessa grinned. "Seemed expedient to him."

That made sense. Daire was all temper, and Adam more seasoned. "It did take care of the problem." Bear smiled. "So Apollo is no longer on the streets."

Nessa frowned. "Wrong."

That was not what he wanted to hear. "Who's distributing the drug now?"

"We don't know yet," Lucas said. "For this brief time, can we just have a good night? You're back." He clapped Bear on the arm. "It's been lonely without you."

"Agreed." Bear could worry about the business tomorrow. Tonight, it was time for fun. He looked over Nessa's prim suit. All it was missing was a pillbox hat. Yet with her hair down and a lovely flush over her face, she looked stunning. Her rosy lips didn't hurt her appeal, either. "Wanna go to a party?"

"No." She tapped her high heel.

The woman hadn't even taken those off while healing him? His grin even felt determined. Oh, there was no way the witch was getting out of his hands until he figured her out. Figured her game. Plus, he owed her. So, he'd take care of the asshole who'd put a bounty on her head. No way was she getting kidnapped on his watch. "I pay my debts, darlin'."

"You're not in debt to me." She glanced at Lucas and then back to Bear. "Plus, I haven't done that much."

Translation: he wasn't completely healed. Yeah, he already knew that. But for the first time in too long, he could see clearly and his body didn't feel three billion years old. Apparently, she didn't want Lucas to know her skill. That was fine with Bear. He liked being on the inside of her little world. "You're staying tonight, so accustom yourself to that fact right now."

Fire flared in her stunning eyes.

He held up a hand. "I'll put you up in a nice hotel, if you want.

Room to yourself." The bounty hunter was just off lickin' his wounds; he'd be back at some point for her. "But until I figure out who's after you, you're staying." The idea of mating her was certainly interesting but was never gonna happen. Not with a witch. Yet it was fun to mess with her. "Plus, what about your plan?"

"I believe it might have been ill-conceived." She straightened her jacket. "Yet we should still talk it out." Her slim shoulders steeled beneath the jacket. "I suppose I could attend your party."

Lucas rubbed the back of his neck. "Is there anything I should know? Somebody is after us?"

"No. Her," Bear said. "The stiff out front was a bounty hunter. We need to find out who's looking for her." He settled, his mind finally clicking into gear. Man, it felt good to think clearly again. "Nessa? Do you have any idea who's after you?" Yeah, he should've asked that earlier. But he'd been too busy kissing her.

"No." She swallowed, moving the very fine line of her throat. "I don't."

Bear cocked his head to the side. Was she lying? If so, she was damn good at it. He surveyed her, head to toe. All lady, all prim and proper. She wasn't lying. "I'm gonna help you find out."

She threw out her hands in protest. "I donna' need help."

That brogue just got sexier and sexier. "That's too bad," he said cheerfully. "If you didn't want help, you shouldn't have kissed me like that."

Her blush deepened.

Lucas groaned and headed for the door. "I can see you're just as smooth as ever with the ladies."

"I do have a gift," Bear said amiably, reaching for Nessa's hand. When she tried to tug free, he just held on tighter. Man, she was fun to play with. He'd like to muss her all up—see that mass of dark hair spread out over a pillow. Or his lap. "Has it stopped raining?"

"Yeah. I have a four-wheeler around the corner but no top on it yet." Lucas grinned. "Had to cut the engine to sneak up on the cabin. Didn't know it was you."

"You did a good job," Bear said, all but dragging Nessa onto the porch.

"I'm not sure—" she started.

He stopped and looked at her shoes. Man, he'd love to see her in nothing but those dangerous spikes. "You're right." Leaning in, he lifted her against him. "Those things will stick in the mud."

She yelped and slapped a hand against his chest. "*What* in the world are you doing?"

"Walking." Bear ignored the curious look on his buddy's face as he strode down the worn steps for the trail. Man, she felt good in his arms. Almost too good.

Lucas followed behind. "You forgot shoes."

Bear looked down at the mud covering his feet. "Well, shit."

Chapter 5

Nessa settled on Bear's lap on the four-wheeler. The thing definitely had four wheels. The seats were leather, the engine quiet, and the mud—everywhere. His big frame encircled her, keeping her easily in place as Lucas drove much too quickly down an incredibly dark trail. "Don't you need shoes?" she asked, trying not to curl right into Bear's hard body. His muscle mass was already increasing to normal, but he had a long way to go internally.

"I have boots at the club," he said, his breath hot on her ear. "They're probably still where I left them."

She swallowed.

The night air whipped at them, but his body gave off enough warmth that she barely felt the chill. He tugged her closer, giving her no choice but to be right where she really wanted to be. She settled her face against his neck and let her body relax into his hold.

"There you go," he rumbled, tucking her more safely against him.

This was insane. She'd heard rumors that Bear was crazy—yet she hadn't seen that in him. And while he seemed to take his time, he was more deliberate than slow. How many people had he charmed with his easygoing facade? Did it really hide a killer? She stiffened.

"Relax, baby," he whispered, his big hand spread across her back. "You're safe."

She barely stopped herself from scoffing. Safe? Yeah, right. Not. Not even close. He had no clue. "Thanks," she whispered back.

What would it be like to really belong with a male like him—*if* he was a good guy? He didn't kiss like a good guy, and that's why the kiss had been so incredible.

Lights soon came into view. She turned her face just enough to see the back of Bear's sprawling clubhouse and garage. "I've never been to a motorcycle gang party," she said. Was her outfit all right? "Club. Motorcycle club," Bear said, sitting straighter. "We'll grab my boots and then head to the party. Drop us by the office, Lucas."

Lucas nodded, yet another male of few words. He whipped the vehicle around the side of the building, and they landed on wet pavement. "There you go."

Bear stood, still holding her.

She looked around. Big garage doors took up nearly a block, while the wide-open windows of a clubhouse showed a party in full force: dancing bodies, loud music, and the smell of tequila. "Oh my."

Bear chuckled and moved toward a man-sized door that he nudged open with his hip. He set her down gently inside. "Give me a sec to wash off my feet with the hose. I'll be right back."

She found herself inside a room smelling of dust and paper. Fumbling for the light switch, she gasped when her fingers flicked it on and the area was illuminated. Papers, manila envelopes, and file folders covered every surface. A desk seemed to take up the far wall, with a couple of mismatched chairs stuck around it. A fan spun in the corner, and papers on top of a battered metal file cabinet ruffled from its wind. Even the floor was covered in loose papers.

Bear ambled inside.

She moved to calm him. "I think you've been robbed."

He looked around and frowned. "Robbed? What do you mean?"

She paused. "Well, this room." She swept her hand out at the complete disaster. "Somebody tossed the place."

Bear grinned. "Nope. This is exactly how I left it."

Horror. True and real horror filled her. "Who-why?"

He moved into the corner and kicked some temporary file boxes out of his way. "It's organized. I can find anything." He reached down for a pair of huge black boots to pull onto his feet.

This was beyond terrible. Dust filled her nose, and she gave a delicate sneeze.

"Bless you."

"Thank you." Her hands fluttered, actually fluttered, with the need to organize the space. This was insane. She calmed herself. Wait a minute. This might be a godsend. "You know, I find myself at loose ends right now."

He turned. "You're not on the Council anymore?"

"Did I not mention that fact?" she asked, trying to appear innocent.

"No. No, you didn't." He crossed his arms, looking more than a little dangerous. "Why would anybody give up a seat on the Council of the Coven Nine?"

When only telling half a story, it was imperative to use as much truth as possible. "Well, to be honest, I was just put on the Council during the turmoil, to observe Peter Gallagher. It was a temporary assignment."

Bear breathed out. "Was it, now?" His eyes glittered.

"Aye." She cleared her throat. Gallagher had put a death sentence on Bear's sister's head while also expunging the Council of pretty much all the other council members. "As you know, he was up to no good." Now that he was dead, the Council had been set to rights, with the correct members back on. "I am no longer needed on the Council."

"Who put you in place?" Bear asked, his lips thinning.

No need to lie. Not really. Okay, kind of. "Vivienne Northcutt," Nessa whispered. Vivienne had led the Council for centuries until Peter had her removed. Now she was back in place. She was also Simone's mother, and she apparently didn't want Bear in her daughter's life.

"That fucking figures. She gets fired, but only after she appoints people to spy for her." Bear shook his head. "How my sister came from that woman, I will never know."

Nessa frowned. Simone was just as brilliant and ambitious as her mother. "Your sister is a lot like her mother."

Bear growled.

Nessa held up a hand. "Vivienne was trying to protect the Council and the witch nation. Even you can see that."

He shrugged.

"You'll recall that I voted against your sister being put to death." Of course, she'd lost the vote. But now Simone had been cleared of any wrongdoing, the death sentence had been lifted, and she was back on the Council.

"I know," Bear said grimly. "That's why you're still allowed in my territory."

"I thought it was the kiss," Nessa blurted out. Bollocks. Why had she said that?

He moved toward her. "That, too."

She backed up until her hip hit the door. "Bear?"

"Why you?" he asked quietly. "On the Council. Why you?"

She couldn't breathe. "My uncle is friends with Vivienne, and I have experience with bookkeeping. I'm methodical." Talk about downplaying her skills. "Viv trusts me, so I was a good choice."

"And you look all innocent and sweet, so you'd definitely fool many a man," Bear said.

She had to get him off that topic. "I have an idea."

"Do you?" he asked, continuing forward until his boots touched her shoes. "Your ideas are intriguing, that's for damn sure. What are you thinking now?"

She plastered on her most sincere smile. "How about you hire me to organize this place?"

His head jerked, and panic lit his eyes. "Organize? What? I mean, why? It is organized."

She reached for him, setting her hands on his hard abs. "Bear, this place kills me." Truth. All truth this time. "I'll have nightmares forever about it. Please. Hire me to organize it." She meant the words, she really did. However, she'd also be able to go through his files and papers. Maybe find evidence. "Please."

He looked around, his shoulders tense. "I don't know."

"While I'm doing that, while I have a purpose here, I can continue to heal you." She tried not to sneeze again. "You need to be healed."

"That's blackmail," he said, admiration lighting his eyes to bourbon.

Whatever worked. "All right."

He leaned into her. "Here's the deal. You heal me, I'll hire you to destroy my nice system here, and you let me go after whoever put a bounty on your head."

What? She released his abs. "I can take care of myself." Didn't he see her beat up the bounty hunter earlier? Sure, Bear had jumped in, but she'd been doing fine. "I can fight."

"Sure you can, but if you're doing me a favor, I'm doing one right back."

She looked around the horrible office. "You're doing me a favor by letting me fix this place. If it can be fixed."

He tugged on her hair until she concentrated on him. "It's not the same, and you know it. That's part one of the deal. Agree."

Part one? Well, it would get her what she wanted, but if Bear was to be healed, he had to remain there. So he wouldn't be able to track down the people behind her attempted kidnapping. "All right."

"You sure you don't know who's after you?" he asked.

"Nope," she lied. There was no need to blend lives, now was there? That was the key to undercover work. "What's part two of the deal?"

"Your mating proposal, of course."

Was he just messing with her? Something about him seemed to be making fun of her. She sighed. "The reasons I gave for us to mate are still valid. I might gain fire, and you'd gain more time with me to heal." Not once in her life had she expected to mate for love. From day one, from her first training session, she'd known it'd be either part of a mission or some sort of treaty. Yet lately, she'd wondered. While serving on the Council, she'd seen so many happily mated couples. Real couples in real love.

Was it possible?

"I guess that would give us time to get to know each other," he said easily.

She didn't react. Oh, how many people in the world would look beyond his simple and grumpy facade? Though his body was relaxed, tension rolled off him. Though his tone was easy, it held a slight edge. Though his spectacular honey-brown eyes were calm, they were also sharp. Incredibly sharp. She gave him a shy smile. "I guess that would work." Two could play at this game.

"Wouldn't it, though?" he asked thoughtfully. His chin lifted. "I need to tell you, baby. I'm fine with a couple of secrets or a little intrigue, but you lie to me and you'll be sorry. Tell me you get me."

"Of course," she said, moving away from the door. "I've always found lying to be a waste of time." Until it wasn't.

"Uh-huh." He pulled open the door. "Let's get a move on."

She looked toward the boisterous party. "I don't do well in groups." A true fact, unfortunately. Being raised by her eccentric uncle had been exciting but a little lonely. "I never know what to say."

Bear slipped an arm over her shoulders and pulled her into his heat. "I just don't talk. People seem okay with that."

People were afraid of the big bear. She straightened her shoulders. "All right. Let's do this party."

He chuckled and steered her toward the wide double doors. The second he opened them, heat rushed through. "Bear." More than one guy shouted his name, and he was ripped away for hugs and claps on the back. He turned, and she waved him off.

"I'm fine," she mouthed, looking around the room. A huge bar took up one wall and a large television set another. Couches had been pushed to the side to make room for dancing. She studied the multitude of bodies: many bear shifters and just as many humans. From her research, she knew that the Grizzly MC only let bear shifters be members. Apparently, they partied with humans—mainly female humans with incredibly tight jeans and low-cut midriff tops. "I am not appropriately dressed," she muttered.

"I don't know about that." Lucas moved in from her right and handed her a beer.

She took a drink and smiled, grateful for a friendly face. Ugh, she hated beer. "Thank you so much."

He walked around her, checking her out.

What in the world? She waited until he'd returned to her front. Bear's second-in-command had thick brown hair and warm brown eyes. His face was rugged, but not as rugged as Bear's. And he was almost the same size as Bear—large and broad. "What are you doing?" she asked.

"Helping you," he said simply. "Give me the jacket."

Her mouth gaped open. "Excuse me?"

"You wanna fit in?" he asked.

She looked around to see more than a couple of young females giving her hard looks. Yet a few of the men were checking her out. Sigh. She so did not have time for this. Bear was over at the bar with several members in black motorcycle jackets. He nodded at her, his eyebrows up.

She nodded back. She was just fine.

He grinned.

"Nessa?" Lucas asked.

All right. She could do this. It was just another undercover op. "Fine." Handing him her beer, she unbuttoned her jacket and pulled it off.

Lucas whistled. "All right."

She looked down at her pristine white silk shirt. "What?"

He grinned and set their beers down on a nearby table. "Give me a sec." His thick fingers tucked into her ribs, and he tugged the shirt free of her skirt. Then he unbuttoned the bottom buttons and tied the silk with a firm knot. "There we go."

She looked down. "I guess it isn't too bad."

"I'm not done." He unbuttoned the first three top buttons.

"Hey—"

He held up a hand. "Trust me." Then he stepped back, surveying her head to toe. "There we go. You're ready for an MC party now."

A statuesque redhead stumbled over and into him. "Lucas. Where have you been?"

He righted her. "Practicing my runway skills." He winked at Nessa. She chuckled.

The redhead turned narrowed eyes her way. "Hi."

"Hello," Nessa said.

"Nessa, this is Angie. Angie, Nessa," Lucas said, retrieving the bottles and handing Nessa's back to her.

Angie had on tight black skinny jeans and a purple halter top. Her breasts spilled out the top, and she smelled like . . . beer. "That's quite an accent."

"I'm Irish," Nessa said easily, looking for Bear. He was still across the room, leaning against the bar, his gaze solidly on her.

Angie followed her gaze. "Bear is back. Wonderful." She leaned into Lucas, her hand caressing up his shirt. "Would you introduce my friend Sally to him? She had such a crush last year before he took off."

Nessa's hand tightened around her beer bottle. What did she care who Bear dated? Unless they decided to mate. Then she'd care. Except she didn't want to care. She had a job to do.

Lucas took a long swig of his beer. "I think Bear is otherwise engaged."

Angie pouted way-too-red lips. "He just got back. How could he have hooked up so quickly?"

Nessa only partially listened.

Bear tilted his head, ever so slightly, and crooked his finger for her to come to him.

Lucas chuckled. "Smooth."

Nessa grinned at him. "Most women probably would troop right on over there."

"They surely would," Lucas agreed, his eyes twinkling.

Never, in her entire life, had Nessa Lansa been like most women. There was absolutely no reason to start now. "Angie? How do you feel about tequila shots?"

Angie pouted more. "I don't know. I guess they're okay."

Nessa focused on her. "I've never tried one."

Lucas motioned for a couple of younger-looking men who were pouring drinks. "We should change that."

She looked back toward Bear and his now heated eyes. "I totally concur."

Bear refused his tenth offer of a whiskey shot from yet another club prospect he didn't recognize. After being in animal form for months, his system wasn't prepared to get plastered. So he leaned against the bar, sipped his beer, and kept his eye on the club. His club.

And the woman.

Nessa surprised him. Normally Bear didn't like surprises—at all. Yet watching her gracefully dance on the makeshift floor with her hair flying loose was a pleasure. He wasn't the only male watching her, either. By his count, she'd been propositioned by at least ten men, if not fifteen, by this point.

Yet she just smiled or kept on dancing. She'd even managed to charm several of the hard-core women in the crowd. They usually kicked a newcomer out on her ass.

Not Nessa. No. She was suddenly best friends with everyone.

Why that gave him pause, he'd have to figure out later.

Her laugh rose through the music as Lucas twirled her wildly, somehow managing not to slam into anybody. Even on the four-inch heels, she moved like she didn't have a care in the world. What had it been—at least fifteen hours in those shoes? Her feet had to be killing her, yet there was no sign of it. He could probably own her soul if he offered her a foot rub.

"Hey. You're Bear." A kid of about twenty sidled up to him. "Want a shot? There's gold tequila."

Bear turned toward the prospect. He had slicked-back brown hair, thick muscles, and old eyes. He was human. They didn't take human prospects, and yet the kid wore a prospect badge. What had been going on in his absence? "Who are you?"

"Leroy Johnson." The kid turned and watched Nessa. "Who's the new bitch?"

Bear's shoulders went back. "Motorcycle clubs have a lingo of their own. Some call women bitches, skanks, honeypots."

"Yeah." The kid grinned tobacco-stained teeth.

Bear pivoted and trapped the kid against the bar. "We don't."

"What?" The kid frowned and stood taller, his chest puffing out. At a closer look, his eyes were dilated and unfocused.

"I said, you call a woman a name like that again, and I'm gonna remove all your teeth and use them to tattoo your face." Bear leaned into the kid, letting the bear in him show.

The kid didn't back down. A couple of his buddies—ones Bear didn't know—crowded close. "You've been gone a long time, old man."

Old man? The kid didn't have a clue. Bear might be over a hundred, but he looked thirty, tops. "Meaning what?" Bear rumbled, the alpha inside him stretching awake.

"Things have changed." The kid shoved him.

Ah, hell. So much for a relaxed evening. Bear smiled. Then he set his beer down on the bar. "I don't believe they have." He grabbed the front of Leroy's jacket, lifted, and easily threw him across a wide span, to fly right out the double doors and into the falling rain. Lucky for the kid they'd opened the doors to let out some of the heat.

Leroy fell hard on the wet pavement and bounced twice. With Bear's animalistic hearing, he could make out at least two bones breaking. Sounded like a wrist and maybe a rib. That was odd—a rib at that angle. Bear shrugged.

Three human prospects moved in toward him, no doubt to defend their buddy. Damn it. Oh, he could take three humans, but he truly wasn't at full strength. Not even close. His lower back ached just from throwing Leroy. "You can't be serious," he muttered.

The three kids straightened as Lucas appeared at Bear's side. "Problem?" Lucas asked, his voice hard.

"He threw Leroy," the first kid, still with acne, said.

"Leroy is lucky he still has legs," Lucas shot back. "The last man who challenged Bear is still walking around muttering about butterflies and kumquats, after his beating. Are you mellowing, Bear?"

Bear bit back a smile. "No. Just trying to figure out why we have new prospects." Who weren't bear shifters.

Lucas's jaw hardened. "Yeah. We should talk business tomorrow. For now, you assholes back off before Bear stops goofing around."

The kids looked toward their buddy outside.

The acne-riddled kid nodded, his gaze not meeting Lucas's. "Yeah. Fine." He slapped his friend's arm. "Let's see if he's okay."

They moved past, the last kid gingerly contorting his body on the way by so he didn't brush against Bear. Smart kid.

"Humans?" Bear muttered, turning to see Nessa toss back a shot with a human named Angie.

"Long story." Lucas clapped him on the back. "We should have a business meeting tomorrow."

Yeah, they should. Apparently, Bear needed to step up as alpha of the pack and president of the club . . . sooner rather than later. "The kid was on something." So long as his members and guests didn't hurt anybody, he didn't care if they poisoned their own bodies.

The women finished the shots, and Angie stumbled through the crowd to fall against Lucas. "Hey, sexy. My new BFF Nessa just agreed to a threesome with you."

Lucas coughed out, interest definitely crossing his face, then disbelief. "Really?"

The hair on the back of Bear's neck rose fast.

Nessa came into view, and he reached out to snag an arm around her waist. She laughed as he pulled her in. "You having fun?" he asked mildly.

She nodded, her wild hair tumbling. "I truly am. It's a lovely party."

Lovely. God, she was cute. "Letting your hair down a little?" Bear asked, trying to ignore his best friend checking out her breasts.

"Yes." Her face was flushed and her eyes sparkling with fun. "I've been working too hard, Bear. Way too hard."

The word *hard* made him exactly that. Quickly. "So Angie just mentioned that you'd be up for a threesome with Lucas."

Nessa paused. Her head tilted to the side. "A threesome?"

"Yeah," Angie said, pressing in. "It's fun. You're in for fun, right?"

Nessa arched one very fine eyebrow. "Well, I do appreciate fun."

Bear stiffened. She was *not* saying what he thought she was saying. He couldn't have been that wrong about her.

Nessa's foot tapped to the music. "But a threesome with me would be a bad idea, and I certainly did not agree to participate in one."

Bear tilted his head down to see amusement dancing in her deep eyes. "Why a bad idea?" He'd bite.

She sighed. "I'm too much woman for one man. Add in another woman? We'd kill the guy." She gave a delicate snort.

Bear laughed, his tension dissipating.

Lucas hung his head. "So no threesome?"

"No," Nessa said, partially turning in Bear's arms to look at him. "You haven't asked me to dance all night."

"I've been watching you dance," he said, liking the feel of her entirely too much.

Her lips twitched. "Have you enjoyed yourself?"

"More than I have in a long time," he said honestly. Who the hell was this woman? More important, why did she look guilty every time she seemed to let her guard down? "Unlike Lucas and his threesome hopes here, I've figured out a way to your heart." More important, to her body.

"Indeed?" She snuggled even closer. "What's the way?"

He leaned down, his mouth next to her ear. "A foot rub."

She drew in a breath. "Oh my. You have figured me out."

Bear grinned. "I know."

She clasped his hand. "First, we dance."

When a beautiful woman full of secrets asked a guy to dance, he danced. Even if he was a bear. Bear handed his beer off to Lucas without looking and let Nessa lead him toward what worked as the dance floor. He'd wanted to get his hands on her all night. "I'm leading," he rumbled, turning her toward him.

She smiled. "Of course."

The song was hard rock, the beat fierce. Yet he tucked an arm around her waist and drew her in, moving slowly.

She sighed and pressed her face against his chest, her body one smooth line of relaxation. He moved her, enjoying the feel of her against him.

"Are you having fun?" she asked, her voice dreamy.

"Yes and no," he replied, his hand covering her entire lower back. "It's good to see friends, but there are too many people here I don't know." Which was something he'd remedy soon. "I'm sure Lucas has his reasons, but I don't like it." He usually didn't like being around people. Not really.

Bodies gyrated around them, creating a cocoon for the two of them. Maybe with her guard down, Bear could really get honest answers from her. "Who wants to kidnap you and why, Nessa?"

She stiffened slightly and then relaxed again. "I was a member of the Council of the Coven Nine. Anybody could be after me just for the information I may have picked up. We have enemies even in peacetime, you know."

He inhaled her rose scent. "I have a simple life."

She snuggled even closer. "Sure you do."

Was that sarcasm? "Your point?"

Her lips were close to his collarbone. "You're a bear shifter with dragon DNA. Your sister is on the Council, and your half brother leads a secret dragon nation on an undetectable island."

"That's their lives. Not mine."

She leaned back and tilted her head. "Family is always part of our lives. Our struggles, hopes, and complications."

He paused. There was more to what she was saying than he grasped. "Maybe." Yet his life was a quiet one, with motorcycles, trees, and freedom. "I don't do intrigue, baby."

A veil drew down over her eyes. "Of course you don't." She pressed her cheek against him again, hiding those expressive eyes.

His instincts remained on full alert, even with the warm woman in his arms. Too much was happening around him, and he didn't like being in the dark. At all. "How long will it take for me to heal completely?"

She breathed against him. "I donna' know." Her shoulders slumped. "I may not be able to mend all of the damage. Not without—"

"Mating," he murmured, his breath stirring her hair. Mates often gained the skills of their partners, and if he mated her he might get her ability to heal—perhaps not other people but definitely himself. She'd possibly gain the ability to throw fire, which certainly seemed a needed skill considering bounty hunters were after her.

Yet he didn't have the full story. His instincts told him that much, at least. As they moved, his feet started to ache. Then his legs. He sighed.

She lifted her head again. "You need rest."

"I'm fine," he said shortly.

She rolled her eyes. "I can sense your pain, tough guy. I've been inside your skin, you know?"

That was weird. "Did you see my soul?" he teased.

She didn't smile. "What do you think you ripped apart?"

He couldn't think of an answer. Was she serious? A ruckus flared up on the other side of the room, and he turned them, easily seeing over her head. "Shit."

Angie had fallen against the bar, her body convulsing. A red flame rushed down her arm. Bear released Nessa and shoved his way over just as Lucas reached the woman.

"Get her to the back room," Bear ordered tersely, trying to block the woman from view of the crowd with his body.

Nessa reached his side and gasped, looking down.

Another flame danced along Angie's full lips. Red and purple streaks marred the whites of her eyes, which were wide open in pure panic.

Lucas grabbed her up and ran around the bar, shoving open the door to the back room. Nessa hurried behind him. Bear paused at the doorway and caught the attention of two of his lieutenants. "She's fine. Too much to drink." He motioned around. "Take care of things. Party is over." Both bear shifters nodded. He paused. "Keep the music on."

They might need to cover Angie's screams as people left.

He shoved into the massive storage room and slammed the door.

Shelves filled with alcohol and bar food lined all four walls. Lucas had set Angie down on the floor in the middle of the room, and her body was convulsing wildly, her fingers randomly shooting flames. Bear jumped out of the way of a stream of fire. "What the fuck? Apollo?" The only way a human could create flames was by taking too much of the drug.

Lucas knelt and pressed both of her shoulders to the floor, trying to hold her still. "Angie? How much did you take, darlin'?"

Angie struggled against him and let out a high-pitched scream.

Bear's stomach rolled. The drug was burning her from the inside out. Why wasn't the shit off the streets? The main distributor had been blown up.

Nessa crouched down and placed her hands on Angie's upper chest.

"Wait a minute." Bear leaned and grasped Nessa's arm. "This is a drug that harms witches, too. Will this hurt you?" He wasn't going to allow her to harm herself helping somebody who'd taken an illegal drug, probably knowing the risks. "Nessa?"

"Let me see how far gone she is," Nessa said, her body stilling. She shut her eyes.

Fire burst from Angie's mouth, and Lucas sat back. The flames danced for a second on Nessa's face and then disappeared.

Lucas gaped. "What the hell?"

Nessa breathed in and settled herself. "She took a lot."

Angie whimpered. Her body jerked several times.

Nessa grimaced.

"That's enough." Bear tightened his hold on her arm.

She shook her head wildly, dislodging him. "No."

Angie reared up and let out a scream of pure agony. Fire flashed from all her fingers, shooting across the room and lighting the alcohol-laden shelves on fire. A bottle dropped and shattered.

Vodka spread across the floor.

Almost in slow motion, a flame arced from a shelf to the liquid. The wooden shelves ignited.

Chapter 6

Nessa kept her hands pressed against Angie's chest, trying to push a healing balm around the woman's burning internal organs. Fire crackled around the two of them, but she had to concentrate.

Apollo was made from a mineral called PK that harmed witches. Most witches used fire. So when humans took the drug, they created fire until they burned up. Using her knowledge of PK, Nessa tried to counter the drug. Water beat fire, so she imagined water and healing gel throughout Angie's body.

The woman cried out, the sound full of pain.

"It's okay," Nessa whispered, looking up.

Bear had taken his shirt off and was trying to slap out the flames on the floor. The cotton instantly caught fire, and he dropped it, giving a snarl. Lucas shrugged out of his leather jacket and threw it at Bear while turning for the nearest shelf, where he shoved bottles away from the flames.

Smoke clouded the room.

"Open the door," Bear ordered, pressing the leather coat onto the flames.

Lucas coughed and shoved open the door. Smoke followed him. He hustled out to the bar and returned with a bucket of ice to throw across the floor.

Bear finished extinguishing the flames.

Nessa breathed shallowly, keeping her head low. Black smoke spiraled up, trapped against the ceiling.

Angie convulsed again.

Nessa closed her eyes and pictured the interior of a human body. She usually couldn't mess with human physiology, but the Apollo drug was created by altering planekite, which only harmed witches. Nessa was used to dealing with planekite poisoning, so, this once, she might have a chance to help a human. The smoke burned her lungs, but she couldn't stop. The balm she'd created soothed Angie's body, and Nessa felt the moment its protection kicked in.

Angie's head jerked back. The heat inside her cooled. The young woman settled back to the floor with a sigh. Her eyelids closed, and she passed into unconsciousness.

Lucas knelt down again, soot across his brow. "What are you doing?"

Nessa didn't have the strength to answer. She swayed.

"Whoa." Bear dropped to his haunches and supported her. "Nessa?"

She leaned against him. "Angie will be okay." She lifted her shaking hands. Her stomach felt hollow. The alcohol she'd consumed settled like a lump, and her head spun. Wildly.

Lucas smoothed hair back from Angie's sweaty face. "How did you do that?"

"Long story," Nessa said wearily.

Bear stood and assisted Nessa to her feet. "Lucas? Get Angie somewhere safe for the night."

Weakness swept through Nessa, and her knees gave.

Bear caught her before she hit the floor.

"I'm fine. Just tired," she mumbled, shaking her head to regain focus.

"Right." Bear lifted her, barely taking a step back as he took her weight.

Her lips trembled into a smile. They were both weakened. "We need sleep and safety." Neither one of them would win a fight at the moment.

Bear nodded. "I want guards on full patrol all night, Lucas. We've had two bounty hunters on the property already today, and that can't happen again."

"Understood." Lucas bent and lifted Angie. "I'll take her to my place above the second garage and keep an eye on her all night."

Bear strode out of the storage area into the now vacated clubhouse. Beer bottles and dirty glasses littered every surface. "Have somebody clean this up by morning. Apparently, we have several prospects now who can be put to work."

Was that irritation in his voice? Nessa looked up at his implacable face. No expression crossed his hard features, but his eyes glittered. "What's wrong with prospective members?" she asked.

"They are human." Bear loped through the shambles to the four-wheeler outside. Cold wind swept against them. "We don't have human members. It's not smart."

Rain slashed down, and Nessa moved closer to Bear as he ignited the engine. "Feels like snow is coming," she murmured.

He tucked an arm around her waist. "I can smell winter. Should snow soon."

Her eyelids fluttered shut, and she tried to hide her face from the wind and rain. They were back at the cabin before she knew it. "I can walk."

"Not in those shoes." He tugged her across his seat and stood, striding up the cabin steps.

Her head lolled, and she rested her cheek against his bare shoulder. "You're stronger already," she said. His chest seemed wider.

"Maybe." He kicked open the door and then shut it behind them.

The fire had died down but still lent a nice warmth to the small space. The scent of pine and male filled the air.

He set her down, his eyes flaring.

She glanced at her wet, white, and now very see-through shirt. Her breasts were clearly outlined and fully on display. "Might I borrow a shirt?" she asked.

"I should say no." He turned and moved for the dinged-up dresser to draw out a green jersey with a porcupine covering the back and a label of PONTSEY PORCUPINES above it. Holding the tee, he stalked toward her. "Take off the wet shirt."

Not a chance. She took the T-shirt from him. "Turn around."

"My shirt is off," he rumbled, his cheek creasing.

No kidding. His broad chest was hard to ignore, as were his ripped abs. But his ribs were still clearly visible, showing he'd lost weight. "Turn around, Bear," she murmured.

He rolled his eyes but did as she'd asked. "Where is your luggage, anyway?" he asked.

"At the Five Winters Hotel in downtown Seattle," she returned, removing her soggy wet shirt and pulling on Bear's T-shirt. The soft material reached her thighs, so she pushed her skirt to the floor as well. With a sigh of pure relief, she kicked off her shoes. Ah. So much better. "What is a Pontsey Porcupine?" she asked.

He turned back around. "It's a local baseball team. Must've picked up the shirt at a game or something." He moved past her to stoke the fire. "You lied to me."

She stiffened. "No, I didn't."

"Yeah, you did." He set the poker back in the metal holder and dusted his hands, pivoting. "Healing people hurts you. Saps your energy."

Oh. That lie. She faced him, searching for the right words. "I never said that healing people didn't take energy. It does. The action takes a lot of energy, just like when somebody runs a marathon. I also said the action hurts."

"You said it barely hurts," he said, standing with only a threadbare rug between them.

The sofa sat to her right, and she fought the urge to move behind it. "So?"

"So? I saw the pain in your eyes when you healed Angie. Felt the hurt in the air." He rubbed the scruff on his jaw.

She sighed. "The pain is temporary and not blinding. I mean, it's not horrible." The rubber band analogy had been fairly accurate. "'Tisn't something you need to concern yourself about."

"I like your brogue," he said abruptly.

She was briefly thrown by the switch in topics. Her abdomen warmed. "Excuse me?"

"Turns me on. All the way."

Her knees weakened. The direct and deliberate Bear was back. "Do most people fall for your simple act?" She tilted her head to the side.

His lips twitched. "My simple act?"

"Aye. The good-ole-boy, cranky, simple guy who uses small sentences. You know, that guy?" She'd been inside his skin, and there were complexities on top of complexities within Bear.

"I am a cranky, simple guy who doesn't see the need for many words." He surveyed her, his gaze stopping on her bare feet. "How drunk are you?"

She curled her toes into the wood floor. "Not very. Witches have high metabolisms, and I burned a lot of the booze when trying to heal Angie."

"You're clearheaded?"

"Aye." What was his point?

"Good. Then I can ask you a straight question." His eyes were molten chocolate in the firelight.

She swallowed. More questions about her motivations? Lovely. "All right."

"You wanna fuck?"

Bear liked catching the classy witch off balance. Her face flared a bright pink, and she actually took a step back. "Too direct for you?" he asked quietly, humor bubbling up through his chest.

Spirit seethed in her eyes. "You're not up for it."

"Wanna bet?" He tucked his thumbs in his damp jeans and studied her. Wearing his shirt, without her heels, she was petite and somehow all smooth, long leg. Her toenails had been painted an intriguing blue. He would've guessed a simple beige or light pink. But they were bright blue.

The woman had many layers to her personality and a wild side. He just knew it. Yeah, he wanted to tap all that. Wanted to figure her out.

She lifted her delicate chin. "We just met." With her hair wet and curling down her back, she was pure temptation.

He had never been a guy to ignore temptation. So he loped toward her, appreciating the fact that she remained in place. When he reached her, the scent of roses grabbed him around the neck and squeezed. "Who cares? You asked to mate me." Which definitely was not going to happen. However, he'd still like some naked time with her. He brushed her hair away from her face, tangling his fingers in the heavy mass.

Need shone in her eyes, but defiance flashed across her face. "I have to conserve my energy for healing you."

"I'd rather fuck." Might as well give her the truth. She was the one who'd offered to mate him. "If you were serious about your plan, then don't you want to see if we're compatible?"

She rolled her eyes. "I'm no' worried about that."

He'd take that as a compliment. "Your little plan has a couple of flaws, doesn't it?"

She blinked, her gaze turning wary. "I'm sure I don't know what you mean." Her throaty voice coated his skin and wandered right down to his balls.

He shifted his weight. "Sure you do." Her pretty pink lips all but invited him to take a bite. "Get here, mate me, get fire, and go. This might be a bit more complicated."

"You don't know me," she burst out.

He twisted his wrist in her soft hair, effectively forcing her to lift her face. "I have no doubt there's a lot I don't know about you." He leaned down, his lips hovering right over hers. "You know what I do know?"

She breathed in sharply. "What?"

"You want this." Holding her in place, he lowered his mouth and took hers. There was something infinitely delicate about Nessa Lansa, but he'd already kissed her gently once. There was only so much softness in him, and it was gone. He'd never been that guy. From day one of his life, he'd fought hard for every single thing he had. Everything he owned.

Fighting was what he knew. He thrust his tongue into her mouth, tasting tequila and something that was all Nessa, something sweet with a tiny bite.

She stilled for about two seconds and then kissed him back, her hands snaking over his shoulders. Her lips were soft and lush, and they felt shockingly good against his. A low moan rose in her throat.

The sound. The soft sound clawed through him with the force of a heated storm. He deepened the kiss, taking what he wanted, asserting himself. Oh, he wouldn't hurt her and he'd try for gentleness when he could, but she needed to know who he really was. What he really was. There was no changing him, so if she wanted a classy guy who got a manicure once in a while, she was looking in the wrong place.

His free hand swept down her back and over her ass. If she wanted a ride on the wild side, she was in the right place. She pressed against him, and his mind went blank. Her soft body against his hardness stole his thoughts and banished any good intentions he might've drummed up.

His fingers spread over her scalp, and he held her still, plundering even deeper. His heart sped up, and his blood pounded through his veins in a hard cadence. He could almost hear the drums—feel the animal inside him take over.

Kissing her, he stood on a precipice. A new one. This was different. *She* was different.

This was real.

He growled low and lifted his mouth. "Tell me you want this."

Her eyelids opened, but her eyes remained unfocused. Her chest moved against his with each hard breath. A tremble took her, and he felt the full roll against his body. His entire body.

Using his hold on her head, he moved her closer into him, his cock nearly punching through his jeans as it rubbed against her.

Her eyes widened.

His dick hardened even more.

The primal need to take snaked through him, clawing with demand. His nostrils flared, and he inhaled her scent. Woman, roses, and arousal. Sweet and edgy . . . an addictive smell. "Nessa?"

She swallowed. "Wait a minute. I, ah—"

He was too aroused to grin, but he came close. The woman was beyond adorable, all mussed up and confused. "I normally don't like witches," he whispered, his gaze dropping to her slightly swollen lips. He groaned. What she could do with those.

"Y-you don't?"

"No." He could see her pulse hammering in her neck. "Too many secrets and long-held intrigue." He shuddered. "But you're different."

Did she wince? He focused on her entire face, but only curiosity and need crossed her expression. "I am?" she asked.

He nodded. The woman had let her hair down and partied with some serious partiers. Then she'd jumped into action to rescue a human she'd just met. "Yes. You're not like most witches." There was an honesty to her, a clear sense of motivation, that most of those lying jerks didn't have. Oh, he still didn't want to mate a witch. But this one? This one he liked. "I was thinking that while you're here healing me and organizing everything to your heart's content, why not have some fun?"

"By, ah, making love?"

He barely kept from grimacing. "Not exactly."

She huffed out a breath. "Fine. Then by having sexual intercourse."

The words were said like she was reading from a health manual, but they still heated him right up. "Fucking."

Her blush rose from her chest to her face. He tugged on her shirt and tried to look down it.

She slapped his hand. "What are you doing?"

"Seeing if that blush goes all the way down." He couldn't see. It was too dark. "How about you take this off?"

A sharp rap sounded on his door. "Bear?" Lucas called.

"Damn it." Bear released the woman and stomped over to yank the door open. "I might have to kill you, Luke."

Lucas brushed wet hair away from his forehead. "Guards called in. We have two dead near the main road."

Chapter 7

"I really need to return to the hotel for my clothes," Nessa said, once again on Bear's lap in the four-wheeler. She was wearing Bear's ripped gray sweats rolled up way too many times, a huge sweatshirt, and a pair of his thick socks. The idea of putting her feet back into those heels had almost made her cry.

He set a baseball cap on her head, protecting her from the wind and rain. "You don't have to come."

"I may be able to help if they're not dead," she said quietly.

"They're dead," Lucas said, increasing speed. "Humans with burn marks around their mouths, noses, and ears. Oh, and hands."

Bear growled. "How the hell do we have people taking Apollo on our property? I banned the drug a year ago."

"I don't know," Lucas snapped. "With the human prospects, we've had a new group of folks in and out for parties."

"Why are there humans here at all?" Nessa asked.

Bear nodded, his chin bumping her head. "Good question."

"Money," Lucas said simply. "Our accounts are frozen, and we need income. The five prospects are excellent mechanics, and they're bringing in a good income. I had to make them prospects to gain their agreement."

"What about Lars, Brinks, and Duncan? They're the best mechanics around—except for me," Bear said.

Lucas cut him a hard look. "When the DEA started sniffing around so intently, Lars and Brinks headed for Alaska."

Bear winced.

Nessa looked up at him. "I don't understand."

"Lars and Brinks may have robbed a few banks back in the day," Bear said quietly. "They need to lay low and keep off human radar for at least fifty more years."

"Oh." She blinked against the rain. "What about, ah, Duncan?"

"Haven't seen him," Lucas said, taking a turn down the asphalt toward what Nessa thought might be the main road. "He took off when you did, Bear."

Bear frowned. "That doesn't sound like Duncan."

Nessa tried to think through the dossiers she'd read about Bear and his crew. The files were sparse because Bear had tried to stay off the radar himself for so long. But if she remembered right, Duncan was a three-hundred-year-old bear shifter who liked the quiet of the Pacific Northwest. Perhaps he'd just liked hanging out with Bear.

Lucas turned the wheel and drove between two dripping pine trees and down a rocky trail. The prone human bodies came into view shortly, illuminated by the vehicle's headlights. Lucas stopped the four-wheeler a mere foot from the bodies.

The stench was nearly unbearable. Burned flesh and hair. Nessa coughed. Two human males lay on the ground, their clothes in tatters from flames. Scorch marks marred the bodies, and burns were everywhere. "Apollo," she whispered.

Bear stood. "Stay here." He strode over to the bodies and dropped to his haunches. Lucas followed along but remained standing. Together, they just surveyed the carnage for a few moments. Bear reached out and felt the jugulars of both bodies, but his expression didn't change. "Who are they?"

"I don't know," Lucas said. "I think they were guests at the party, but I don't know who invited them."

A man dressed in all black moved out of the trees. "I found the bodies and called Lucas." He shoved wild red hair away from his wide face.

Bear stood and clasped the guy's hand. "It's good to see you, Trapper."

Trapper shook his hand. "Welcome back. You all healed?"

Bear looked toward Nessa. "Not yet, but I will be."

Nessa could feel that stare to her core. He didn't trust her, but he definitely wanted her. She'd had the feeling back at the cabin that he was perhaps starting to believe her story. Guilt put a lump in her throat.

"How many people might know these guys were here tonight?" Bear asked grimly, turning back to Lucas.

Lucas shrugged. "I don't know." He wiped rain off his face with both hands. "We just wanted to let off some steam with a party like we used to have. It's been tough without you, Bear. I should've vetted the guests better."

"Not your fault," Bear said. "I'm the one who took off."

Nessa made to get off the four-wheeler.

Bear swung his gaze toward her. "Stay put, Ness."

She paused. Ness? Only her uncle called her that. Hearing the intimate nickname and seeing Bear so completely in charge stirred something in her. So she sat back to watch.

Bear sighed. "All right. I've been out of the loop. Why is Apollo still a problem in Seattle?"

Trapper wiped rain off his head. "After Titans of Fire broke up, things settled down for about two months. Then the last month, it's like a new distributor has gotten seriously ambitious. There were five overdoses just last week. But we don't know who's behind it."

Nessa leaned out of the vehicle. "How about witch deaths from Apollo?"

Trapper stared down at the bodies. "Dunno. The witches usually keep that quiet, you know?"

Aye, and she hadn't heard anything; she would have if something had happened. But Bear didn't know that, so the question was necessary. Aye. More guilt for her. "I see." She settled back against the seat. The wind and rain whipped into her, but at least the cap protected her face.

Bear shook his shaggy hair out. "Trapper, get some men here and take the bodies into a known drug area in Seattle, where the deaths won't be questioned. Don't get caught." He looked toward Lucas. "Find out everything about them. Family, backgrounds, everything. And definitely who invited them to a Grizzly party." He lifted his chin. "Anybody still back at headquarters?"

Lucas nodded. "A few of the guys crashed in the rooms above the garages."

"Good. Call in and have somebody bring my truck, would you?" Bear asked.

Lucas pulled a cell phone from his back pocket and texted something while Bear rolled the bodies over and took out their wallets. "Josh Lindon." Bear flipped open the other wallet. "Rick Alton." Nessa made a mental note to find out more about the deceased men. They were both dressed in jeans and dark shirts, one a Caucasian blond and one an African American with a shaved head. They appeared to be in their late twenties. Other than that, the burn marks covered any tattoos or scars.

Lucas took the wallets. "What if people saw them at the party? Humans, I mean?"

Bear shook his head. "Then we say that they left here before overdosing somewhere else. Hopefully, nobody will mention the Grizzlies." His tone didn't exactly sound hopeful.

A lifted black truck, shiny and tricked out, came into view up the road. When it got close, a guy jumped out of the driver's side and gave Bear a respectful nod. Bear strode over to Nessa and easily lifted her from the four-wheeler, carrying her through the rain to deposit her in the passenger side of the truck.

"I'm getting used to you carrying me," she murmured.

He wiped rain off her cheeks, his gaze serious. "We're not permanent, baby. It's fun to tease you, and I definitely wanna see you naked, but a bear shifter and a witch don't mix. I'm tired of messing around. That's the truth." He shut the door before she could respond.

Her mouth opened and then abruptly closed. What in the bloody world? The shifter, the *bear shifter,* was actually rejecting her? Did he not know where shifters stood in the hierarchy of species? Waaaaaaay below witches. Way below. He was an animal. Her chest heated, and the skin on her shoulders pricked. How dare he?

Several deep breaths later and she managed to subdue her temper while Bear continued talking to his men. She looked around. The truck was luxurious: new-smelling leather and heated seats. She flicked hers on high. A computer console took up most of the dash. If she had time, she'd make good use of it.

She focused back on the oh-so-very-honest shifter just as he strode through the rain, a powerful man wearing a firm frown.

He opened the door and slid into the driver's seat, bringing the scent of rain and male with him. When he shut the door, an intimacy settled throughout the cab. He backed out of the trail and turned onto the private road, heading for the main road.

"Where are we going?" Her voice was just a mite shrill.

He glanced her way. In the dim light of the cab, with the rain pelting the windshield, he looked like the predator he was known to be. "I'm sorry if I hurt your feelings."

Her eyebrows lifted almost to her hairline, and she forced them back down. "You did not. I'm fine."

He sighed, the sound weary. "We don't mix, and you know it. Oh, we can have some fun, and I like our agreement—without the mating—but I wanted to be clear with you."

There would have been something honorable in that statement if it didn't piss her off so much. Apparently the seriousness of the dead bodies had made Bear stop goofing around with her. "I understand holding out for happily-ever-after." Kind of.

He shook his head, and water sprayed. "I don't believe in love and all that."

She stiffened. "Oh?"

"Just don't like witches."

She jolted.

"Not you. I mean, I do like you." He scrubbed a hand through his hair, untangling it. "You're sweet and kind. Honest."

"Okay?" All Saints, did he have her wrong.

"But witches and bears don't work well together. You guys have too many secrets, treaties, and hidden wars, you know? I mean, your own Council split apart recently, ordering hits on pretty much everybody. It took blowing up a Seattle motorcycle club, a fight to the death, and the Enforcers working together *against* your Council to set things right."

Well, since he put it that way. "It was an unfortunate series of events," she said primly.

"Huh. Seems normal for witches." He kept his gaze on the road.

"Bears are simple. This is us, everyone else is them, and that's the end of it."

"We're allies," she retorted.

"Now," he shot back. "We're allies today. Tomorrow, who knows? You might send a spy right into the Grizzly camp and decide to burn us all to a crisp."

There wasn't a good answer to that, considering it was true. "I'm not desperate to mate, but you have to know, I may not be able to heal you completely without that bond."

"Just do your best, and time will take care of the rest," he said easily, flicking the windshield wipers on stronger.

He was her best chance to gain fire, but there was another alternative. If he wouldn't help her, she'd go elsewhere after she'd healed him and concluded her investigation into Apollo and the Grizzlies. She needed the skill of throwing fire in order to survive, and she knew it. There were too many enemies coming for her. "I donna' suppose you'd introduce me to your half brother?" she asked, her mind quickly sorting facts into logical columns.

Bear glanced her way. "He's a full-bred dragon."

"Exactly." Though she'd have to finish the current case before she tried to fix her personal problems. "Fire, right?"

Bear's frown deepened. "You're not mating my brother."

"Why not?" She turned to face him.

"Because you and I are going to be intimate, and you know it." He calmly turned back to the raging storm outside. His tone was both tired and absolute; the determination in it couldn't be denied. He tapped his fingers on the steering wheel. "Protest all you want, but you know it's gonna happen."

Now that was an ego. A huge bloody ego. "I think I can control myself, *shifter*." It was only a couple of kisses. Sure, they were the best kisses of her life, but who said his brother couldn't kiss as well? Maybe it was a family thing. She crossed her arms.

Bear cut her a look. "I don't appreciate the way you just said 'shifter,' baby. Lose the attitude or you're gonna see how dangerous a pissed-off *shifter* can get."

In his current state, she could probably beat him senseless. The temptation to do so caught her off guard. She wasn't bloody violent, damn it.

He rolled to a stop at the end of the private road and turned the truck toward the city. "You're welcome to stay here and heal me, Nessa. If you do, I'll take care of the bounty hunters and whoever hired them to kidnap you. It's a good deal. Take it."

She lifted her chin. "I still get to organize your office."

"You have OCD?"

"Close enough." She needed to get her hands on his records, and that was the easiest way to do it. Investigating people in plain sight was usually impossible. "And no more kisses. Period." The tequila she'd downed earlier rolled in her stomach. Most of it had burned away, but just enough remained to make her feel slightly off.

"I'll agree to the organization but not to the kissing rule."

The city lights came into view. "You are unbelievable. If I say you can't kiss me, then you can't." She huffed back in her seat, wishing for her high-heeled shoes.

"I won't kiss you against your will, but you'll have to tell me no in the moment." The smile he flashed was full of dare. "We both know that won't happen."

"You are such a jackass," she returned, planting her feet on the dash. The wet socks made a squishing sound.

Bear took in her feet and sighed. "This is my truck, darlin'."

"Speaking of which. Why is your cabin such a dump and your truck so nice?" She ran her fingers along the lush door.

"This is my truck." He frowned again at her feet. "Money should go into trucks and motorcycles. Not cabins."

Okay. They were certainly opposites. He had hurt her feelings with his rough rejection, and he'd just given her means to pay him back. The male would probably love to see his cabin spruced up a little with floral patterns and delicate furniture. "I see," she said.

He eyed her. "What are you planning?"

Her eyes opened wide. "What do you mean?" Man, he read people well. She hadn't even fully formed a plan, but so far it involved Internet shopping and interior decorating.

Bear concentrated on driving through the city, finally reaching the high-end hotel.

"You can just drop me off in front." She smoothed down her hair.

"I'll valet park," he returned, driving into the front vestibule.

She forced a smile. "I'm not inviting you up."

"Yes, you are." He stopped the truck by the valet station. "Per our agreement, I'm on your ass until you're safe. That means, we stay in the same place."

She sucked in air to keep from belting him across the mouth.

He grinned. "I'm thinking you'll give me a good-night kiss."

Chapter 8

Bear followed Nessa down the hotel hallway to the suite at the end.

Her ass somehow swayed in the overlarge sweats, and she held her head high as if she had no concerns in the world. In his socks, without her traitorous heels, she didn't even reach his chin. Man, she was small. What was it about the woman that made her seem so much taller?

His boots left tracks in his wake. "Are you mad at me?" he asked, as she opened her door with a key card.

"No," she said shortly, flipping on the lights.

The suite was luxurious, with fancy furniture. Bear admired the glittering Seattle skyline outside the full wall of windows. He stepped inside and was instantly transported to the first part of his childhood, when he didn't belong and knew it every day. Yet she would be right at home surrounded by the comfort of wealth. "You'd like Fire Island."

She paused and turned, looking perfectly at ease in the opulent surroundings, despite her hand-me-down clothing. "Excuse me?"

"Where the dragons live. Fire Island—off the coast of Ireland. Far from here." Bear shut the door gingerly and toed off his thick boots in the tiled entryway. He might be a mutt, but he knew not to drag mud across white carpet. "It's all gold and diamonds there."

She tilted her head to the side, her skin smooth and her eyes curious. "What makes you think I need gold or diamonds?"

He snorted. "Come on." Gesturing toward the sofa—no, *settee*—he forced a grin. "You belong in a place like this." Man, she must've hated his cabin. He liked his place. Even though he could afford more, he didn't want more.

She looked around. "It's a hotel suite."

"Yeah, it looks like the island."

"Did you grow up there?" she asked quietly.

He shrugged, and his gut ached. "Just until my teens. Then I left and came to the States." After his asshole of a father had died, he'd had to run. But he'd created a home for himself in the wilds of Washington.

"By yourself?" she asked.

"I prefer life by myself." It was good to remind them both of that fact. They were in a hotel room, for Pete's sake. He'd never taken a woman to a hotel without at least breaking the bed a little. Usually a lot.

She frowned and pressed a hand to her stomach. "Are you hungry?"

His stomach was growling before she finished her sentence. It was three in the morning, and he hadn't eaten since returning to human form. "Starving."

She moved to a phone by a round inlaid table and ordered two steak dinners.

"Three," he mouthed.

She added another order, along with several desserts, before hanging up. "They'll send the food shortly. For now, I'm taking a hot shower." She pointed down a hallway to what looked like a bedroom. "There's the other room, and I think it has its own shower."

He hesitated.

"What?"

"I'm not hitting on you." Especially since he'd just figured out that the witch probably did belong with somebody like his brother. The guy was loaded and liked the expensive stuff in life. Bear just didn't care. "But I don't think we should separate from each other while we're in the city."

She pulled up the sagging sweats, looking way too cute. "You've been hitting on me since we met."

"I'm done." Why did she have to look both adorable and sexy? Who else in the world could pull that off? He discreetly adjusted his jeans.

Her pretty blue eyes narrowed. "Why?" Slowly, she looked around the plush suite. "Because of this place?"

God. Was she gonna make him say it? Fine. "Yes. I just realized . . . you might have a shot with my brother. He has fire, and it'd work. And you have a lot in common." She put her hands on her hips and the sweats fell down again. She yanked them up. "I'm not a snob. For God's sake, Bear. I grew up in a thatched-roof cottage in the middle of rolling hills. I can sew my own clothes, and I can cook over an open fire."

"Then you became an expert bookkeeper and a member of the Council of the Coven Nine." There was a lot more to the woman than she'd admitted. "You have political allies that might be the most powerful in the world. Don't tell me for one second that you're a dedicated accountant just living a quiet life." How stupid did she think he was?

"I never said that."

He warmed to the subject. "In fact, I'm thinking you're one of the main number crunchers for the Council. Top of the political pyramid, are you?" Yeah, that made sense. It explained how she'd ended up on the Council. The woman was probably a billionaire who liked to be pampered.

"I'm very good at my job," she said primly. "Now, go take a shower."

"I'm not leaving you alone," he growled.

Her small nostrils flared. "We're safe here. I'm registered under an alias, an untraceable one, and there's no way anybody can find us. So go take your shower, and I'll do the same." She turned to storm off.

He caught her easily around the bicep and turned her around.

She grabbed the waistband of the sweats to keep them from falling. "What are you doing?"

"Alias?" he asked, his mind spinning. Wait a minute. Why would she use a fake name?

The color drained from her face. "I, ah—"

"You knew," he whispered. "You knew there were bounty hunters after you." She opened her mouth, and he cut her off. "Don't lie to me again. I mean it." Betrayal burned down his throat. Fucking witches. They always lied and had an agenda. She'd brought danger onto his land without even thinking of giving him a heads-up. He released her so he wouldn't shake some sense into her. "Tell me the fuckin' truth."

She sighed. "You are so overreacting."

He growled low.

She stepped back. Smart girl.

"Now, Ness," he ordered.

She looked longingly toward double doors at the other side of the living area. Dark circles stood out beneath her eyes. "Fine. Yes, I did have knowledge of a possible bounty for my capture."

Even the way she strung the words together pissed him off. "Continue."

"Would you just trust me that we're safe for the night?"

"I don't trust an inch of you," he said, his voice hoarse. Shit, he was hungry. Her scent wrapped around him, upping his tension. "Who is after you?" In her eyes, he saw the second she finally decided to give him the truth.

"His name is George Flanders, and he's one of the few healers I know of still alive today." She bugged out her eyes. "Happy now? There's the truth." Her voice rose. "He's one of the richest guys on the planet, and he thinks he can buy anything—everything."

Bear held up a hand. "Slow down. If he's a healer, why does he want you?"

She clapped her palm against her head.

All right. When Little Miss Irish got tired, she got a little dramatic. Why he liked that about her, he'd never figure out. He sighed. "I'm tired, too." But he wasn't slow. Why would another healer want her? Wait a minute. Why would she want to mate Bear? Sure, the idea of her getting the ability to throw fire made sense, but since when had witches done things for just one reason? Their reasons were often multilayered and complex. "For Christ's sake," he muttered.

"Exactly." She nodded vigorously.

"He wants to mate you. The two of you—healers. Just what kind of an offspring might you create?" Bear barely kept from swearing about witches again. They were all nuts, really. "You were a member of the Council. A guy just doesn't put a bounty out on a member of the Council."

She sighed. "I'm not a member any longer, and I'm far away from home. This is the first chance he's had to catch me alone and without protection."

As the accountant to the Coven Nine, she probably did have a decent protection detail, not only for her skills but for her knowledge.

Bear's shirt kept dripping on the carpet, but at this point he didn't give a crap. "So the second you left safety, he put a bounty on your head." The woman was batshit crazy for leaving the protection of the Guard or the Enforcers to seek him out with her harebrained scheme. "You said my sister asked you to come."

"She did." Nessa's eyes blazed. "Simone asked me to help to heal you. The mating idea was mine, and I might not have revealed that plan to her."

"You also didn't tell her there was a bounty on your head," he said slowly. No way would his sister put a friend in danger. Nor would she send a hunted woman into Bear's territory without at least warning him first.

"No," Nessa whispered. "I figured it'd take a while for them to find me."

None of this was adding up very neatly. "Lady, I've had it with the half-truths." Bear needed to figure the guy out. Flanders had to have some serious clout to go after Nessa like this. "Do you want to get mated to avoid this whole issue with George?"

"It would be convenient," she said. "However, I was considering an arranged mating for the very reason I gave to you. I want the ability to create and throw fire. This world is just too dangerous not to have that."

"It's dangerous because you left the safety of your home and job," Bear shot back. "I can't believe the Enforcers let you leave."

"The Enforcers work for the Council," she said helpfully. "They protect the council members and also go on missions."

Why the hell was she giving him a civics lesson? "Your point?"

Exasperation filled her exhaled breath. "I'm not *on* the Council. Even when I do their work, I have protection from the Guard. They're the police force for our people."

The facts turned over until they made sense. His temper roared right awake. "The Guard doesn't know you have a bounty on your head." There was no way the Guard would have let her go, with her vast knowledge of the Council, if there was a known threat. He sighed. "You crazy-assed spoiled brat."

She reared back. "Watch your mouth, *shifter*. I might not be able to throw fire, but I can fight."

That quickly, at the derisive tone of her voice, he lost the control he'd kept on himself. He reached her in one stride, grabbing her arms and lifting her straight up. "Can you, now? Let's see."

She moved fast, her knee hitting him square in the gut. Air shot out of his lungs, but before he could regroup, she slammed both hands down on his shoulders in knife-blade formation. Pain ripped through his neck and arms as his nerves vibrated from the impact, and he released her.

The woman landed on her feet, pivoted, and kicked him square in the knee. He dropped fast.

She'd forgotten he was part animal. He grabbed her on the way down, flipping her onto her stomach in one smooth motion. She countered with an impressive somersault, ending up on her feet.

She kicked him in the cheek, and he rolled over onto his back with the woman standing up by his head.

He saw stars. Manacling her ankles, he pulled so hard she flew forward. Then he yanked her down.

She landed on him, and he spread his legs to keep her face from smashing into his knees. She landed on her hands and knees, her butt toward his face. Without any thought, he let instinct take over, shooting an arm between her legs to flatten on her abdomen. He shoved up and rolled, effectively forcing her onto her back next to him. Then he rolled on top of her.

Swearing an impressive litany of insults, she bucked and squirmed beneath him. Her nails raked his neck.

Pain lanced through his skin. He grabbed her wrists and pinned them above her head. With all the fighting, her sweats had ended up by her ankles. He kicked them out of the way, leaving her only in the thick sweatshirt and what looked like wild pink panties.

The woman didn't give up. She kicked and squirmed, her eyes ablaze.

He settled more comfortably against her, letting her fight it out. The more she struggled, the calmer he became. God, she was something.

Finally, she stopped moving, glaring at him. "I'm stronger," he said mildly.

She blew a piece of hair out of her eyes, fury spinning a glorious red across her cheekbones. "At the moment, only. I'm exhausted."

So was he. Yet he was suddenly appreciating their positions.

Her eyes widened. "You're aroused."

"Yep." He shifted to the left and put his raging cock right where it wanted to be. Or rather, close to where it wanted to be. His jeans and those panties kept him out of pure heat. "So are you."

The uptight little accountant had a few layers to her. He liked that, damn it.

She opened her mouth to deny it, to lie, and he just gave in. He took her mouth like the animal he was, hard and fierce, letting the hunger ripping through his veins free. The fight she'd just given him, the scratches on his neck, were all foreplay in his world. An invitation to take and tame.

White-hot lust coursed through him. He pushed her wrists up more, stretching her out, forcing her breasts against his chest.

She moaned deep, and her tongue swept against his as she kissed him back. His heartbeat thundered in his ears. She was the only thing in the world. The only thing he wanted. When she lifted her knees to the sides of his hips, he rocked against her.

"God," she gasped against his lips, arching up into him.

A brisk knock on the door shocked him into awareness. Fuck. He'd totally forgotten where they were. Who they were. He jumped to his feet and took her with him.

She sagged against him for a moment and then pushed him away. "Room service." She started toward the door, staggering a little.

He stopped her by hooking the back of her panties. The second his fingers slid past the waistband and brushed her smooth skin, he nearly came in his pants. "You're not wearing enough. Go to your bedroom, get some clothes that'll stay on, and I'll open the door." He twisted his wrist and nudged her toward the bedroom. "We'll eat something and talk." His body, even on fire for her, suddenly felt a thousand years old.

She obeyed him. This once. "I'll be right back."

Yeah. Then they really had to talk.

Chapter 9

Morning light cascaded into her sprawling bedroom, highlighting the antique oak furniture. The hotel really had put some time into perfecting the feng shui. Nessa hustled to dress casually in a pink pencil skirt with a ruffled blouse. Her earrings were small and gold, her lipstick muted, and her hair up and out of the way. After she and Bear had eaten the previous night, or rather in the morning, they'd been too tired to fight.

But after five hours of sleep, she was raring to go. If he wanted another round, she'd give it to him.

This time she'd win.

First, she had work to do. Opening her laptop, she quickly typed in a series of codes. Then she initiated a string of fail-safes that sent out signals from her computer so nobody could listen in—especially not the nosy shifter with super hearing in the other room. Soon, a handsome face came into view.

She smiled. "Morning, Jasper."

Jasper Marks took shape on the screen from Guard headquarters. Brown hair, green eyes, hard jaw. "Nessa. I was about to send out a search party."

She rolled her eyes. "I'm fine and still in Seattle."

"News?" the Guard lieutenant asked quietly.

"None yet." She made the decision on the spot to keep silent about George Flanders and the kidnapping bounty he'd put on her head. This was a mission, and she didn't need any more complications. She could handle George. "There were at least two deaths from the Apollo drug last night, and distribution seems to be flowing again."

Jasper sighed. "Human deaths, I assume?"

"If they had been witch deaths, I would've already called," she muttered.

He straightened. "Of course. I'm sorry."

"No worries." She straightened her posture. "I've infiltrated the Grizzly Motorcycle Club compound, and two of the deaths occurred there. Another human female overdosed, but I was able to save her." He reared back. "We'd wondered."

"Aye." Nessa swallowed. "Turns out I can assist humans with Apollo because of the PK."

Jasper's eyebrows drew down like they did when a junior officer screwed up. "You took too great a risk in finding out."

"It was worth it." She leaned toward the computer screen. "The Grizzly MC is definitely in the middle of the new Apollo trafficking, but they're covering their tracks well. Has anything happened at home?"

"Not yet, but we're keeping a close eye on Dublin. Sources say Apollo darts are set to arrive soon, but we haven't been able to track down a date." His eyes sizzled. "All intel points to Seattle as the location of the manufacturer still. I think you should have backup there."

She shook her head. "No. I barely got into the Grizzly compound. If I add another witch, it'll jeopardize the entire investigation."

"The dossier on Bear McDunphy says that he strongly dislikes witches. Except his sister," Jasper said.

Nessa nodded. Bear hadn't seemed to dislike her too badly when he'd been kissing her senseless the night before. "I know. He's a wild card. He's back in human form now."

"Tell me you haven't tried to heal him."

Nessa widened her eyes. "I promised Simone I would. So I am."

Jasper glanced over his shoulder and then back. "I guess that would inspire his trust." He leaned in and lowered his voice. "From all indications, if Bear discovers you work for the Guard, he might try to kill you."

"Good thing I can fight," she returned. "If you remember."

Jasper rubbed the area above his right eye where she'd clocked him during their last training session. "Aye. I remember." He stared directly into the camera. How many times had they communicated this way over the years? Too many. "It goes against all the regulations for you to be on assignment without backup. With only the two of us knowing about it."

Apollo was that deadly. "If the drug gets to Dublin, and those darts are used in any setting, we'll lose witches. A lot of them." She appreciated her friend worrying about her, but national security trumped safety. "This is too important, Jasper." They'd been buddies who had covered each other's backs many times through the years, and she trusted him. "If I need backup, I'll let you know."

He typed for a moment. "There's chatter, Nessa. Operatives are checking in all over the world having observed coded chatter. Odd movements of enemies and mercenaries."

She straightened. "You think there's a worldwide campaign commencing?"

"Aye," Jasper said.

Bollocks. They'd always known there was an endgame to the Apollo drug and that it involved harming a lot of witches. Possible targets would be anybody in government, medical research, or politics. Probably private citizens as well. "Get coverage on anybody we think might be a target, and no group assembling for the time being. Is there any intel we can pursue right now?" she asked.

"No, but the clock is counting down. The attack is imminent. We need to find the manufacturer, and now." Jasper leaned even closer to the screen. "Is Bear McDunphy behind the distribution?"

"I don't want to think so, considering his sister is a witch," she said slowly. Of course, her opinion might be clouded by his hot body and drugging kisses. "He's lying about not shifting for the last three months. His body would be a little better healed if he'd stayed in bear form for an entire season."

Jasper's eyebrows lifted. "When did he shift?"

She was doing her best to be logical, but her stomach ached at the thought that Bear might be trying to kill her people. "I don't know. It seemed like his crew didn't know he'd shifted back. They acted as if they hadn't seen him in a long time."

"Did anybody expressly say it had been three months?" Jasper asked.

Nessa thought back to the party. "No. I don't think so."

"Perhaps it had just been a month. Or even a couple of weeks. They still might be glad to see him." Jasper's gaze darkened. "Step very carefully, Nessa. Besides the council job, you haven't been undercover in a long time. The entire motorcycle club might be organized around the Apollo drug, and you're over there all alone."

She shivered. "I know, but it doesn't make sense. Why would Bear want to harm witches, especially when his sister is one?"

"I don't know," Jasper said. "Witches and dragons have never gotten along very well, and he is part dragon. Plus, whoever is selling Apollo in the States is making millions. Humans are loving the drug. Well, those who don't overdose."

Aye. The drug made them feel godlike for a few hours. "Bear doesn't seem to care much about money," Nessa said. Darn it. She needed to think logically and not let her hormones get in the way. "If he's behind the manufacture and new distribution of the drug, it'd be about something else. Revenge, maybe." She needed to dig deeper with him.

"Revenge?" Jasper asked.

"Yeah, but for what? I mean, his dad died when he was a teenager, and he moved to the States by himself." She tried to remember the facts from the information compiled about him. "I think Vivienne Northcutt forced him out of Dublin and away from her daughter—his sister."

"Trauma in his teen years would certainly give him motivation," Jasper mused. "But he would've had to amass a fortune in order to mine the PK in Russia, ship it to the States, and then create Apollo with it. Does he seem smart enough to do that?"

"Definitely," Nessa said. "He's incredibly intelligent." But would he use his energy that way? "I'm uncertain he'd want to spend years planning a terrorist campaign. He's more of a rip-your-head-off kind of guy." The planning this took would have required great patience.

"Keep alert, and if you need anything, call," Jasper said.

"I will. Before we sign off, have you seen my uncle?"

Jasper grinned. "Aye. He took part in the field exercises the other day. First he kicked everyone's ass, and then he healed any bones he broke."

Nessa chuckled. "He still thinks I'm on vacation after the council job?"

Jasper sobered. "Which is a very bad idea. Tell him the truth."

"He's retired." The man was over two thousand years old and deserved a break. Oh, he'd be back to work at some point, but for now he was mentally recharging. If Nessa told him about her mission, he'd be in Seattle in a heartbeat. "He stays out of this one, Jasper."

"Your decision. Check in as soon as you can."

"Aye." She clicked off the call and stood, smoothing her hair into place. She'd been undercover before, but even when pretending to be part of a group, she knew she was alone. Aside from her uncle, she'd always been on her own. Nothing new. Drawing her courage around her, she slipped into muted beige heels and finally exited her bedroom.

Bear was at the table, eating what looked like several platters of food. "Mornin'." He was in the same faded jeans and dark T-shirt, and he'd pulled his hair back at the nape. Scruff still covered his angled jaw, and his bourbon-colored eyes were clear, but dark circles slashed beneath them.

She paused and then continued toward him. "Hungry?"

"Yeah. I'll pay you back." He gestured toward a chair. "You?"

"A little." She took a piece of toast and ate it. "You look tired. Are you hurting?"

He finished his eggs. "No."

"Liar," she said softly, a part of her needing to ease his pain. It came with healing. "How about I heal you a little?"

He leaned back, studying her. "You up to it?"

She tilted her head toward the settee. "Let's find out, shall we?"

Bear took in her pink skirt. While it was probably meant to be businesslike, it hugged her ass perfectly. He followed her to the sofa, enjoying the distraction from the pain thrumming through his chest. He'd overdone it the day before, and he was paying for it.

She paused, her lips pursing. "Hmmm."

"What?" he asked, his fingers itching to yank out her hair clip.

"I'm not sure how to do this." She looked around the room. "It'd be easiest if we sat across from each other, but I'd have to lean the whole time, and I need to concentrate just on you."

"Easily solved." He sat on the couch and pulled her onto his lap to straddle him.

"Wait—" she started, her hands flattening on his chest.

He pushed her skirt up her smooth legs and pulled her closer. "There."

Her mouth slightly opened, and she barely shook her head. "What are you doing?"

With her legs on either side of his, with her core so damn close, what he was doing was losing his fuckin' mind. "Solving the problem." He glanced pointedly at her hands on his chest. "See? You're in position and you don't have to lean."

One of her shoes dropped to the carpet. Her mouth tightened. "This is not appropriate."

The woman should know by now that there was nothing appropriate about him. He'd thought about it all night, and fixing her up with his brother made sense. She'd be better off with a full dragon mate who had lots of fire and money and lived on a safe invisible island in the middle of nowhere.

But his gut had ached the whole time. For the moment, she was in his hands. Temporarily. Ah hell, why not? He gave in and grasped her hair clip, opening it and tossing it across the room. All of that glorious hair flew around. The smell of roses heated through him and settled.

"Bear," she protested.

He landed his hands at her waist. He was a rough bear shifter and not a smooth dragon shifter—so be it. "I thought I heard you talking to somebody in your room." But then when he tried to really listen, all he got was silence. Was he imagining things now?

"Sometimes I mumble to myself when I'm planning my day." She spread her fingers over his chest. "Close your eyes."

"Wait. Will this hurt you?" While he wanted to be whole again, he wouldn't use her to do it. Not if it caused her pain.

She rolled her eyes. "No. Stop worrying and shut your eyes."

Man, she was bossy sometimes. "All right, but if it starts to hurt, you stop."

"Of course."

He shut his eyes. His chest warmed and heated, and then the solid flow of energy moved inside him, going deep and massaging. He groaned and let his head roll back on the sofa. For the moment, he forgot about the sexy woman on his lap and just felt the healing balm going deep inside him. The feeling was nearly indescribable. His body relaxed, taken away. All pain disappeared, and tension soon flowed down his arms and out his fingertips.

Deep down, where he hadn't been able to find himself, he started to mend. He could feel it happen.

The world floated by outside him, and he couldn't care less. He became energy in that moment—free and healthy. No worries, no pain. No anger, either.

Soon, an alertness wound through him. The world returned. He was aware of the woman on his lap and the scent of roses. Her taut thighs clasping his. Smooth hands, fingers wide, sending warmth through his entire body. When he came back into himself, he did it with one word. "Nessa." His eyelids opened.

She leaned back, her eyes dark pools of pure violet light.

He breathed.

As he watched, her eyes morphed back to the violet blue he already knew well. She blinked several times, as if coming back into herself.

"Are you all right?" he whispered.

She barely nodded. "Aye. That was . . . unique."

His hands felt just right on her hips. "For you, too?"

"Yes. I've never experienced anything like that." A cute frown drew down her eyebrows. "I've been out of it before, but never a part of somebody else's essence, you know? I always figured that kind of connection only happened between family."

"Or mates." He said the word she was obviously trying to avoid.

She looked down at her hands on his chest. "We're not mates."

No, and he'd never given one inch of credibility to fate or destiny, even though many of his people did. "No, we're not." The fabric beneath his hands was high-end and silky, and the hips beneath it firm and narrow.

A small smile played on her mouth. "Did you feel your muscles return to health?"

He rolled his shoulders. "I did. It was weird. I could sense them strengthening and getting healthy, but it was different from whatever went on deeper. I guess my messing with physics and turning into a dragon was a very bad idea."

Her smile lit her face. "You violated physical laws. That was a very bad idea."

His chest was wider—almost as wide as before he'd gotten sick. His legs felt strong again. A rumble came up from his chest that was all bear. "I feel like myself again." Like the alpha of the grizzly nation.

"Your physical strength has returned," she said thoughtfully.

Did that seem to worry her? He tilted his head to the side. "I won't hurt you, Ness."

"I won't hurt you, either." She dropped her hands and looked to the side.

"Wait." He flexed his fingers and fought the strong need to pull her closer to his now very awake groin. "Thank you."

She smiled and shimmied her hips to dismount. "You're welcome."

He bit back a groan. She had to stop wiggling on him. "I thought about what you said yesterday, and I think you should go meet my brother."

"The dragon," she said, irritation swirling in her eyes.

"Yes."

Her other shoe dropped from her wriggling. "Because I'm superficial and need a lot of money."

"No." Bear frowned. "You deserve luxury and safety."

She sighed. "You don't understand. If I want luxury, I can make my own money. And I can definitely keep myself safe. Get a clue, Bear." She grasped his hands and set them to the side before sliding off him to stand. "However, we agree that our mating is definitely off the table, so to speak. So let's finish the rest of our agreement, and we'll go our separate ways."

He opened his mouth to say something, anything, when the door blew open with a fiery blast. "Nessa!" he yelled, leaping for her.

Chapter 10

The explosion blew Nessa over the marble coffee table. She landed hard, the air whooshing from her lungs. Training kicked in and she rolled, coming up in a crouch.

She gained her equilibrium in time to see Bear bound over the back of the settee straight at three men in black with ski masks covering their faces. He plowed into two of them, propelling them sideways into the doorframe. Wood cracked and splintered. Sheetrock blew out. One guy dropped to the ground and the other pulled up a green gun and fired.

The shot went wide, toward Nessa. She yelped and leaped to the right. Then she set her stance and focused on the third guy, concentrating on his energy. Human. He was tight and tall—definitely in fighting shape. But she could take a human. Several, probably.

He lifted an odd, narrow, long gun.

She paused, panic rippling through her.

He fired. Several yellow-tipped darts shot out. She yelled and jumped out of the way, dropping hard to the floor. The darts flew over her head and embedded themselves in the drapes behind her. There was only one reason to use darts in a firefight with a witch. The damn things had to be full of Apollo.

A body flew over her to crash on the dining room table. She gaped. The human bounced to the floor and then expelled air before going limp. Smoke billowed in the room, and a small fire from the explosion licked up the wallpaper by the entryway.

Don't think. Act. On her hands and knees, she lunged for the dart shooter's legs, taking him down in a tangle. He chopped at the side of her neck, and she saw stars. Pain rippled down her entire arm and through her rib cage. The guy fumbled for his gun again, his eyes cold behind the mask.

Panicking, she kicked the gun out of his hand, and it went spiraling across the lush carpet. She punched him in the throat before following up with a jab to the nose. Blood sprayed, and she tried to duck, but it arced across her blouse. Bollocks.

With a fierce roar, the human tossed her off him. Her shoulder hit the coffee table, and pain flared through her torso.

Another body flew over her head, this one smashing into the window and dropping to the carpet with a bone-breaking crunch. Bear was throwing bodies everywhere.

She looked up.

He stalked toward her, fury sizzling off him and choking the atmosphere. Through the light smoke, he looked like a destructive god.

"No." She shoved to her feet. "This asshole is mine." Her feet scrunched into the carpet as she advanced on the human.

He looked from her to Bear, obviously thinking Bear was the bigger threat.

Bear crossed his arms, blocking the exit, his gaze beyond pissed. "Hurry up, then." He paused. "You might want to give him a message for George."

"He doesn't work for George," Nessa said, jumping up and kicking the human beneath the chin. His head snapped back, and he dropped to his knees. He did not get right back up.

How disappointing.

"Not for George?" Bear asked.

"No." She moved in and yanked off the guy's ski mask. He swayed in place. About thirty, black hair, blue eyes, very thick jaw. Nessa punched him in his smashed nose again.

He howled and grabbed his nose.

She sighed and looked at Bear. "He's just not giving a good fight."

Bear nodded soberly. "Your kick probably gave him a concussion. How do you know he doesn't work for George?"

Nessa jerked her head toward the dart gun several feet away from her. "Apollo darts."

Bear straightened and lost his lazy amusement. His eyes darkened to a violent hue. "Apollo? This is a kill squad?"

"A crappy human one." She grabbed the guy's hair and jerked

back his head. Blood flowed freely down his face and over his mouth. "Who hired you?"

He sputtered and spit blood.

She swallowed down bile. "I donna' want to kill you, but I will. Tell me who."

Bear growled, letting the rumble sound just like a real bear.

The human trembled. "Frank J hired us."

"Who is Frank J?" Bear muttered, gingerly touching a cut in his lip.

"He's a bartender at Slam downtown," the human said. He coughed, and more blood came up.

Nessa backed away from the mess. "Did he say why?"

"Nope. Just offered us a grand each." The guy wiped off his mouth, spreading blood over his chin even while his nose continued to spurt. "It's just darts. Frank said they'd only knock you out and give you a hellacious hangover. Something about a boyfriend you cheated on."

For Pete's sake. Nessa moved around him and gingerly picked up the dart gun.

The guy started chuckling with an odd wheezing sound.

She paused. "What?"

"We're not alone, lady."

Her eyes widened. A bizarre buzzing sound came from outside, and she slowly turned her head toward the window. Panic shook her. Her muscles bunched and she turned to run for Bear, her head down. "Run," she yelled.

He was already in motion, grabbing her and rushing for the exit. They reached the double door just as the window shattered and something landed on the coffee table to bounce loudly with resonating tings. A grenade?

Bear wrapped his arms around her waist and propelled them both into the hallway. The grenade blew, and the atmosphere changed, electrifying with energy that threw them both high into the air. They flew several yards. Bear twisted at the last moment, reversing their positions and landing on his back with Nessa on top of him.

She landed hard, the air knocked out of her. Pain detonated in her head when her forehead hit his chin. Red and white sparked behind her eyes, and she whimpered, the sound muffled against his shirt.

Human shouts of fear sounded from behind closed doors.

Then she was up and the walls were flying by, smoke chasing them and fire crackling in their wake. Bear had a tight hold around her waist and was all but carrying her, his speed amazing. A light fixture dropped from the ceiling, and he sidestepped it, not losing momentum.

She regained her faculties and pushed his ribs. "I can run."

"Okay." He set her on her feet without missing a stride. "Elevators are probably safer than the stairs."

True. The attack force would cover the stairs. "They might have taken the control room to access the elevators," she gasped, hunching over to avoid falling debris.

He stopped and punched the down button at the elevator bank. "We'll have to risk it."

She set her hands on her knees, bending over, trying to pant in air. Her face hurt, her ribs ached, and now her lungs burned. "The first wave was just a decoy," she coughed.

"Yes." He pushed the button several more times. "Human ones."

"These might be human, too." Trained with explosives. Where was the elevator? At the far end of the hallway, the stairwell door burst wide.

The elevator door slid open, and Bear yanked her inside, repeatedly pushing the lobby button and the close-door button.

Three men came into view, running toward them, all dressed in black gear. Two had dart guns. The one in front fired rapidly. Bear whirled and put his body between the darts and Nessa just as the door closed.

"Fuck," he muttered, looking over his shoulder at his back. He turned around. "Can you take these out without touching the poison?"

She gulped over a lump in her throat. Her hands shook as she reached quickly for him.

"Wait." He stepped away. The elevator started to descend. "Don't panic. Apollo doesn't hurt me, and the darts are just a nuisance. They'll kill you. So make sure you can take them out without harming yourself. I need you at full speed."

"You don't feel anything?" she asked.

"Just the prick of the dart. PK and Apollo only harm witches and humans. The poison won't affect me."

Yeah, but he was part dragon. But he seemed fine. She eyed the five darts sticking out of his back. "The flight and shaft are safe for me." Even the barrel was probably fine for her to touch. "I just need to avoid the point."

"The flight and shaft? Lady, you know your darts."

She gingerly reached for the first shaft and yanked out the dart with one smooth motion. "We know all about darts, with Apollo on the loose." Tossing the first one aside, she pulled out the remaining darts, keeping just one. The flight was a hard plastic, with the shaft and barrel made of steel. Bear turned around just as Nessa lifted it to her nose and sniffed. A very mild smell of spiced oranges and sulfur burned her nose. She threw the dart on the floor with the others. "It's Apollo."

"How does a mineral have a smell?" Bear asked, looking up at the numbers atop the door. Soot covered his cheekbone, and a cut above his left eye bled down his rugged face.

"It doesn't. The chemical agents they use to melt it down and keep it in liquid form have a distinct smell." She followed his gaze, her ears still ringing. They were almost at the fourth floor. "The front and back entrances will be covered, Bear." Her mind spun, and she tried to think of a way they could get out of the hotel without getting killed.

"I know." He pushed the button for the third floor.

She shook her head and then winced at the sparks of pain slamming into her temples. "The stairwell will still be covered."

"Yeah. I'm thinking a different exit." The door opened and he stepped out, his hand holding her back. He lifted his head and scented the air, his shoulders going down. "We're clear for now." Grabbing her hand, he pulled her out of the elevator and down the hallway. "How do you feel about jumping?"

She stumbled, following him to the very end of the hallway and a wide window looking out onto the street. "Jumping?" she croaked.

He leaned his head against the window and pointed down. "There's an awning over the valet station."

She gulped and looked down. The awning was high-end and tight. But Bear was a bear . . . and he was almost at full physical strength and size. "Not sure it'll hold us both."

"Doesn't have to hold us." Bear turned to the side. "Cover your face so I can break the window."

Panic, hot and desperate, rushed through her and burned her lungs. She turned and crouched down.

Glass shattered.

"Got it all," Bear said, roughly grabbing her arms. "Let's go." Without waiting for an answer, he jumped through the window.

Cold air slammed into Nessa a second before she opened her mouth and screamed. They fell and hit the awning. Her ribs protested, and her head ached. The awning creaked and stretched, finally splitting.

Bear held her close, did an odd somersault in the air, and landed on his feet with Nessa in his arms.

She blinked and looked up at him. Stunned.

Without pausing, he set her down, grabbed her hand, and clasped several key chains from the valet box. "Run. Now." He launched himself into motion, and she had to pump her bare feet furiously just to keep up. They barreled down into a garage, Bear dropping keys as they went.

They passed a brand-new Ferrari.

Bear halted, looked around, and pressed a button on the only key fob left in his hand—the one for his truck. Lights blinked from the back of the garage. "Let's go. We have to get out of here."

She couldn't think.

Men yelling orders from the street caught her attention and she hurried behind Bear, running for the truck.

The air gathered and stilled in warning.

Bear stopped cold, and she collided into his back, bouncing to the ground. Her butt hit first, and agony raced up her spine. The truck exploded with a flash of fire. Bear dropped and turned, flattening her with his body. Metal flew over their heads, and a flaming tire rolled by to fall against a pillar.

"Fuck," Bear muttered, shoving himself up and taking her with him. Men ran down the sloped entrance right at them.

"The Ferrari," Nessa blurted, heading toward it.

Bear grabbed her arm and yanked her in the other direction. "No. Can't hot-wire it. SUV." He hustled toward an older SUV and punched through the driver's-side window to unlock the door. Blood dripped from his hand.

The men ran closer, the one in front firing a dart gun.

Something pierced her shoulder. Bear lifted and threw her across the seat. She bounced and grabbed the dashboard to hold herself in place. He slammed the door and ripped wires from below the dash. The engine ignited.

He yanked the car into reverse and hit the gas pedal, speeding backwards to smash into several men. Bodies went flying.

Nessa swallowed down bile. Her temples hurt. Her brain felt heavy. Where were they? Why did everything ache?

The SUV spun around and Bear punched the gas. They careened out of the garage, the back end thumping over a speed bump.

Wind poured through the broken window.

Nessa tried to focus on Bear. He hunched over the steering wheel and zipped around honking cars and yelling pedestrians. Within minutes, they were on their way out of the city.

Her head lolled. Fire lit her blood, and she gasped in pain as she could almost feel her brain swell against her skull.

He glanced her way, not losing speed. "You okay?"

Her mouth went dry until she couldn't speak. The day fuzzed and turned gray.

"Nessa?" His voice came from very far away, as if it were in a tunnel. Then, "Shit. You got hit." He leaned over and pulled something out of her skin.

She cried out at the pinch.

They'd gotten her, and her veins hurt. Her head, on the other hand, had taken a beating with the last grenade. It wasn't her first concussion—not by a long shot. She'd forgotten how bad it could hurt.

The world went black, and she passed out.

Chapter 11

Bear smoothed back the damp hair on Nessa's head and then replaced the cool cloth on her forehead. A slight fire crackled in his fireplace, and a peaceful silence took hold of the small cabin. He'd gotten her back to his cabin two hours ago, and she still hadn't regained consciousness. "Are you sure she'll be okay?" he snapped into the phone at his sister.

"Yes. We already know that Apollo darts don't harm her like they do most witches. It's the fire-making properties, which she doesn't have, that cause most of the internal damage," Simone said thoughtfully. "If she was hit with only one dart, she'll be fine and just needs to sleep it off."

"What if she gets hit with more than one dart?" Bear asked grimly.

Simone sighed. "I assume it depends on the dosage. At some point, even with her mutated genes, enough Apollo would take a toll. Even kill her."

"She isn't mutated," Bear snapped back.

Simone's voice softened with what sounded suspiciously like amusement. "Oh, brother. Do you have a crush?"

"No." He barely kept his growl in his chest.

"Mutations aren't bad or good. They're part of genetics," Simone said, as if explaining the existence of the moon to a toddler.

Bear refused to answer.

She sighed. "It sounds like Nessa has a concussion." Simone's voice was a little tinny on the secure line. "Relax."

"Simone? What the hell is going on?" he growled. "Why was there a kill squad at her hotel? This is different from George Flanders's kidnap plot that I already told you about. These people wanted her dead."

"I donna' know," Simone said. "I'll have the Council start investigating."

Bear rubbed a hand over his eyes. "Help me work this out."

"Always," she said calmly.

"You sent Nessa to heal me," he started, anger slowly building. A beep echoed on his phone, and he looked down to see his sister's face. Long black hair and dangerously intelligent eyes. "Let's do this so we can see each other," she murmured, her full red lips curving in a smile. "Modern technology is so lovely."

He tried to hold on to his anger, knowing he was being manipulated, but it wisped out of his grasp. "It's good to see you," he admitted.

"I've missed you, too." One of her dark eyebrows arched. "You need a haircut."

He brushed his hair back from his face. "Back to the topic."

She sighed. "Fine. Yes, I sent Nessa to heal you. Or rather, I asked her nicely."

"You emotionally blackmailed her because the Council screwed up while she was a member," he returned, sitting on the bed and managing not to jostle Nessa.

Simone shrugged. "That is nicely."

Probably true in the witch world. Damn witches. "You took advantage of a friend."

"Aye. I'd take advantage of any friend in order to save you, my brother." A fierceness echoed in the words. "So deal with it."

"I'm trying to deal with it," he growled back. "But you sent a woman who looks like Jackie O, fights like Jackie Chan, and has more secrets than Jackie Fiddleton."

Simone burst out laughing. "Very nice. I always thought Jackie Fiddleton got a bad rap."

The former witch spy had been killed a century ago, but during his long life he'd worked on nearly every treaty created by the witches. And he'd been a hell of a spy. "The guy is legendary. Even the shifter nations know about his exploits." Bear glanced again at Nessa. "She's not safe out in the world right now."

"Witches rarely are," Simone returned. "She's the top forensic accountant for the Coven Nine, Bear. She's accustomed to danger."

Bear's head jerked. A ball of ice dropped into his gut. "Excuse me?" Simone faltered. "Ah, well . . . hmm. I guess you didn't know that. Nessa is a forensic accountant—one of our best. She traces money like nobody else."

The silent witch on his bed held top-secret clearance. "Isn't she full of surprises," Bear muttered, wanting to shake her awake.

Simone nodded. "Probably."

He'd deal with Nessa and her lack of trust in him later. "One enemy at a time. For now, find out everything you can about George Flanders and what kind of a reach he truly has. By the end of the day, I want to know his favorite ice cream. Give me every weakness he has." Bear's hands twitched with the need to wrap them around George's neck. "I'll not let him force Nessa into a mating just because she's a healer."

Simone's eyes gleamed. "I already have our techs on a deep background check. But he's not the enemy to focus on."

"I'm aware," Bear muttered, not able to look away from the too-quiet woman on his bed. "Somebody wants her dead."

"Yes." Simone sobered. "We'll start an investigation immediately."

Bear focused. "You don't know anything? No leads or clues?"

"No," Simone said, meeting his gaze evenly. "This is definitely unexpected. Also, I'm not sure if you're aware, but yesterday there was a dramatic increase in worldwide chatter. Movements of operatives and a lot of Internet correspondence and positioning."

Bear's head dropped. Why hadn't he just stayed in the woods? "You think the attack is coming together." They'd known from the onset of the Apollo trafficking that there would be a full-out assault against the witch nation at some point.

"Aye," Simone said. "We're pulling in informants and trying to find a pattern, but nothing so far. We're on full alert."

"I'll get my people up to speed," Bear said.

"Good. For now, I'll send the Enforcers over to escort Nessa back home."

Nessa stirred. "I'm not leaving," she said, her eyes remaining closed. "Bear isn't healed yet."

Relief shook Bear so hard he barely bit back a gasp. "Ness? You okay?"

"Just tired," she said sleepily. "Don't want to leave."

"You don't have to leave, baby." Bear had made a promise to take out George Flanders, and now he made a mental vow to destroy whoever was trying to kill her. He focused back on his sister. "She stays here."

"Really?" Simone drawled, her dark eyes sparkling.

Bear kept his gaze stoic. "We have a business arrangement." That had involved more than a couple of kisses. "We're on lockdown here with full patrols. Assure the Council, Enforcers, and Guard that Nessa is safe in Grizzly territory." The idea of her leaving made his chest feel hollow, but she couldn't stay long-term. Once he made her safe, he'd have to deal with that fact. He made a mental note to have the patrols tripled.

Nessa rolled over, sighing into what looked like a deep sleep.

"She'll be fine after she sleeps and heals her brain," Simone said. "Stop worrying."

"I'm not. I'm pissed. They blew up my truck." Bear lowered his chin and studied his sister, now that he'd issued the orders. "You look pale. How are you feeling?"

She smiled, and her face was transformed from beautiful to unbelievably stunning. "I feel fine. Carrying a demon baby isn't for wimps. The kid is already doing somersaults in there."

"And your mate?" Bear asked. Truth be told, he'd liked Nick Veis from the beginning, even though he was a demon soldier—the top soldier for the demon nation, right alongside his best friend, their leader, Zane Kyllwood. "Is he preparing for this kid? Could be a girl, you know."

Simone nodded. "Nick is driving me crazy. Did you know there are little plugs humans put in electrical outlets? They're impossible to remove, even for an adult."

Amusement swept over Bear. "You still have five months to go. Why plug the outlets now?"

She leaned in. "I have no idea. He's lost his mind." Love filled her words. "Crazy demon."

Oh, there was no doubt insanity ran in the demon nation. But Nick would keep Simone safe, and that's what mattered to Bear. "You mated him," he reminded her.

"Aye, I did." Her smile was happy. That's all Bear had ever wanted for her.

He sighed. "I have work, sis. Call with updates tonight."

"Wait." She leaned in. "What's going on with you and Nessa? I mean, I thought maybe you two might—"

He clicked off. His personal life was just that. Sliding the phone into his pocket, he felt Nessa's pulse at her wrist. Steady. Good. He stood and paused, staring down at her. Her hair was splayed all over the pillow in a silky mass. Beneath the blanket he'd draped over her, she looked small. Defenseless.

Something harsh and fierce rose in him. "You'll be safe here." Without a thought, he leaned over and kissed her brow, inhaling the scent of Irish roses—the wild ones that grew in the high country. "I promise." She didn't move.

He turned and strode for the door, shoving his way outside to find a light snow falling in the dim afternoon. The first snow of the season. It'd disappear within an hour, but soon it'd be winter. He nodded at the guards on the porch—two of the men who'd been Grizzly brothers of his for more than three decades. They both still looked twenty-five and were in excellent physical shape. "Nobody gets in there."

"Copy that," they said in unison.

He clomped down the steps in his thick boots and walked along the trail toward headquarters. The snow fell lightly around him, and the muddy ground had hardened to crisp cracked dirt with frost. His normal metabolism had returned: he didn't feel the cold even while wearing just a T-shirt.

But he stopped in his office to tug on his leather jacket and cut with the Grizzly logo on the back. There were people he didn't know in his organization, and that had to end.

Lucas came in the front door, brushing snow off his hair. "I've had all members in the area come in. They're waiting in the main rec room."

"I want everyone recalled," Bear said, rolling his neck. Being in human form still felt weird. "I don't care where they are, what they're doing, or who they're with. If they want to continue to be members or prospective members of the Grizzly Motorcycle Club, then they will be here by the end of the week." He also wanted to reach out to members of the grizzly nation who weren't part of the MC. While many of them roamed in independent packs, at the end of the day, he ruled them, too.

"Understood," Lucas said. He'd also changed into his cut. "Listen, Bear. I've known you a long time."

Bear paused. "Yeah?"

"Now's not a good time to do what you're about to do." Lucas's eyes glowed a serious hue.

"What's that?"

Luke shut the door behind him. "Get rid of all the humans. You're going to go in there, tell the humans to get out, and then put the entire club on lockdown."

Bear lifted his head. Yeah. His friend did know him. Well. "Humans can't be members of the club. Sometimes we shift. We talk shifter nation business. You know we can't have humans here unless we're having a big party." What the hell had Lucas been thinking to allow humans in?

"We need them," Lucas said simply. "At least until everyone gets back—especially Lars, Brinks, and Duncan. We have full appointments all next week for repairs and a whole lotta snow tires. We need the funds, Bear."

"My men will return," Bear said evenly. "I'll fund the motorcycle club until then." He'd made money for years and didn't see any need to buy shit he didn't want, so he'd invested most of the money. His private accounts could support the club indefinitely.

Lucas shook his head. "We agreed the business would stay separate. You can't fund it."

Bear rolled his eyes. "If you weren't so shitty with money, you could've loaned the club money while I was gone." He grinned. His buddy was the worst with money—just terrible. Never had any. "Remember that biofuel company you bought a couple of decades ago?"

Lucas sighed. "I thought tree sap would make a good fuel."

Bear snorted. "I'll loan the club money, and when the guys get back, we'll be fine."

"I know, but when? I haven't been able to track down any of the three. If they wanna be lost, they're lost. We also have about thirty members roaming the earth elsewhere." Lucas wiped snow off his forehead. "At least let the humans stay the week to get the work done. Even if we have money, we need good mechanics. We don't need any more bad press, either. If they leave and start badmouthing us around town, we could be harassed again by the bloodsucking DEA."

That's all Bear needed, especially with Apollo overdoses already having happened on his property. "How many human prospects are there?"

"Just five," Lucas said. "All good mechanics. We have four shifter prospects as well."

Bear blew out air. "Fine. They can stay the week, but then they're gone."

Lucas nodded. "Thanks."

Bear paused. "I'm sorry I dumped all of this on you."

"No choice." His friend grinned. "I get it. Plus, it was fun being in charge for a little while. Lots of tail."

Bear snorted. "You've never had trouble with the ladies." But had Lucas ever been serious with anybody? "You ever think of settling down? The whole mating and cubs thing?"

Lucas sobered. "Yeah. Now that the war has ended—the most current war, anyway—I've been giving it some thought."

Bear perked up. "Is that a fact? Anybody I know?"

"Nope," Lucas said, nudging the door open with his hip.

Bear followed, noting the snow had almost stopped falling. "Wait a minute, here. Are you 'in lurve,' Lucas?"

"Shut up." Luke punched him in the arm hard enough to break a human's bone.

Bear just grinned and punched him back as hard. "Come on. Tell me who. Is it Angie?"

Lucas cut him a look. "Of course not. I'd never mate a human."

Yeah, they stayed frail even when they became immortal. It was an odd combination. So Lucas must have his eye on a bear shifter. Bear ran through the available women. "Is she a member of the MC?"

Lucas rolled his eyes as they walked over the snowy pavement and past the garages. "You are being such a girl. Forget about it."

Bear clasped a hand to his chest. "Oh. She doesn't know you're alive."

Lucas growled. "I've been leading the Grizzlies. Of course she knows I'm alive."

Bear bit back a laugh. "She doesn't like you, then."

Luke hunched his shoulders. "Get your mind in the game. You're about to face a room full of shifters who'd die for you and a few humans who have no clue we aren't of the same species. You clear?"

Bear sobered. "I'm clear. When we're finished with this meeting, I need you to investigate a bar downtown called Slam and especially the bartender, a guy named Frank J. He hired out the hit on Nessa."

"Copy that," Lucas said. "We'll get right on it."

"Good. When you find the guy, I want to question him." Bear followed Lucas inside the warm rec room. The sofas had been pushed to the side again, but the place was pristine clean. Maybe the human prospects weren't so bad. Men and women sat around on chairs, on the bar, even on the pool table.

He looked around at the assembled group, recognizing most of them. Many looked back at him and gave relieved smiles.

"Welcome back," said Polly Risen, a bear shifter who'd been his friend for decades. Her long brown hair flowed around her shoulders, and her even darker eyes sparkled. "We missed you."

Bear smiled. Was Polly the woman Lucas wanted? He lifted his eyebrows at Lucas, who glared back. That might be awkward. Bear and Polly and torn up the sheets more than once—but just for fun and only as friends. Lucas had to know about that, so if it was Polly, then Luke had made peace with the fact.

Who cared, anyway?

Bear cleared his throat. "I'd first like to thank Lucas for covering me these last few months. He stepped up, and he did the club proud."

Catcalls, whistles, and clapping ensued.

Lucas just sighed.

Bear then lost his grin. "We had an overdose of Apollo in our territory, in our *clubhouse*, last night. The woman is fine now, however." He didn't mention the two dead bodies. The fewer people who knew about that, the better. The group instantly went sober. "I want to know this second if anybody here is messing with that poisonous drug."

Nobody moved.

"Who invited the guests who brought Apollo?" Bear growled.

"How are we supposed to know what guests bring in?" asked the human prospect Bear had thrown out the night before. A bandage covered his broken nose, looking right at home between his two black eyes. His arm was in a sling, and he sat slightly to the side as if in pain.

The room went deadly silent.

The kid moved on the seat uneasily.

Bear looked at him, unmoving.

The kid next to him, another human, swallowed loudly. "I agree. We're not responsible for what other people do."

And that was the exact wrong answer. Bear strode toward the five humans sitting together. "You're out. All five of you." He could barely make out Lucas's quiet sigh. "We don't need new prospects, and we sure as shit don't need dumbasses who invite people with Apollo into our world. Get. Out."

The second kid lunged to his feet, his chest bumping Bear's.

The hackles rose down Bear's back. He grabbed the kid by his T-shirt.

"Bear," Polly murmured. "Murder is illegal."

The kid paled.

Bear leaned into the kid's face. "Get your buddies and get out before I throw you, too. This time I might miss the door."

The kid jerked away and huffed toward the exit.

"Now," Bear said to the rest of the humans. "You have five minutes to get out of my territory. Then I get cranky."

They all stomped off, and the kid Bear had thrown stopped at the door. "This isn't over," he muttered.

Bear moved toward him, and he quickly escaped outside. Taking a deep breath, Bear looked at his brothers and sisters—all shifters, as they should be. "So. I guess we have a lot of work to do now."

Chapter 12

"Nessa? Stop it, baby," a low voice rumbled in her ear.

She jerked awake, her gaze catching on the rough interior logs of the cabin. The very first rays of dawn were trying to poke through the darkened window. A fire crackled happily and warmed the entire room, while the wind whistled furiously outside. Blankets cocooned her . . . and a hard body held her from behind.

She blinked.

Bear's arm was banded around her waist, and her butt was flush against a full erection. The bear slept in the nude. Not a surprise. His nose was tucked into her neck, and his voice had been hoarse and sleepy.

"What are you doing?" she whispered.

"Waking you. Sorry about that, but we fell asleep, and you were healing me," he mumbled, his lips moving against her nape.

She shivered, and desire flowed through her as if she'd poured heated wine into her veins. How was she half-nude in bed with the sexy shifter? "I was healing you while sleeping?"

"Yep."

All right. Whether she wanted to admit it or not, they had a connection. No way could she do that without something more than mere friendship or intent between them. Her mind slowly awoke. "Wait a minute. I was hit with a dart."

"Yesterday morning," he said. "You've been sleeping for almost twenty hours. How are you feeling?"

She stretched her legs and took inventory. Just one dart wouldn't have seriously hurt her. "Pretty good. Like I got hit in the head and had twenty hours to heal. I'm not harmed by just one dart."

"I know. Talked to Simone. How do you know that fact, by the way?"

Nessa swallowed. "I took a dart to the neck months ago while working for the Council. Didn't hurt me, but the theory is that several darts at a time would. So I've avoided that possibility." Her knees felt a little weak, but it might be from having a half-naked and very ripped male body holding her. He gave off warmth like a heater she had in her office back in Ireland. "Why are we in bed together?"

"I was tired, and you were snuggly." His heated breath brushed her ear.

That heat flowed through her, zinged around her chest, and landed between her legs. She bit back a moan. This type of need couldn't be healthy. She was far more dangerous than most people knew, and yet she might not have survived the fight without him. He'd saved her. Repeatedly. When the grenade had gone off, he'd covered her with his body. Protected her from the debris and fire and smoke.

She rolled over to face him, and he loosened his hold on her waist to let her. "Bear."

In slumber, he was all sexy male. Rumpled hair, whiskered jaw, relaxed body. But those eyes. Those primal eyes were bright and hot—lust filling them. As if he was just taking his time and deciding when to pounce. At his leisure.

That look. All male intent. She cupped his jaw, smiling when the whiskers scratched her palm. "Thank you for saving me."

His nostrils flared. "You owe me a truck."

"Aye," she whispered. She'd forgotten about his demolished vehicle.

"I had somebody fetch your possessions from the hotel after the police finished with the scene," he said. "Good thing you used an alias."

She didn't care about her job right now. Her gaze sought his lips. Tension rolled from him. "What game are you playing?"

"No game." She'd been hit with an Apollo dart. If he hadn't jumped in the way when they were in the elevator, she would've been hit with five, and she might be dead. No sights, no sounds, no need—she'd be buried and gone. But she had lived. She was *alive*. And she was in bed with the sexiest, deadliest, most protective male she'd ever met. How could he be a bad guy? The intel had to be wrong. She just knew it. "Why did you save me?"

He swallowed, moving the cords in his neck. "I don't like being attacked."

"They weren't after you." She caressed across his jaw and down the strong muscles in his neck. "They were after you and you were with me. That doesn't happen." His voice roughened.

Now wasn't that sweet? Slightly arrogant, but sweet, too. "You brought me back here. This isn't safe for your people. I'm in danger."

"Not here, you're not. I've upped our security." His arm flexed against her waist. "Your defenses are down; you need to go back to sleep."

And gentlemanly. In all the files she'd studied about him, not one notation had even hinted that a gentleman lived in Bear's rough skin. She smiled.

"Sleep, Nessa." Warning was clear in those clipped words.

"No." Oh, this was wrong on so many levels, and if he ever found out about her, who knew how dangerous he could really be? Having him for a friend wasn't exactly comfortable. Having him for an enemy would be disastrous. But for now, he'd saved her. She felt alive. Forget intrigue and reality. She wanted him—wanted to enjoy the fact of survival. So she cupped his neck and kissed him.

His body jolted.

Power rushed through her. She slid against him, her body shuddering when her core met his hard erection. There was so much to him, and she wanted it all. Maybe just for this morning. That could be enough. Reality would return soon enough. Lifting her head, she let her lips wander over his.

"Nessa," he said, his mouth moving nicely against hers. "This is a mistake."

"Aye." Tightening her hold on his neck, she pressed against him, sliding her tongue inside his mouth. Honey and some sort of bourbon awoke her taste buds. "You taste good," she whispered.

He growled.

There was nothing like a bear growl—so real. Tingles rippled through her, lighting every nerve with a fiery need.

She continued to explore him, feeling feminine power. She licked his lips, the corners of his mouth, and then slid her tongue inside his mouth again. The play aroused her as much as him. He remained perfectly still, his body one tense line, the atmosphere clogging with that tension. She breathed him in, caressing down his neck to smooth her hands over his impressive chest. Slowly, deliberately, she fastened her teeth on his bottom lip and gently pulled.

His control snapped.

In one smooth movement, he planted a hand across her entire upper back and one on her ass, jerking her so hard against him her panties were pushed inside her. She gasped, opening her mouth just enough for him to thrust his tongue inside. His lips were fierce and strong on hers, overwhelming her in every sense.

Bear McDunphy didn't kiss.

He consumed.

Rolling on top of her, he continued to work her mouth, giving her so much pleasure from the simple act that she'd never be the same. He ripped off her shirt. "I want all of you," he whispered against her lips, his hands stroking down her body.

Yes. *Everything*. More.

Cool air slid across her nipples, forcing them to become even tighter. His mouth released hers and he caressed down her neck, licking and sucking, his mouth an inferno hotter than any fire.

Everywhere he touched, everywhere he licked, she heated just for him. It was as if he had the key to her and wanted to unlock every single thing she'd ever feel. Need. Crave.

The rasp of his tongue against her nipple made her cry out and arch into him. His stubble burned between her breasts and stole her breath. His hand moved down, and he circled her clit outside her silk panties. "Oh, you're wet, baby." Chuckling, his mouth lava-hot on her breast, he snapped the sides of the panties and threw them across the room. "Open," he whispered.

She gladly spread her legs, so much need in her that this couldn't be real. It had to be a dream. "Bear," she whispered. He slid a finger inside her, and sparks flared behind her closed eyelids. It was too much. "Now." Grabbing his shoulders, she tried to pull him up into her.

"Wait."

"No. Now." She used all her strength, and he still didn't move. "Please. Gonna die."

He kissed his way across her skin, nipping and biting on the way. "I wanna taste you."

"Later." She clawed down his back and sank her nails into his very firm butt. "Edge off first." God. She couldn't even talk in complete sentences.

He gently lowered his body to hers. "You sure?"

"Aye. Sure." She pushed against him.

"All right." He grabbed her hands and pushed them above her head, holding her captive. "Then it's gonna be my way."

She couldn't move. The idea, the simple act, nearly threw her into an early orgasm. Her thighs trembled, and she lifted her knees, slapping her skin against his to hold him in place.

He looked fierce. Angled face, hard body, full determination.

Then he thrust into her. Not gentle, not seeking. He drove deep, filling her completely, and she cried out at the perfect fullness of him. Oh, he was so big it hurt, but pleasure quickly overtook the pain. Finally—she was with a man not afraid of her position or skills. One who didn't want to use her for political gain. One who, basically, just wanted to fuck her.

But it was more than that. *He* was more than that.

He pulled out and plunged back in, rocking the entire bed. Pleasure increased and flooded through her. Her entire body tightened as a release rolled over her—so perfect. So complete.

But he kept thrusting, hard and fast, his body in complete control. The hands over hers allowed for no movement, and with his body pounding into hers, she was trapped on the bed.

Even her thighs were spread wide by his hips.

All she could do was feel.

Every thrust, every touch of skin on skin, every tightening of his muscles—she felt them all.

He hammered harder and harder, forcing her to take more of him, forcing her to take all of him. She climbed, her tension rising, need uncoiling inside her again with razor-sharp edges. She opened her eyes wide and gasped as the next release took her. The explosions inside her jerked her entire body, and she cried out, curling her fingers through his and trusting him to keep her tethered.

She rode out the waves, finding a pleasure deeper than she'd known existed.

When she relaxed with a heartfelt sigh, he dug his face into her neck and shuddered with his own release.

His canines brushed her skin.

She stiffened, her heartbeat out of control. If he bit her, they might mate. Then he slowly licked his way up her jugular. She relaxed again. He released her hands and cupped her face, kissing her so gently on the mouth that tears pricked the back of her eyelids. She batted them away.

"Are you okay?" he whispered, leaning back.

She could only nod.

"Good." He turned them and curled around her from behind again. "Go to sleep for a few more hours. We'll talk about it when you wake up." His chuckle brushed her hair. "Or we'll do that again and then talk. Yeah. Good plan."

She smiled sleepily and closed her eyes, cuddling closer into his safety. Just for now.

A quick knock on the door destroyed the peaceful afterglow.

"You are kidding me," Bear snapped. "What?" he bellowed.

The door opened, and Lucas stomped inside, shaking snow off his hands. He was in faded sweats and a ratty T-shirt with his hair a mess, obviously just out of bed. His eyebrows lifted at seeing them in bed and the clothing on the floor. "Just got word from a local contact. The DEA is going to raid us in about twenty minutes."

"Damn it." Bear sat up. "All right. I'll handle it."

Chapter 13

Bear leaned against the wall in the rec room, with Lucas on one side and Nessa on the other. He flipped to the second page of the warrant, heat filling his chest.

"Perhaps you should call your solicitor?" Nessa asked, her gaze on the five DEA agents methodically going through every drawer in the bar and video console.

Solicitor? Bear didn't twitch. "I don't need a lawyer."

DEA agent Brenda Franks strode in from the swirling snow. Wearing high boots, the woman was over six feet tall, with brown hair, very blue eyes, and too-red lipstick. She clapped her black gloves together. "I have men searching your office and the apartments, McDunphy. Give me the truth now and I'll run interference for you with the federal prosecutor."

Bear flashed her a smile complete with canines.

She narrowed her gaze and took a step back.

Ah, humans. They thought they were so tough. "I'll give you all the truth you want, Agent Franks." He knew all about the woman. She'd forced one of his friends to be her informant about the Apollo drug, so he'd researched everything he could about her. She was raised in Wisconsin, was twice divorced with no kids, and had an ambitious streak three miles long. "Ask away."

"Are you distributing Apollo?" Franks asked.

"Of course not," Bear returned easily. "Anything else?"

She leaned in, trying to assert dominance. "I have two dead bodies that were dumped on the other side of town after having overdosed on Apollo the same night you had a raging party here at Grizzly."

Bear stepped in, showing her real dominance. "I don't know anything about dead bodies, agent. The warrant says you have three anonymous tips that we're running Apollo out of here. It doesn't mention overdoses or bodies."

She didn't back down. "Oh, we will tie those bodies to you. The second we do, the very second, I'm taking you in."

Either she had fabricated the anonymous tips in order to get the warrant or else somebody was talking. It had to be the humans. He needed to track down his group and see exactly who knew about the dead bodies in the woods. Hopefully, the human prospects he'd just thrown out on their asses didn't have a clue. "While I'm sure it'd be nice to spend time with you, I'm otherwise engaged." He put an arm around Nessa's shoulders and drew her into his body.

Having her right there felt good.

Franks rolled her eyes. "Speaking of which, who are you?"

The urge to protect rose in Bear so quickly he growled.

Nessa instantly intervened. "Your warrant has nothing to do with me. Who I am is absolutely none of your business." The words were clipped and the Irish brogue . . . gone.

Bear barely kept from looking at her. She sounded like a twenty-something from Maine, with perfect inflection. How had she done that? Why would a number cruncher, even a specialized forensic accountant, need to be able to banish her accent? Just who was this woman?

She carried his scent after their time in bed, but he really didn't know her.

Franks stared. "I can have you arrested for hindering a federal investigation."

"I'm not hindering anything," Nessa returned. "I was just on the property for a booty call with Bear here and don't know anything about the Grizzlies, Apollo, or bodies. Sorry."

Booty call? Had the prim and proper Irish belle just used the phrase *booty call*? Bear tightened his hold around her shoulder. She stiffened but didn't fight him. Good damn thing, too. His control was never a sure thing, and at the moment he felt like tethers were tied around his neck and all he wanted to do was snap them in half, along with anybody in his way.

Franks studied Nessa for a moment and then turned to check on her agents.

The search took three hours, but by afternoon the agents finally gave up.

Franks again approached Bear. "You have a tequila problem. There are bottles everywhere."

"They're legal," Bear countered, his patience long gone. His rooms were torn apart, and even the pool table had been set on its side. Did they really think he was running a drug manufacturing plant in his pool table? "Get the hell off my property, Franks."

She studied Ness again. "I want your name."

Nessa tilted her head to the side in a curiously smartass way. "My name is none of your business, and its relevancy has nothing to do with your warrant." She smiled, her eyes darkening. "But I assure you, I have the best damn lawyers on retainer if necessary. Do you like your job?"

Bear pressed his lips into a firm line. The woman sounded fully American and well educated. How the hell had she done that?

Franks snarled and motioned for her men. "I'll be back. Next time for both of you." With a strong stride, she finally left. Within minutes, the five DEA vehicles roared away down the snowy drive.

"Jesus," Lucas muttered, surveying the damage.

Bear breathed out and looked around. He'd deal with Nessa in a moment. "Get the prospects here to clean up. The shifter prospects." The others were gone. "And I need to know exactly who was aware of the bodies the other night."

Lucas tugged a cell phone from his back pocket. "I'll get on it right now."

Bear tried to figure out a way to find peace, and there was only one path. "We're gonna have to solve this ourselves, Luke."

Lucas stopped with the phone halfway to his ear. "What?"

Bear snarled. "This whole fucking Apollo disaster. The Enforcers had to go back to Ireland, so now we're on our own. It's a drug that harms witches, who are our allies. And it's a drug that has found its way into our club—even just for a night. The DEA ain't gonna leave us alone until the whole thing is solved."

Lucas looked at the mess of wires spilling out from the enormous television set. "We are not private detectives."

Bear had to agree. They'd formed their little slice of the world away from people on purpose. "We have to shut down the distributors and find the manufacturer of this drug."

Lucas nodded. "All right, but the Enforcers couldn't track down the manufacturer, and they worked the case here undercover for months."

"Yeah, but they're smooth and were worried about relations with the human law enforcement community. We don't give a shit. It's time to end this." Bear looked down at the woman listening quietly. "I believe you and I need to have a little talk." She opened her mouth to protest, apparently read the rage in his eyes, and then remained silent. Smart girl. Very smart girl.

Outside, twin Harley engines zoomed up the drive, pipes roaring. "Who's riding bikes in the snow?" Lucas snapped. "If they're ours, I'm killing them."

Bear shook his head. "If they're young bear shifters, they're idiots. We were, too."

The bikes came to a stop, and loud boot steps echoed across the pavement. The doors opened.

Bear took one look. "No fucking way. Get out. Right now."

Nessa remained still as Bear set her to one side and strode toward two twenty-something men. Powerful men. The kid to the right had metallic gray eyes, dark hair, and a strong build. She felt for his power. Ah. Vampire. Interesting. His buddy had world-weary green eyes, thick black hair, and just as powerful a build. Another vampire. No. There was more to him. She focused on his odd energy signature. Interesting. He was a demon-vampire mix.

Ah ha. "Don't tell me," she said. "Garrett Kayrs and Logan Kyllwood." Of the vampire and demon ruling families. She had dossiers on them, but they'd grown up since she'd last studied them. Rumor had it they were best of friends since their siblings mated. Sure looked like it.

Garrett sent her a charming smile. "Miss Lansa. My uncle said you were staying in Grizzly territory for the time being."

Bear crossed his arms. "No. Get the hell out. Right now."

Nessa frowned. "Your uncle knows I'm here?"

Garrett shrugged. "He's the king. Dage pretty much knows every-thing, and he really hates it when people seem surprised by that."

Logan snorted. "Isn't that the truth?"

She faltered. King Dage Kayrs was the ruler of the Realm, which was a coalition of all immortal species except for the Kurjans, who were off licking their wounds after getting their asses kicked in the last war. Just what else did Dage Kayrs know? "I see."

"Get . . . *out*," Bear continued.

Garrett looked beyond him at the mess. "Whoa. What kind of party did you have?"

"The DEA dropped by," Nessa said. What was Bear's problem?

Lucas remained silent and just watched the exchange, his gaze resigned.

Garrett nodded at him. "Hey, Lucas."

"Boys," Lucas finally said. "Please don't tell me—"

"Yep," Logan replied cheerfully. "We're new Grizzly prospects. Isn't it great? I love watching games on that big television over there."

Bear growled low and long and hard. "No."

Nessa rubbed an aching bruise on her shoulder. Must've been from the dart. She mentally ran through her files on the Apollo op. Hadn't there been something about those boys being undercover as prospects at Titans of Fire? She hadn't paid much attention to Titans of Fire. Of course, the Titans' clubhouse had been blown up. So now the boys must want to go undercover with the Grizzlies, considering it was the only game left in town. "You boys are here on behalf of the king to figure out who is manufacturing Apollo," she said slowly, putting the puzzle pieces together.

"No," Bear said shortly.

Garrett strode into the room and righted the pool table with one hand. "You don't have to let us stay, Bear."

"I agree," Bear snapped.

"But my uncle would like to call in a favor." Garrett's grin was cheerful, but a clear predator gleamed in his metallic eyes. "I believe you owe him?"

Tension rolled from Bear, but he didn't answer.

"For what?" Lucas asked quietly.

Nessa cleared her throat. "I may have heard something about Bear being kidnapped by the Council and the king interceding and getting him home quickly. Maybe. Didn't something like that happen recently?" Of course, she knew all about it. It felt wrong to keep facts from Bear now. She'd just slept with the shifter. What had she been thinking?

"Yes," Bear said through gritted teeth.

"So we're staying," Logan said, moving toward the bar to start putting bottles back into their places.

Garrett sighed. "Listen, Bear. Logan and I have been on this case since the beginning, and we really want to see it through to the end. You're missing three of your board members, and you could use backup for now. Logan is a genius at tracking people. We'll get right on it."

"You are missing members?" Nessa asked Bear, her thighs still tingling from his touch. She needed to calm down, and now.

"They've been recalled," he said, looking at Garrett. "I knew owing Dage would bite me in the ass. All right. Here's the deal. You can stay, but you do what I tell you, when I tell you. The last thing I need is for one of you to get dead."

"We love you too, man." Logan continued with the bottles.

Bear turned on him. "I don't even like you two idiots. But if you die, then I have either the vampire or the demon nation on my ass. Probably both." He righted a chair that had been overturned. "You two can't even go on vacation without ending up in trouble and forcing the king to put your asses to work."

Garrett's mouth twisted. "Fair enough."

"We are *never* gonna live that down," Logan groused, pushing a drawer closed. "One wild week on a beach—that's all it was."

Garrett's watch dinged, and he glanced down to read the face. "Oh. Uncle Dage wants to have a conference call. Is that cool with you?"

Bear looked like he'd chewed and swallowed shards of glass. "Your uncle is now setting up my calls?"

Garrett shrugged. "I figure he probably just wants to share his intel on the case. We've had the computer guys working the issue around the clock for the last month, ever since the drug reappeared on the streets of Seattle."

Bear sighed loud enough to stir the air. "Fine. Let's go to the conference room and see what the king knows." He turned and took Nessa's hand.

Electricity jolted up her arm.

"This way." Bear maneuvered through the demolished room to a door to the storage room behind the bar.

Nessa followed, her curiosity buzzing. "We're going back into the storage area?" The room was black and sooty from the fire.

"Yep." Bear led her to the far back wall and moved a panel to the side to show a keypad. He punched in numbers and a door slid to the side, revealing a situation room.

"Wow." Nessa stepped inside. Twelve people could sit comfortably around the burnished teak table, which held the Grizzly MC emblem in the middle. Notepads and pens were placed before thick leather chairs. A huge screen took up the far wall, while smaller screens were spaced across another wall. A third wall held computer consoles.

Bear sat at the head of the table and put Nessa on his right. She sat, her gaze taking everything in. Bear reached for a keyboard and smoothly punched in several codes.

Wasn't he full of surprises.

Within seconds, the big screen lit and King Dage Kayrs sat with a green board behind him. "Afternoon," the king said. Dage had black hair, silver eyes, and a hard-cut face. He grinned. "I see the boys made it."

Bear snorted. "Do you have intel?"

Dage looked around the room. "Hello, Nessa." He nodded at Lucas. "Luke."

Lucas nodded back. "Hi."

Nessa smiled. "King."

"Intel?" Bear snapped.

Dage rolled his eyes and tapped a keyboard that was out of sight. "We're still working on new intel. I'm bringing in Simone to update us on the Coven Nine research."

Simone Brightston came into view, on a split screen now that showed both her and Dage. "Bear," she said, her face lighting up.

Bear's eyes crinkled. "Hi. You look better. Not so pale."

Nessa's heart turned over. The cranky shifter obviously loved his sister. What would it be like to have a family beyond just her uncle? To have that backup in life no matter what? She shook herself out of her thoughts. "Hi, Simone."

Simone waved. "Nessa. So good to see you."

"Hi, Aunt Simone," Logan and Garrett drawled in unison.

Simone scowled, but the displeasure didn't reach her eyes. "I am not your aunt. Either of you. We are not related by blood, and I have not married nor mated an uncle of either of you. How many times do I have to explain this?"

Logan shrugged. "You mated my brother's best friend, who's more like an uncle, so that makes you my aunt."

Garrett grinned. "His aunt is my aunt. We're family."

Simone huffed out air, her lips twitching. The amusement sparkled in her eyes.

"Enough," Bear said. "You should be resting. Give us the info, and then you're out of this, sis. At least while you're pregnant."

Simone shared a look with Nessa, barely rolling her eyes.

Nessa kept an eye on Bear. His sister was on the Council. Surely he understood undercover ops and the secrecy required in governmental work. He wouldn't be angry that she hadn't really been honest with him even though they'd been intimate. He'd understand.

Yeah, right.

Chapter 14

Bear kept a close eye on his sister to make sure she seemed all right. Truth be told, Simone looked healthy and happy. He'd have to be nice to that demon she'd mated next time they were in the same room. "I haven't paid a lot of attention to the Apollo problem until recently," he admitted. "We provided support for the Enforcers, but we stayed out of it."

"That has now changed," Lucas added.

Simone nodded. "Agreed. You're in place to hunt down the manufacturer, Bear. We need you."

"Of course," he said. He'd do anything for his sister. "Whatever you want, Simone."

Nessa smiled next to him.

His chest warmed. He liked making her smile during this brief time they had together. "Catch me up, sister."

Simone smiled prettily at his use of her title of sister. "All right. After Titans of Fire MC was destroyed, the distribution of Apollo in Seattle almost stopped until a month ago. Then it picked up dramatically, so there's definitely a new distributor. We've identified witch residents in the area, and I'll send the list to you."

"You want a protection detail on them?" Bear asked.

"No. We have that taken care of already. I'm just keeping you in the loop," Simone said.

"How rare for a witch to say that," Bear said, his chin down.

Simone glowered and then smoothed out her expression. "Like you tell us everything. For now, we need you to infiltrate the Seattle bars and trace back to the source."

Bear grimaced. "My people don't like venturing out."

"This is important," Simone said, her eyes shining with intelligence and determination.

"That's also something we can do," Garrett piped up. "Logan and I were undercover all over Seattle last spring, and we have contacts. We just need to reach out to them."

Bear kept his hands lightly on the table. How was he gonna keep both kids safe? When he got his sights on the creator of Apollo, he was going to end him for good. Period. "You guys can start with a bar called Slam downtown. As soon as Lucas has intel on the place, we'll talk about it."

Simone smiled. "See how well we can work together?"

Not in a million years. But Bear did like seeing his sister smile, so he let the comment pass. "So you have no idea who this new player is. You must have some grasp on the manufacturer of the poison."

Simone typed something. "This is what we have." A picture of a pretty blonde with deep blue eyes came up on the screen. "Her name is Grace Sadler, and she used to be on the Council of the Coven Nine. She had two sons, and both have been killed during the Apollo investigation."

"Phillipe Sadler, her son, was the one who kidnapped you, correct?" Bear had been put out of commission briefly, and his sister had been taken. She'd survived and killed Phillipe Sadler.

"Aye, and he said he and his mother wanted to strip my powers." Simone sighed. "Grace and I dated the same man way back when, and then my cousin Moira defeated Grace and removed her from the Council. So she definitely has a grudge against not only me but the entire witch nation."

The king leaned forward. "Agreed, but I don't see how she could have amassed enough money to create an enterprise this large after being tossed from the Council."

Simone shook her head. "She's also not a mastermind. More of a follower. We're trying to trace her activity for the past twenty-five years, but we keep running into roadblocks. She's the key, though. I know it."

The blonde actually looked like the girl next door. Damn witches. Bear watched Nessa from the corner of his eye. How much of this was news to her? Probably most of it, if she usually just worked with numbers. But she had gone undercover on the Council—so maybe there was more to her job than she'd said.

She turned and met his gaze, hers eyes unblinking.

A mere few hours ago, he'd been inside her—holding her tight, feeling her convulse around him. His nostrils flared.

Dage cleared his throat. "What's the plan?"

Bear turned toward the king. "We spend today putting my headquarters back to rights. Any help you could provide with the DEA would be fantastic. Tonight, our new prospects hit downtown Seattle and try to find any lead on the current distributor." He clicked through the plan. The king's computer experts would provide intel, so that was covered. "Is Chalton on it?"

"Yes," Dage said. "He has about five computers going with different searches. Whoever put this plan together is brilliant."

"Everyone makes mistakes," Bear said shortly. Had he just made one? With Nessa? One night with her in his bed and he wanted her there again. Right now. "Thanks, Dage. Check in."

"Affirmative." The king's screen went dark.

Simone smiled. "So. How are things?" She focused on Nessa.

Nosy sister. Bear leaned forward. "You stay safe and out of trouble. Please send us info the second you have it." He disconnected the call before Simone could start asking embarrassing questions.

Nessa gave him a look. "That was rude."

"That was smart. Believe me." Bear straightened as an alarm beeped. He grabbed a remote control and turned on one of the smaller screens to see two men breaching his territory from the north. Zeroing in his camera, he could make out the bounty hunter who'd attacked earlier.

"Who's that?" Garrett asked.

Bear took in the two kids. "That's Lark Redmond."

Logan perked up. "The bounty hunter?"

"Looks like he brought a friend," Lucas said.

"Yeah. There's a bounty for kidnapping Nessa, and this is Redmond's second attempt," Bear drawled. "You guys want to let off some steam?"

The kids jumped up.

Bear bit back a grin. "All right. Catch them, torture them to your heart's delight, and then kick their asses off my property."

Anticipation lit both boys' faces.

Bear held up a hand. "No killing, though."

Logan sighed. "All right. We'll be back."

Bear waited until they'd left the room before laughing.

Nessa rolled her eyes. "You're terrible. Do you mind if I go start getting organized in the office?"

Lucas leaned back, his eyes going wide in horror. "What are you saying? It is organized. I mean, it was, before the DEA went through it."

"I promised her," Bear said sadly. "That's fine. But you stick close."

Her smile made him feel way too pleased. "I promise." She all but danced out the door.

Lucas reached beneath one of the computers to open a fridge and draw out two beers. "You are so whipped."

Bear started. "I am not."

"Dude." Lucas slid a beer his way. "You're letting her *organize* the office. Your office. I mean, with all the papers and files. Organize. It's crazy."

Bear flipped the cap off the beer and drank half of it. "Organization won't hurt us." Hell, it sounded lame even to his ears. "Okay. She's pretty, and she wants to help. You've done a lot stupider things for a woman." There had been a woman in the fifties that Lucas had even dyed his hair for. Geez.

Lucas took a drink of his beer. "Yeah, I know." He settled back, his gaze on the bounty hunters on screen one. "It's been you and me and the club for so long."

Bear took another drink. "Yeah?"

"You now have a sister and a brother. Family." Lucas held up his beer. "I'm happy for you."

Bear clinked and then paused. Was there a hint of melancholy in his old buddy's tone? Man, he'd chosen the wrong time to disappear for a while. "Luke? You're my family. You and this club. Have been for thirty years."

Lucas's eyes softened. "Yeah, I know. It's just, I used to imagine finding out my parents were alive. Or that I had a sibling somewhere. I'm glad it happened for you."

"We're brothers." Bear said the words, and it was a vow. "That means that Simone and Flynn are yours now, too." He could share all his siblings, and frankly, he could use some help with them both. They were wild and dangerous . . . and they both thought they were invincible. Nobody was. "I promise."

Lucas took a long drag of his beer. "Simone seems like a pain in the neck as a sibling." He grinned. "Maybe Flynn the dragon and I could bond over a couple of tequila shots. I wouldn't mind seeing him spit fire."

Bear chuckled. "Simone is not a pain—she's just dangerous. Period." His sister was awesome. Lucas wasn't any more of a talker than was Bear, but maybe it was time to work through some shit. "You never talk about your folks."

"Didn't know them." Lucas shrugged. "They were supposedly part of a smuggling ring in between wars. They got caught, and they fought to the death."

Bear had known they'd died, but Lucas had never wanted to talk about it before. Were the two of them mellowing? No. No way. But the story did make sense. Shifters had often turned to smuggling back in the day. "What did they smuggle?"

"I've heard it was gold, but who knows. Enough talking about my dismal past." Lucas leaned back. "Does this thing between you and Nessa have legs?"

"She's a witch," Bear said automatically. His hand shook, so he put it under the table. Damn it. Just when he'd thought he was healed, the symptoms were coming back. Maybe he'd really screwed himself by shifting into a dragon. He'd never admit it, but he'd tried to do it again just a month ago. To see if he could. He could not. That talent, or trick, or whatever, was now gone.

Lucas just watched him, waiting for an answer about Nessa.

"A. Witch." Bear could still smell roses. "We've never been close to the witch nation. Never wanted to be."

"Your sister is a witch, and she's back in your life now," Lucas reminded him. "There's no turning from that."

Didn't mean he had to mate a witch. His stomach ached in the center. He sighed. Maybe he'd messed himself up too badly with that dragon shift and was gonna die anyway. But he'd saved Simone, so what the hell. "What about you? Who's the woman?"

"I've just been playing around. Nothing serious," Lucas said, finishing his beer.

"I thought you said—"

Lucas reached for another beer in the fridge. "Was just messing with you. I am nowhere near ready to settle down with one woman." He shuddered. "Forever." Then he paused and gestured toward the screen. "The boys have caught a scent." He grinned. "That's why we're still here, right? We want to watch those boys in action."

"Exactly." Bear wanted to see how Kayrs and Kyllwood would handle things. See if he could trust them to stay alive in the Seattle underground. He took another drink of his beer, his gaze on the screen.

The bounty hunters were moving smoothly between trees, navigating through the snow and barely leaving any trace of their presence.

Garrett and Logan circled around them, moving as gracefully as any shifters. Not a branch stirred.

"They move well together," Lucas mused.

Yeah, they did. "They also move like they've been hunting prey for centuries," Bear noted. They hadn't.

"They've seen some shit, Bear."

True. The boys zeroed in from different directions, still somehow in sync. "I like that they're not playing around," Bear said.

Lucas nodded. "All business. Even with something simple like this. Sometimes it takes centuries to learn that."

Bear leaned forward. "It's as if they're hearing the same beat. Watch their footsteps."

"They probably train together daily," Lucas said. "What was the story about their getting in trouble on vacation?"

"Something about too many girls," Bear muttered. "They were being stupid kids, and the king yanked them home and put them here. To give them direction."

Lucas set down his bottle. "The king wants to keep tabs on us. On everyone."

"He is a busybody." Bear didn't care. He kinda liked the kids. His heartbeat picked up. "They're about to make a move."

"Yeah." Lucas kicked back in his chair.

The boys attacked at the same time, each taking a bounty hunter.

The hunters fought fast and hard, showing impressive training. Some of the punches were too fast to see clearly. Fire danced down Redmond's arms, and he threw plasma at the boys. They ducked and dodged, hustling in to punch. The other hunter also threw fire, but he lacked Redmond's speed. The fight continued, bloody and precise.

In the end, Garrett and Logan stood over two unconscious witches. Each boy hefted a body over his shoulder and stomped to the edge of the territory, throwing the witches across the road.

Garrett, blood pouring from a cut above his right eye, turned and saluted the camera.

"Smart-ass." Bear grinned.

Approval curved Lucas's smile. "I guess we don't need to worry about them in Seattle."

"No. I'd say not. Track down all the information you can on Slam downtown and that bartender. As soon as we have decent intel, we'll send in the boys." Bear finished his beer. The scent of roses still tempted him. "I think I'll go see how Nessa is doing in the office."

Lucas didn't even try to hide his grin. "Whipped."

Bear flipped him the finger and strode through the war room to the storage room. His vision narrowed. He kept going, trying to appear nonchalant to the prospects already cleaning up the rec room. Nobody stopped him.

He stepped outside, and the freezing snow slapped him in the face. His knees went weak.

Damn it. He had to get himself under control. Why wasn't he staying healed? He didn't want Nessa to see him like this. Not again. Biting his lip, he turned into the second garage and staggered up the steps like an old man, finally reaching one of the small rooms they kept for anyone who wanted to crash. He shut the door and dropped to the bed. Just a small rest, and he'd go find Nessa.

With that last thought, he passed out.

Chapter 15

Nessa sneezed for the seventh time but kept organizing papers into neat piles. Payables. Receivables. Correspondence. Within an hour, she'd created file folders for each and set up a system in the file cabinet, after she'd taken several engine parts out of the various drawers. Apparently, Bear had a pretty good business going.

The shifters worked on just about anything with an engine or motor, and they seemed to have a consistent clientele.

Another hour later and she'd set the entire office to rights. Even the desk drawers contained neatly organized supplies.

She angled her head and looked outside. Club members had come and gone, several giving her a wave. The sense of belonging was foreign, and she tried to pretend it was real. Oh, her uncle was more than enough family for anybody, but she'd missed having siblings. With her work, she didn't have close friends.

The Grizzlies seemed like family.

It was funny, because Bear was such a loner. Yet he'd created this family in a safe place for himself. But he'd still shifted from bear to human form in the last few months, and it seemed nobody around here knew about that. What kind of a secret was he keeping?

She sat at a surprisingly new computer and booted it up. If she had time, she wanted to digitalize all of Bear's records. There was no need for so much dusty paper.

But for now, she had a job to do. She backtracked through the Internet to a secure site and then put in several of her codes. Soon there was a beep, and Jasper came into view. He had a black eye, a broken nose, and a fat lip. Static came across the line, and she tapped the monitor. "Jasper?" she gasped.

"I've been trying to get you," he said, wheezing.

What in the world? Jasper was one of the best-trained members of the Guard. "Are you all right? Were we attacked?" She partially stood.

His eyes were hangdog. "Where's your phone, damn it?"

She took out her phone and shook it. "Dead." Bloody hell. She'd been too busy having sex with Bear to remember to charge it. "I've been a bit busy. What happened, and do you need me?"

He winced. "I'm sorry, Nessa. I really am."

Her lungs seized, and her breath stopped. "What?" she whispered.

"Your uncle. We were having dinner at his place—"

"What?" She stood upright. "Where is he? What happened?" God, she had to get home.

Jasper held up a hand. "I don't know. We were at dinner, and a force of ten just showed up. I have the entire Guard searching for him. It's our top priority."

She gulped, and tears filled her eyes. Okay. She could handle this. "He was taken?"

"Aye."

All right. Boondock Lansa had more money, knowledge, and secrets than anybody else in the witch world. There were a multitude of people who might have taken him. "Has there been contact?"

"No," Jasper said.

So no ransom. As of yet, anyway. "Send me your report," she said. Jasper would've immediately written a report after the altercation.

"I will. I was knocked out for several hours," Jasper said, pain in his eyes.

Translation: Boondock could be anywhere.

Nessa's shoulders shook. "Are you all right?"

He nodded. "Just bruised."

Good. Time to think. "We've handled kidnappings before." She kept her voice strong and her gaze as direct as the tears would allow. "This is just another one. Keep on top of everything, and I'll be there as soon as I can."

Jasper nodded. "You need to check all your e-mail accounts. See if there's a ransom demand or if he somehow got word to you."

"Affirmative."

"And charge your damn phone."

She clicked off before she started bawling like a frightened baby. The blank screen stared back at her. Okay. She needed to get busy. She opened up her accounts and booked a plane ticket under one of her aliases, one of the names that even her uncle didn't know. He was the one who'd taught her to create identities that nobody else in the world knew.

He had to be okay.

She flashed back to when he'd taught her how to grapple and choke out an opponent without messing her hair. God, he was funny. Sweet and kind and strong—and he'd raised her by himself. He'd taught himself how to braid hair and paint nails and cook. For her.

She'd find him. He'd be okay. Hunching over the keyboard, she began checking her several e-mail accounts. There was nothing interesting until she reached her more public account. That one held about three hundred e-mails, but the one at the top caught her eye. The subject line: Uncle Boondock.

Her stomach dropped. She sat back down. Her hands shook, but she reached for the mouse and clicked open the message.

A video was embedded in the e-mail, and she hit the play button. She gasped.

Her uncle sat tied to a chair, his face a bloody mess, his blue eyes furious. An old rag was stuffed in his mouth, and it looked like his hands were tied behind his back. Somebody kicked his chair, and he fell over.

Nessa cried out.

The camera shuffled, and a man crouched down.

Bloody hell. Nessa glared into the face of George Flanders. The witch was several hundred years old, but didn't look more than thirty, with dark brown hair and deceptively placid green eyes. His face was angled, his nose crooked, and his mouth full. To most women, he was handsome. To her, he was a dangerous pain in the ass.

"I've underestimated you," she whispered to the monitor.

He pushed a button on the camera. "I hope by the time you see this that I haven't just killed this old bastard for fun." He turned toward a ruckus offscreen. "He is making it far too tempting to slice off his blustering head."

Rage lanced through Nessa, and she struggled to sit still. Oh, she was going to kill him. Dead.

George focused back on the camera. "Nessa? My sources tell me you're in Washington State. That's rather convenient, since your uncle and I will be in Los Angeles by tomorrow night. I need to check on some of my businesses."

Like that impressed her.

"I'm sorry it has come to this, but you just won't listen to reason. So be in Los Angeles tomorrow night at 9:00 P.M. I will send a message to this e-mail address with directions for you once you're in in LA. We shall mate, as is our destiny, and you will get your jerk of an uncle back. If you don't show, I'm cutting off his head."

Nessa slapped a hand on the battered desk.

"And come alone. If you have anybody with you, especially the Guard, then I kill Uncle." George smiled. "Part of me hopes you don't show, by the way."

The video stopped.

Her hands shook, but she dialed up Jasper.

"Did you have contact?" he asked without preamble.

"Aye. Send me everything you have on George Flanders, and especially anything about his California interests." She didn't trust that LA would be her final destination, but it was a start.

"Does Flanders have Boondock?" Jasper asked, leaning forward.

"Affirmative." She needed to schedule her flight to Los Angeles.

Jasper quickly started typing. "I can be in LA by tonight and will bring forces."

"No," Nessa said sharply. "George will kill Boon if the Guard shows up."

Jasper paused, his gaze narrowing. "You're no longer a field operative, Nessa. You haven't been for a long time."

"Yet here I am in the field," she shot back. "This is a one-operative mission, and I'm it. You know the meet won't be in LA. He's setting us up, and he wants to kill Boon." She cleared her throat. "He may have a plane waiting to take me back to Dublin. Stay put until we know more."

Jasper lowered his chin, looking like the warrior cop he was. "Then I want full tactical gear on you. Got it?"

"Affirmative." She'd have to go shopping in LA.

"Camera, too," he snapped.

"Right." She stood, panic gripping her again. What was happening with her uncle right at that moment? "I have to go. I'll be in touch when I set down in LA." She disengaged the call.

Her head hurt, and her stomach felt hollow. Okay. She had to go, and now. Sucking in air, she hustled out of the office and ran through the snow and down the narrow trail. The jog helped to clear her mind, and her limbs were just loosening up when she reached the cabin steps.

She shoved open the door and went for her luggage, quickly repacking a small bag. Then she paused.

The cabin smelled like Bear. All musky male. Her gaze dropped to the bed, and her stomach tingled. He might try to stop her, so she couldn't tell him she was leaving. Should she leave a note?

And say what?

That was silly. Shaking off regrets, she quickly pulled her phone out and plugged it in to an outlet. After a frustrating call with a taxi service, she finally got a driver to agree to meet her at the end of the private drive.

Now, all she had to do was get there.

Bear stretched awake, feeling mildly better. He shoved himself off the saggy cot and lumbered down the stairs to the garage, his joints aching again. Maybe Nessa would take time to heal him a little.

He was getting the uneasy feeling that her healing only lasted for a short time, like how an aspirin soothed a headache but didn't fix the underlying cause.

The wind slapped against the garage door, and he looked around for his jacket. Where had he left it?

Oh well. It was time to check on Nessa, anyway. He pushed outside just in time to see a flash of pink down the private drive. What the hell? He focused his eyes, trying to peer through the storm. Yep. It was Nessa. She was struggling through the wind, her shoulders hunched, a bag over her arm.

She was *leaving* him?

A bomb slammed into his gut and exploded. The woman was deserting him without even a good-bye? Had their night together meant that little?

Fury swept over him. Where was she walking in the storm? He ducked his head and moved into a run, his head reeling and his lungs burning. Pain grabbed his ankles and held on, but he shoved it away, ignoring everything but the anger propelling him.

She must've heard him coming, because she whirled around, her wild hair flying in the snow. Her mouth dropped open.

He reached her and looked beyond her to see a taxi waiting at the end of the Grizzly private road. A growl ripped from his chest. "What the fuck are you doing?"

Her chin snapped up. "I have to be somewhere." Then she turned on her stylish and snow-covered boot.

He grabbed her arm and spun her around. "Excuse me?" Steam poured out on his breath.

Her blue eyes glittered. "I'm sorry, but there isn't time for this. I'll call you when I can."

There was hurt behind his anger, and that pissed him off even more. "You're not going anywhere," he bellowed over the storm.

She drew in air. "I donna' want to fight you." In her pretty pink suit with her little boots, she looked as dangerous as a baby rabbit he'd once had for a pet. "But I will. Just back off, Bear."

How could she leave like this? He yanked her bag off her arm and stomped toward the taxi. She followed, but his stride was much longer.

The taxi driver rolled down his window.

Bear flashed his canines. "Go. Now."

The driver's dark eyes widened, and he jerked the cab into gear. Without rolling up his window, he sped off, sliding on the icy road.

"Damn it, Bear," Nessa yelled, throwing up her hands.

He turned on her.

She took a step back.

"Too late, baby," he snapped. "Now explain yourself."

Fury rippled red across her high cheekbones to match her pink nose. "I have to go." Desperation lit her words and gave him pause.

"Why?" he thundered.

She looked down the very empty main road, and her shoulders slumped. "George has my uncle. He'll kill Boon if I don't show up in LA by tomorrow night."

Bear's temper cooled. Slightly. "You're being blackmailed?"

"Aye."

"Why didn't you tell me?" He gestured toward the snowy road. "Why just leave?"

"I didn't think you'd let me go," she mumbled, her face pale in the snowy day.

He sighed. "Does this kind of thing happen often?" Damn witches. She shrugged. "Often enough."

His leg tingled. So she was throwing herself into danger to save her uncle—and she still lacked the ability to create fire. Oh, she could fight, but size mattered, and she didn't have it. At some point, some asshole with a dart was going to hit her, and she'd be gone. He couldn't let that happen. "Is it possible that your healing attempts are temporary? I mean, on me?"

"I donna' know," she said. "It's possible. You really harmed yourself."

He looked down the now vacant road to the city. His mind spun. His only chance for survival might hinge on actually mating her— which was what she'd wanted from the beginning. "You want the ability to throw fire so you can defend yourself."

"So I can fight." She nodded, looking incredibly delicate standing in the angry snowstorm. "I could really use it."

His chest heaved. Oh, this was crazy. "If you're mated to me, then George Flanders has no reason to keep your uncle." That didn't mean Flanders wouldn't harm Boondock, but the bounty for Nessa's kidnapping would cease to exist. This was beyond insane. Nothing in Bear wanted Nessa to mate his brother. He didn't want to examine why, but he wasn't that clueless. He wanted her for himself. At least for now. "Do you still want to mate me?"

Snow fell on her pert nose, but she ignored it. "Aye." She faltered, sticking her hands in her jacket pockets. "With conditions."

The animal in him rose up, quickly pushing logic aside. "No conditions." The blood pounded through his veins. She needed fire, and he needed to heal completely. Matings for convenience had been part of their cultures for centuries. But this was more. Her scent. Her mind. Her spirit. She called to him, and he was tired of denying it. "The only thing I agree to is a mating. Right now." The rest he'd figure out later.

His body tensed in anticipation, and the bear inside him roared awake.

Like a doe who's caught a predator's scent, she stilled. Completely. "All right."

His vision narrowed to her—only her. "Do you understand what's entailed in a shifter mating? We're not like witches."

Arrogance firmed her chin. "You have the same working parts, Bear. Come on."

"I'm a fuckin' animal, baby." She had to know what she was agreeing to. "We don't nip your skin and soften it with a kiss. We *bite*. Really bite." He'd seen a shifter lose a shoulder after a mating. Sure, it had eventually grown back, but still.

"I understand." She faltered. "So. Well. All right. The cabin?"

"No." His voice dropped to a hoarse rasp. It was decided then. "Run."

It took her a second to catch his meaning, and then her instincts kicked in. She bunched her legs and sprang toward the road.

He caught her around the waist and whipped her around to face a trail through two pine trees that led into Grizzly territory. "That way," he growled, setting her down and smacking her on the ass.

Hard.

She yelped and then launched into a run.

The beast inside him broke its shackles.

Chapter 16

Nessa careened through the trees, snow falling all around her, her breath panting out. The thrill of the chase rippled through her, making her faster. She dodged to the left and between barren huckleberry bushes.

Silence came from behind her.

She didn't relax. A hunter never made sounds.

But she had hunted plenty in her youth. Her limbs tingled with life—with energy. Every mating was primal, but mating an alpha, an alpha shifter, took it to another level. She wanted this.

For now, for today, she became lost in it.

Instead of running away, she circled around. There he was.

Tall and strong, he strode through the trees, his head up, scenting the air. He stilled.

Oh, he'd caught wind of her altered course. Thank goodness she'd worn her boots with traction. Something told her she was going to need it.

For now, she pressed closer, planning an attack from behind. He pivoted. "Ness."

She halted, hidden by several young cedar trees. Her heart beat so hard her ribs expanded.

His gaze swept the trees and then settled right where she stood.

Her mouth gaped open. No way could he see her. Excitement pumped through her, followed closely by arousal. Why this turned her on, she'd never know.

But she felt *alive*.

"We're done playing now. Come out," he ordered, warning glittering in those primal eyes. "If you make me come and get you, you'll regret it."

The male didn't know her at all. Even so, she didn't want this to end. Not yet. So she pushed her way out of the brush, stopping only yards from him. With his warning about shifters, had he really thought she'd run and hide? Cower from him? Not a chance in blooming hell. "Tired of chasing, shifter?" she asked.

A low rumble spilled from his chest.

Her thighs trembled in response. Yes. This.

"Come here," he rasped.

She forced a laugh. "Why? You too tired?"

Warning flared hot and bright in his eyes. His fists clenched. "No. You turned and started running the wrong way."

She frowned. The wrong way? Oh. He'd wanted to chase her to the safe and warm fire in the cabin—because she wasn't a shifter. She wasn't as strong as a shifter mate. Boy, did he have that wrong. "The trail leads to your cabin."

"Yeah." He cocked his head to the side, looking not quite human. Like something more . . . something that stalked prey.

A shiver trembled down her back. If she was going to do this, she wasn't holding back. More important, she wasn't going to let him hold back. Not with this. "Don't think you can take me out here?" She spread her arms through the falling snow. "Too much for you?"

His breath steamed the air. "What are you playing at?"

That was just it. She wasn't playing. Keeping his gaze, she walked toward him, noting how his shoulders relaxed with each step.

"Good girl," he said.

Her smile should've provided warning. "I'm not that easy, shifter."

His eyes burned. Yeah, he didn't like it when she called him that. Her smile widened. "You want me? You're going to have to earn it." Before he could respond, she twisted her body and aimed a round-house kick to his ribs, followed by a side kick to his left knee. He coughed and went down, surprise darkening his face.

Leading with her left, she punched him in the cheek. His head rocked, and he fell sideways.

Sucking in as much air as she could take, she turned and ran.

Instinct grabbed her tight, and she let it rule, jumping over bushes and between trees—away from the main trail.

A roar echoed through the entire forest from behind her. She stopped breathing. God. What had she done? He was already up and after her.

Rain mixed with the snow, soaking her suit jacket. Water matted her skirt, hindering her movements. Her boots squished in snow turning muddy and sticking. At least there were only a couple inches on the ground.

Bear yelled her name from somewhere behind her. The anger in it, the passion, made her run faster.

Thunder cracked the sky open as if in agreement.

She slipped on a patch of ice, her arms windmilling. Regaining her balance, she leaned against a cold spruce tree and panted in air, trying to get her bearings. The trees, their limbs dusted with snow, rose high and quiet around her. No other sounds pierced the forest.

Silence.

The silence of a stalking predator. His essence, his determination, his very intent rode the wind.

A sense of urgency shot through her limbs. She moved deeper into the forest. A branch cracked to her left. She turned right, hustling for a narrow trail, hunching her shoulders against the wind. A shiver took her.

The cold engulfed her hands, and she shoved them into her pockets, trying to keep her balance.

A sound to her right.

She switched directions again. Then again.

A thick stand of trees stood in her way, so she maneuvered around them, emerging at the back of the cabin. Bear's cabin. Her ears rang. He had *herded* her there. She whirled around to find the threat.

He strode out of the forest, his shoulders wide, his face hard. His clothes were plastered to his body, outlining every defined muscle and tendon. His shaggy hair was wild in the crazy wind. But his eyes. They glowed a supernatural color. With something feral and unreachable.

She took a step back, unable to stop herself.

Thunder cracked, and she jerked.

"Why did you kick me?" Low, guttural, the primal tone cut through the storm.

The lump in her throat kept her from answering.

"Nessa." His tone owned the word. Owned her name.

She was stronger than this. A woman like her would never cower. "This is all or nothing."

The animal in him reacted to her words, visible just beneath his skin. Anger, dark and primal, overtook the wind. Even the snow felt like a touch from him. "Cabin. Now."

She could go to the cabin like a meek little human. Or she could show him. Show him she was strong enough to be his mate, whatever that meant. At least for this moment. After, there would be intrigue and undercover work, and probably more hidden agendas. But in this time and this place, he was all male, and she was female. If this was going to happen, then that's all that mattered right now. It was all that could matter. So she stood her ground. "Make me."

His head snapped up. The growl he emitted was darker—deeper—than she'd ever heard. The female inside her heeded it. She turned and ran, seeking safety. Adrenaline lit her on fire, and she aimed for the river.

He caught her by the nape before she'd cleared the cabin, sending them both sprawling through the snow. He wrapped himself around her as they tumbled end over end, keeping her off the rough ground. Even so, snow and ice splattered her, and she shut her eyes. The world spun in every direction.

They landed with him on his back and her on him. She gasped and jumped up, pushing off the impossibly hard ridges of his chest.

He stretched to his feet, his gaze pinning her in place, his body between her and the rushing river. Rips marred his T-shirt, and the talons of the dragon tattoo nearly glowed a dark omen.

She'd forgotten. Oh, he was mainly a bear shifter—a predator of the forest. But deep inside his flesh, inside his very bones, a dragon still lived. Unpredictable and deadly. A primordial being not understood by many. "Bear," she whispered.

He stalked toward her. Broad and dangerous, his body moved fluently. But his face. Hard ridges and predatory planes. His eyes glittered with masculine intent.

She backed up. If he was still hampered by his illness, he didn't show it. In this time and place, nothing else mattered but the two of them. A week ago, she had never been within a foot of him. Now? There was just *them*. For this slice of time, her entire world narrowed to the beast of prey deliberately stalking her.

Because she'd wanted this—and she'd challenged him.

It was too late to stop him, even if she'd wanted to. She quivered, caught. Reality tried to creep in, and she looked around almost frantically.

"There's nowhere to go," he whispered, the deliberateness of his steps toward her all the more threatening than if he had charged. "Cabin."

She stood straighter. A witch didn't submit any easier than did a shifter. Her people were long on this earth, and they created fire from ice. They understood the laws that sustained the entire world. They were power, and they were strength. She was part of that flow. "No."

His lids half lowered.

She turned and ran again. What had she been thinking? Panting, she dodged around a tree and smashed right into his body. He didn't grab her.

Freaking out, she ran the other way, her legs pumping and her arms swinging. She rounded a series of bushes and collided with him again. She bounced back, her butt hitting a sapling.

He towered over her, not saying a word.

Desire slammed through her so quickly she swayed. Coupled with fear, it left her entire body alight with a shocking anticipation. She couldn't back up any farther.

"This is what you wanted," he said, his eyes glittering way beyond lust. The animal shifted beneath his skin, shimmering, always present. He remained in human form, but he was no longer anything close to human. Maybe he never had been. His eyes blazed, and red flushed across his rugged cheekbones.

Her knees trembled with the instinctive need to flee. Her blood pounded, hard and fierce, wilder than the storm vibrating through the air. She moved to run, and he stepped into her space, pinning her between his body and the tree. Hunger, primitive and deadly, shone in his eyes.

Hunger for her.

A preternatural silence surrounded them both—all from him.

She shot her knee up, and he swatted it down, his hand clapping hard against her thigh. Her gasp burned up from her compressing lungs.

"Enough." His mouth slammed over hers, furious and forceful, knocking her head back against the tree. He kissed her deep, taking everything he wanted, penetrating her mouth with his tongue. All male, all alpha, all-controlling. His canines were elongated, and they scraped her lips but didn't cut.

Their threat remained.

Her knees gave, and he held her upright, kissing her as if to squash any defiance, any challenge.

She moaned into his mouth, lava rushing through her veins. Digging her nails into his ruined shirt, she stretched on her toes, trying to get closer.

He didn't let her move. Not an inch.

Thunder cracked again.

Faster than she would've ever believed possible, he ducked his head and tossed her over his shoulder. Her ribs impacted his solid shoulder with a dull ache, and the breath whooshed out of her lungs. Shock kept her immobile for several seconds. By the time she lifted her head to fight, he'd kicked open the cabin door.

She flew across the room and landed hard on the bed, bouncing several times. The man had *thrown* her? Her eyes widened, and she gaped at him. Without saying a word, he kicked the door closed.

Whoa. What had she done? Her mind spun, and if there were any words she could use, they were out of her reach.

He kicked off his boots and drew his shirt off over his head.

She swallowed. Her body trembled. So much need raced through her it was difficult to breathe. But the need was edged with caution. Maybe with fear.

"Clothes. Off." His wide chest gleamed in the firelight. Standing there in wet faded jeans and bare feet, he was every inch the determined male. "Now."

She pushed from the bed and stood, having to tilt her head back to meet his gaze. It was too late for submission. "No." Her voice trembled, but she didn't care. His animalistic senses were no doubt in full control, and he could smell her fear. Her arousal. Especially her defiance.

Raw pain flared in her right palm, and she winced. Slowly, she opened her hand to see the perfect mark of a delicate Celtic knot. The mating mark. It was said fate decreed it would only appear when a mate was near, but biology and science probably had more to do with it. She'd decided to mate. There it was.

His gaze caught the marking. "Clothes," he growled, his fingers flexing.

She eyed the door behind him.

Color spread across his face, and he turned slightly to the side to give her a clear path.

She had to try. Gathering her strength, she lunged.

He stepped in her path at the last second, and she rushed into him. Using her momentum against her, he swung them around, landing them both on the bed. It protested with a loud creak and plunged to the floor.

Ignoring the splintered wood legs, he flipped her around to her hands and knees, ripping off her skirt and tights. Her panties were next.

She panicked, bucking against him, fighting his smooth movements. He countered every move, almost easily, and her jacket ripped down the back. She gasped—that was her favorite jacket. Claws shredded her shirt, barely touching her skin. She stilled completely and gathered herself. Oh God. He had to be in human form. He had to be.

She slowly looked over her shoulder to see him in full human form, all male.

He flashed his teeth. Mostly human form—his canines had elongated. Keeping her gaze, he unhooked her bra. It sailed over her head to land near a lamp.

Then his fingers found her core, the claws nowhere in evidence. Pleasure snared her, shooting up her entire body.

"Wet." His chin lowered, and he scraped a nail across her clit. "For me."

She arched and cried out, electricity coiling tight inside her. He pinched and released her.

Her head dropped from raw need. So much. She had to get him inside her now. "Bear," she whispered. It was all she could say.

He knelt behind her, unzipping his jeans and shimmying out of them. Strong hands grabbed her hips.

She elongated her back, tossing her hair down it.

He growled. "Spread your legs."

The order was sexy, the idea of submission a challenge. She gave a slight roll of her butt but otherwise didn't move. Then she held her breath.

His fingers tightened before releasing her hips.

No. Her body rioted. They couldn't stop.

Rough hands clamped onto her inner thighs and pulled. Her thighs spread, her knees pointed in, and her face fell forward to the blankets. She tried to push up, and his hand planted itself firmly across her upper back, holding her down. She struggled, trying to find leverage with her hands, but she lacked the strength.

The hollow ache between her legs widened to a painful emptiness—a furious need.

His erection probed her sex.

God. Now. Please. She bit into a blanket to keep from begging.

One of his hands manacled her hip, while the other remained on her back. He pressed against her opening, and then he stopped.

She tried to push back against him but couldn't move. He controlled her—he controlled everything. She shut her eyes, trying to dispel some of the hunger. Any of it. God, she needed him.

"Are you sure?" he growled, his voice barely recognizable.

It took her a second to translate. She was naked, vulnerable, and wide open for his use. There wasn't a thing she could do to stop him. And he'd stopped himself.

Somehow, he'd paused and was asking her. Giving her control. For the moment.

Her body had wanted him, was open to him. Her mind had accepted him as a mate. At his question, at his strength, her heart opened just as wide. "I'm sure, Bear," she whispered. "I'm sure."

His grip tightened, and he shoved inside her, instantly yanking her back into him. Shock ripped through her at the sudden pain. Just as quickly, pleasure exploded around the pain, combining them until she couldn't tell the difference. Until she didn't care.

He hammered into her, hard and fierce. Relentless. Her first orgasm shredded her, frying each nerve, and she screamed his name. Her body ignited as he continued to pound, forcing her to climb again and fall over the edge. She whimpered with the second orgasm, her face in the pillows. Wave after wave of harsh pleasure took her under.

She'd barely had time to catch her breath when he changed his angle, driving her up again.

Leaning over her, his lava-hot body bracketing her, his mouth enclosed her shoulder.

She stiffened, but coils of electricity were sparking inside her, hitting every corner. Her heart kept galloping.

His canines slid in slowly, deliberately. Pain slashed through her. He kept going, holding her, embedding those dangerous blades in her bone. She cried out, struggling against him, not able to move.

The hand at her hip released. Then the one at her back.

She lay there, gasping, a tear winding down her face. Only his mouth and his cock held her in place.

She still couldn't move.

Her heart beat several times, and silence echoed around the cabin. One gentle hand caressed down her spine. She relaxed into the bed, accepting him.

The second she did, he grabbed her hip again and started to pound. His teeth remained in place. White hot lights flashed across her vision, and she exploded, the world going black for a moment. He increased his thrusts and ground against her with a powerful orgasm.

The canines retracted, and he gave a lazy swipe of his tongue, healing the wound. He withdrew, flipped her over, and shoved back inside her. "We're just getting started."

Chapter 17

Bear rolled his hips, trying to get even deeper inside this stunning woman. The witch. His mate.

The taste of her blood was still in his mouth, still driving him to take and tame. She looked up at him, her blue gaze shocked. Never in his life would he have believed what she'd unleashed in him.

But they weren't done. Not yet.

He smoothed damp hair away from her lovely features. Moving inside her, going deep, he felt his entire world settle. For a century, he'd been alone. Sure, he had friends, brothers he'd claimed as his own. And he'd had two siblings across the world.

But this bond was different. There was only one mate—and his had her hands on his biceps. Her nails cut in, and the slight pain drove his hunger higher. Would he ever get enough of her? "I'll never let anything hurt you," he vowed, caught up.

Denial chased surprise across her face.

Oh yeah. Independence and all that. She didn't get it, and that was okay. But he'd never let anything harm her again. The need to protect lived in him, somewhere too deep to define, and he'd never fought it. He had no intention of doing so now. So when she opened her mouth to argue, to remind him this was an arranged mating, he covered her lips with his.

Her taste was even better than her smell. Her lush lips curved under his, accepting him. She moaned low, her hips arching up into his.

She'd searched him out for an arrangement, but he no longer cared about agreements. He wanted more from her. All of her passion— her dreams and fears. Everything.

He let her pull back to breathe, and her lips were red and wet from his. The woman was addictive.

"More," she whispered, her ankles locking at his back.

"Give me all of you," he murmured back, his voice soft but his gaze direct.

Her pupils dilated and she gave a short nod. Yeah. She got him. There was no question what she had to do next. "Where?" she asked, her neck stretching as he hammered harder inside her, those soft hands caressing him everywhere.

His balls sparked and electricity burned down his spine. "Your choice." If he was gonna carry a witch's mark, she could choose where to put it.

She licked her lips, inevitability in her gaze. It was way too late for either of them to turn back.

At the thought, he increased the speed of his thrusts. Her eyes widened, and she stiffened, biting her lip as the orgasm took her. Her delicate inner muscles squeezed him, rippling along his cock, sending him into paradise.

A piercing pain burned along his back and he jerked, coming harder as raw pleasure pierced him. The orgasm rung him out and took everything he had. He settled against her, careful not to crush her, his heart pounding harder than if he'd been in battle. "Are you all right?" he managed to gasp out, running a knuckle down her cheek.

Her gaze dropped to his neck. "You're a mite heavy." Her tone was . . . bemused.

So he wasn't the only one feeling completely overwhelmed. Good. He rolled to his side and pulled her to face him, grabbing blankets to spread over them both. "I asked you a question." He lifted her chin with two fingers. They might as well get a few things straight right now. "If you don't want to answer something, tell me. But there will be no hiding or evading. Definitely no lying." He had no clue where they were gonna end up, but some things were absolute.

She gingerly touched her bright red shoulder. "What is up with you and no lying? You're a fanatic about it."

He leaned in and rubbed his nose against hers. "I don't like subterfuge." His father, the asshole, had been full of lies and deception—when he wasn't kicking the shit out of Bear. "There's no need."

She winced and rolled the same shoulder. "I work in the Coven government, Bear. My life is full of confidential information."

"That's fine. Your professional life can be all about secrets and lies." He pushed her hand away to examine the wound he'd left on her. "But in our life, this life, we use the truth. *All* of it."

She scoffed. "You trust me? Really?"

He paused. Did he trust her? He'd just mated her. Would he really mate a woman he didn't trust? They had too much to learn about each other still. Good thing they were immortal. "I'm choosing not to answer that question because I'm not sure what to say at the moment. Other than, heal that shoulder. Now."

She rolled her eyes. "You don't get to become all bossy now." Tingles cascaded from her as she sent healing cells to the wound.

"I'm the alpha, Ness. I am the boss." It didn't hurt to remind her. "Can you heal yourself faster because of your gift?"

"No. Not faster." Her skin regained a healthy color and lost the swelling. But his mark, that strong bite, remained in place for all to see.

She glanced down. "You marked my entire shoulder."

Yeah. His bite was visible from her front and her back. Satisfaction filtered through him along with a powerful sense of possession. *His* mark. Her body. Yes. Though he hadn't been the only one to brand tonight. He looked over his shoulder but couldn't see her marking. It still burned, but he chose not to send healing cells to the area.

The burn felt right.

She snuggled sleepily against him, her eyelids closing. "We broke your bed."

Probably wouldn't be the last time. "Go to sleep. We'll figure things out tomorrow." The wind rustled against the cabin as the night descended.

She nodded, her hair brushing his shoulder like fine silk. "I have to go to LA tomorrow." Then she dropped into sleep, her body relaxing completely.

He pulled the blanket up to her neck and studied her. Long black lashes lay against her pale skin, hiding those spectacular eyes. Her hair was a wild mess over her slim shoulders. He reached out and ran his finger across the bite.

She shifted and mumbled something, her legs moving beneath the blankets, one hand clutching the material up by her neck. He touched her fingernails and slim fingers. So small, so feminine. Yet the woman could punch.

What was he going to do with her? So far, a known enemy wanted her kidnapped, and an unknown threat wanted her dead. All of that had been brought to his attention just during the last few days.

How many times would he need to protect her in a whole month? He sighed and tugged on a wayward curl. It was time to start training his people again, and they needed to increase their numbers. With shifters only. His eyes closed, and he tried to feel his internal injuries. A healing balm was already spreading, and his constant pain had quieted. He stretched; now he could send his own healing cells throughout his body to start repairing damage. The mating, for him, was already a success.

What about her? He might not have given her the gift of fire. If he hadn't, he'd make sure he kept her safe, whether she liked it or not.

After he was certain she was asleep, he slid from the bed and made his way to the small bathroom beyond the fireplace. Curiosity held him while he shut the door and tugged the string for the light. The small room lit up. He moved toward the mirror above the sink and turned, surveying his back.

The dragon he'd had tattooed there faced to the side so its talons could wrap around his shoulder and bicep. The tail was long and its scales appeared razor-sharp. The creature had bright eyes in a narrow face. Right in the middle of the dark beast now glowed a perfect Celtic knot with sharply delicate lines.

"I'll be damned," he murmured. She'd marked the dragon right where its heart would be.

Exactly.

Nessa fought the urge to rub her branded shoulder as she typed rapidly on the keyboard, canceling her flight. While her shoulder no longer hurt, the whole thing tingled as a reminder.

She'd mated Bear.

He'd barely spoken to her this morning before escorting her to the office and telling her to cancel her ticket. Then he'd said he'd be right back, before disappearing toward the main rec room of the headquarters. That had been an hour ago.

She punched up a series of codes, and soon Jasper came into view.

"Any news?" she asked, her stomach churning. Was her uncle all right? He had to be.

Her friend shook his head. "We know nothing. Our only lead to Boondock is you. Are you sure you don't want me to send backup to Los Angeles? You shouldn't be going on your own."

Her uncle had to be all right. "I doubt I'll be alone." Looking around, she tugged down her shirt to show him the bite.

Jasper gasped and sat back. "You did it. You really did it." His eyes widened. "The idea was crazy, and I thought you'd change your mind. Are you all right? He's a shifter."

She swallowed. "Remember when you had that weekend with the twin demonesses in Antigua a decade ago?"

Jasper's eyes widened. "Those females almost killed me. But it was worth it." He grinned.

"It was like that times a billion." She tried to smile, but it was all just so overwhelming. "It's hard to explain."

Jasper rubbed his mouth. "So what now? After you save Boon, you're going to stay in the wilds and have a bunch of bear-witch babies?"

She sat up straighter. "Of course not." The idea of a baby warmed right through her belly, and she banished the sensation. "I have a job to do, and I'm damn good at it." It was also a job that required a lot of travel, and she didn't see Bear just trooping along all the time. "I said this was a mating of convenience, and I meant it." But that was before she'd spent two nights with the shifter. Leaving him would hurt. Maybe. Why couldn't she trust him completely? She should. There was nothing wrong with going on faith.

"Nessa?" Jasper asked.

She started. "Sorry. Mind wandered."

He leaned in. "I support you and always have. But there are going to be repercussions. About this."

"Aye." A woman in her position mated to a bear shifter? "I know. That's a problem for tomorrow, though."

"I'll back your play. I always have."

Yeah, he had. She and Jasper had started training at the same time decades ago, and they'd instantly become friends and confidants. Maybe she could talk him into mating a female bear shifter. Wouldn't that be handy? She smiled.

He straightened. "Whatever you're thinking, you must stop. I hate that smile."

"You're a good friend, Jasp." Besides her uncle, Jasper was the closest thing she had to family. Well, before she'd mated Bear. "Thank you for everything."

His dark eyebrows rose. "That had better not be a good-bye. Just say the word, and I'll send backup of the kind the USA has never seen before."

"I'll call if I need help. Is there any update on the worldwide chatter?"

"No. Still going on, and an attack is definitely coming. But we haven't been able to find out any more details."

Her chest hurt. "Please check in with any news." She clicked off.

It was time to figure out more about Bear. She leaned over and started typing in a command to reach hacking software created by the Guard. It was the best out there, and moments after she'd employed it she was scanning through Bear's accounts.

Bloody hell.

She squinted. Bear was loaded. Not just kind of wealthy, but incredibly so. He had accounts all over the world in addition to land holdings and stock in a multitude of companies. Yet he lived in a ramshackle cabin and wore jeans so faded they looked more white than blue.

What was he hiding?

The old phone on the desk rang. She looked at it. When was the last time she'd answered a landline? Interesting. She picked up the bulky handset. "Hello?"

"Hey, yeah. Is Bear around?" asked a gruff—very gruff—voice.

"I'm sorry, he isn't here." She reached in a drawer for a pencil and a message pad, right where they should be, in an organized pile. "I'm taking messages for him. What can we do for you?"

"Tell him Smitty called. I heard that he was back in town and just wondered if he still wanted me to meet him on Thursdays in Plato Park, or if he was going to handle things now from his end."

She took the note. "Thursdays?"

"Yeah. Except for the Tuesday two months ago. In fact, tell him I still have a pair of his jeans and an ugly green shirt if he wants them back. Last time he shifted back to bear form, I forgot to drop them off at his cabin."

Her ears rang. Bear had been meeting this man every Thursday and had left behind clothing when he shifted to bear form? "Um, Smitty? Just curious. How long have you and Bear been meeting up?"

"Why?" Smitty's voice lowered.

"I'm just wondering."

"Give him the message, girlie." Smitty hung up.

She stared at the quiet phone receiver. Talk about secrets. She'd known Bear hadn't remained in bear form the last three months. Just who was Smitty? More important, why had Bear been shifting into human form every Thursday? Was it to pick up Apollo?

It couldn't be. But he had so many accounts with so much damn money. Bear could certainly finance a new drug—both the manufacture and the distribution. In fact, if he was the manufacturer, it would've been brilliant to have another motorcycle gang distribute the drug, to keep the Grizzlies clean and off the DEA's radar.

Until one of her people had blown up the rival motorcycle gang, and its members had scattered in every direction.

Bear wasn't a drug runner.

Right?

He nudged the door open with one hip and carried in two cups of coffee. "There's a plane meeting us in three hours to head to Los Angeles." Snow swirled in after him, and he handed her one of the cups. "Now, you're going to tell me all about George Flanders, your uncle, and everything else I don't know."

She looked at him, no longer surprised by the intelligence shining in his eyes. "Right. Because we don't keep secrets from each other. Correct?"

He took a sip of his steaming drink, his gaze intense over the cup. "Exactly. Glad you're finally on board."

Chapter 18

The private plane was too confining. Bear shrugged off unease and tried to stretch out his legs. After nearly two hours in the air, Nessa sat next to him, staring out the window, while Lucas played poker with Logan and Garrett up ahead of them.

Bear glanced at the woman. His woman.

She'd been out of sorts all day, but looked sexy as hell in a blue pencil skirt, white blouse, and black boots. She'd ignored him the entire flight. Maybe she was just worried about her uncle. "Every one of my contacts is trying to track down your uncle," he said evenly.

When she turned her head, a couple of curls escaped the clip she'd used. "This is a bad idea. We shouldn't have Lucas and the boys with us." Her eyes glowed, and concern deepened the hue. "George was very clear that I had to come alone. I knew I couldn't talk you out of coming, but this is too much. They're too much."

Bear reached for her hand, but she jerked it away.

A growl filled his chest, and he cleared it. "I understand your concerns, but we're all trained in combat missions. Going into something like this without backup is fuckin' crazy."

Anger poured off her. "Aren't you the strategic fighter today."

Was that sarcasm? It was. His temper stretched to meet hers. The silent treatment had grated on him the entire day. Now she was being a smart-ass? "I'm tryin' to be real understanding here, baby. Your uncle is taken, you just got mated, and life must be overwhelming." He bit back a threat or two. "How about you lose some of the attitude?"

Her smile lacked any charm whatsoever. "You're right. Thank you for the plane ride. It sure is nice to have friends with money, now isn't it?"

The hair rose at the base of his neck at the derision in her tone. "What is wrong with you?" he snapped.

Lucas looked back, and Bear glared until he turned around again. Nessa crossed her arms in a huff and focused out the window once more.

That was it. He grabbed her waist and lifted her right out of the seat, plunking her on his lap to straddle him. Her legs went on either side of his hips, and she slapped his chest.

He grabbed her forearms and drew her in. "Talk. Now."

She snarled. Actually snarled. "Let me go or you lose a testicle."

"Mom? Dad?" Lucas called back, chortling. "Stop fighting. You're scaring the kids."

Bear ignored him and yanked the offensive pin out of Nessa's hair. She protested, pushing against him. Her hair cascaded down and all around them, scenting the air with roses. For once, the smell didn't calm him. He leaned in until his face was right at hers and whispered. "You want a fight right here and now? I'll make it happen. I don't give two fucks who's in the plane with us."

Her glare could burn through concrete.

He kept his voice low so only she could hear—probably. "If not, tell me right now what has crawled up your ass."

Color bloomed across her face. "You're a crass bastard."

"Yeah. I am." He gave her a slight shake. "I'm also not fuckin' around. What the hell is wrong with you?"

"You believe in truth and not having secrets. So much truth." She rolled her eyes. "You're a damn liar, you are. Seriously."

The words should have sent him into orbit, but there was a hint of hurt behind the sarcasm. What could he have possibly done to hurt her? He breathed out slowly and tried to calm himself until he could figure out the truth. "All right, Nessa. What have I lied about?"

Her eyes sparked. "You're rich," she hissed. "Not a little, but a whole bloody shitload of a lot. You're loaded, Bear McDunphy."

He frowned. "So?"

"So?" Her voice rose. "You live in a shack. Your jeans are older than anybody on this plane."

He shook his head. What was wrong with his jeans? "Again, so?"

She sat back. "You're hiding your money. Pretending you're poor."

He scratched his chin. Had she lost her mind? "I'm not pretending or hiding." Man, life was confusing. No. Forget that. Women were confusing. "I like my cabin and there's nothing wrong with my jeans. Not once did I tell you I was poor." He grimaced. "This plane is mine. I don't like it, and I really don't like flying, but I have a plane. It's better than flying with other people. With humans."

She blinked several times.

He relaxed his hold on her, but he wasn't ready to let her up yet. The hurt had been real, and it wasn't just about money. "Why are you bothered if I have money, Nessa?"

A guilty flush wound over her face.

He watched, fascinated. Then he clicked facts into order. "Wait a minute." She worked for the Coven Nine. The Enforcers had been recalled, and now Apollo was back on the streets. Humor bubbled up through him, and he snorted. "You think I'm distributing Apollo?"

She shifted uneasily on his lap.

It slapped him then. "Oh my God. You thought I might be the manufacturer?" His breath heated, even as his mind spun. Part of him wanted to laugh his ass off, and the other wanted to beat hers. "So you're investigating me?"

Her shoulders went down. "Aye."

Wow. That kinda hurt. "Ness? Did you really think I was behind Apollo?" He smoothed curls away from her face.

"No," she mumbled. "Not until I saw how much money you have."

"By hacking into my accounts?" he guessed. That should piss him off, but truth be told, he didn't much care. "Why not just ask?"

She tilted her head. "If you were behind Apollo, would you just have admitted it?"

Okay. Good point. "No." But she should've said something the second she'd found the accounts. Of course, if she was half as thrown by their mating experience as he was, he could understand her wanting to regroup a little. "Witches always have multiple agendas," he muttered. So she'd come to town to heal him, investigate him, and mate him to gain the ability to throw fire. Yep. It figured. "I'm not creating or running Apollo, baby."

"All right." Her gaze fell again.

He ran his thumb across her bottom lip. "What else, Nessa?"

She sighed. "Smitty called. Wanted to know if you were meeting him this Thursday."

Dumbass Smitty. "Damn it. Smitty has a big mouth." Bear shifted uncomfortably in the seat.

Her gaze rose. "You admit it. You've been shifting back to human once a week for the last few months. When everyone thought you were in bear form the whole time."

Heat climbed up the back of his neck and spread to his chin.

She watched, her gaze interested. "Bear? What exactly have you been doing once a week?"

He cleared his throat. His ears burned. "Does it matter? Maybe I just had some human stuff to do."

Her shoulders hunched. "Fine. Okay."

No, it wasn't okay. He'd demanded honesty. "Remember the shirt you borrowed? The Pontsey Porcupines shirt?"

She leaned back to study him. "Aye. Why?"

He looked away and back. "Fine. All right. I coach a baseball team—the Porcupines. Games are on Thursdays, and I couldn't think of a way to just disappear. Too many of these kids have had folks leave them already." His chest filled. He felt like an idiot. "They're a mismatched group of lost human teenagers, and I've got them playing baseball." Defensiveness rose in him, and he sat straighter.

"Baseball?" Her eyes softened to the color of spring bluebells.

Why did they have to discuss this? "Yes. There's the answer. Enough." He moved to put her back in her seat.

She stopped him, her arms winding around his neck. "That's one of the sweetest things I've ever heard."

Geez. He rolled his eyes. "Good. Let's stop talking about it."

She kissed his nose. "Why don't you want people to know you're a nice guy?"

His ears got even hotter, and he could see Garrett's shoulders shaking up ahead with what had to be muffled laughter. Hopefully the kid choked on his chortles. Bear pressed a hard kiss to Nessa's lips. "The alpha leader of a shifter nation isn't a nice guy. Ever."

There was no way she could understand that.

She leaned back. "Of course. Your secret is very safe with me."

Why wasn't she understanding him? "It's not a secret. I just don't go around telling everybody about it." He wanted another taste of her. So he leaned in and indulged himself. If she thought he was sweet, he'd run with it. Within seconds, the kiss deepened, engaging his whole body.

She pulled back first, her expression bemused.

They weren't alone on the plane. He had to get himself under control as they moved into battle mode. He'd shared his secrets, and it was time for her to share hers.

The tablet next to her seat dinged.

She stiffened, head to toe.

He caressed down her arms. "You understand how to do this?"

Her eyebrows rose. "I've been doing this a long time." With that statement, she rolled off him and back into her seat to grab the tablet.

He stood and crossed to sit facing her as she straightened and pressed buttons on the tablet.

A male voice came through the speakers. "Hello, Nessa. Are you alone?"

Bear shut down all emotion before he lost his mind. The familiarity in the voice made him want to crush the other male's throat with his bare hands. He would at some point.

Nessa's face remained mildly polite. "George. Where's my uncle?"

So that was good ole George's voice. Kind of nasal.

"He's safe. A little the worse for wear, but still spitting fire." George had a grating chuckle. "Well, not fire. But you know what I mean."

Nessa's expression didn't alter. Not by an inch. "I see." If anything, she sounded bored.

Bear watched her, his admiration growing. She was a helluva lot tougher than he'd realized. His interest piqued, he forgot all about temper and murder.

"Are you in the air?" George asked.

"Aye. Should be over Los Angeles in about ten minutes," she said as if reciting a recipe. "What's the plan?" Her gaze remained on the tablet screen as if there was nothing else to look at in the plane. "This is getting tedious."

George laughed again. "You are so cool under pressure. I've always liked that about you."

Bear focused on Nessa. Just how well did the two know each other?

Nessa sighed. "I've never thought much of you. The plan?"

"I'm assuming you're in a Guard private plane?" George asked.

"No." Nessa shook her head, and her hair tumbled. "You said to keep the Guard out of this. I borrowed a plane from a friend."

Nice job. George's question had been a trap, and Nessa had easily sidestepped it. Bear rubbed his chin as the men behind him remained perfectly silent. Nessa was interesting to watch in action. She truly was a phenomenal actress.

Should that concern him?

George cleared his throat. "I'm sending you the coordinates of a private airstrip in southern Oregon. You might need your pilot to turn around. Come here, land, and get out of that plane alone, or I'll send orders to have your uncle beheaded." There was silence for a moment. "By the way, I like your hair down. A lot."

Nessa waited and then slammed the tablet down, screen first.

Bear reached for her hands. They shook so hard he enfolded them, trying to add warmth. Tears gathered in her eyes, and her shoulders trembled. Wow. She had given away nothing—not one bit of the turmoil that was consuming her. He pulled her across the way and snuggled her into his arms.

Lucas reached around Bear and grabbed the tablet. "I'll give the pilots the new coordinates." Without waiting for an answer, he moved toward the cockpit.

Bear ran a soothing hand down her back. "I can take you home and send forces, Nessa. Just say the word."

She lifted her face to his, tears on her lashes. "He's my uncle. My only family."

Bear brushed tears off her smooth skin. "He was your only family. Now you have me." His job was to protect her.

Her eyes softened. "The plan is good. Are you sure you don't mind jumping from a plane?"

Hell yes, he minded. "No." He stood and let her slide to her feet. "It's time to suit up."

The boys hustled into motion, fetching bulletproof vests, weapons, and parachutes.

"You ever skydive?" Garrett asked, handing over several knives.

Bear shook his head. The very idea of allowing gravity to have a hold on him in midair made him want to puke. But he kept his face stoic. "Nope. But just pull the purple cord, right?"

"Right." Logan checked a clip and slid a green laser gun into the back of his jeans. "It's fun. Just relax and float."

Bear grasped a smaller vest and pulled it over Nessa's head. Then he handed her the shirt button containing a tiny camera, which she placed at the top of her blouse.

She tightened the Velcro. "This will work. It has to."

Bear shoved an earbud into his ear. "Don't leave the plane until we're in place. No matter what."

She nodded. "Affirmative."

The woman was right in character. Bear eyed her. She had better be telling the truth. "I mean it. You stay put until I give the okay."

She pressed an earbud into place. "Of course."

Why didn't that reassure him?

She tied her hair back at the nape. "If my uncle isn't at the airport, you have to let them take me. Follow all you want, but I'm going with them."

Bear hated that part of the plan. "Tell me you've at least trained for this type of thing." As an accountant for the Nine, she'd have had some training. At least a little, right?

"I have," she said. "Don't worry."

Lucas returned and quickly suited up. "Just got a call. There were two Apollo dart attacks in Seattle earlier today. Both witches living in Bellevue, and both took enough darts to be killed." He sobered. "I'm sorry, Nessa."

Her head lifted. Anger lit her features. "Thank you. We'll deal with them next."

Damn it. Bear rolled his shoulders beneath the vest.

Garrett opened the back door. "Time to jump. It'll take us about fifteen minutes to run from where we land to the coordinates of the private airport. Let's go." He disappeared into thin air.

Bear leaned down and pressed a hard kiss to Nessa's lips. Everything was jumbled, but he needed her to stay safe. The idea of not having her with him hurt deep inside, surprising in its intensity. "See you soon, baby."

Chapter 19

Although Nessa had been in the field, she hadn't been in combat in much too long. Frankly, she'd never spent much time in combat. Strategy was her specialty, and she liked how numbers lined up. The fighting and shooting were just bonuses.

After the men had jumped from the plane, she'd secured the door and sat back down, waiting for the plane to land. The two pilots, both shifters, were armed and trained to fight. They'd stay in the cockpit unless she yelled a distress signal. She had absolutely no intention of yelling anything.

Her body felt different since the mating. Stronger, somehow. More attuned to Bear, that was for sure.

Yet . . . she held out her hand and tried to imagine the oxygen molecules morphing into plasma. Nothing happened. She tried harder. Nope. She spent the next twenty minutes trying as hard as she could to make fire. Nothing even sputtered.

Well, her uncle had trained her to hone her healing skills. Maybe she just needed a fire-thrower to teach her how to do this. Plus, she'd just gotten mated. It might take time for her chromosomal pairs to change and adapt. She'd studied the science extensively before approaching Bear with her rather unusual plan, and time was needed for sure.

For now, she'd have to rely on her fighting skills. The plane continued descending, finally touching down on a small strip with just a lone warehouse at the side. She looked out the window to the trees surrounding the place. Talk about deserted.

The plane rolled to a stop, and she opened the door and waited for the automatic steps to stretch out to the concrete. The slight wind stirred her hair, but Oregon seemed to be having a much milder winter start than Seattle. She looked around, trying to find any immortal signatures.

Nothing.

Her men were well hidden in the forest, if they'd made it. Anybody in the building was well shielded, most likely with countermeasures she'd helped to develop through the years. She centered herself and tried again, finding a familiar energy. Bear. He was in the stand of trees to the far left.

Keeping her head high, she descended the stairs. The lights outside of the warehouse turned on, illuminating the area. She paused on the tarmac, and the wind blew her hair around her face.

The front door of the warehouse opened, but only darkness was visible inside. Keeping her hands free, she strode forward, each step light on the tarmac. Her gun was tucked nicely in her back, and she had three knives hidden on her body. The one on her thigh would be tough for anyone to find. That's why she liked skirts.

She reached the door and stepped inside. It instantly shut behind her, and the lights turned on to reveal a small waiting area with a sofa in front of three private planes. Four soldiers guarded the planes with automatic weapons in their hands and green laser guns at their waists.

George sat on the sofa, a gun pointed at her. For the meet, he'd worn dress slacks, a button-down shirt, and brown boots. His wavy dark hair curled around his ears. "Nessa. It's good to see you again."

"I canna' say the same," she said, her brogue deepening. "Where is Boon?"

George stood and moved toward her, tucking his gun away. "If you move, they'll shoot you." Then he brushed her hair back.

She showed her teeth.

"Please." He tugged out her earbud and then scrutinized her. "There it is." With deft fingers, he removed the camera button from her shirt. Then he casually tossed the camera and bud on the floor, crushing them beneath his boot. "This isn't my first op."

"This isn't an op," she hissed. "Where is my uncle?"

"Safe," George said. "You can have him the second we mate."

She relaxed her stance. George wasn't paying attention, or he'd sense her mating. She all but smelled of Bear. If needed, she could jump to the side and go for her gun. "Not garna happen. So hand over Boon, and I won't put the Guard or Coven Nine on your ass."

George sighed. "You have always been such a bitch. Why can't you just see how strong we'd be together?" He took one step away from her. "Even your uncle agrees."

Nessa snorted. "He most certainly does not."

A tall figure exited the nearest plane. "That's not exactly true, sugar plum." Her uncle smiled as he crossed the painted concrete toward her.

Her breath deserted her. Completely. "Boondock?" she whispered.

He smiled, a handsome man in full health. "Aye." Instead of being a bloody disaster, he was clean-shaven, with his dark hair slicked back. His movements were smooth in his pressed green slacks and gray Armani shirt. "You might want to step away from her, George. She can get violent when riled."

George took another step back.

Heat clawed down Nessa's throat. What was happening? She shook her head, trying to get a grip on reality.

George sniffed her.

She shoved him farther away with one hand.

He frowned and sniffed her again. "Sonuvabitch. You smell like bear. A blooming bear."

Heat climbed into her face.

"Nessa?" Boondock asked, reaching the sofa. "Please tell me I'm not too late."

George slammed his hands on his hips. "You said you'd talk her into mating me if I helped you. You promised."

Boondock rolled his eyes. "Please. You can't handle a woman like my niece. She'd chew you up, spit you out, and then bat you around for fun. You're an idiot, George. Always have been."

George's face turned a mottled red. "Oh yeah? Shoot them!"

Nessa set her stance and reached for her gun, but nobody else twitched. She paused.

"They're my soldiers," Boondock said smoothly. "Guard soldiers."

Nessa looked at the four. She didn't recognize any of them.

Boondock took in her surprised expression. "They cover Australia. There's no reason you'd recognize them."

Realization started to dawn. "You didn't. Please tell me you did not set this whole situation up just to get me here. Uncle?" Her temples pounded. "I cried about you."

"Ah, that's sweet." He quite wisely kept his distance. "I don't like being unaware of your location."

Anger ripped through her so quickly her entire throat felt scorched. "I was on mission."

"Yes, but I didn't know where." His smile twinkled in his eyes. "When I got Jasper drunk, he may have let your whole mating plan slip."

"You got Jasper drunk?" she snapped. Not Jasper. He was the one who'd told her about the kidnapping. "He's in on this?" That betrayal cut deep.

"Of course not." Boondock waved a hand. "We legitimately had him beat up trying to protect me. The boy gave it a good shot, I'll have you know. Took out three of my men." Boondock puffed out his chest. "You two are well trained, if I do say so myself. I did a good job."

Oh, she was going to kill him. Her hands trembled, and not from fear. "How could you?"

He sobered. His shoulders went back. "How could I? Are you jesting? You fly all the way across the world, by yourself, on a mission? One involving Apollo and PK? One where you might mate a bear shifter? A shifter." He moved toward her, his eyes blazing. "How could I not? You've lost your bloomin' mind."

George sniffed again. "She mated the shifter. I can smell it."

Boondock stopped cold. He paled. "You did not."

Heat burst in her face, but she kept his gaze. "I did." Slowly, deliberately, she tugged her shirt to the side to reveal the mating mark. "I burned the hell out of his back, too."

Boondock gasped.

"Damn it," George yelled. "I knew I couldn't trust you. Attack."

Men poured from the other two silent planes, guns blazing. The Guards turned to defend themselves. George grabbed Nessa and pushed his gun to her throat.

The warehouse door burst open, and several flash grenades rolled across the floor, blowing up and sheeting the room in blue light. Nessa dropped fast and swung out, nailing George in the knee.

Her head rang, and she couldn't see. The smoke was thick and blue. Combat boots poured into the room. Bear grabbed her up to her feet, Lucas covering him. "Nessa?" Panic gripped his voice. He shook her, running his hands down her body. "Are you all right?"

She nodded, her head lolling. The flash grenade had been too close to her. "Fine. Don't kill the soldiers in black—they're actually with us. The ones in green are fair game."

"Fine." He set her to his side.

His men rushed forward and into the fight as Garrett yelled a war cry.

Boondock lunged up, firing green lasers at Bear. Nessa screamed. The lasers would turn into hard bullets when they hit flesh, and too many could kill even a bear shifter. Several hit Bear's vest and he growled, reaching up and slapping the gun away. He swung out and nailed Boon in the temple. Her uncle dropped like a rock.

"Why was your uncle shooting at me?" Bear asked.

Nessa coughed, her eyes burning. "Long story. He's fine."

"Fucking witches," Bear bellowed.

She cringed but couldn't quite blame him. Just then, George rose from the smoke, firing rapidly at Bear's face.

Out of pure instinct, Nessa jumped in the way. One bullet hit her neck, and she cried out, pain ricocheting up to her ear. She fell, her cheekbone hitting the concrete.

Bear lunged over her, connecting with George and taking him to the ground. It was no contest. George fought with all his training, but Bear methodically countered every move with another intended specifically to cause pain. Blood flowed freely—all of it from George. Bear played with him like an animal with prey until George was pretty much sobbing. Bleeding and sobbing. He grabbed his ear, screaming.

Nessa rolled over. "Bear," she croaked, holding her neck. "Don't kill him."

Bear turned her way, the thirst for blood bright in his eyes.

"Please," she whispered, trying to stay alert.

He looked at her for a moment. Then he punched George square in the face, breaking his nose and several facial bones. The witch flopped to the ground, unconscious.

She lifted her head and tried to smile, but her strength deserted her. Bear slid on his knees and caught her head before her nose smashed onto the concrete floor. "You're okay." He gingerly pulled her hand away from her neck. "You have to be."

"Ouch."

The sounds of men fighting slowly died down.

She looked over at her unconscious uncle. "I can't believe——"

An explosion blasted against the side of the warehouse, buckling the metal siding. "Damn." Bear jumped up and hurried to the door to look outside, turning almost instantly to yell, "Transport blown." He tapped his ear. "Need plan B. Now. He turned back to Nessa just as the entire rear of the building blew in.

Shock and fury sizzled across his face. So, that wasn't part of his plan.

The plane had been blown up? She gasped, turning almost in slow motion. The blue smoke flew out into the night. A squad of five ran inside wearing full tactical gear with even their faces covered. The first two held dart guns. Apollo dart guns.

One spotted her and gave a signal. They ran for her, all shooting rapidly. Darts flew all around her.

"Shit." Bear grabbed her and raced for the main door, rushing through it with a shattering of glass. "Secondary vacate, now. Now," he yelled, running out onto the tarmac near the smoldering mess of his plane.

Nessa struggled until he put her down. "We can't run. Have to fight," she gasped, whirling around.

Two of the men with darts leaped through the broken glass doors.

Bear roared a battle cry and rushed them both, ignoring the darts impacting his body. He ripped the guns away and threw them onto the burning roof. "Get the other dart guns," he ordered. Hopefully, everyone else still had their comm units on.

One of the dart soldiers tackled Bear, taking him down. He fought furiously, smashing his hands against the attacker's ears.

The other soldier ran around them, coming straight for Nessa. Her vision was fuzzy, and her head hurt. Blood flowed down her neck to soak her blouse. She'd lost her gun in the fight, but she reached for a knife from her boot.

The soldier smiled and yanked out his own knife.

His was bigger.

He circled her, his movements fluid and graceful. She waited, her heart thundering, her stance set.

He charged.

She only had one chance. Pivoting, she dodged back and then in, drawing her knife across his jugular. He grabbed his neck and dropped to his knees, his eyes bugging out behind the mask. Drawing on strength she hoped she had, she kicked him in the temple. His eyelids fluttered shut, and he fell sideways.

He smelled like shifter. The guy would live, but he'd need some time to recover.

She stumbled back.

Bear reached her, blood flowing from a cut in his lip. "You okay?" He sounded very far away.

"Aye," she said, her hand going to her neck again. She had to stem the blood.

"Where the fuck is plan B?" Bear yelled.

Lights pierced the clouds above, and a Mil Mi-24 attack helicopter descended rapidly and landed. Nessa stilled in place. What? This was Bear's plan B? The side opened, and Bear hustled her aboard, pushing her into a seat along the wall and buckling her in. The pilot turned and nodded. "Stay here," Bear ordered.

She coughed, her brain shutting down as her body tried to repair itself. "My uncle. Don't leave him here with the darts." Those darts would kill witches. Was he okay? He had to be all right. She shuddered. "George, too. He's a witch."

Bear turned and ran back into the building. Seconds later, he ran out with her unconscious uncle over his shoulder. Lucas, Garrett, and Logan followed with the two shifter pilots from Bear's other helicopter on their heels. Thank goodness they were okay. They all jumped in, and instantly the helicopter rose off the ground. Bear dumped Boondock on the floor and moved to sit by Nessa.

She raised her head. "George?" she croaked out.

"He's fine. The Guard soldiers took him," Bear said, reaching to hold her hand. "He wasn't hit with any darts."

"Y-you have an attack helicopter," she whispered, her throat on fire.

He tightened his hold. "I'm the leader of the grizzly nation, sweetheart. I have several attack helicopters." His free hand reached for her head, and he tugged her toward his shoulder. "Close your eyes and heal your neck. Now."

"This is such a mess," she mumbled. "Is everyone okay?" Blackness dotted her vision.

"Yes. But you owe me a plane now."

A truck and a plane. She passed out with a smile on her face.

Chapter 20

Bear stretched awake, his body feeling like his own again. If his mate hadn't been in danger the night before, he might've actually enjoyed the fight. There was so much intrigue to figure out that he just wanted to bury his face in Nessa's fragrant hair and stay there all day.

She'd slept the entire way home, even while he'd brought her to the cabin on the four-wheeler. Good thing he'd had Lucas put the plastic roof on it.

The fire popped across the room, and a quick glance out the window showed a nice snowfall . . . puffy and mellow. The wind had given up the fight for a time, and the day almost seemed peaceful. Oh, it wouldn't end up that way, he just knew it. There was one key question that had bothered him before he slept. Who would've sent soldiers with Apollo darts after Nessa? More important, who had known where to find her? It hadn't seemed that George had wanted her dead, so who was this outside threat?

Maybe the dart soldiers were George's plan B. If so, and that was the only thing that really made sense, then he should've killed George. Now he had to hunt George down to kill him. Bear sighed.

She murmured and stretched against him, her smooth legs rubbing against his as she rolled onto her stomach and stretched her arms up, her face toward him.

"Morning," he rumbled, sliding his hand down her back to cup her butt.

Her eyes opened, blue and a little cloudy. They slowly cleared. "Bear."

Yeah. Bear. He squeezed, letting his hand roam. Arousal spiraled through him, but he kept his movements gentle. His woman had been hurt the night before, and although he'd felt her healing herself for a couple of hours last night, he needed to be gentle with her. She deserved it. "A couple of things became clear to me last night," he said, appreciating her other buttock.

She arched an eyebrow. "What became clear and why is your hand on my rear?"

He grinned at the rhyme. "My hand is on your rear because your butt is tight and firm." He caressed her, enjoying the interest that leaped into her eyes. "As for what became clear, you did. Sweet little healer raised by a half-crazy uncle witch who set her up in an op the previous night instead of just tracking her down to find her." Bear could see her clearly as a kid being raised by the lunatic. "The man is a crackpot." No wonder she seemed so alone sometimes.

"That's Uncle Crackpot to you." She grinned. "He probably meant well. Where is he?" She lifted her head. "We're back at the cabin . . . on the bed that's on the floor." Her face fell. Her frown was adorable. "You have billions, Bear. Billions."

"That's how I afford attack helicopters that save our asses," he reminded her, looking around his perfect cabin. "If you wanna make a change or two, feel free." That felt like a mistake. He twisted his lip, considering. "Maybe." His fingers skimmed her upper thigh.

She breathed in. Rolling onto her side, she flattened her palm across his heart and shut her eyes. Warmth spread through his torso and slid down to his balls. Her smile brightened her entire face. "You're healing. Completely."

Her pleasure at his health took him by surprise. Much of his life, nobody had cared if he was hurt or alone. But she did. His being healthy made her happy. That one little fact slid deeper than her healing touch and landed hard. He leaned over and nibbled on her mouth. "Something else became clear last night, Ness."

A slight tremor took her. Yeah, she liked the little nickname. He kissed her, taking his time and enjoying the moment. When he lifted his head, her lips were a pretty pink, and her eyes a deep blue.

"What became clear?" she asked, her voice throaty.

He ran a thumb across her bite mark. This time, she shivered hard. Yeah. That. "I decided I'm keeping you."

Her eyes widened. "Excuse me?"

"You have impressive enemies, well funded and organized."

Maybe George was one of them or maybe not. "In addition, your family, such as he is, is a nutjob." Bear squeezed her ass.

She gasped and arched her back. "None of that has anything to do with you."

Ah, she wasn't getting him. Not at all. "You're my mate." He let the words stand alone for a moment. They should say everything, but he figured she needed more of an explanation. "Your safety is my duty. It's my right." The only place to keep her safe in the world was in his territory, with his guards. "So you're staying here." Plus, he liked having her around. A lot.

She shook her head. "Listen, Bear—"

"No. I made you a promise." The idea of her leaving him and getting harmed forced a growl up from his chest. "I'll take out whoever is trying to kill you. And I think I need to hunt George down and kill him for the darts last night."

Her gaze went to the side and up as if she was thinking. "George would not have used darts like that. He doesn't have that kind of drive, and while he's a moron, he's not a killer." She caressed up to Bear's neck. "I like your caveman routine here, but I'm fine taking care of myself. I have work to do."

He'd never ask her to stop working. "I'll get you the best computer system in the world so you can do your accounting work from here. You'll be secure enough even for the Coven Nine to be happy." At her frown, he continued, "I'm sure you like to go heal people sometimes. There's a human hospital just thirty minutes away. They always need help."

"Oh, I can't heal humans." She brushed the thought away. "And I need more than a computer."

He rolled her over and flattened himself on top of her. "What do you mean you can't heal humans?"

"Huh? Oh." She threaded his hair with her hands. "Humans aren't strong enough."

"What about Angie? The human who overdosed on Apollo. You saved her," Bear said, his body feeling alive.

"That's because of PK and Apollo," Nessa said. "I can help a human who's fighting Apollo, but that's the only time. The fire properties of the mineral make it possible. But if I try to repair a human bone, it ends up a pile of dust." She lightly tugged his hair.

He felt it to his balls, and he bit back a moan. He liked this morning flirty side of her. "Bones are bones."

She snuggled her nose beneath his jaw, kissing down his neck. "Immortal bones are different from human bones. That's like saying a cat's brain is just like a human's brain. They're not."

That was a good point. He slid the shirt up and over her head, baring her breasts. Her pink nipples were already hard and ready for a kiss. So he gave them one each. "Have you tried to heal a human?" he asked, before taking a nipple into his mouth.

She gasped and arched up into him. "Yes. I've taken human bones and animal bones and tried to mellow my abilities. Everything turns to dust. It's sad." She held his head with her hands, right above her breasts, and widened her legs, allowing him to settle more comfortably against her core. "You're not wearing any clothes."

He reached down and ripped off her panties. "Neither are you."

She laughed and pushed her groin against his. "What in the world shall we do about that?"

He could feel her wetness against his cock. "Between the two of us, we're pretty smart." He slowly pushed himself inside her wet heat, pausing a couple of times so as not to hurt her. Finally, he was balls-deep right where he wanted to be most in the world.

She kissed him, her hands on his neck as her body vibrated around him with so much warmth his head pounded. She released him and nipped his bottom lip. "I never said thank you for last night."

"You are right now." He licked the mating mark on her shoulder.

She shivered. "I mean it. Thank you for the op, for saving my uncle, and for saving me from the darts. And for plan B, which you, by the way, hadn't told me about."

"All ops should have a backup retreat plan," he said, grasping her hip and withdrawing before plunging back in.

Her chest pushed against his. "True that."

Cute. Definitely cute.

She ran her hands down his biceps and hummed. "Your muscles are coming back, and fast. Feel your strength."

He'd rather feel exactly what he was feeling right now. The stronger he became, the more he needed to be careful.

"Stop worrying." It was as if she could read his mind. Her nails curled into the top of his ass. "Don't hold back. Please, with me, just don't ever hold back."

The words released the tether he was trying to hold on to. He pulled out of her. "It's a promise." Giving free rein to the animal inside him, he licked her breasts, scraping his whiskers down her stomach. Her abdomen clenched. He nipped and licked, moving right down to where he'd wanted to be from the first second he'd seen her.

She grabbed his shoulders. "Wait, I—"

"No." He manacled her hands and pushed them up. "Hands above your head. Now."

She lifted her head and stared down at him, her fingers curling over her palms but not moving.

He blew on her exposed sex, his gaze remaining on hers. "Now."

She slowly lifted her arms above her head, and her breasts rose with the motion. With her hands up and her legs spread, she was the perfect image of submission. Oh, she hadn't come close to submitting to him yet. But she would.

He grinned and slowly licked her clit with one swipe.

She started, and her hands slammed down on his shoulders. He stopped and fought another smile. The scent of her beckoned him, causing a hunger that had to be satisfied. But not yet. "Hands. Up. Now." To enforce his order, he nipped her clit.

She gasped and shot her hands right back up.

He chuckled around the sweet little button, and tremors shook her legs. God, he wanted this. Wanted her. He licked her, nipping once in a while to throw her off balance, and even bit her thigh. His fingers worked her, and he found her G-spot, rubbing it. Within minutes, she was writhing against him, her hands obediently up, little gasps of need escaping her.

He could do this all fucking day.

But her cries, soft as they were, turned to pleading. So he increased the pressure of his tongue on her clit and twisted his finger inside her. Her thighs clamped onto his shoulders and she arched, springing into an orgasm with a tightening of her entire body. She rode out the waves, and he felt them against his mouth.

The second she paused, he surged up and pushed into her. Drove deep—as deep as he could go. He pushed back onto his knees and grabbed her hips, pulling her back to meet each thrust. Hard and fast, he took her, his fingers tight on her skin.

Tremors echoed inside her, around him, and she frantically reached out with her hands for something to hold, finally grabbing the pillow above her head.

Her breasts bounced, and her abs clenched so hard he could see them. God, she was perfect. So damn perfect. And he might've lost her the night before. When the darts had shot out, he'd had a vision of the world without her. A lonely, dark world.

He was a simple guy. She was good, and she made the world better by being in it. She made his world a lot better. So that meant she belonged there. And he'd never met anybody in more need of protection than her. Not only from enemies but apparently from her own family. He could provide that. He wanted to.

He tightened his hold and yanked her up into him.

Her legs spread on either side of his hips, and he hammered harder, taking everything he wanted. Giving much more than he'd intended.

She threw back her hair with a sharp cry, and waves pummeled through her, smashing around him. Fire shot down his spine to his balls, and he came hard, pounding into her as far as he could go. She went limp first with a soft sigh. He finished, the blood coursing in his veins, his heart beating way too hard.

For her.

He released her and withdrew, grasping the covers before flopping next to her on his back.

She rolled over so her chest was on top of his and lifted up to kiss him on the chin. "Good morning to you, too."

He grinned and stretched lazily. "How about we do that again in about five minutes?"

"All of that?" she said, a grin tipping her lips.

"Yeah," he said softly, running a hand down her hair. "We need to stick close to home today anyway. Well, for the immediate future."

He really didn't want to ruin the soft glow they had going on, but she deserved to know what he'd done.

She blinked and drew soft circles across his chest. "Why is that?"

"Don't be mad." He traced her spine with two fingers down to her very fine ass.

"Mad?" She stopped playing and looked him in the eye. "Why would I be mad?"

"I took advantage of the situation last night," he said, running his knuckles along her cheekbone. He could play with her all day, memorizing every inch of her. "As any soldier would."

"Like you got me almost naked?" she teased, resting her chin on his chest.

He really liked her in the morning. "Not exactly." Okay. Grow a pair. It was a good plan, and she'd understand that fact. "The Guard soldiers saw the dart soldiers come in, and they saw you go down."

She stiffened. "Oh?"

"Yeah. So when I went back for your uncle, I may have told them you'd taken eight darts." He waited for her to figure out it was an awesome plan.

She was silent for a moment. "You. Did. What?"

He winced. Okay. She hadn't figured it out quite yet. "I told them you were dead and I was bringing you here to bury on my land. Then I sent them home to Ireland."

Her head snapped up, hitting his chin. Pain ripped through his entire skull. She jumped up, buckass naked. "Oh my God. Tell me you didn't do that. Tell me you did not send the Guard soldiers back to headquarters in Dublin in the belief that I was dead. And you kept the body. My body." She scrambled over to the other side of the cabin to rifle through her suitcase.

He stood and stretched. "Yes. Think about it." He was going to keep her safe whether she liked it or not. "Somebody wants you dead, somebody with access to Apollo-filled darts. Somebody with phenomenal intel, good enough to find you at a warehouse in the middle of nowhere last night."

She yanked on a thick white sweater and some dark designer-type jeans. "You don't understand. You have no clue what you've just done."

"If the world thinks you're dead, then you're safe here," he explained patiently—very patiently. "It's a good plan."

"Oh God." She quickly pinned her hair up at her nape. "I have to stop this. It's probably too late."

Just then, warning sirens blared to life around the territory. He lifted his head to discern the direction, but they came from every which way. What was going on? Either his security system had just completely malfunctioned, or he was being attacked from all four directions.

She stilled, her head lifting, her eyes full of panic. "It's too late. They're here."

Chapter 21

Nessa grabbed her phone and ran out into the sweetly falling snow, her central nervous system screaming in panic. She'd thrown on her sturdiest boots, so she ran toward Grizzly headquarters, crunching icy snow on the trail. This was a disaster. Several attack helicopters and troop transports were already descending rapidly.

She reached the garages and skidded around the front, with Bear on her heels.

A ground force had already breached the area, soldiers in black with green emblems on their arms pouring out of the forest from every direction. Two tanks, actual tanks, roared down the private drive toward them.

Bear grabbed her arm and stopped her cold.

She shrugged him off. "Step away before they kill you," she snapped, shoving her useless phone into her pocket. It was way too late for a cease and desist order.

The doors to Grizzly headquarters and garages burst open, and men and women rushed out, several holding guns. Two shifted right into bears, and the percussion shock threw Nessa back into Bear.

He caught her and she shoved herself away from him. "Let me go."

Lucas ran out in full tactical gear and tossed a gun toward Bear, who instantly shoved Nessa behind him. Hard. "Get your ass inside. Now," Bear commanded.

Several Grizzly members engaged with her soldiers, fighting hard, blood instantly spraying. A couple of the witch soldiers were already using fire, throwing and burning quickly.

The world slowed to barely moving. She knew it was the adrenaline, but she seemed to see everything at once. The troop helicopters touched down, and the tanks roared to a stop. The attack helicopters remained hovering, their weapons pointed at strategic targets.

Her uncle strode out of the rec room area, munching on a bagel. Somebody had given him a Grizzly Motorcycle Club sweatshirt, and it hung low over his dress pants. He took in the scene, smiled, and leaned back against the building to watch. Garrett and Logan took up posts on either side of him, watching the melee carefully.

Lucas took up position next to Bear. "I called for backup. Shifter nation's on the way, but it'll be an hour."

"Missiles and explosives armed?" Bear growled, his stance set.

"Yes. Armed and waiting for the go order," Lucas affirmed, handing over a phone. "I'll give our people the signal if you want to blow the land."

Bear looked at his people fighting and the attacking soldiers coming from the helicopters. "They're Guard soldiers." He looked over his shoulder at Nessa. "I told you to get inside the office and stay there. I'm going to blow this entire area." He lifted the phone to his ear, his gaze furious.

Panic gripped Nessa. She lunged for him, grabbed the phone, and threw it as far as she could. It landed on a fighting Grizzly soldier's head and bounced off, the screen visibly shattering before it sank in the snow.

"What the hell?" Bear bellowed.

She shoved past him and hurried to the center of the area, holding her arms up. "Cease and desist. Now." She yelled the order as loud as she could. The sound of the helicopter might have drowned out her voice, but everyone around her froze. Even the fighting Grizzlies.

A Guard soldier ran her way, ripping off his dark green mask. "Nessa? Nessa?" His voice rose as he reached her.

"Jasper." She gave a muffled *oof* as he picked her up and swung her around. "Jas."

"Oh." He set her down and stepped back, emotion in his eyes. "We received word that you were dead."

She nodded, just as Bear reached her side, raw displeasure on his face. He not so subtly edged between them.

"Jasper, I don't have a comm unit. Call off the attack order," she said.

Jasper's dark gaze took in Bear, who looked like he was about to launch his own attack.

"Now," Nessa snapped.

Jasper shook himself out of it and quickly relayed the order after tapping his ear. The drivers of the tanks cut their engines and exited their vehicles, as did the pilots of the helicopters on the ground. The Guard soldiers on the ground ceased fighting and turned. Only the attack helicopters in the air remained in place, providing cover just in case.

Jasper gave another order.

All the Guard soldiers, what looked like about sixty of them, ran toward them and lined up in formation, their gazes on her. They kept their fighting masks on, and in full tactical gear, looked incredibly dangerous. They stood at attention as one.

Even though this was a debacle of enormous proportions, she couldn't help the pride that filled her chest.

The Grizzly soldiers hovered to one side, guns at the ready. The two who'd shifted into bears patrolled behind the Guard formation.

Bear turned on Jasper. "You're the idiot in charge of this shit show?"

Jasper turned and took his place next to the troops, facing Nessa. "No." In one smooth motion, they all saluted her, fists to heart.

Her shoulders straightened. Honor and humility washed through her, and she saluted them back.

Bear stiffened to rock next to her. Furious tension rolled off him, its heat actually melting the snow that had been falling near her.

Her knees wobbled. She cleared her throat, needing to keep it together.

"These are your soldiers," Bear said, sounding like he'd been swallowing jagged chunks of gravel all night.

"Aye," she said softly. "All of them."

Jasper stepped closer, taking up a protective stance. "Commissioner Lansa? I recommend we immediately vacate the area. We have a safe zone set up an hour away."

"Commissioner?" Bear growled in a much lower tone than normal. The air shimmered around him.

She gasped and tried to move away, but he manacled her arm. Her soldiers instantly tensed. She held up a hand. "Retain formation," she called out.

"I'm not gonna shift," Bear gritted out.

"Bear?" she whispered. "You have to let go of my arm. They're ready to attack."

He turned and looked at the soldiers all watching him carefully, ready to shoot him in the head. "No."

All right. There had to be a way to diffuse the situation. "Please," she whispered.

He slowly released her arm. "You're in charge of the entire Irish Guard. The witch police force. You're *the* commissioner."

"Aye," she said softly, facing her soldiers.

"Ma'am?" Jasper asked, his gaze on Bear and not on her. "We vacate?"

She kept her face stoic. The wrong move from Bear and things would get bloody before she could stop it.

"You're not fuckin' going anywhere," Bear hissed.

She swallowed and stepped forward to address her people. "You are the finest police force in the world, and this action only proves that fact. To mobilize in such a way and conduct an attack on foreign soil before meeting any interference is something only we could do. Well done. Very well done." Man, she was going to have to soothe some international feathers, and soon. She turned to Jasper. "You and six soldiers remain here at post to set up a command center for an Apollo task force. Vacate the remaining troops for home. Full movements go dark." The fewer people who found out about this, the better.

Jasper paused for a brief moment.

"Now," she said.

He turned and gave the order. Trained perfectly, the troops filed back into tanks, helicopters, or silently into the forests, to return the way they'd come. The helicopters lifted, did a sweep, and headed out toward the sea.

Silence descended.

"Jasper? Set up a command post," Nessa said, already clicking through the next few hours. "I'll need to reach out to world leaders to avoid a war." If she could. Any witch forces in the USA were already going dark and creating battle plans, she had no doubt.

Lucas stood at attention next to Bear. "You're not using our war room."

"Donna' need it," Nessa said easily, as her men started erecting a field tent on the other side of the rec room. Computers would be arriving within the hour, she suspected.

"Plans?" Bear asked shortly, not looking at her, his body visibly vibrating.

Her lungs refused to work properly. As his mate, she was already in tune with his moods, with his emotions, and right now he was on a dangerous precipice of raw fury. "I have to reach out diplomatically. Fast."

His head lifted, and he focused on Lucas. "They use the war room. Ours."

"No—" Nessa started when Bear turned to her, his eyes deep pools of anger. If her soldiers weren't near, she would've taken a step back.

"Our war room is surrounded by multiple layers of concrete block, among other materials," he gritted out between tightly clenched teeth. "A series of bombs wouldn't even shake the room. You. Will. Work. From. There."

Jasper looked back and forth between them, curiosity in his gaze. But no challenge. "Commissioner?"

At her title, Bear growled again.

She drew air in and slowly breathed out. With a slight struggle, she plastered on her most diplomatic expression and softened her voice to pure politeness. "Very well. Thank you for the use of your facilities." She turned to Jasper. "Let's start with the king. No—with the Coven Nine and then the King of the Realm."

"Give me five minutes," Jasper said, his eyebrows lifting.

"Lucas?" Bear asked.

Lucas cut Jasper a hard look. "This way. Break anything and I break you." They strode together toward the rec room and the hidden areas behind it.

Nessa nodded for her men to follow them.

Bear looked at his forces. "The fight is over for now. Get back to whatever you were doing, and we'll have a meeting later today to discuss updates . . . and options."

Nessa shivered. The shifters all went back inside. "Bear?"

"Hold on." He focused on the boys. "Garrett and Logan? Escort Uncle Boondock through the war room and into my private offices underground—Lucas will show you the way. Keep him there."

The boys nodded, all serious.

Boondock gave a little wave. "Let's grab a couple of coffees on the way," he said congenially, pausing at the door. "Nessa?"

"I'm fine, Uncle," she said. The last thing she needed was her uncle fighting with the boys. She'd hate to see either one of them get hurt. Oh, they were fine soldiers, but her uncle had been fighting for more than two thousand years. He had skills. "We'll chat later." The man had a lot of explaining to do.

He grinned at the boys. "Either one of you play chess?" They disappeared inside.

"Options?" Nessa asked, turning on Bear.

He towered over her, his face losing all expression. She'd seen the predator in him, and she'd seen the man. This was the first time he'd shown the cold soldier very few people knew he could be. "Your forces breached my territory and committed an act of war. Do you realize what this means?"

"Of course." She was the head of one of the most powerful police forces in the immortal world. In any world. "But you started it."

His chin lowered. "Excuse me?"

"You told them I was dead. I'm their leader." She tried to use reason when all she wanted to do was run for the forest. His anger, although completely hidden, still choked her. Even with her soldiers around her minutes ago, she'd felt a vulnerability that had shocked her, all because of the male now standing in her space. "They did what your people would've done in the same situation."

"The grizzly nation is ten thousand strong," he said quietly, snow falling on his hair to melt instantly. "The wolf nation another ten, and the feline nation twenty."

She swallowed, her nose turning cold. Perhaps hiding her true calling from Bear had been a bad idea. She hadn't realized how bad until right this second. "Aye."

"Add in the dragons, and you've just declared war on a nation large enough to blow Ireland off the world map. You get that, right?" He cocked his head to the side and looked at her as if trying to drill inside her head with his question. "I say the word and we're at war. One word."

"You don't want that any more than I do," she whispered. "We just found peace."

"You could've kept it, too," he said quietly, retreating from her in a way she couldn't explain, even though he remained standing in place. "Instead, you lied and kept secrets. For no reason."

She had plenty of reasons—some even she couldn't avoid. "I understand your anger, but I have to fix this mess."

"Think so?" he asked silkily.

Her stomach dropped. "Aye. Come on, Bear. You just gave orders for me to use your command center—your very safe and protected command center—to do my job. You don't want anybody to harm me." If that's where they needed to start, then she'd do it.

"You're right. I don't want anybody else to harm you," he said, standing so tall and dangerous in the light snow.

She blinked. Twice. "Anybody else?"

"Aye," he said, mimicking her brogue. "I want to kill you myself. Mate."

Chapter 22

Bear didn't blink as he made the most ridiculous threat of his life.

Nessa gasped and then smiled. Oh, she tried to hide the smile, but she failed miserably. "You're not going to kill me."

"Of course not." He grabbed her arm and started walking toward the main building, though he was incredibly tempted to wrap his hands around her slim neck. "Right now, we have to focus."

She stumbled, and he righted her. "Focus?"

"Yes." He yanked open the door, adrenaline flooding his system. "You're right. Forces around the world just went into Def-con Delta, and we have to diffuse the situation." He thought of the last war and the friends he'd lost. His stomach ached. Determination quickened his stride. "The only way to do that is with a united front. For now."

She looked at him, surprise and then admiration in her eyes. "Right."

The surprise slapped his ego a little bit. "I didn't become alpha of the grizzly nation because of my roar," he muttered. He understood strategy better than most. He just didn't like it. The direct approach was best.

"Wh-what about us?" she asked, her voice wavering.

He steeled himself against her tone. "There is no us." Betrayal had gripped his chest and ripped out anything inside, leaving him completely empty. Even now that he was thinking straight and planning, he felt like he'd been kicked in the balls. Multiple times. "Our people are what matter. We don't."

"Bear—"

They reached the storage room and the keypad, where he paused, turning to her. "We're done, Nessa." He meant every word, even though they sliced through him like a sharpened blade. The woman hadn't just lied. She'd kept herself distant from him and hadn't even given them a chance. More important, she'd put his people in danger. *All* people in danger if another war had just started. It could've been avoided if she'd just told the truth. Witches kept secrets, and witches lied. It's who they were. "Let's stick to business."

Her eyes widened, and hurt swirled for a moment.

The look slammed him in the gut, and he steeled his body, wanting to comfort her. Fuck, it was way too late for that. He needed to get this business done, and now.

"We're mated, Bear," she reminded him, spunk filling her eyes.

"I know." Hell, did he know. "We can look at options after we deal with this crisis." What they might be, he had no clue. There was a virus that might negate mating bonds, but it could be dangerous and not worth the risk. Right now, he had enough to worry about. His code opened the door.

Lucas stood at one end of the room, Jasper at the other. They seemed to be guarding their respective areas, tension pouring from both.

Vivienne Northcutt, the head of the Council of the Coven Nine, was already up on the screen. A stone wall made up her background, giving no clue as to her location. Of course, she was in Dublin. The centuries-old witch wore a smart black business suit, her dark hair pulled back in a bun. Her makeup was muted, her skin clear, and her eyes extremely intelligent. "Commissioner Lansa. I am very glad to hear that the news of your death was greatly exaggerated." The leader smiled politely.

Nessa moved into the war room and drew out a seat, somehow taking over the room. "Now we're quoting Mark Twain?" she asked smoothly.

Vivienne's smile widened. "He was a friend. As you know."

Bear's teeth started to ache. He hated diplomatic games. Slamming the door with a bit more force than was necessary, he shoved Nessa's chair to the side and pulled another up to sit next to her at the head of the table.

Northcutt turned her attention to him. "Mr. McDunphy. How lovely to see you again."

Two could play at this game. Bear smiled, letting his canines show. "Hey, Viv. Kidnap anybody lately?" If the woman thought he'd forgive her for having her soldiers fly him across the world without his permission months ago, she hadn't figured him out at all.

"Alas, no," she said smoothly.

Damn witches didn't give a shit about other species. Not really. Most of them, anyway. "How's my sister doing?" he asked.

Vivienne's expression didn't alter. "Simone is at demon headquarters in Idaho, as you know. As *my daughter*, she's hard at work for the witch nation."

He hid a wince. The next call had better be to Simone, or she'd come charging in to save him from invasion.

"You might want to ring her up," Viv said, as if reading his mind. "For some reason, she's not only fond but rather protective of you."

"I bet that bites your ass," he drawled.

Nessa cut him a look and cleared her throat. "Councilwoman Northcutt, I wanted to let you know that the Guard conducted a foreign training session here outside of Seattle this morning. It has come to our attention that we might have been remiss in informing you of our plans."

"Why yes," Viv said smoothly. "I understand the session went well?"

"Aye," Nessa said evenly. "The troops have been sent back home after a job well done. I appreciate your understanding."

Viv spread her hands out. "Of course. What else would I do? Tell the world that the Guard up and invaded foreign land based on only a rumor? That the troops waged war, completely out of control and with no structured chain of command in place?"

Bear's muscles tightened.

"No," Nessa said agreeably.

Viv smiled. "However, I believe this incident does demonstrate a problem, aye? Our Enforcers and personal guards might have to step up their training, and we need a decent facility. The one just created on the twenty acres outside of Galway would suit our purposes so well. You're not using that for the Guard training, are you?"

"We are," Nessa said.

"Well then. It would still be good form for you to sign that land over, don't you think?" Viv sat back, clasping her hands together.

Bear remained perfectly still. This was a shakedown? Seriously? The witches even blackmailed each other?

Nessa tapped her nails on the table. "I would like to transfer that land to you and your Enforcers," she said mildly.

Viv's eyes gleamed.

"However," Nessa continued, "after the mess the Council has been in the last year, with members issuing kill orders on other members and with the Enforcers being fired and rehired, the Guard has had to take the reins, so to speak. What would the world think if it discovered that I, the Guard Commissioner, had to go undercover on the Council, just to protect our nation?" She mock shuddered. "You surely understand how badly we need our training facilities in case the Coven Nine screws up again to that degree."

Bear bit back a smile. The entire conversation pissed him off, but Nessa was good. Damn good. Not many people alive could handle Vivienne Northcutt face to face.

Vivienne smoothed back her hair. "You make an excellent point. Perhaps we should move on from here and just write off recent events. To protect the nation."

"Agreed. Have a nice day." Nessa tilted her head, and Lucas cut off the feed.

Lucas winced and tapped an earbud. "The demon nation is yelling at me."

"On-screen," Bear ordered. Might as well get this over with. Nick Veis, the second-in-command of the demon nation, took shape first. He'd tied his blond hair back at the nape, and it looked like he'd already changed into combat gear. Next to him, Simone appeared, her hair a wild mass around her shoulders, her eyes glittering. "Hi, Sis," Bear said.

Simone stilled and looked him over. "You okay?"

"Fine. Just watching my mate and your mother try to blackmail each other," he said.

Nessa glared at him. Then she turned toward Simone. "Councilwoman Brightston and Lieutenant Veis. Nice to see you."

Nick lifted a dark eyebrow but didn't speak, letting his mate take the lead.

Simone stepped closer to the camera. Her red silk shirt covered a barely there baby bump. "Did you say *mate*?"

"Yep," Bear said. "Bitten and branded. Of course, that all happened before the Guard decided to drop helicopters and soldiers on my land."

Purple fire flitted up Simone's arms and then was snuffed out. Nick sighed and patted out a flame on his arm, leaving a round burn in the dark cotton.

Bear's chin dropped. "Was that purple? Purple fire? Really?"

Simone sighed. "Yes. Pregnancy hormones mess with the hue." Then she straightened. "Nessa. Seriously? My mother just texted me with the news. You're the Commissioner for the Guard?" Her eyes widened, and she shook her head.

"Aye," Nessa said quietly.

Bear coughed. What in the world? "You didn't know?" he asked his sister.

"Of course not," she shot back, her contemplative gaze on Nessa.

"Wait a minute." He held up a hand. "How could you not know? You've been a member of the Council of the Coven Nine for a century."

Simone looked at him like he'd lost his mind. "Nobody knows who the Guard Commissioner is. Well, except for the head of the Coven Nine, so Mother knows. Interesting."

"Why the hell not?" His voice rose. Their police leader was a secret? Seriously?

Simone sighed. "A couple of reasons. One, secrecy protects the commissioner from assassination. Two, secrecy allows the commissioner the freedom to move among agencies to investigate. Such as Nessa taking a turn on the Council when things got so bad."

"So she couldn't even tell her mate," Bear muttered.

Simone focused on him. "Not without committing treason and breaking a blood oath." She smiled. "So you're the one who has brought the Guard into the current century lately. Computerizing everything and diverting funds to scientific pursuits. It's been you."

Nessa smiled. "Aye."

So the woman was impressive. Bear sighed.

Simone looked back at him. "Let's talk about this mating."

"Let's not," Bear retorted. Nessa should have told him everything. There were more important issues than countries and oaths. Mating superseded all that. He settled back in his seat. "Veis? Why you all geared up to fight, and where is Kyllwood?" Zane Kyllwood led the demon nation.

Nick slid a comforting hand down his mate's arm. "Zane is at Realm headquarters planning an attack on the Guard in order to defend the shifter nation. You might want to call the king next."

"I am coming to Seattle," Simone said, taking Nick's hand.

"No." Bear softened his tone so he didn't hurt her feelings. "We're right in the middle of an Apollo epidemic, and witches were attacked yesterday outside of Seattle." He still hadn't read the intel on that. "Somebody is trying to kill your good ole commissioner, also known as my mate, and this is not a place a pregnant witch needs to be. Even a badass witch like you, Simone." He turned his focus to Nick. "Keep your mate there."

Simone's instant frown of irritation matched Nessa's.

Nessa sat straight. "Lieutenant Veis, on behalf of the Guard—"

Nick raised a hand. "Is the grizzly nation declaring war on the witch nation or asking for assistance from the demon nation?"

"No," Bear said shortly. He'd handle the Guard himself.

"Good enough. Check in with the Realm, and I'll let you know if we'll be visiting." Tugging Simone into his side, Nick leaned forward and disengaged the call. The screen went black.

"Well," Nessa huffed.

"Sorry he didn't try to blackmail you with something the demon nation wants from the witch nation?" Bear asked dryly.

She lifted a shoulder. "A little bit."

Amusement—very unwanted—wandered through him. Damn witches. Though she could certainly handle her own, now couldn't she? He didn't want to be impressed by that side of her—not at all. But hell. She'd fooled him. Easily.

Lucas clicked a remote control, and the King of the Realm came up on-screen. In battle gear, Dage Kayrs looked every bit the warrior he was known to be. He'd also tied back his thick hair. An odd, narrow swatch of gray cut from his temple through the black from a virus he'd survived, but the king was still as dangerous as they came. "The fight is over?" he asked, sitting back in his thick leather chair.

"Yes," Bear said.

Dage kicked at something out of camera range. "Oh, all right. Very well, then."

"Sorry to disappoint you, King," Bear said.

Dage lifted a shoulder. "I'm pleased you're all right." He nodded at Nessa. "Commissioner."

She started. "You've already heard about my position?"

Dage rolled very silver eyes. "I've known since you were sworn in decades ago. I'm. The. King."

Bear sat forward. "You knew about her and didn't say a word? You and I just spoke the other day when I agreed to allow your nephews a safe haven and a job."

"Eh." Dage steepled his fingers beneath his chin. "Wasn't my secret to share."

A more likely story was that Dage wanted to see how it all played out between Nessa and Bear. The king might be a badass, but he was also a helluva matchmaker. "I would've appreciated a heads-up," Bear snapped.

"All right. Then how about this? The woods around your land are teeming with sharpshooters and a strong ground force. All witches." Dage smiled.

Nessa flushed a light pink.

Bear turned on her. "I thought the Guard went home."

She swallowed.

Dage coughed. "She's their commissioner, and she has a kill order on her head. It's time you learned how to work with the witch nation, Bear. Especially since you mated one."

Bear started. "How did you find that out so quickly?" They hadn't gone public yet.

Dage's chin lowered. "The. King. Me. I'm the damn king." He shook his head. "My satellites have quite the view. Speaking of which . . . Commissioner."

Nessa pressed her hands to the table. "Yes, King?"

"Your people conducted not only an operation but a full-on assault on another Realm member, on foreign soil, and without informing me." His voice hardened.

Bear stiffened. "King—"

"Yes, we did," Nessa interrupted Bear, her eyes lighting up. "Our apologies. It won't happen again."

Dage furrowed his brow. "I'm afraid that's not good enough."

"I hate politics," Bear groaned. "Just hate it."

Nessa eyed him, obviously enjoying the interchange. "Then stay out of it." She turned back to the king. "What do you want, Dage?"

"Access to Satellite Alpha Delta," Dage said smoothly. "We're not interested in your other three. Just that one."

Nessa didn't miss a beat. "Alpha Delta? Never heard of it. You know all witch satellites are controlled by the Council of the Coven Nine, right? You should contact Vivienne."

Dage sighed. "I'm aware of the Nine's satellites. I also know that the Nine only knows of two of the Guard's satellites, and AD isn't one of them. Give me access, Nessa. The technology on it is better than on any other satellite, and I need to keep an eye on the Kurjans."

Nessa paused for a moment. "If such a satellite existed, I might agree to sharing surveillance from it. No way, and I mean no way, would I agree to sharing the proprietary design and function of said satellite. Take me to war, out me, do what you must do, but we will not provide that."

"Accepted," Dage said, sitting back, his lips twitching into a smile. "Wasn't that easy?"

Dage nodded at Bear. "If you wouldn't mind, get *your* damn satellite out of my orbit, McDunphy. We're not going to descend upon you, using today's events as an excuse."

Bear gave a curt nod. "All routine, King."

"Also, Nessa. I'd like to talk about a Realm position for you," Dage said.

"She's not going to Idaho," Bear said.

Nessa looked his way. "Excuse me?"

Bear just held her gaze without speaking. He had no right to dictate where she went, considering he'd said it was over. But the idea of her in the Realm's belly didn't sit well with him. He looked back to the screen.

Dage rolled his eyes. "Sorry about this."

A white lab coat came into view, and the queen plopped down on the king's lap. She smiled, her hand on her protruding belly.

Bear grinned back. "Hi, Emma." He'd met her a few times, and she was a pistol. "How are you feeling?"

"Bear," she said, her eyes sparkling. "So good to see you. I'm fine. Soon this babe will finally be here." She wrapped an arm around Dage's neck. "Nessa? It's very nice to meet you. As part of the agreement here, I need a test tube or five of your blood. Thanks."

"No," Bear said before Nessa could answer. "Ma'am."

Emma rolled her eyes. "You know I hate being called that. Come on. Nessa, you're a witch just mated to a shifter, and I'd love to track the changes in your blood as the mating completes on a chromosomal level. I'd really appreciate it."

Bear sighed. The queen was a world-class geneticist who worked around the clock. She wouldn't give up.

"Plus," Emma said, "since you can't throw fire but can heal wounded immortals, I'd love to compare your blood to others."

Nessa gasped. "How did you know that?"

"The. King," Dage bellowed.

Emma patted his arm. "Dage may have mentioned it. He also told me that one Apollo dart doesn't hurt you. Perhaps I could use your blood to find an antidote to planekite and Apollo. Just think about it, okay?"

The screen fuzzed out and went blank.

Nessa sighed and turned toward Bear. "So. I guess we should talk."

Chapter 23

Bear pushed away from the table and held out a hand to assist Nessa up. She took it and barely kept from jumping at the electrical jolt of anger that shot up her arm.

"Jasper—" Nessa started.

"Here's what's going to happen." Bear spoke over her. "Lucas? I want a full command center ready to go in one hour, dedicated to a sole mission: finding the manufacturer of the Apollo drug. Work with Jasper, but don't let any other witches into my private offices. I want Garrett and Logan involved and providing backup." He drew Nessa to the door.

She cleared her throat. "Jasper?"

"I know what to do," Jasper responded.

Bear opened the door and partially turned. "The witches can continue patrolling the boundaries, but if one of them, and I mean just one of them, sets foot onto our land, I want you to blow him or her to bits. Got it?"

"Copy that," Lucas said, flashing his teeth.

"Bear," Nessa protested. "There are witches outside the garage right now."

Bear nodded. "Jasper? You have fifteen minutes to get those witches off territory, or I set bears on them." Without waiting for an answer, he manacled Nessa's hand and strode through the storage room.

She could either accompany him or let him drag her, so she quickened her steps. His command of the situation was a turn-on, but his bossiness with her was infuriating. His huge hand swallowed hers as he led her through the rec room and into the gray day, his boot steps sure and determined. The area was already empty of both witches and shifters. The snow had been replaced by freezing rain, and it pinged off concrete around them.

Once outside, she yanked her hand back, her body going cold. "I still need to call the shifter nations."

"Lucas will take care of that." Bear grasped her again, his head down, heading for the trail to the cabin. "You wanted to talk, we're going to talk."

Her pulse sped up. That was enough. She bunched her back leg and swung, hitting him in the back of the knee with a roundhouse. His leg buckled, but he didn't release her hand. His knee hit the pavement and he was right back up, stepping into her and throwing her over his shoulder. Her hair escaped its clip and cascaded down his back and past his butt.

He had not. He had not just done that.

Thank goodness her soldiers were out of sight. She levered herself back and punched him as hard as she could in the left kidney. He growled and turned on his boot, heading into his office. The door slammed shut behind him, and he plunked her on the desk, stepping between her legs and forcing her to catch herself with her elbows.

Fury engulfed her. She balanced on one elbow and hit him with a jab and an uppercut, nailing him in the mouth and neck. She punched again, and he grabbed her hand midstrike. Pain ripped up her arm.

"You done?" He released her.

"No." The stupid male had thrown her over his shoulder. Again. She secured her legs at the back of his waist and lunged up, wrapping her arms around his neck and yanking down his head, putting him in a capture hold.

He struggled, but she held on tight.

Then he stopped, his head turned, and she trapped him against her chest.

"Bear, we need to talk. I don't want to hurt you, but I bloody will." She emphasized her words by tightening her hold.

He breathed out against her, and his hands came up to clamp around her biceps.

She settled in. There was no way for him to break the hold. "You can't win this."

Slowly, methodically, he started to pull.

The tendons in her arms stretched. Then her muscles protested. She tightened up, trying to resist him, but his strength was just too great. Without pausing once, he broke her hold and stood.

She sat up, her legs still around his waist. "You're stronger. That's just biology . . . and me." She'd healed him, damn it.

Something fired in his eyes. Something hot. He grabbed her thighs and tightened his hold until she released him, letting her legs drop. Then he grabbed her hair and yanked her from the desk, nudging her to the middle of the room. "You want to fight? Let's fight."

Anticipation lit her so quickly, her limbs tingled. "I've been training since birth. You can't beat me without brute strength." Her chin lifted.

"Think not?" he asked, his voice a hoarse rumble, his jaw clenched and hard. He reached behind himself and locked the door. With the shades drawn, nobody could see in. "Let's find out, shall we?"

Warning ticked down her spine. Why, she wasn't sure. There was plenty of room to fight between the desk and the battered chairs, but the floor was bare concrete. It'd hurt to grapple on it, but she'd been in worse conditions. She was well trained, but Bear had surprised her repeatedly with his strategic command and intelligence. "You've trained?" she asked, circling to the side.

"Yes." He didn't move.

She shook out her hands. "With whom?"

He watched her legs, his eyes hard. "Everyone I could find. First dragons, then everybody I met in the States when I came over."

She kicked up, a testing movement, and he casually blocked her with an almost gentle swipe. "Why?"

"Why?" His eyebrows lifted. "I was a teenager alone in a foreign land—a bear shifter to boot." He stretched his neck as if preparing for a good match. "Do you think I ended up leading the grizzly nation because I always win the July chili cook-off?"

They had that in common. Lonely childhoods where they'd had to learn to fight in order to survive the world. Why did she get the feeling there were parts of him she didn't see? "You're not an open book, either." On the last syllable, she faked with a left and shot forward, tackling him into the door. He flipped her sideways, just using his left arm, and pinned her to the floor without causing a bruise.

She panted, twisting. "Why just the left arm?"

"Want to make it fair." He lifted up, taking her sweater with him.

She rolled and stood. "What are you doing?"

"Wanna make it interesting." He threw the sweater over the fan. "I'm not an open book, but I've never lied. You've never asked."

Had she? Not really. She'd never asked if he was rich, trained, or had a brain. "You hide who you are," she hissed.

"No." He dodged forward, hooked a leg behind hers, and dropped her on her ass. Two seconds later, her bra joined her sweater. His gaze caught on her nipples, and the room heated. The entire room.

She tried to focus, but her nipples hardened, and a pulse pounded between her legs. How could this be turning her on? Worse yet, he was just playing with her. He hadn't come close to making a real effort. She ran through a couple of moves in her head that would take him down, and hard, trying to figure out which one to try first.

A hard knock on the door stopped her.

"Go away," Bear called, his gaze not leaving hers.

"Bear? We have a problem," Lucas answered.

Irritation rippled across Bear's face. He turned and poked his head outside. "What?"

"Attack on witches along the northern perimeter from an outside force and not us—we just caught wind of it on the cameras. Apollo darts—looks bad," Lucas said.

"No," Nessa breathed, rushing past Bear to grab her sweater.

"Get a squad, and we go in bear form," Bear ordered Lucas before turning, his face a solid mask of fury. "Ness, whoever attacked has darts. They don't hurt us, but they kill you. Stay here until I get back." He leaned and grabbed the back of her head, yanking her toward his face. His mouth crashed on hers, his lips firm and determined. Then he released her. "Don't fuck with me on this. Use that computer and do all the diplomatic shit you need. But be right here when I get back."

He slammed the door in her face.

Bear stomped out into the freezing rain to meet Lucas and a squad of shifters. "Where the hell are Lars, Brinks, and Duncan? You called them back, right?" He needed his best soldiers.

Lucas pulled his shirt over his head as everyone else did the same. "Yeah. When they go underground, they do it right. I'll find 'em."

Damn it. All right. Bear stripped and tossed his clothes next to the garage. "How many attackers?"

"About fifteen," Lucas muttered, dropping his jeans. The rain mashed his hair to his head. "All with dart guns. What is going on?"

"I don't know." Bear kicked off his boots. "Did you see any witches go down?"

"Yeah. Bad," Lucas affirmed. "I called for medevac. Our pilots just put the helicopters away, but they'll be back in about fifteen minutes."

"Good thinking." Bear surveyed the naked group. "Kill anybody with a dart gun. They came onto our land, and they die." The next words hurt. "Don't kill any of Nessa's witches. Today, anyway." He turned and leaped, shifting into bear form in the air. God, it felt good.

He was healthy and strong again. The shift had been effortless. Finally.

His paws hit the ground, and he bounded forward, his senses already enhanced: sights and sounds . . . and soon smells. Witches and humans. Another scent. What was that?

Colors flew by even in the gray day. The rain punished him, but he didn't feel it. His coat was thick, and his body heated. Within seconds, he came upon the fight—eight witches and at least fifteen unidentified attackers with dart guns, all shooting. There were two large trucks on the dirt service road, both empty.

The witches threw fire, trying to cover each other, letting their gear take the darts. Several witch soldiers already lay on the ground. Their fellow soldiers covered them. One of the fighters was hit with a dart in the face, and she jerked it out, not stopping her fire.

Bear leaped over her and right into the man shooting at her, his canines slashing into the guy's neck. It hit him then.

Wolves.

The guy twisted beneath him, and the air shimmered. Fuck. Bear jumped back and covered the female Guard member. A series of pops echoed all around. When the air had settled, he lunged back up.

Fifteen fully grown and pissed-off wolves snarled at him, teeth bared. Their dart guns lay on the ground, discarded.

Wolf shifters had dared to breach his territory. They were after

Nessa, his mate. In his animal form, he let go of any hurt feelings or pride. He wanted her. He'd bitten her, and he'd given her his heart in that moment. He didn't know any other way. And these killers had come to his land to kill her.

To kill his mate.

Bear stood up on his hind legs and roared, the sound echoing throughout the entire forest. All humanity disappeared from him, leaving only the predator.

Lucas bounded by, colliding with the first wolf, claws already slashing through flesh. The wolf yelped, and another one, this one black with brown markings, jumped on Lucas's back.

Bear rushed forward and swiped off the wolf, following up with claws across the jugular. Going for the kill, he sank his teeth into the wolf's neck, ignoring the animal's furious struggles. Claws raked down Bear's snout, but he barely felt the pain. Growling and snarling, he bit clean through the wolf's neck. The animal's body exhaled in death as its head rolled through the sleet.

Two wolves instantly jumped Bear. He swung around, fighting furiously. Fangs dug into his neck. He grabbed the nape of the wolf biting him and threw the beast over his head.

A fireball flashed from the trees and burned straight through the wolf's neck. Nice.

Bear turned to get three wolves off Lucas, biting and clawing as fast as he could. He finished off two more wolves, his mouth full of blood. He spit it out and roared.

His squad was bleeding but winning. Dead wolves littered the ground. One leaped for him, clawing down his back. He turned to fight. Five ran, wounded and growling, toward the first truck, shifting to human form as they reached it. Piling inside, they roared away down the road. He finished off the nearest wolf and glared at the speeding truck. He'd hunt them down later.

Another scent caught his attention.

Everything in him stilled.

He turned to see Nessa and Jasper run out of the trees. Nessa slid on her knees to one of the wounded, instantly putting her hands on the witch's chest.

The remaining three wolves turned their attention to her.

Bear lost it, barreling into all three. Lucas joined him, and they fought furiously, spilling blood. Bear broke the last wolf's neck and threw him toward the remaining truck. Then he turned to find his mate.

She was with another downed witch, her hands over his chest, her eyes closed. The witch sat up and gently pushed her away. "I'm okay."

Jasper stood to her right, balls of fire on his hands, ready to throw. Bear looked around at the battlefield. Blood, fur, and sleet mingled together.

Almost in slow motion, one of the truck doors opened and a man stepped out, dart gun in hand. He fired a long series of shots right at Nessa.

Jasper yelled, as did the witch on the ground, both jumping up and putting their bodies between the darts and Nessa.

Bear roared and leaped through the air, taking ten darts in the chest. He kept going, rushing the shooter and bashing him back against the truck. Rage took hold of Bear, and he snapped his teeth through the wolf shifter's neck, decapitating the bastard with one righteous bite.

The head rolled away.

Bear turned around just as his helicopter made a fast descent behind the truck. He shook out his fur and stood on his hind legs, shifting back into human form with barely a twinge of pain. "Load them up," he yelled.

His men shifted quickly and ran for the injured witches, rapidly loading them into the waiting helicopter. A couple had taken more than one dart, but Nessa had helped to heal them. Bear loaded the last witch into the helicopter and leaned around to talk to the pilot. "Take them to the Realm hospital north of Vancouver." Canada offered the best hospital nearby.

The pilot nodded.

Bear ducked and hurried from the helicopter, the scent of Irish roses filling his head and unadulterated fury filling his body.

Garrett and Logan pulled up in a four-wheeler, quickly dispensing the clothes that had been left at the garage.

Bear didn't give a fuck about his clothes. His mate had come out into pure danger, a place where darts flew, against his express orders. Worse yet, the lies she'd told him still poisoned his gut. It hurt, and he hated hurting. He found her standing near a tree, her face pale, her eyes wide.

There was a lesson to be taught. Now.

Adrenaline ripped through his body, intensified by the anger heating his blood. Stalking toward her, he slowly pulled out each of the ten darts still stuck in his flesh, one at a time.

She turned even paler.

Finally, he reached her and grabbed her arm. "Let's go."

Chapter 24

The ride back to the cabin was made in total silence. Nessa tried to concentrate on the mystery of wolves being after her. Why wolves?

Bear had ordered his soldiers to find out how the hell wolves had ended up on his property, while Nessa had sent Jasper to check on the rest of the troops and then answer the same question. He'd looked at her with concern, but she'd given a clear order, so he'd followed it.

Why would wolf shifters have Apollo darts, and why would they want her dead? They'd attacked witches on the perimeter. Were they trying to get inside to her? They'd certainly focused their darts on her the second she'd been recognized.

Nessa tried to focus on these very important questions, but the half-naked male driving the vehicle all but commanded her attention. For once, there was no give on his face or in the lines of his body: no humor, no laziness, no amusement.

Bear McDunphy was pissed. Not pissed—furious. Was there a word past fury? Rage? No. Rage connoted out-of-control behavior.

Bear was one hundred percent in control. Cold, methodical, deadly. And pissed.

God, was he pissed.

She swallowed over a huge lump in her throat. Her breath came in shallow gasps, and her lungs felt as if a belt was banded around them. Okay. She was tough and trained, the leader of a police force. Sure, she worked mainly from a desk creating strategy and not fighting on the front lines, but still.

Her hands trembled.

His anger filled the small space, heating her skin. Steam came off his wet jeans as they dried, and his bare chest was already dry. Probably from the fury inside him.

Freezing rain hit the top of the plastic cover, making it fog inside. She tried to logically work through what was scaring her. All right. He'd ordered her to stay in the office.

She didn't take orders from him.

He'd wanted her to stay away from the poison darts.

Her soldiers were fighting, so she couldn't just sit back and do nothing.

He'd had the situation pretty much under control.

She hadn't known that.

By the time they reached the cabin, she'd worked up a good dose of self-righteousness. Without a word, she jumped out of the vehicle, her boots sliding on the icy ground. Regaining her footing, she stood straight. "This is ridiculous."

He paused and then shut his door, facing her across the front of the four-wheeler. "Get inside." His voice was a low growl.

The rain slashed against her hair and pelted her arms, chilling her. But she didn't care. She lifted her face. "No."

He changed. Nothing obvious, but something shifted beneath his skin, something more than just the bear shifter inside him. His eyes flashed black. "Excuse me?"

Her knees went weak. So her spine snapped straight. In that moment, she realized she was actually afraid of him. That thought, that one simple thought, exploded her temper as nothing else could have. She flung out her arms, stomping around the vehicle. "You are not the boss of me, so just lose the attitude," she screamed through the sleet.

The black in his eyes glittered hot and bright. "Not the boss of you?" he yelled back.

"No," she screamed.

"This is my territory," he bellowed. "My men were out there. In danger. For you."

"My men were in danger, too." Her voice rose even higher. "I'm the head of the Guard."

His chin lowered. "Exactly." His low tone was even more frightening than his bellow. "You're the president. The queen. The one that everybody will jump in front of a bullet for. It's your fucking duty to stay safe and behind, to keep your people safe. To keep *my* people safe."

The fact that he had a point just spurred her anger higher. "I do what I want." Plus, she was a damn healer.

"Not on my land." He took two steps toward her. "Not wearing my bite."

Her mouth went dry, even as her body flared to life. This side of him—this dangerous, deadly, raw side of him that nobody else saw . . . she'd bet her entire fortune that he didn't let anybody else see him like this. "Your bite does not give you any rights over me," she yelled, her recklessness matching the storm around her. She couldn't help it. There was more to him, and she wanted it. Didn't understand it, but she knew how to get it.

They were on opposite pages, and that had to change and now. She needed to change that. So she challenged the alpha, knowing full well what she was doing.

He stepped into her space, his entire body vibrating. His muscles clenched and grew defined. Determination glowed like lava in his eyes. "My bite gives me every right, and it's time you learned that. I've tried so hard to be somebody else. Something else. That's fucking over."

She shoved him in the abdomen. Hard.

He didn't move an inch.

"You said we're over," she snapped, shoving freezing wet hair out of her eyes, hurt bubbling through the anger. "We're done. Over. So get the hell out of my life."

"No." He tugged her wet sweater to the side and ran his thumb across his bite mark.

Electrical jolts swept down and around her, hitting every nerve. Panic mixed with her anger. "Yes."

His gaze remained on the bite. "You're reckless, dishonest, and a pain in the ass." He looked up, his hard eyes making her breath catch in her throat. "You came here. You wanted to mate a shifter. Me. An alpha grizzly."

"So?" she challenged, her legs outright trembling.

"You did exactly what you'd planned in your nice safe office a world away. You wanted to mate a grizzly bear alpha." His hand slid up her neck to cup her head. "I tried to be nice. Gentle. Patient." Twisting his wrist, he shoved her toward the cabin. "I tried to be what you probably thought you wanted."

She stumbled and then pivoted around to face him. "Fuck you."

"Yeah." He planted a hand against her upper chest and pushed, sliding her backward over the ice as he moved. "It's time you got what you really wanted."

Her hands windmilled and she tried to plant her feet, but he was too strong. Before she knew it, the porch steps stopped her slide.

His hand remained planted across her chest. "Get. Inside. Now."

She stared at him, so many feelings bombarding her that she couldn't find just one. Rain slashed down on him, and in the gray day, his features were all rugged planes of strength. His eyes glowed. Steam rose from him. The smart thing, the safe thing to do would be to turn around and go into the cabin. That movement would give him a few seconds to control himself.

She didn't want his control.

Now she wanted all of him. Logic didn't explain it; neither did strategy. But deep down, in a place she'd never explored, she needed to know all of him. He wasn't the only one with ancient, wild, and passionate blood pounding through his veins.

So she lifted a foot to the next step.

Satisfaction gleamed in his eyes.

And she kicked him right in the shin.

He stilled. Sleet blasted around them, shattering against the wooden porch. She panted, her face wet, her sweater plastered to her, waiting. Watching him. Wanting to run but knowing she wouldn't get an inch. She lifted her foot again to kick.

And didn't make it.

He took her down, and hard.

Her ass bumped the porch. Before she could strike, he flipped her over, her knees on the bottom step and her elbows landing on the top. Pain shot up her arms.

He shredded her sweater, ripping it apart in the back. "Kicking me is something you won't want to do again. Ever."

Exhilaration streamed through her along with caution—warning she couldn't heed, even if she'd wanted to. She struggled, slapping back, aiming a kick at his gut.

His groin pushed against hers, holding her in place and immobilizing her legs. "I warned you." Cold air swept her bare back, and rain pummeled across her skin. Even so, she could *feel* his heat. He ripped off her bra, forcing her arms up to let the straps free. Challenge rose in her, hard and fast, with a dark female edge. She rose up and swung back, swiping her nails across his abs. She dug in and smelled blood. His growl rolled inside her, deep and full, setting her on fire. Her desire was turning to a hunger that hurt.

Leaning over her, he manacled her wrists before her in one hand, ignoring her struggling shoulders. He wrapped the bra around her wrists—tight.

She used her hands as a club and struck sideways.

With a growl, he loomed above her, his hips forcing hers down as he punched a board in the porch, his skin hot and bare on hers. The narrow plank disintegrated into shards of wood. Her eyes bugged out. "What are you—" He punched another plank, leaving just one in the middle. Oh, he did not—

He wrapped the bra beneath the remaining plank and tied it firmly.

She yanked back, fighting, trying to free her hands. They remained in place. A startled laugh escaped her, even with the desire and warning coursing through her. She stretched, trying to dislodge him, her palms flattening on the rough wood.

"No hitting," he whispered in her ear, his breath hot.

She shivered and bit back a whimper. "You ass—"

He yanked off her jeans and panties, leaving her nude in the pelting rain. The sleet cooled her, while the male behind her heated her right up. She fought the restraints a moment longer. Then she stopped, panting. She couldn't move.

His hand wandered down her back, and she arched into his touch. Her head dropped. This was so crazy. She'd driven him as far as she could, and she'd never in her entire life felt so alive, wanted somebody else this much. She was outside in the elements, naked, on her hands and knees.

She threw back her head.

Her icy hair flew back, a powerful mass, and smashed into something.

He growled.

Was that his face? She pressed her lips together and then gave up, laughing. She'd hit his face with ice from her hair.

He palmed her core. Shock powered through her and she went silent. Mini-explosions rocked her entire bottom half, and her legs shook on the wood. He leaned over her and bit her ear. "You're wet. For me."

She blinked and tried to swallow. "Oh yeah?" she gasped out. "That isn't a gun in your pocket." He was rock solid against her.

He chuckled, and the sound of a zipper releasing cut through her. His hand twisted, and he stroked two fingers inside her. Pleasure bombarded her, teased her, took her over. She gyrated against him, needing so much more. His thumb brushed her clit, once and then twice, and she shut her eyes as tiny pinpricks of sensation overcame her need to challenge him.

His fingers were ruthless, driving her high but not letting her go over. Every time she came close, he slowed down or moved. Finally, she was one long mess of frantic nerves. "What do you want, little witch?" he rumbled, stroking her too gently.

She whimpered in pure frustration.

His thumbnail scraped her clit.

Jolts snapped through her. "You. I want you," she gasped, trying to find words—any words. She no longer even felt the rain or the cold, just him and what he was doing to her.

His hand flattened under her pelvis and he lifted, tilting her hips up even farther. Then he paused. His shaft pushed into her, getting instantly wet, and he shoved in with one incredibly hard thrust.

Her head snapped up, and she arched her back. Pain and pleasure edged together, whipping through her. He was so big. Bigger than before—fuller. He took up every centimeter inside her and then some. His cock pulsed in her, caressing needy nerves, teasing her even more.

He tongued her ear. "Breathe, Ness."

She expelled air.

"Good girl."

The words should piss her off. But all she could do was feel. "Move. Now," she panted.

A hard slap on her ass resonated throughout her body, and she moaned. Her sex quivered around him. "This is the one place in your life you don't give orders, baby. Never again." He bit into her earlobe.

She tilted her head to give him better access. Oh, she'd challenged him to this, but she hadn't expected to feel so . . . taken. She was utterly and completely beneath his command. He'd stolen the control as if it had been his in the first place. "Bear. You've made your point."

"Have I?" His chuckle warmed her neck. "I don't think so." He reached around her and rolled her nipples between his fingers.

She moaned, her head dropping, the feeling too erotic to escape. Then he tapped his way down her abdomen to her clit.

Her eyes opened and barely focused on the closed cabin door. Passion pulsed in her veins. "Wh-what are you doing?"

"Whatever I want to do." His tongue lashed the bite mark on her neck.

She exploded around him, her entire body rolling with an orgasm that left her breathless. But it wasn't enough. He was still inside her, stretching her, taking her.

To her shock, his fingers found her clit again. "No," she moaned.

"Yes," he corrected, his fingers slick from her wetness. Something tugged in her hair, and then shocking cold touched her clit.

She arched and cried out.

"You like ice. Remember?" he asked, swirling a small piece around her clit.

The cold sensation with the hot shaft inside her pushed her into a craving that shook her entire body. "Bear."

He rocked against her just enough to make her gasp. The ice melted, and his fingers heated her again. He touched where they were joined, where she was stretched around his size. Then he ran a finger over her clit again. Sensation pounded through her. "Move," she whispered.

His ruthless finger circled her clit, enticing it into hardness, holding her on the edge. "You're done with demands. Feel free to beg."

He licked along his bite while his fingers tortured her, holding her in place easily. Way too easily.

She couldn't take it. He won. White flag. Game over. "Please, Bear."

"Ah, you're giving me what I want now." His voice was pure rock and gravel—raw and hoarse.

"Aye." She'd give him anything right now. Who cared? Her mind fuzzed. Her entire core was in need, throbbing uncontrollably.

"Good." He drove her higher, circling and lightly pinching, forcing pleasure through her. She panted, moaning, losing any ability to think. He pulled out and pounded back in. She arched her back, taking him all the way. Then he slowly slid out and back in, enhancing each electric jolt.

A rough hand tangled in her hair and jerked her head to the side. Even that sensation was somehow erotic. Her neck was elongated and exposed, and now not even her head was hers to move. She tested him, tugging, and only ended up pulling her own hair. She bit her lip.

His bare chest heated her back as he leaned closer, his thighs pushing hers into the step. "Who did you mate?"

"You," she panted, her body on a very thin edge. So close. So damn close.

"Right. Who am I?"

Words. He was saying words. She tried to follow, but he pulled out and slammed back in. Hard. "Ah, Bear. Alpha. Grizzly." Those were right. Those had to be right.

"Yes." His fingers played with her again. She whimpered. "I'm claiming you, Nessa. Right here. Right now."

She may have gurgled.

He slapped her clit. Her head jerked, and hunger flared hotter.

"What are you, Nessa?" he demanded, his hold absolute.

She opened her eyes. This was beyond what she'd wanted. But here they were. "Claimed," she whispered, her body relaxing into his hold. Ready for whatever he wanted to give to her. Submission she felt much deeper than anything she'd ever imagined.

"Yes." His hands closed over her hips in a ruthless grip, and he hammered into her with hard strokes, driving her forward.

Never in her life had she felt such raw pleasure. He pounded, increasing his speed, and everything inside her exploded. She cried out, her body stiffening and shaking, sensation after sensation careening through her. He ground against her, his body shuddering over her.

She went limp.

Quick hands untied her, and he lifted her, carrying her into the warm cabin. There was nothing left to her. She was done. Sleep claimed her before he'd even placed her in the bed.

Chapter 25

Finally, a morning without sleet or snow. The sun even tried to peek between the clouds. Bear hustled toward headquarters, his mood too dark for the day. Even the slight sun didn't cheer him.

He'd left Nessa sleeping peacefully in bed with two guards outside. She'd been exhausted.

What the hell had he been thinking, taking her like that the night before? Nothing. He hadn't been thinking. Period. Damn, he was confused. His life had been nice and orderly before she'd shown up. Okay, maybe a little boring. Could he return to that? He stormed into the rec room and stomped back to the war room, where Lucas was manning several screens. "News?"

Lucas looked up, circles beneath his eyes. Scrapes from wolf claws were red and swollen along his neck. "Not yet. I've been trying to track down that wolf pack all night."

"Did you contact Vilks?" Terrent Vilks led one of the most powerful packs.

"Yes. He doesn't know who they are and guesses it's just a rogue pack. Seemed rather pissed we were attacked. Wants to send reinforcements."

"No," Bear said. He had enough new faces around there for a lifetime.

Lucas rubbed his left eye. "I told him we appreciated the offer and would let him know but were fine for now."

Bear studied his friend. "Why don't you heal your neck?"

"I will. Had a couple of broken bones to do first and am just recharging." Lucas stared at his full cup of coffee.

Guilt heated through Bear. It was his job to protect the nation and go without sleep, not Lucas's. "Get some sleep, Luke."

"In a few. After this search." Lucas glanced around. "How long are the witches staying?"

Probably not long. After last night, Nessa would want to run for the hills. He couldn't blame her, but he wasn't sure he could let her go. His life had been calm and colorless before she'd arrived. Now it was chaos filled with color. "I don't know. Just keep an eye on them."

"Copy that. I'm also sending out another order for our men to get back here." Lucas grabbed a manila file off the table. "Here's the intel on Slam Bar downtown and the bartender. Interestingly enough, he's a wolf shifter."

Bear stilled. "Is that a fact?" He read through the file quickly. "Excellent. Come up with a strike plan, and we'll talk about it later. For now, I have some interviewing to do." Bear turned and slid a panel to the side near the door. Another keypad came up, and he entered his code, revealing concrete steps going down. "Have you checked in on Uncle?" he asked.

"Nope. The boys are in charge of the damn witch," Lucas said cheerfully. "It's great having prospects—even if they are undercover." He cleared his throat. "They're, ah, not down in the underground rooms."

Bear's head jerked. "Where are they?"

Lucas sighed. "River house."

"What the fuck?" The uncle had set up Nessa and might have hired people to kill her. He'd known the airport location, obviously. That made him a key suspect.

Lucas shrugged. "You put the boys in charge, and they think he's safe. Don't worry. They're both trained and won't let Boondock free."

Right. Bear slammed his fist on the keypad, and the door closed. "I'll be back." He loped through the storage room and headed outside for a trail on the other side of the garages.

His thoughts kept returning to Nessa. Had he bruised her? Part of the reason he'd never gotten serious with a woman was because he knew of the beast inside him. Nessa had almost purposefully unleashed that part of him.

But it was his fault. He was in control, and if he'd hurt her, he'd pay. She'd been sleeping peacefully, and she had orgasmed several times. But still. The woman deserved a softer touch.

He was an ass.

If anybody else so much as made her cry, he'd end them. Man, he had it bad. This had to stop. He needed to get himself under control, save her, and then get back to his peaceful life.

His peaceful, boring, lonely life.

He hunched his shoulders and jogged through a forest still dripping from rain and sleet. But the sun helped. He kept his pace fast as he reached several forks in the trail, easily picking his way. Fifteen minutes later, he arrived at a sprawling house of wood and stone sitting over a wild river. He climbed the steps and then knocked on the door instead of opening it with the keypad. No need to get shot.

"Who's there?" Garrett asked from the other side, sounding like his mouth was full.

"Bear. Open up."

The door opened, and Garrett stood there with a plate of scrambled eggs. "We're almost out of food," the kid said, chewing thoughtfully.

"I'm sending Dage a bill," Bear muttered, walking into a sprawling kitchen with granite countertops. The floor-to-ceiling windows looked out on a rushing river, gray and churning.

"Morning," Boondock Lansa said, an apron around his waist and a spatula in his hand. "Hungry?"

Bear turned on Garrett. "I told you to secure him in one of the rooms."

Garrett kept munching contentedly. "He can cook, and he doesn't seem to want to go anywhere."

Bear pinched the bridge of his nose to keep from swiping the kid's head off his shoulders. "Where is Logan?"

"He's downstairs in the rec room playing Xbox," Garrett said. "We were up late last night with a Bastion Warrior Seven tournament, the three of us, and he's moving slowly."

Bear blinked. Several times.

Garrett's eyebrows rose. "So, um. Tell you what. I'll grab his plate and take it down to him. Let you guys talk." Fetching another oversized plate of food, he hustled to the carpeted stairs on the other side of the living room and disappeared.

"Nice kids," Boondock said, his eyes twinkling. "You sure you're not hungry?"

"No. Sit down." Bear motioned to the living room with the huge stone fireplace and comfortable couches. The house had come with the land when he'd purchased another twenty acres on his perimeter last year, and so far he'd just let guests crash there. It had five bedrooms, more than five bathrooms, and a couple of rec rooms. "You're a prisoner, damn it."

"Eh." Boondock untied his apron and followed Bear into the living room, a steaming cup of coffee in his hand.

Bear took the coffee. "How old are you?"

"Couple thousand years," Boondock said easily, looking about thirty-five. He was fit, with intelligent blue eyes—the exact hue of Nessa's eyes. "Where's my niece?"

"Sleeping," Bear said shortly, his ears heating. "She's the commissioner of the Guard." He still couldn't believe she'd kept that little tidbit to herself.

"Aye." Boondock wiped his hands down his black dress pants. With his polo shirt, he looked like he was off for a day of golfing. His dark hair was slicked back. The guy could be a banker. "Nessa is a special girl and always has been. She's made strategic and fundamental changes to the Guard that has made our entire species safer. The woman is brilliant."

"But the Guard Commissioner," Bear said quietly.

Boon smiled. "Aye. She's gifted, but she really has wanted nothing more than to have a big family and love all around."

"So she joined the Guard?" Bear growled.

"Yes," Boon said. "The Guard is a tight organization full of loyalty. Even if most of her troops didn't know who she was, she took care of them. Nurtured them. Was part of something bigger. It's all she's ever wanted."

Bear shifted uncomfortably on the sofa. "I see."

"Isn't that why you joined the grizzly nation and then created this motorcycle club?" Intelligence shone hot and bright in Boon's eyes.

Bear shrugged. If Nessa wanted a family, a real one, he could give her that. Give her security and a lot of lost shifters to watch after and nurture. "Why the hell did you set her up to be in danger? The whole kidnapping thing? She could've been killed."

Boondock flushed a hot red. "I had George and his men in hand. Never, in a million heartbeats, would I have expected a kill force armed with Apollo darts to show up." He shook his head. "I've been over and over who could've possibly known we'd be in that warehouse in Oregon."

"Besides you?" Bear snapped.

George lifted his head, his gaze direct and sober. "Absolutely not. Nessa is my only family. I'd die for her." His gaze probed deep into Bear. "As would you, apparently."

Seemed to be telling the truth. "The attack force was after her and not you, so you weren't the target."

"I noticed." Boondock rubbed the back of his neck.

"Any ideas about who?" Since Nessa was the leader of the Guard, the reasons didn't matter. Bear just needed the *who*, to go take them out for good.

"No. George wouldn't have done that, but I don't know about his men. Maybe somebody got to them." Boondock's chin firmed. "It could've been one of your people."

"Never," Bear said. "None of my people would be involved with Apollo or want Nessa harmed. They just met her." Although *now* he could see it, since they'd gotten to know her. He bit back a grin.

"That's what I figured." Boondock cleared his throat. "What are your intentions toward my niece?"

Bear took a long drink of coffee, letting the fragrant liquid burn down his throat. "I'm not sure. She mated me for business reasons. To gain fire."

Boondock threw back his head and laughed. "That's hilarious."

Bear frowned. "Excuse me?"

Boondock wiped his eyes. "She might have convinced herself of her grand plan, but no way would my little girl mate just for business. She must've seen something in you. Sensed something. The woman is not that logical and cold."

"You think?" There was nothing cold about Nessa. She also didn't seem all that logical. Bear's heart thumped hard. Was there more to their mating for her, too?

Boondock smiled. "You've got it bad."

Yeah, he did. And he might have screwed it all up the night before. There was no doubt she wasn't safe with him. The woman deserved better. "I'm still pissed about your little escapade," Bear said, searching for heat to add to his words.

"Understood," Boondock said cheerfully.

"You made her cry. She was worried," Bear snapped.

Boondock sobered. "I didn't mean to make her cry. Shoot. Sometimes I forget how sweet she really is." He sighed. "She's going to miss the Guard so much."

Bear's heart leaped. "You think she's leaving the Guard?"

Boondock's eyebrows rose. "Of course. You outed her when you lied about her death and the entire Guard arrived here. Everyone knows who she is now. She can't go on being the commissioner."

"Oh." Bear wiped a hand across his eyes. "I didn't know. When I sent out the false information, I thought I was keeping her safe."

"You think that's your job now?" Boondock challenged.

Bear met his gaze levelly. "Damn straight."

Boondock's smile widened. "I knew I liked you."

Oddly enough, the feeling was mutual. Bear growled.

Nessa stretched awake in the bed and winced from all sorts of little aches and pains. Everywhere. Even with those erotic reminders of her wild night with Bear, her body was more than satisfied. She hadn't been this relaxed in years. Maybe decades.

A fire heated the small cabin, and she turned toward the flames, surprised to see Bear sitting on the sofa, reading something, his back to her.

Tension rolled off him.

She rested her head on the pillow and then noticed her bags packed by the door.

Hurt slid through her, and she breathed deep, trying to focus.

"I spoke to the king, and he'll give you refuge at Realm headquarters until I find whoever's trying to kill you," Bear said, without turning around.

Ouch. She bit back a harsh retort to keep from striking out in pain. How had last night not meant anything to him? At all? He hated witches that much?

His shoulders hunched. Very slightly, but they hunched. "Did I hurt you last night?"

The entire day cleared. Oh. Sweet big bad bear. They'd both lost control, and he'd turned as primitive as a male could. Now he felt afraid . . . and guilty.

She banished her own hurt in an effort to understand him. In doing so, her heart swelled even more. Man, he was a keeper. She tucked a blanket around her and slid from the bed, an easy feat considering the damn thing was on the floor. The wood chilled her bare feet as she padded around the sofa and plopped into his lap. Her internal muscles, well used and sore, protested.

He dropped the papers, his eyebrows raising. "Nessa?"

She snuggled her nose beneath his jaw. "I'm cold."

His arms instantly came around her.

She smiled against his skin. Such a tough-ass bear. "You didn't hurt me."

His chest stiffened. "I took you in the *storm* on the porch steps." Guilt and anger filled his voice.

"Aye," she yawned, still awakening. She could make light of the evening, say it was fun. But fun wasn't the right word. Not even close. "I liked last night," she whispered, opening herself up completely to banish his guilt. She played with a string on his worn T-shirt. "I, ah, I trust you or that wouldn't have happened." At the realization, she leaned back to look into his eyes, when all she wanted to do was hide her face. "I like you. The deep-down, way-beyond-dominant side that you wouldn't share with anybody else."

His eyes flared.

She'd faced down a mass of terrorists once, and this was harder: Facing one male. Giving him the truth.

"I pushed you on purpose, and I don't regret it." She stretched again and winced. "I'll probably do it again. But not right now." Maybe not for quite a while. Even after a good night's sleep, she was feeling way too vulnerable. Exposed.

He studied her, his eyes softening to honey brown. "Look at you being so honest."

Truthfully, it didn't come easy to her. "That seems to matter to you." Oh, he'd been furious she'd put herself in danger, but not nearly as angry as he'd been when he'd discovered she'd lied to him. "So no more untruths or even half-truths."

His eyes deepened. "Loyalty is everything to me."

Loyalty meant honesty to the bear. She understood that finally. "Agreed."

He sighed. "You know why I packed your bag?"

"You wanted to play with my underwear?"

His grin eased the knot in her stomach. "No. I packed it because I'll definitely take you like last night again if you stay. I like you begging."

Desire bloomed in her abdomen, even as she forced a frown. "Next time you'll be begging."

He tweaked a curl. "I seriously doubt that, but challenge accepted."

He sighed. "You couldn't have pictured a life with a shifter. Didn't you see yourself with some brilliant witch having intrigue-driven dinner parties where you fleece your guests?"

She laughed out loud. "No. Any man I've dated before got boring quickly. Either the male was threatened by my ambition or was too cold and focused."

Bear sighed. "I'm neither."

Exactly. She smiled. "I don't want to go to the Realm headquarters."

Bear lifted her chin, his gaze turning serious. "That's your choice, but I want you to take some time to make it."

She frowned. "Why?"

"Because once you do, it's absolute." He pressed a kiss to her lips, sending very nice tingles through her body. "If you decide to stay, you're staying. Nothing in me does anything halfway, and I can't be in limbo. Won't be. We mated for convenience, or for sex, or maybe for something deeper. Regardless, if you decide to stay, I'm not letting you go."

The possessiveness was both sexy and a mite alarming. He meant every word, and she knew it. But she also knew she wanted to stay. With him. To see if this was as big as it felt. "I have a job." One she needed to resign from. But then she'd find another.

"I have no problem with you working, but your home base is here. With me."

Yeah, she couldn't imagine Bear moving to Dublin. But she liked it here. Uncle Boondock would probably like it here, and it wasn't as if she couldn't bring in witches to work with her, whatever she decided to do. Maybe some sort of consulting business. "How much land do you have?"

He patted her ass.

Slight bruises jolted. "Hey."

"You are not building homes on my land."

They'd see about that.

He caressed up her back. "At the moment, we have more important issues, don't you think?"

"Yeah. We have got to find the manufacturer of Apollo." She started to work through the problems.

"That, too."

She blinked. Oh yeah. "And somebody wants to kill me." She bit her lip. "It'd be nice if it was one and the same person."

"Unlikely," Bear said, rubbing her nape.

She closed her eyes and moaned in pleasure. "I know. I'll come up with a list of possible enemies, and we'll start from there." He hardened beneath her thighs. "In a few moments."

He kissed her temple. "In a few moments . . . we'll move out of here. There's another place we could stay that's close to the office."

"Wonderful." Hopefully, the new place had a working bathroom and a bed that wasn't on the ground. She lifted her face.

His mouth met hers in the sweetest kiss imaginable. Then Bear relaxed, taking care of her, giving her more than she ever would've thought he could give. His kisses were soft, his caresses gentle, and his attention absolute as he removed her clothing and then his own.

Not once did his mouth leave hers as they moved to the bed.

When he entered her, she actually felt all of him. The beginning and the end, the hopes and the fears, the anger and the love. She closed her eyes as he thrust inside her, his mouth on hers, his body shielding her from the world. Heat uncoiled inside her, building higher, pushing her off the peak.

She sighed his name as he ground against her and came, his mouth still working hers.

Bear. He'd asked her to make a decision and take the biggest risk of her already risky life.

She loved a good risk.

Chapter 26

Bear watched as Lucas, Garrett, and Logan manned the computers in the war room. Jasper had gone to patrol with his men. Nessa and her uncle sat at the conference table, creating a list of possible enemies that might want her dead.

The list kept growing.

Irritation swept over Bear. "If your job was secret, how in the hell could you have so many enemies?" he growled.

She looked up, her pretty blue eyes clearing. "We're creating a complete list, just in case somebody found out about me. It's a starting place." Turning back to the papers, she muttered something.

"What was that?" he asked, a little too loudly.

"Nothing." She went back to work. The woman had been a little out of sorts since he'd taken her to the river house. It was like she thought he'd been hiding it from her. He hadn't been. It just wasn't where he lived. His cabin was his cabin, and he liked it.

His frown started to ache. They were both off-center after the *way* too emotional lovemaking earlier that day. It wasn't fucking. Not even close. It was the whole emotional "becoming one" bullshit he hadn't believed existed until right that second, and neither one of them knew how to handle it. So they sniped and glared at each other.

He focused on Lucas. "Do we have a full recall?"

Lucas nodded. "Almost all motorcycle club members are back in our territory. The grizzly nation, as well as other organized shifter nations, are on alert and ready to engage if we call them up."

"What about Duncan?" His other two lieutenants might be further underground than he'd thought, but Duncan was always dependable and ready to watch his back.

Lucas shook his head. "Still looking. He's somewhere on the other side of the globe—I know that much."

"Damn it. Find him." Bear eyed the code running across the computers. "Do you have a mission plan for that bar?"

"Yes. I'll print it out," Lucas said.

"Any news on the rogue wolf pack?" Bear asked. "Check specifically if they have ties to that Slam bar."

"It's coming," Garrett said, hunched over a keyboard. "The camera caught a good shot of the man who stepped out of the truck at the end of the fight—the one you killed—and I'm tracking him down. He seemed to be in charge, waiting for the final moment to go for Nessa."

"Great. Logan?"

The vampire-demon glanced over his shoulder. "I'm on it. Full security installation for the river house—top of the line. You're gonna need equipment for the escape tunnels, and I suggest at least three." He turned back to the keyboard.

Nessa shot Bear a look.

"What?" he asked.

"That's overkill, don't you think?" Her frown was somehow adorable.

"No. It's necessary, if we're going to live there." Somebody wanted her dead. Hell, half the time *he* wanted to kill her. After they caught this guy, or this organization, and Bear killed them all, the woman was still going to be in danger. "The witches have cloaking mechanisms for underground tunnels."

Nessa's head snapped up, and Boondock's gaze narrowed in contemplation.

Bear rolled his eyes. "Please. I'm the head of the grizzly nation." Now he knew how the king felt. Of course he knew about their cloaking abilities.

"Ah, we have incoming," Lucas said, straightening in his chair. "Helicopter transport with two gunships."

Bear slammed his hand against the wall and the keypad came into view. He typed in his code, and the screened wall opened to his armory.

Boondock half stood, whistling. "Nice."

Nessa craned her neck. "Is that one of the Realm's new guns?" She pointed to a far rack of assault weapons.

"Wait a sec—" Jasper typed on his keyboard, and one of their cameras zoomed in. "Demon designation on two of the copters, Realm emblem on the third."

Garrett and Logan leaped to their feet, heading for the door. Logan paused and turned, throwing Bear a smart-assed grin. "Guess who's coming to dinner?" He followed his friend out of the war room.

Bear looked longingly at his guns before shutting the door. "There are more people coming on our property, Lucas. *People.*"

Lucas sighed sympathetically. "The place is turning into a bed-and-breakfast."

It was Bear's worst nightmare, without question. The very idea kept him up at night. "Luke? Cover Nessa and Boondock here. They don't leave the room."

"Happily," Lucas said, swiveling his chair, gun at the ready.

Bear would give anything to change positions with his too-happy buddy. Oh, Luke was thrilled to stay away from newcomers.

Nessa glared at Bear.

He glared back. "Stay secure." Without waiting for her argument, he shut the door and strode through the building and out into the chilly but sunny day.

The center helicopter set down, scattering ice still remaining on the ground. The door opened, and Nick Veis jumped out, reaching back to assist Simone to the ground.

Pleasure burst through Bear so quickly he could barely keep his frown in place. It was an effort. He strode forward, approaching his sister in long strides. "Simone." What in the hell was the witch doing coming into dangerous territory while pregnant? When she launched herself at him, he easily caught her, enfolding her gently. Her baby bump nudged his abs.

The thought of the babe propelled him into motion. He picked her up, running for the safety of the rec room.

"Bear," she protested, laughing and holding on. "Careful. I throw up often."

He swung her down and rounded on her mate, who was right behind him. "What the holy fuck are you doing bringing her here?"

She punched him in the kidney, and he ignored her. "Nick? I have dart-wielding wolves making attacks. Darts that hurt witches. Like my sister," Bear snapped.

Nicolai Veis had power that could choke a whole room, even when he was smiling. He'd tied his blond hair at the nape, and even in slacks and a sweater, he looked like the dangerous killing machine he was. His eyes were black pools of warning, and when he spoke, he had the rough, almost mangled, vocal cord tone of a full-bred demon. "Hello, brother."

Ah, geez. The demon thought they were brothers. Bear shook his head. "You can't tell her no. She's knocked up, all pretty and sparkly, and you can't tell her no." No matter how close Bear and Nessa became, even if she bounced his heart around like a basketball, he would never be this whipped. If Nessa needed to be told no for her safety, he'd say it. "Nick," Bear said sadly.

Nick clapped him on the arm. "We're family, buddy. Suck it up and deal."

Did one of the most dangerous demons on the entire planet just tell him to suck it up? Bear growled.

Simone punched him again and shoved her shoulder beneath his arm, sliding her arm around his waist and snuggling close. "I have been so worried about you. Are you better?"

He paused. "Yes." Nessa had healed him. Oh, he wasn't at a hundred percent yet, but he was feeling damn good.

"Excellent," Simone said cheerfully. At almost six feet tall, she brushed his cheekbone with her forehead. "Also, you are mated. I just couldn't stay home and wait this out. Somebody must welcome her to the family."

Nick flashed sharp teeth in a smile. "Simone really wanted to come to make sure you didn't screw it up." Simone smacked her mate, and he grabbed her hand, lifting it to his lips. "Watch it, little bunny."

Bear gagged. While the nickname for his tough-as-nails sister was hilarious, Bear didn't need to see them all cooing. He might actually puke. "No flirting."

"How do you think I knocked her up?" Nick asked easily, amusement curving his lips.

The other two helicopters landed, and soldiers poured out of all three. Garrett and Logan met with a Realm soldier carrying an impressive number of guns. They began pointing out areas on the land to him.

Bear's hackles rose. "What is happening?"

"Protection detail," Nick said easily. "We trust your people, but mine will be on close detail for the day we're here. Covering Simone and the babe."

Demons and vampires. Bear couldn't breathe. "There are witches on my perimeter. Now demons and vampires close in. Oh God. It's purgatory. I'm in fucking purgatory. I have to move. There must be property in Antarctica you haven't found." His head spun.

Simone patted his chest. "Hey. You're all badass and full of muscles again. Nessa has cured you."

Bear stilled. "Did you say just one day?"

Nick grinned. "You're welcome. I needed to come check on the boys, and Simone was determined to interfere in your personal life, so I agreed to twenty-four hours only. That's it."

Bear brightened. "All right, then."

Simone pouted. "You donna' want me here?"

He instantly pressed a kiss to her forehead. "I want you here any time and all times." He meant every word. "But not with Apollo darts around. Once I take down the manufacturer, you and the babe can come stay here. Live here. It'll be great."

Simone bit her lip, her dark eyes sparkling. "What about Nick?"

"He can visit," Bear said softly. "Once a year."

She laughed.

Bear's chest eased, and his body relaxed. He'd made his sister laugh. That was good.

Logan and Garrett jogged over, each giving Nick a quick hug before reaching for Simone. She good-naturedly hugged them both, pulling on Logan's ear hard enough he winced.

"We gave Max key locations to cover, and he's having the soldiers fan out. After that, he wants access to the computer and surveillance equipment for maximum coverage," Logan said, brushing his dark hair back.

Bear sucked in air. "I'll think about it."

Simone patted him again. "Cooperate. It's just for a day."

He didn't answer, but they both knew he'd do as she asked.

"How are they doing?" Nick asked, all serious, jerking his head toward Garrett and Logan.

The boys paused and looked his way.

"I'm sending a grocery bill to the king," Bear said, messing with them.

Neither twitched, and no expression crossed their hard faces. But they did watch him closely. They also seemed to have stopped breathing.

Oh, all right. Bear let them off the hook. "Other than that, the boys have done an excellent job. They're good hunters and fighters, and their computer skills are helping enormously." Especially since his three key lieutenants hadn't been located yet. Logan was conducting his own searches, and Bear appreciated the initiative. "They can stay as long as they want."

Simone gasped quietly.

Yeah, that was the highest praise he could give. Bear rolled his eyes. "Would you like to start interfering now? Nessa is in the war room." The most secure room in the entire facility was a good place to put both of the women in his life. "Tonight you can stay in the river house in the same room as last time." He drew Simone toward the bar and looked over his shoulder at Nick. "You'll probably want to patrol or something."

Simone chuckled.

"That horse is out of the barn, brother," Nick drawled from behind him.

Bear gagged again. "I had plans to kill you before you got her with child," he said mildly, leading her toward the storage room.

"It's all in the timing, my friend." Nick chuckled.

Wasn't it, though? "I guess it could happen at a later date. You do deserve to see your child," Bear said magnanimously. But there was no need for anybody to get too comfortable around him. People got comfortable and they not only stayed but invited all their friends to drop by. Enough with the guests.

He opened the door to the war room, and Simone brushed in.

Nessa looked up from a pile of papers, and a wide smile brightened her already stunning face. "Simone."

"Hello." Simone shook hands with Boondock and Jasper before hugging Nessa. "I guess we're family."

Nessa swayed, her eyes widening. "I guess we are."

In that second, Bear could see the little lost girl searching for a family, the little girl Boondock had tried to describe for him. Apparently, so could Simone, because she hugged Nessa again, this time longer. "Don't worry about Bear. I'll teach you how to handle him," she whispered, loud enough that he could hear.

Nessa smiled and leaned back. "You shouldn't be here, Councilwoman."

Bear crossed his arms. "That's what I said."

"I still lead the Guard," Nessa said gently. "Your safety is priority one. You can't be here, as much as I'd like for you to stay."

Look at his woman getting all businesslike and duty bound, when she obviously wanted nothing more than to bond with Simone. How fucking sweet was that? "You're gonna be an aunt, Nessa," Bear said gently. If she decided to stay with him. Hell, even if she didn't, they were still mated. He still had a say in her life. A big say. In fact, she'd better decide to fucking stay.

Emotion darkened Nessa's eyes, and she glanced down at Simone's barely protruding belly. "I'm greatly looking forward to it." Nessa cleared her throat. "Now we need to get you to a safe location."

Simone smiled. "The Enforcers guarantee the safety of the Coven Nine, sister. The Guard is our police force."

"Aye," Nessa agreed, her chin firming in a way that made Bear want to take a bite. "But the Guard provides backup and military strength. This is not a safe place for you."

Man, it'd be a fun fight to watch between the two of them. Bear cleared his throat. "Ness? We have shifter, witch, demon, and vampire soldiers surrounding us at the moment. Simone is only staying for the night and will return to the safe haven of Realm headquarters tomorrow."

"Demon headquarters," Nick corrected.

Same damn thing. They were located less than a mile from each other on the same Idaho lake. "Whatever," Bear said.

Nessa turned her head toward him. "You've allowed demon and vampire forces *into* the territory?"

"Just a protection detail for Simone," Bear said hastily, uncrossing his arms. "They leave tomorrow. It's temporary." If he didn't watch his step, he'd be surrounded by witches. Even now, his forces were patrolling in tandem with the witches guarding the perimeter. The walls were starting to close in on him.

"Interesting," Simone said, her eyes absolutely twinkling.

Garrett pushed his way into the room and took up his post at the computers, already talking jargon to Lucas, who'd stayed behind. It was nice those two had bonded. "The search should be about finished," Lucas said, hunching over his keyboard.

"Where's Logan?" Nick asked.

"Flirting with a bear shifter," Garrett said absently, his fingers flying across the keyboard.

Bear looked around. There were way too many people in his war room. People who shouldn't even know he had a war room.

"Breathe, brother," Nick said quietly. "I've been there."

"It gets better?" Bear asked.

"Actually, no." Nick's lips twitched.

Wonderful. Just damn wonderful.

Lucas straightened. "Hey. I have something."

Thank God. Bear could always trust his friend to come through for him. Maybe somebody was bombing them or something, so he could get away from people and just fight for a while. "What?" Bear asked, blanching at the hope in his voice.

Lucas typed in a series of codes. "Got 'em. Vilks sent over all the intel on rogue gangs, and I traced that one wolf shifter to a group known as Riot—after combining the search with the one on the Slam Bar."

"Riot?" Bear asked. "Never heard of them."

"They're a small-time wolf gang. Theft, kidnapping, some robberies." Lucas kept typing. "Last known headquarters north of Seattle. Definitely hired thugs . . . who are known to frequent Slam Bar. And here it all comes together."

"Exactly. Now they've moved on to attempted murder," Bear growled. "You already have an attack plan ready. We go tonight." This time, he clapped Nick on the shoulder. "You up to a mission?"

Nick's eyes darkened. "God, yes."

Chapter 27

Tension grew in Nessa as the day wore on and night began to fall. She'd created a list of people who might want her dead, and the number on the list caught her off guard. How odd. She'd turned the list over to Boondock to start investigating, before sitting down with Simone and going over a list of witches who'd been attacked in the US.

She flipped open a file on the two most recent deaths. "They were young," she murmured, looking at two smiling women in their early twenties—their real early twenties. "Why were they alone in the States?"

"College," Simone said, her fingernails tapping on a legal pad. They had papers and manila files scattered across the conference table, while Lucas worked one computer bank and Boondock the other. Bear, Nick, and the boys had disappeared to plan an attack.

Nessa reached for the remainder of a sandwich somebody had brought in at some point, her gaze on the photos of the dead bodies. The PK mineral harmed witches if it touched them, but the Apollo drug? It was melted PK forced into liquid form, for darts and for distribution. The advantageous side effect for the manufacturer was that humans could take it and get high—if they didn't overdose—so it came with an automatic income stream. For the ultimate purpose of what? Killing all witches? "Who wants to hurt us this badly?"

Simone sat back, her dark eyes thoughtful. "I don't know. Whoever is behind it wanted to fracture the Council of the Coven Nine, and they were successful for a while. So it might be some sort of takeover, but it feels more personal than that. Angry, even."

That was in line with Nessa's analysis. "Has the Council had any luck tracking down Grace Sadler?"

"No, but we're on it full-time." Simone sipped a cup of tea. "Grace and I dated the same man for a while, you know. Decades ago."

"Yes." Nessa knew the entire case. She put the pieces together. "Wait a minute. Didn't he kidnap you, along with Garrett's mum? Put you in a jail cell?"

"Aye," Simone said softly. "Cara went into labor, and I delivered that little vampire pain in the butt."

Nessa laughed. "No wonder Garrett hovers around to be sure you don't trip. Or get shot."

"He is devoted," Simone said, sighing. "You help one kid get born, and he attaches for life. Vampires."

Nessa chuckled and turned back to the matter at hand. "Why didn't the Council keep a closer eye on Grace Sadler when she was defeated and had to leave?"

Simone shrugged. "We were in the middle of a war. Her powers were stripped, and it'll take a century for her to rebuild them. Put simply, we had more important things to worry about."

Aye. "Her sons are both dead now because of this Apollo campaign. If she's behind it, she'll be out for blood."

Simone nodded.

"What about other disgraced council members?" Nessa asked.

"Council contests usually end in death," Simone mused. "Grace is one of the few who was allowed to live. But we're also tracking down anybody else we can think of."

"As is the Guard," Nessa said.

"Aye," Simone said softly, her hand on her belly. "Speaking of which."

Nessa's shoulders slumped. "I know. I need to make it happen either today or tomorrow." The idea of resigning from the Guard hurt a little, but it also opened up possibilities. Maybe it was time to move on and do something else. She'd done a good job, and it was time for new blood in the top position.

"Will you be involved in choosing your successor?" Simone asked.

"No," Nessa said easily, lying through her teeth.

Simone took another sip of tea. "How does it happen? It's all a mystery, even to council members."

Nessa smiled. "That's the point."

Simone laughed. "My brother hates secrecy and intrigue. I mean, really hates it."

"Aye. I've noticed," Nessa said, her gaze on Simone's bump. What would it be like to be pregnant? To have a baby? Bear's baby?

"Nessa?" Simone asked softly.

Nessa looked toward her new sister-in-law. "Yes?"

"If you hurt him, really hurt him, I'll gut you before I burn you to a smoldering pile of screaming ash."

Nessa grinned. "Your imagery is impressive."

"Aye. So is my ability to gut people and throw fire," Simone said seriously.

"Understood." Nessa stretched her arms over her head. "He asked me to stay."

Simone turned her chair. "He did? Like, really asked you?"

Nessa thought through the words. "Aye. Said to make a choice now, because it's absolute. If I decide to stay, then there's no leaving."

Simone pressed her hands to her chest. "That is so sweet. And so many words for Bear to say at one time."

Nessa frowned. "He's kinda bossy."

"Just wait until you get pregnant," Simone murmured. "It gets a lot worse. But they're worth it."

Aye, but only if love was involved. Bear hadn't said he loved her—not once. Sure, they'd had wild sex, and he might've said he liked her at some point. But they had much different lives, and they needed more than sex and liking. She needed more. Looking at Simone's contentment, Nessa realized she wanted more. All of it. Could she have that with Bear?

"You're mated," Simone said, her lips curving. "Stop thinking like you're just dating. If you want him, you have to go for it."

Hadn't she done that just last night?

"I have surveillance of Slam Bar and intel on the wolf pack." Lucas texted something on his phone, and within a minute Bear and Nick loped into the room.

"Slam's on the rough side of town—very rough." Anticipation lit

Lucas's eyes as he stood. "There are twenty known members of the gang, and we took out ten the other day. But they might have local friends as well."

Bear nodded. "Get me the schematics of the bar and the entire neighborhood. We want to go in small: the boys, Lucas, Nick, and me." He looked toward Nessa. "Jasper will be in charge of your protection, while Max will be in charge of Simone's. Both are outside coordinating with troops."

"Isn't it nice when we all work together?" Simone asked dryly.

"Nessa. Come outside," Bear said, turning around and disappearing.

"See? Bossy." Nessa pushed away from the table and followed her mate, flexing her fingers. She'd been writing all day and could use a good training session or jog to let off some steam.

He waited for her, his big body leaning on the pool table. "You figure anything out?"

"Still working on it." Both work and personal issues.

"All right." He'd changed into black cargo pants with a dark shirt, and his combat boots appeared to be around a size eighteen. "So. I was thinking."

"That doesn't bode well for me."

He grinned. "Funny."

She fought the urge to preen. For goodness' sake. "You were saying?" Could her voice sound any more prim?

He brushed her hair away from her shoulder. "When I said that if you decide to stay, that's the final decision?"

Her breath caught. Had he changed his mind? "Yes?"

"I thought I should tell you that I want you to stay. I'd like for you to make that decision." He kicked a cushion out of the way. "Thought you should know."

Her heart did a funny somersault. She smiled.

He tapped her lip. "Okay. Back to business. I have snipers set up in multiple locations, ground forces in place, and satellite backup around the clock. You and Simone will be safe here tonight until we return."

"I won't let anything happen to your sister, Bear," Nessa said softly. "Stop worrying."

The knife secured to his thigh glinted when he shifted his weight. "You're both vulnerable to Apollo." He frowned. "Just because one dart didn't harm you doesn't mean several won't."

"I know. Did you call the doctor to come take blood? I kind of promised the queen."

"Yes. We'll overnight it to the queen to take a look and see what's what. But under no circumstances are you to use yourself as a guinea pig," he said.

Even if she had access to Apollo, which she did not in her present location, she wouldn't stick the stuff in her veins. "No worries there."

"Good. Sometimes the queen takes research too far, and I won't allow that to happen with you." Arrogance was stamped hard on his rugged face. "Now, come here. Please."

Her abdomen did a little wiggle. She stepped toward him, her boot tips touching his. "I'm here."

He widened his stance, pulling her between his legs. "Closer."

She settled in and lifted her face. "Yes?"

His lips brushed hers, and then he kissed her. He tasted of mint and male, taking her under, shooting desire through her blood. Finally, he lifted his head, his gaze soft. "Promise you'll stay safe tonight."

"I promise," she whispered, cupping his whiskered jaw. "You make the same promise. Don't get shot."

He grinned. "I promise. When I get back, I want a decision about us." With another hard kiss to her mouth, he set her aside and turned to stride out into the night.

Beneath his jacket, Bear tugged his bulletproof vest down to ease the pressure on his chest. The thing barely fit him, and it had been specially made for shifters. They'd parked the trucks several blocks away from the bar, running through alleys and deserted streets after that. Most buildings in the area were boarded up, but a few small businesses still existed. They were all closed for the night, complete with strong security bars over doors and windows.

Clouds flitted above, letting the moon shine through on debris and broken glass littering the asphalt.

He kept to the shadows with Nick and Garrett on his flanks. Lucas and Logan covered the other side of the street.

A bum stumbled out of an alley and fell on a garbage can, which toppled over, spilling out papers and fast-food containers. Bear led the way around him. They'd save people tomorrow. Tonight was for fighting—and gathering information. "I need at least one of them alive," he said through his comm unit.

A series of affirmatives came in loud and clear.

They finally reached Slam Bar, on the corner of hell and this place sucks. A metal sign hung haphazardly from a couple of stripped wires, blowing in the wind. Raucous laughter came from inside, and somewhere a woman screamed. Sirens wailed from a distance, their shrill cries echoing through empty streets, making it impossible to discern their location.

Bear used hand signals to send Lucas and Logan around back. They both slipped silently into the night.

"Stay alert," he said quietly, pushing open the heavy metal door.

Heat and noise hit him first, followed by the stench of old beer and piss. An enormous bald bartender shoved glasses of whiskey across a scarred wooden bar, his arm muscles bigger than a tire. Bottles lined the shelves behind him, and matted red velvet covered the walls. Dirty velvet.

Barstools and high round tables were scattered throughout the space, with a couple of lower tables toward the back near several dartboards and pool tables. The stools were ripped, and cotton wadding stuck out.

About ten people were inside, heads down, drinking heavily. Smoke hung in the air, choking it. Five additional men sat around a table in the back.

Bear recognized one guy from the pictures Logan had downloaded of the wolf gang. Good ole Frank J. "It's a go," Bear said into his comm unit, striding toward the back of the room. The men there, wolves really, watched him approach, their gazes alert but their postures relaxed. The closer he got, the more he could smell the stench of wolf.

Frank sat in the middle and had dark eyes, light hair, and a scar down his face. His nose was crooked and his clothes dirty. "What the fuck do you want?" His buddies watched carefully, going on alert.

"You know who I am?" Bear asked, setting his stance.

"Yeah," Frank said, downing a glass of whiskey. "You're a friend of Goldilocks."

His buddies chuckled and snorted.

"What an idiot," Bear muttered to Nick.

"Yep. It's always the idiot," Nick said, letting his fangs slide free. "But they talk fast enough when they're holding their intestines with both hands and trying to keep them from sliding to the floor."

Two of the wolves pushed back from the table, their chairs scraping the filthy floor, and stood.

"We don't want a fight," Bear said, catching himself. "All right. We would like a fight. But we won't hurt anybody if you just tell us who hired you to attack Grizzly territory. Just a name."

"Fuck you," Frank said.

Bear smiled. "I was hoping you'd say something like that. Maybe not those exact words, but something that indicated I get to hit somebody tonight." Barely leaning over, he yanked the nearest wolf off his chair. A quick pivot, and he threw the man across the bar to hit the back door. The wolf bounced off and slammed to the ground. The door didn't move.

Solid doors. Interesting.

Frank stood and lifted a green gun, pointing it at Bear's head. "That wasn't very nice."

The wolf already had a gun in his hand? Nick stiffened next to Bear.

Bear slowly turned his head to see every patron in the bar concentrating on the three of them. Even the losers who'd seemed lost in their drinks were watching intently, not so drunk.

The bartender lumbered over and locked the front door, setting a metal bar across the entire thing.

Ah, shit. Bear lifted his wrist to his mouth. "We need backup."

No answer.

His shoulders shot back. "Lucas? Logan? We need backup." Nick and Garrett fanned out from his right, surrounding the table of wolves and putting most of the bar in their sights. Something had happened outside. Lucas would never fail to answer. As Bear watched, the wolf he'd thrown slowly stood, staggering, with blood sliding down his face. He engaged the locks on the back door and then pushed a metal rod into place so the door couldn't be breached.

"Am I the only one thinking this might be a trap?" Nick asked congenially, his body tense and his gaze sweeping the entire bar.

"No," Garrett said. "Logan? Call in. Now." His voice deepened, and he sounded much older than twenty-five.

No answer came from Logan.

Bear moved toward Garrett to cover the kid. "First things first. Let's handle this and then go find him. Lucas will protect him." If Lucas was still alive. Bear couldn't think about that. Not now.

"Logan can fight," Garrett said.

Bear cleared his throat. They were so outnumbered it wasn't funny. Not even close. Maybe there was a way out of this mess without spilling blood. He increased the volume of his voice. "So. We need information, and you need, what? How about a decorator?"

The bartender moved back to the bar and lifted a semiautomatic green weapon—one that no doubt shot laser bullets that turned into metal upon piercing flesh. "We like money."

"We have money," Bear said, sizing up the situation. Three of them, and about sixteen enemy—all wolves.

"The odds aren't so bad," Garrett said, dropping into a fighting stance.

The odds were fucking terrible. Worse yet, Bear had the king's nephew and the demon leader's best friend at his side. If either died, it'd be a diplomatic nightmare, not to mention the fact that he actually liked both of them. And at the moment, Bear's best friend and the demon king's brother were outside, alone and not responding to calls.

"I'd sure like to know how they knew we were coming," Garrett growled.

The bartender smiled, showing a gap between his front teeth.

"I'd rather find out later and get free of this fuckup now," Nick countered quietly.

"Agreed," Bear said, focusing on the bartender. The huge guy seemed to be more in control than the wolf who'd first spoken. "How about a civilized exchange? Money for a little bit of information?" The bartender cocked the gun. "There's a mite of a problem, mate. We've already been paid."

"Now," Bear bellowed, backflipping over the table and taking three wolves down with him.

The entire bar sprang into life, and gunshots ripped through the melee.

Chapter 28

Nessa finished pouring another cup of tea for Simone and took it into the living room of the comfortable house. Beyond the dark windows, the river churned. Every once in a while, the clouds would part enough for the moon to shine down on the rapidly moving water. "They're all right, Simone."

Simone sat on the sofa, her legs extended on an ottoman, stacks of paper in her hands. "I know. They're all good fighters, and the wolves have no idea they're coming." She set the papers down to accept the tea. Her dark eyes glowed in her pale face, which looked even paler next to the thick waves of her black hair. The elegant witch wore light pants with dark high-heeled boots and a red tunic.

"Shouldn't you be sleeping? It's after midnight," Nessa asked.

"Not until Nick gets back."

Nessa couldn't sleep, either. Every time she'd sent Guard members into battle, she'd wanted to join them, to protect them. But that wasn't her job. It wasn't her job tonight, either. She picked up a legal pad with names already scratched off. Who wanted her dead?

Her phone rang and she jumped for it. "Bear?"

"No. It's Jasper."

"Oh." She tilted her head at Simone's quizzical look. "What's going on?"

"You have a phone call from the king. I can transfer it to the river house if you'd like," Jasper said.

Nessa fumbled for the remote control that managed the wide screen above the fireplace. She pushed a couple of buttons. "All right. Send it to the main system. I think I can find him in here."

"Copy that." Jasper cut off.

The screen fuzzed for a moment, and then Dage Kayrs came into view. "Evening," he said, looking impeccable in a black dress shirt and black pants. His silver eyes blazed. "Simone. How are you feeling?" His gaze seemed intense.

Simone sat up. "Fine, Dage. Why?"

He surveyed her. "Just checking in. Everything is all right?"

The hair on the back of Nessa's neck rose. "Why are you asking? Have you heard anything?"

The king visibly relaxed. "No. I just wanted to see how everyone was doing. Have you quit your job yet?"

Nessa shook her head and relaxed along with the king. "No. Probably tomorrow." Once Bear was home safely. "I still need to write a quick speech."

"Since I have you, I'd like to offer you a job as Coordinator between Realm Allies," Dage said smoothly. "You'd deal with all the different allies and coordinate agreements and disagreements. You'd answer only to me. Five million a year."

Simone sat up. "Not a bad salary."

No—it was an amazing salary. The job seemed perfect for her and a logical extension of her diplomatic experience with the Guard. "King. I don't know what to say," Nessa murmured.

"Say yes, and feel free to rename the job whatever you want. I just need somebody to coordinate the relationship between witches, demons, vampires, and shifters. Please." He eyed his wristwatch. "You can hire a staff of up to ten if you want. There will be some travel, and you'll have to move to Idaho. I want you at Realm headquarters."

Her stomach dropped. "The job can't be handled remotely?"

"No." He focused right back on her. "This is senior staff level, and meetings occur on the fly and at my convenience. The job is here. Think about it." He reached for an area above the camera and stilled. "Oh. I'm supposed to ask you if a doctor took your blood and sent it our way today."

"Aye," she said weakly. The doctor had shown up hours ago. "Expect the vials tomorrow morning."

"Great. We're hoping there's something in your blood to help counter PK and Apollo. So far, our labs haven't come close to finding an antidote. Have a nice night." He reached again, and then he paused. "Are you sure you're both all right?"

Simone huffed out air. "Why do you keep asking that?"

The king sat back. "I honestly don't know. It's just a feeling." He gazed beyond the camera as if listening. He stood up, and his eyes flared from silver to a deep blue. "Get out. We just received satellite pictures. You're under attack. Get out of the house right now."

An explosion rocked the entire house. The screen fell to the floor and shattered.

Nessa jumped up, grabbing Simone's arm and running for the master bedroom. The door there had the best lock in the entire house.

Another explosion echoed, shattering the windows. Nessa stumbled and fell, glass cutting into her hands. Simone grabbed her by the waist and tugged her up.

Nessa turned to the windows to see two helicopters in position with guns pointed inside, fully armed. They'd sent helicopters? She scrambled and shoved Simone out of the way. Any weapon would hit Nessa before Simone or the baby.

Alarms blared from outside.

Gunfire pattered toward them, and Nessa tackled Simone, trying to cover the taller woman with her body, turning to see the threat.

The sound of zip lines came clearly from outside, and two men landed on the porch, quickly releasing the ropes. The first guy, his head covered with a red mask, yanked a gun from his hip and jumped through the broken window.

He had a dart gun.

Nessa yelled and jumped up, putting herself between Simone and the attacker. "Get in the bedroom. Now." She ran forward, her head down, and tackled the asshole through the window. Glass cut her arm as they flew into the night. She punched and kicked, aiming for his trachea.

A ball of fire whizzed past her head, and she ducked, turning quickly.

Simone stood behind her, balls of morphing fire on her hands, her hair streaming behind her. She threw hard at the other man, hitting him center mass. He flew through the air, landing in the middle of the river and quickly disappearing downstream.

The guy beneath Nessa punched her in the face, and she fell back. Pain burst through her skull.

Soldiers rushed out of the forest, firing up at the helicopters. Jasper came around the house and leaped over Nessa, grabbing her attacker and spinning him across the icy deck. Max, the vampire soldier, ran around the other side of the house, already firing rapidly at the closest helicopter, with Uncle Boondock on his heels. Max hit the pilot, who slumped forward.

The helicopter swung around, its nose dipping.

Bloody hell. Nessa jumped up and turned, running for Simone. The tail boom flew their way, the propeller cutting through the side of the house and then the sofa, sending tufts of cotton everywhere. The helicopter kept going, spinning around and crashing right in the middle of the river.

Simone pivoted to run and slipped, falling and turning sideways, protecting her belly. Nessa reached her, grasping her and pulling her up. She turned to see the closest threat.

Everything somehow slowed down.

The other helicopter swung in close, a man leaning out of the side. He fired several darts.

Nessa cried out and tried to shield Simone. One dart hit Nessa in the arm, and she hurriedly yanked it out. The helicopter rose and turned around, flying away with multiple soldiers shooting at it.

She gulped, turning to look at Simone.

Oh, shit. Simone had three darts sticking out of her arm. Her eyes wide, she slowly looked down at the darts.

"It's okay," Nessa said frantically, pulling each one out. "It's okay."

Simone swayed. Panic filled her eyes. "Nessa?"

"Yeah?" Nessa asked, sliding her shoulder beneath Simone's arm and gently prodding her toward the bedroom.

"I, ah, I think I'm bleeding." Simone stopped moving and looked down.

Nessa swallowed and looked at Simone's beige-colored pants. Blood showed at the vee of her legs.

"The baby," Simone whispered, anguish in her tone.

A knife blade slashed across Bear's thigh before he landed, men bouncing on either side of him. Flipping to his feet, he drew his gun and fired rapidly, hitting each man in the neck. There wasn't time for nuance.

He turned just in time to get hit with a blast to the chest that threw him back to the metal door. His head snapped into the metal, and stars exploded behind his eyes as he went down. The vest had protected him, but his entire torso felt like it had been hit by a truck. Sucking up air, he rolled and shoved the table over, taking cover for a moment. Gunfire and the sound of flesh hitting flesh overwhelmed the song on the jukebox.

Garrett sailed over the table and scrambled on his belly to Bear's side. Blood poured from a cut beneath his eye. "We're outgunned. Too much firepower," he gasped, spitting out more blood.

Nick hurtled over, his left pant leg shredded and covered with blood. "I'm thinking they don't want to negotiate." He dropped his clip and grabbed another from his back pocket before leaning up and firing a volley.

Something crashed.

The song on the jukebox stopped playing.

Bear dragged over the three guys he'd shot and quickly frisked them, finding three guns and two knives. Good. More firepower.

Bullets sprayed above their heads, and they ducked. "Ideas?" Nick asked, leaning around the side of the downed table and firing quickly.

"I could shift." Bear levered up and fired several rounds at the bar. Bottles shattered, and alcohol poured down.

"You'd knock us out with the shift," Nick gritted out, wincing as he moved his leg. "And you wouldn't have your vest. There are too many of them for one bear to take out."

Yeah. His face hurt, his head pounded, and a bone in his chest felt like it might be broken. He wasn't completely healed yet from his brush with being a dragon.

Garrett leaned around the other side and fired quickly, ducking to avoid the return fire. "I'm almost out," he said. He shook his head, and blood arced across the back of the table. "One other thing."

"Don't say it," Bear snapped, handing over two of the stolen guns. "I know."

Nick checked his clip and snarled. "They knew we were coming, so that means they know headquarters is without us."

"You said it. I said not to," Bear hissed, leaning up and shooting toward the bartender again, who ducked quickly. The man had the biggest gun, and he needed to be stopped—now. "We have more guards than ever at territory. Unless there's an air strike, Ness and Simone are safe." Their enemy had hired rogue wolves for an attack. If they had had an army, they would've used it. "Let's just get out of here."

Garrett fired and then stopped. "How? I'm out of my bullets." He picked up both extra guns. "We need a plan."

Bear handed over his gun and the final extra one to Nick. "This is all I have left."

Shots pinged into the table, several bullets penetrating the wood and going right through. One whizzed by Bear's ear. "Shit." He had to think. This was his fault, damn it. There were at least ten men facing them, all armed and probably prepared to shift into wolves if necessary.

It probably wasn't.

Nick fired again and then dropped down, a bloody slice cut along his temple.

Bear grabbed his head. "You got hit."

Nick shrugged him off. "I'm fine." The blood slid down to coat his collar.

Bear swallowed. "All right. You guys duck and cover your heads. I'm going to shift in the air and go for the bartender. The second I clear the bar, you shoot with the remaining bullets."

"I could perpetrate a mind attack," Nick said. "But it'll take you guys out at close quarters, and I won't be able to shoot during. If they rush me . . ."

"No. I shift." Demons could attack minds, but Bear needed his intact to get out of this. He drew in air. "It's the only way."

Something banged against the front door. Hard.

Static came across the comm units. "Get to the back of the room. Now," hissed a hoarse demon voice.

"Logan?" Garrett asked.

"Yeah. Get ready." An engine roared, and suddenly the entire front wall of the bar crashed in. Bodies went flying. Garrett shoved a gun into Bear's hand, and they all three stood, firing in every direction, running for the truck.

Logan shoved open the passenger-side door, firing through the window toward the bartender.

Garrett jumped inside and fell over the center console to the back seat. Bear shoved Nick in and then jumped in behind him, turning and firing. A bullet pierced his arm. "Go, go, go."

Logan slammed the truck into reverse and punched the gas. They squealed out of the bar and flipped around.

Men stumbled out of the demolished bar, two still firing guns. Bear plugged one between the eyes, while Nick caught the other in the neck.

The bartender ran out, pumping his huge gun. Bear and Nick fired simultaneously, hitting the asshole in the head. He went down, his gun flying into the air. A head shot wouldn't kill him, but he wouldn't be shooting at anybody for a while.

"Where is Lucas?" Bear asked.

"Dunno," Logan said, leaning over the steering wheel. A purple knot swelled on his temple. "When they locked the back door, he told me to take point, and he ran around the front." Logan flipped the lights on.

Bear looked frantically around. "God. There he is." Lucas's legs stuck out from a side alley. He had to be okay. Bear leaped from the truck and ran over to his friend, grabbing him up. "Luke? Luke." He shook his second-in-command.

Lucas's head lolled, and he blinked. A raw gash bled across his entire forehead. "Bear?"

Thank God. Bear dragged him back to the truck and lifted him inside, jumping in after him. "Go, Logan. Go."

The kid stomped down on the gas, and they lurched down the street.

Nick grabbed a cell phone out of the jockey box. "I'll call it in." He dialed and held the device to his ear. "It's Veis. We—" The demon stopped speaking.

Tension, raw and fierce, rolled through the cab. Horrible pain and images slammed into Bear's brain, and he shut his eyes. "Nick."

The demon mind attack stopped. Bear opened his eyes, feeling as if a boulder had landed in his gut. "What?"

"We're on the way," Nick said, disengaging the call. "Attack on headquarters—from the air. Both Simone and Nessa were hit."

Chapter 29

Nessa settled Simone on the wide bed in the master bedroom, fluffing her pillows. Simone groaned and clutched her stomach, pulling up her knees.

Panic choked off Nessa's breathing. "You'll be okay." She shucked her sweater, leaving only her blouse. "Hold on. Take deep breaths." The dart she'd taken was slowing her movements, and she tried to shrug it off.

"It's too early," Simone gasped, her face twisting in pain. "Even for immortals. Four months is too early."

Nessa soothed the hair back from her face. "Deep breaths."

Jasper came to the door. "We've secured the premises and ordered the helicopters up for air support."

Nessa tried to calm herself. "Thanks. I need my uncle. Send Boondock."

"He's out cold, Nessa. Took several knife wounds to the neck and upper chest." Jasper wiped blood off his chin. His face was a bruised mess, and his lip double its usual size. "Boondock will be out cold for hours. Can I do anything?"

"No." Nessa shot him a smile, her body seizing. "Just shut the door. Thanks."

He shut the door quietly.

Nessa moved up the bed to sit next to Simone. "All right, Simone. Let's see what we can do to heal you." She kept her voice soft as she placed her hands over Simone's chest. Heat instantly burned her. "You have some Apollo damage going on, but we can fix that."

"W-why aren't you slower? I saw a dart," Simone panted out.

"Dunno," Nessa said. "The dart just glanced me. I feel fine. Let's work on you." Actually, she was nauseated and her head hurt like she'd been kicked in both temples, but she could do this. She had to do this.

Tears slid down Simone's aristocratic face. "I can't lose this baby. I just can't."

"Shhh." Nessa kept one hand on Simone's upper chest and placed her other one low on the woman's abdomen. She breathed in and shut her eyes, trying to feel the damage.

A little heartbeat pressed against her energy. "Okay. The baby is all right." She searched for damage, easily finding an amniotic sac ripped down the side. Though she couldn't actually see the damage, she could feel it. "Simone? I need you to breathe in and out and try to calm yourself. I know it's tough."

"What's going on? What do you know?" Simone's voice was shrill. She moved restlessly and tightened her body. Pain flared through her, transmitting itself to Nessa. "Please."

"Two things are going on. First, your body is reacting to the Apollo by heating your internal organs. I can counter that. Second, the baby is in danger, but I can sew up the sac and make sure she's nice and safe."

"She?" Simone panted.

Nessa widened her fingers across Simone's abdomen. "Aye. You have a very strong demon-witch female in there, and we're garna help her to survive. Both of you will survive." There was so much damage. How could Nessa secure the baby and still fight the Apollo in Simone's blood and organs? "But you need to help me." She wasn't that strong. Nobody was that strong.

"How?" Simone arched off the bed, fire dancing on her lips.

"I need you to shut your eyes, breath in and out, and calm your body. You have more control than you think. Let's slow your heartbeat. Come on." Nessa imagined a chilly healing balm spreading around Simone's heart. At the same time, she created a gel-like bandage to cover the sac holding the baby.

"I'm still bleeding," Simone whispered.

"Doesn't matter." Nessa soothed another layer of gel over the sac. "The baby doesn't need that blood. The baby needs you to breathe and slow your heart rate. Now."

Simone settled back on the pillow, another tear leaking out of her eye. "Okay." She drew in air, pushing out her chest, and then exhaled slowly.

"Good," Nessa said, her hands and arms starting to shake. Another layer around the baby. Then she turned her attention to Simone's liver, which was vibrating with heat. The organ shook as it started to burn. Simone moaned but kept still, breathing as evenly as she possibly could. Nessa sent ice over the liver.

"I need Nick," Simone whispered.

"He'll be here," Nessa said, trying to force coolness around the kidneys. "Keep breathing. I need your blood to slow down a little." Her thudding heart was spreading the drug too quickly. "You're a tough, take-no-shit Councilwoman for the Coven Nine, Simone. You throw fire like a warrior."

"That's true," Simone whispered, her nails digging into the bed-covers. She groaned.

"Good." Nessa moved back to Simone's heart to cool it more. "How's your head?"

"Hurts," Simone muttered. "Protect the babe first."

If Simone died, so did the baby. "I will take care of her, don't worry." Nessa lifted her hand off Simone's chest and covered her forehead. Heat filled her palm. She dug deep and created another soothing balm, forcing it through Simone's skull.

A ringing set up in Nessa's ears. Blood dribbled from her nose, and she casually wiped it off. Her ears felt wet, and she ignored them.

She rubbed circles over Simone's abdomen, and the sac stitched up, quickly filling with fluid. The baby's heart rate sped up to a healthy level. Nessa swayed and caught herself. She opened her eyes, but her vision narrowed to a pinprick and then went black. Her stomach rolled over. She shut her eyes and concentrated on the baby, keeping the protective gel in place for a while longer.

Blood slid from her nose and over her mouth.

"Nessa," Simone said, not moving. "You're bleeding."

Nessa wiped off her nose and opened her eyes but saw only blackness. "It's all right. That's normal," she croaked, sounding like she was being choked. Her lungs heated until her chest burned.

Simone grabbed her wrist. "Your eyes are bright violet. You need to stop. Rest." She tried to push Nessa's hand away from her chest.

"I'm fine." Nessa fought her, aiming for the kidneys again.

"Your ears are bleeding," Simone said urgently. "Stop for a minute. Please."

Nessa shook her head. "Here's the deal, Simone. If I don't heal you, your baby dies. So keep taking deep breaths and just focus internally." Blood from her ears wound down her neck to her blouse.

Simone gave a frustrated moan.

"It's okay." Nessa was fading, and fast. She tried to heal more, but her strength was tapped. Her ability was gone.

The baby wouldn't make it. Neither would Simone.

That was unacceptable. Nessa sucked in air and dug deep. For Bear. For an animalistic power to survive. She felt inside herself for him, looking for that power.

Her body stilled. Bear. She pictured him—and she felt him. Mating him had changed her on a fundamental level. He wasn't only a bear—he had dragon genes. Those were hers now. She could do this. Bear loved his sister, and that held power.

Gathering her strength, Nessa pushed all her healing powers into her hand, creating a massive amount of imaginary cooling balm that she shoved into Bear's sister's body.

Something exploded in Nessa's head, and then there was only an odd black with violet edges filling her vision as she started to pass out.

Then . . . nothing.

Bear barreled down the trail from the rec room toward the river house, fury and fear roaring through him. "Lucas? Get everyone the fuck off my property. At the end of the next hour, there will be no witches, no demons, and no vampires. Period. Call the entire grizzly shifter nation and get full troops here by the crack of dawn." He jumped over a series of trees that had been downed by missiles. Missiles fired from helicopters.

"Got it," Lucas said, awake but bleeding. He'd taken a hard enough hit that his eyes were still dilated.

Bear turned and grabbed him. "Put Jasper and Uncle Boondock in the cells belowground first. They were the only ones who knew where we were going tonight. Lock them down. Now." He shoved him.

Lucas stumbled back toward headquarters.

Nessa had to be all right. She had to be. Same for Simone.

Bear hadn't felt fear since his childhood, and he'd forgotten how bad it could burn. Nick ran beside him, panic on his breath, murder in his eyes. The boys followed right behind, eyeing the forest, seeming on guard and protecting the two males frantically rushing for their mates.

Bear could barely breathe. He'd left them. Nessa and Simone were on his property, in his protection, and they'd been hit. The intel wasn't complete, so he had no clue what he was about to find.

He almost stopped cold at seeing the shattered window and demolished side to the house. Bodies littered the deck, and he jerked his head at one of his men. "Only bear shifters here. Get everyone else the fuck off the property." The shifter nodded. Bear stepped over his ruined porch, trying not to panic at seeing the damage to the living room. Had Nessa been in there? "If any attackers are alive, stick them in the cells underground."

Then he ran into the living room. "Nessa?" he yelled.

"Simone?" Nick bellowed, shoving what was left of the couch out of the way.

Bear turned for the master bedroom.

He and Nick hit the door at the same time, sending it bouncing against the wall.

Bear's heart stopped. He swayed.

Nessa was on the bed, blood pouring from her nose and ears. Wounds covered her, and her hands looked like they'd been burned in a campfire.

Simone sat next to her, pale and bloody, panic in her eyes. She had tucked Nessa's head onto her lap, and she was stroking her hair. "She won't wake up." Simone's voice croaked as if her vocal cords had been shredded.

Nick shoved his way to the other side of Simone and gathered her close. "Are you all right?"

"I don't know." Her voice trembled. "I got hit with three darts—"

"What?" Nick sat up, raw fury on his face. He looked down at her pants. "You're bleeding." His voice dropped. Pain rolled from him to clog the air.

Bear couldn't move.

Simone nodded, tears spiking her lashes. "Yes. But Nessa put her hands on me, and she made the pain go away. There was a healing balm. She tried to save the baby, too."

Nick placed a hand on Simone's stomach. "The baby?"

"I'm not sure," Simone whispered. "Nessa said she's okay, but then Nessa passed out. I can't get her to awaken." She looked up at Bear.

Bear's legs almost gave out. He stepped slowly into the room, approaching the bed. "Ness?" His hand shook, but he reached out to touch her cheek. "Wake up, baby." He dropped to his knees, his hand flattening over her head. "Wake up."

She didn't move.

He wiped the blood away from her nose. Her breath was shallow and somehow heated. "I'm so sorry," he whispered, tears clogging his throat. He'd failed to protect her. How had he thought for even one second that he could let her go? The woman was everything.

His hands trembling, he lifted her off Simone's lap and sat in the chair beside the bed, cradling her. Holding her close. "I'll never let anybody hurt you again. Wake up, Ness. Please?" He kissed her damp forehead and then her mouth, tasting blood.

"Bear," Nick said quietly, holding Simone close. "Mates can heal each other sometimes. See if you can take away her pain."

Bear had no clue how to be a mate. Obviously. He touched her forehead, trying to feel pain. All he felt was her soft skin. "Wake up." He had no idea how to cure her. She had to be all right. How had he even thought about sending her away?

His entire life had been leading up to her. The idea of no light, no chaos, no Nessa cut through him, sharper than any blade. He'd do anything—be anything. He tried to pull pain out of her head by using his fingers. They tingled. "Ness? I need you to wake up. Please."

She didn't move.

Bear's head hung. "Nick?"

"Yes?" the demon asked softly.

God. This was impossible. "Can you help?" Bear asked, his chest shuddering. He could feel Nessa slipping away.

Simone sucked in her breath.

Yeah. It was unthinkable. Bear lifted his gaze to his friend. "Please."

Nick looked at him, his gaze dark. "I can get into your head, but I can't help you heal her. I'm not sure what you're asking."

Demons could attack or slide inside minds. Bear swallowed. "I need help tapping the dragon in me. There's enough power deep down if I combine it with shifter strength. But I need to bridge the gap."

"No!" Simone said, struggling.

Nick held her tight. "It might kill you, Bear."

"I don't care." There was no reason to fight to live if he let Nessa die. "Please?"

Nick swallowed. "Shut your eyes."

Bear shut his eyes and relaxed his guard. Pinpricks edged into his brain, and he growled. His eyelids flipped open.

Sweat dotted Nick's upper lip. "You have to let me in. The blocks are too strong."

Damn it. For Nessa. Bear nodded and held her tighter, shoving his mental blocks to hell and making himself vulnerable for the first time since he was a kid. Nick could slice his brain in two and kill him if he wanted.

The demon's power touched Bear's brain, sparking lights behind his eyes.

"Look for the dragon," Nick whispered.

Bear nodded and dug deep, closing his eyes, letting the demon navigate inside his brain.

"Simone," Nick said.

Something warm and comforting tilted around Bear's mind. He smiled.

"Nessa," Nick said.

Warm, comfort, hope, possessiveness, and pleasure melded into a lump inside Bear.

"Find the dragon," Nick murmured.

Bear searched inside himself, touching on that power he tried to avoid. He growled as a bear, but his arms tingled like a dragon's.

"Now, Bear," Nick said.

Bear dropped his forehead to Nessa's and searched deep inside her, using both sides of himself. He found her pain, and it was fucking breath stealing. Breathing in unevenly, he imagined taking her pain into his own body.

His spine snapped, and his head rocked. He took more of it. Then more.

"Get rid of it," Nick growled, his voice so hoarse it was hard to make out the words.

Bear imagined the pain spinning into nothingness. He opened his eyes. "Nessa?"

She slowly stirred.

His heart beat more rapidly. "Sweetheart?"

Her eyelids fluttered open. "Bear." She sighed his name, and her body relaxed against him. "I'm glad you're okay."

"I'm fine." He eyed the dried blood around her nose and ignored the residual pounding between his ears. The dragon inside him slowly slipped away. "How about you?"

Her smile was exhausted. "I need sleep. Bad." She pushed away from his chest, and he gave her room. "Wanna check on Simone." She turned.

"No," Simone said. "You need to heal."

Nessa shook her head. "Please, Bear. I just need to check. Donna' need any powers."

He couldn't say no to her ever again. So he silently carried her over to his sister and knelt on the bed, unable to release Nessa.

She reached out and felt Simone's chest. "You're okay," Nessa sighed. "Might take a few days to regain your strength, but your body can handle the remaining bits of Apollo." Her eyelids fluttered shut, and she moved her hand to Simone's abdomen.

Nessa's smile was the sweetest thing Bear had ever seen. "The babe is fine. She's a tough one, she is."

"She?" Nick asked, his voice shaking. The demon looked like he'd been through a meat grinder.

"Yes," Nessa sighed, slumping against Bear's chest. "Need to . . ." She dropped into a deep sleep before she could finish the sentence.

Bear held her to his chest, trying to force his world to settle. "Thank you," he mouthed to the pale demon.

Nick nodded, his gaze warm. "You so love her."

Great. Now a demon knew every secret he'd ever held. Bear

sighed, unable to draw up much anger against Nick. However, there was an enemy out there that needed to go down and now. His men had better be carrying out his orders. As soon as he could let go of Nessa, he was going to go torture her uncle and her best friend.

One of them would break.

Chapter 30

Nessa awoke slowly, her body buzzing with pain. She blinked grit from her eyes to see the master bedroom of the river house. A drill and hammers echoed from the living room. The sound was kind of muffled. She rubbed her ear and felt dried blood. Oh yeah.

She sat up, holding the blankets to her chest. Weakness assailed her limbs, so she concentrated and tried to send healing cells wherever her body hurt. A sensation kind of sputtered and died out. Wonderful. She was useless for the time being—totally out of juice. Pouting, she limped from the bed like an old human woman.

Where was everybody?

Her knees wobbled, but she made it to the bathroom for a very hot shower that served to restore a little bit of her energy. She dressed in jeans and a sweater, tying her hair on top of her head. She wore flat boots out of necessity today. Even thinking of trying to wear heels made her want to cry. A couple of quick swipes of lip gloss, and she steeled her shoulders to meet the day.

She needed to check on Simone.

Allowing herself to limp until she reached the door, she plastered on a smile and stepped out into the living room. All the furniture had been removed and the entire area cleaned. Teams were repairing the wall, installing new carpet, a new window, and what looked like multiple security systems.

She moved toward the kitchen to find Nick and Simone in the breakfast nook eating off paper plates.

Her stomach growled. Man, she was starving. She stepped over a pile of lumber, around a bunch of electrical cords, and moved into the nook. "Morning."

Simone looked up. Dark circles marred the smooth skin beneath her eyes, but her eyes themselves were clear, as was her skin. She smiled, looking both fragile and determined. "How are you feeling?"

"Better. You?" Nessa sat and leaned over to press her hand against Simone's abdomen, hoping with everything she had that the babe was all right.

Nick stilled, his eyes darker than dark, intensity swirling through them. His focus was absolute, which was probably how his people could demolish a mind in a good attack. The idea that he could squish her brains out of her ears was one she needed to forget about.

Nessa ignored the dangerous demon and concentrated on Simone. The witch sucked in air, and then held her breath. A strong and very steady baby heartbeat echoed where Nessa looked. Relief nearly made her sway. Thank God. She tilted her head and just felt for a moment, enjoying the little person's essence. Oh, she was going to be a handful. Everything was healthy around the babe. "Your baby is fine. Spunky little thing." Nessa smiled.

Simone hiccupped and quickly wiped away a tear. Her relief was palpable. "Thank you, Nessa," she whispered, her voice thick.

"You're welcome." Nessa lifted her hand toward Simone's neck and felt. Her pulse was a little sluggish, but Simone would survive. "You're out of danger. Might take a week or so to completely recover." She released her friend and reached for a cup of coffee.

Nick grasped her wrist.

She started and looked up.

His chin lowered, his eyes blacker than the darkest midnight. "Thank you for saving them. If you ever need anything, I am at your disposal." His hold tightened. "Anything." He released her.

Wow. The vow was heartfelt, and she might take him up on it someday. "It was my pleasure," Nessa murmured, pouring coffee, her hand shaking.

Nick took the coffee carafe from her and finished pouring. "You're not all right."

Simone piled eggs on a plate to set in front of her. "You're not. I'm so sorry. What is wrong? Can I help?"

Nessa reached for a fork. "I'm fine. The healing—it was a lot. Not too much, just a lot, and there's a price. I'll be back in good form in a few days. I remember what you did for Bear . . . and me. Thank you, Nick."

"Was my honor," the demon said.

Protein would help. She tasted the eggs. "Where is Bear?"

As if on cue, he strode in from outside, issuing orders to a battered Lucas. When he caught sight of her, he said something quietly and then moved toward her. He knelt down, his hands on her thighs. Her entire thighs. "How are you feeling?" he asked, his honeyed eyes swirling and his voice gravelly.

"Just fine," she said, gently touching a bruise on his chin. He must've had to heal some pretty bad injuries to have been unable to get this one.

He grasped her hand and pulled it away from his skin. "No healing."

"I can't right now," she said simply. "I'm probably out of commission for a week or so. Recharging batteries and all that." She forced a smile. "I was just touching."

"In that case." He put her hand back on his face. "Touch all you want."

She studied him. There was a hardness to him that hadn't been there before. Or rather, that had been hidden behind charm and crankiness before. Now it was out for all to see. "Are you all right?"

"Yes. The wolf bar was a setup. Obviously." His lip curled.

"Wasn't your fault." She grasped his shoulder. "You know that, right?"

He looked toward Simone. "How are you doing?"

"Fine, and the babe is well." Simone's smile was tired but relieved.

"Good." Bear's hands flexed on Nessa's legs. "I'll find out who set us up."

Nick put his napkin on his plate. "Speaking of which, I think I should head that, ah, investigation. It'd be better all around." His gaze flicked to Nessa and back.

"No," Bear said shortly. "You and Simone are allowed to stay as long as she wants, but the rest of your soldiers need to be out of my territory within the hour. Or we start shooting."

Nessa's mouth gaped open and she quickly shut it. "What are you talking about?"

"Grizzlies only." He leaned over and pressed a kiss to her nose. "And one healing witch. That's it."

She tried to make sense of his words. "I don't understand. Why are you making everyone leave? A lot of their soldiers saved us last night. They fought hard."

"The only way I can control this area is to control it with my people." He ran a knuckle along her chin. "I'm not forcing you, but I have to know if you really are resigning from the Guard."

She nodded numbly. "I don't have a choice. It's done."

"In that case, I want you to resign now. The sooner we get it over, the less danger you'll be in." He kept her gaze.

Too much was happening all at once. "Right now?"

"Yes." His implacable face had no give in it. None.

She missed his laid-back attitude. "Even if I resign, I might be a target."

"Maybe, but it's one box checked. What needs to happen?" he asked.

She looked around, her gaze seeking, trying to concentrate. What was wrong with him? He seemed so . . . distant. "I, ah, need to sign a Declaration of Resignation and do so in Coven Nine headquarters in Dublin."

"No." Bear looked to his sister. "She'll sign the letter and do so via video from here. Will that suffice for the Council?"

Simone watched him carefully. "Yes. Bear, you need to take a step back and breathe for a moment. Think everything through. I know you're angry—"

"I'm not angry." Bear turned back toward Nessa. "Finish your breakfast, and I'll have the video room set up for you. Remain here until I come for you."

"I, ah, need my uniform," she whispered.

He looked at his sister. "Get her one." With that, he stalked across the living room toward one of the rec rooms in the back.

"What is wrong with him?" Nessa asked, watching his broad back.

"He almost lost you last night," Nick said, taking a drink of his coffee. "And he almost lost his sister and his niece. He's trying to hold it together, but he's going to blow. Get ready for the explosion."

Nessa shuddered. She couldn't take another explosion, not right now. "Is there anything I can do?"

Nick shook his head, his jaw incredibly tight. "No, and there's no way I'm letting any of my soldiers leave until I take Simone with me, whether Bear likes it or not."

Nessa exchanged a worried look with Simone. Perhaps Bear wasn't the only one about to explode.

Her phone buzzed and she lifted it to her ear just as Simone and Nick both reached for their phones. Her body settled and her mind cleared, her adrenaline starting to hum. "Lansa," she answered.

"Ma'am? The chatter went silent across the world. However, undercover operatives are calling with signs of movement around possible targets," one of her soldiers said, his voice low.

"Affirmative." She held the phone away from her head and focused on Simone. "Whoever is after us is making the move now. You getting the same intel?"

Simone pushed back from the table. "Aye. We need the war room."

Nick stood, stopping her. "Are you all right to move? To do this?"

She looked at him, her shoulders straight. "Aye. It's my job. All I need to do is sit and type today, Nick. It's okay."

The demon drew in a deep breath. "All right. If you start cramping or bleeding, you promise to tell me."

She reached up and soothed his cheek with her hand. "I promise. I won't let anything harm this babe."

"We'll take a four-wheeler. You're not walking," Nick returned.

"Where are Garrett and Logan?" Nessa asked, standing and moving toward the living room while still on the phone.

"War room," Nick said shortly, following her with Simone. "Our techs are interpreting hacked e-mails right now. Whatever is happening is going down today."

Nessa had been waiting for this. They all had. Panic heated her, and she shoved it down. Time to think. "All right. War rooms." She pressed the phone to her ear. "I'll coordinate from the shifter location. Gather intel and be ready with a report in fifteen minutes. I want everything." She clicked off, having to stretch her legs to make it over another pile of lumber.

"You're not fucking going anywhere," Bear said, striding in from the rec room. "We're almost set up for your news conference."

Nick stopped and looked like he wanted to say something. Then he glanced at Nessa. "We'll be outside getting a four-wheeler." Taking Simone's arm, he assisted her around the construction area and into what looked like another snowy day.

Nessa took a deep breath. "I can't resign today. We need somebody in charge, and it's me for now."

"No." Bear put his hands on his hips. "This is the most secure place I have at the moment, and you're staying right here."

"The war room is the most secure." She knew he was acting from concern, maybe even caring, but she didn't have time for this. Not right now. "My people are under attack. This is my job, Bear. Either you understand that fact or you don't."

He looked so hard. Determined and cold.

She wanted to reassure him, head right back to bed and snuggle. But she couldn't. Not right now. "Time matters."

Something softened just a little in his eyes. "Are you up to this?"

"There's no choice." She reached for his hand. "I could use your help."

He turned them toward the exit. "Oh, you're getting my help. If you're in the war room, so am I. But you're either there or here for now, got it?"

Was he turning the entire territory into a secured zone? She'd worry about that later. "I got it." They moved quickly out into lightly falling snow. She'd forgotten her jacket again. What kind of targets would be hit today? Key people in government, medicine, law enforcement were all at risk. How many could she protect? Her hands shook, so she shoved them in her pockets.

They reached the four-wheeler and jumped in.

"Here we go," Nick said, the sound low and ominous.

Chapter 31

Bear followed his mate into the war room, his senses on high alert. He needed to get to Jasper and Boondock, who were downstairs. Logan was on one set of computers, Garrett the other.

Yeah, they weren't bear shifters. But he needed them, and he trusted them. Plus, he'd promised the king. In fact, he'd given Logan all the codes dealing with Grizzly personnel and a challenge to find Brinks, Lars, and Duncan. The kid's eyes had gleamed.

Nessa strode over to the conference table. "We have worldwide chatter of an imminent attack on prominent witches and our holdings. Garrett, I need you to coordinate with the vampire nation and the Realm. Get them online." She grabbed the remote control and turned on the large screen across the room, bringing up a map of the world. "Simone? Get on those computer banks and start coordinating with the Coven Nine and your Enforcers. I want any Level Alpha members of the nation under lockdown. Now."

The woman was impressing the hell out of him.

Bear turned and signaled for three guards—all waiting in the rec room—to set up a perimeter around the headquarters building. "Team of ten," he mouthed.

They hustled off to obey his orders.

Lucas ran in from outside, snow dusting his hair. "We have patrols set around the entire perimeter, and I've given orders that all other species have to leave. I gave them the entire night to do it, but they're not moving. We may have to engage."

Bear bit back a growl. "Hold tight for now." He couldn't have his people fighting the witches while Nessa coordinated a worldwide operation.

Lucas's head jerked up. "We need to get them off our land. We're surrounded by witches. And demons."

"Agreed," Bear said. "But not right now. Have our people on alert."

"Copy that," Lucas said, moving to the side and reaching for his cell phone.

Bear turned back to Nessa.

She looked at Nick. "I need either you or Logan to get on computers with the demon nation."

"I've got it." Nick sat next to Simone at a computer and started typing rapidly.

"Bear?" Nessa looked around. "The shifter nations need to be brought in."

Bear leaned to the side and brought up his contacts, most of whom had already checked in with details. Their intel was as good as the Guard's. "Logan? Be me for about an hour." Bear pulled the demon's chair toward his computer and typed in his code. "Maybe two hours."

It hit him then that he was trusting a demon with his entire life— again. Not just a demon this time, and not one he was related to, but a vampire-demon mix. Interesting.

Logan switched gears. "I've been doing the other searches you asked for. Will update with available information." He leaned in and started typing commands.

"All right. Keep me informed." Bear turned for the wall and revealed the hidden stairwell.

Nessa didn't look his way. "Somebody find Jasper for me. Boondock, too."

Bear paused. "They're otherwise engaged."

She stiffened and partially turned to face him. "Excuse me?"

His shoulders went back. "The people who knew I was heading to a wolf bar in the middle of nowhere, and that you'd be alone here, and that we didn't have air support up . . . are few and far between. Either Jasper or Boondock set us up, and I'm going to find out which one." By any means necessary.

Her eyes widened. With her face still bruised, she looked defenseless. Oh, he knew she wasn't, but he had to harden his heart against what she was about to say.

"Do what you have to do," she whispered. "But I give you my

word, on my life, that neither of those men betrayed me. Not a chance in hell."

He rocked back. "It's often the person you least expect, sweetheart. You're thinking with your heart."

She straightened and reached for a headset to plant in place. "My heart is pretty damn good, Bear. Just remember that you're about to torture two of the only three men in this entire world who I trust. One of them took me in and raised me when my parents died, and the other has covered my back for decades." Then she turned back around and got to work.

"Who's the third man you trust?" he asked quietly.

"You."

His heart clinched. He noted the hard line of her shoulders. If he did this, she might never forgive him. But he didn't have a choice. So he motioned for Lucas to follow him down the concrete steps, and the door closed behind them both.

He strode around a corner to the block of cells. Each cell had a cot, toilet, and sink. Fortified iron bars, covered in planekite, or PK, made them impossible to breach. Jasper sat on the bed in one, his face still bruised, while Boondock leaned against the far block wall of the other.

"Gentlemen," Bear said, standing between the cells and staring at both men. "Whatever attack you've planned for today is being thwarted right now. Tell me everything, and I won't shred your skin off your bodies."

Lucas pulled a green gun from his waistband. "Could I shoot them both? Just to get things started?"

Neither man so much as twitched.

Bear pretended to think about it. "Let's give them a chance to speak, first." The image of Nessa's hurt eyes wouldn't leave his mind, so he shook his head. He had to find out who'd tried to kill her, and it was definitely one of these men.

Fire glowed on Jasper's hands.

Bear smiled, showing his sharp canines. "Go ahead. Throw."

Jasper threw. The fire hit between the bars and shot back at him. He rolled off the bed and came up, his shirt smoldering. Keeping Bear's gaze, he glared and patted out the flames.

Bear cocked his head to the side. "Do you honestly think I failed to take into account your fire when I built these cells?" He eyed the long iron bars. "A demon mind attack can't even make it through." Jasper stepped closer to the bars. "Aren't you just full of surprises. So much for the lazy grizzly hiding out in the woods." Bear moved closer as well. "I'm the head of the grizzly nation. If your people are so arrogant they don't bother to pay attention to facts, then that's your own problem."

"You're also the mate to my niece." Boondock finally spoke, his body relaxed and his gaze shuttered. He had a powerful presence, probably from age and experience. His dark hair curled over his nape, and his blue eyes, so like Nessa's, seemed mildly irritated. "She's not garna like you torturing her loved ones." No concern echoed in his words.

"She'll have to get over it," Bear said mildly.

Boondock smiled then. "She won't. Oh, the girl is brilliant at strategy in a tough business. The toughest. But she's all heart, and she's the most loyal person I've met in my entire life. That's one of the reasons she's been so good at her job."

All true words. "If you've betrayed her, she'll have to forgive me." Bear needed to decide which one to torture first.

"Can't I start shooting now?" Lucas asked, resting back against the concrete blocks, his stance nearly mirroring Boondock's.

"No," Bear said shortly, fully understanding Luke's need to get things moving. Bear was stalling because of Nessa, and he knew it. "Jasper? I bet it chaps your ass that Nessa is in charge. That pretty little thing gives you orders, and you have to take them."

Jasper's lips curled into a sneer that did nothing to take away from his handsomeness. "Oh, I don't know. There are orders from her that I've *loved* taking."

The intentional goad served to settle Bear into pure calmness. "You've never touched her, and we both know it. Does that hurt? That she'd choose a grizzly bear over you? An animal from a foreign land who can't throw fire. A beast several rungs below witches. Maybe she likes it rough, man."

Fire formed on Jasper's arms again, and he whiffed it out. "It won't last. She'll leave your ass before the month ends."

"There is that virus that negates mating bonds," Boondock said helpfully. "We can have her free of you in no time, *animal*."

"Who are the main witch targets today?" Bear shot back, eyeing them both. Watching body language.

Boondock finally showed emotion, heat flashing in his eyes. "Let us out of these cells so we can find out. It's our people under attack, and you have us contained. We need to get to work."

Jasper moved toward the bars again. "Maybe he doesn't *want* us to work. If the witch nation goes down, he can keep Nessa here all for himself. Maybe he's helping whoever wants to take us down. Witches and shifters have never mixed. Ever."

All right. They were getting nowhere. Bear's money was on Jasper. "Lucas? Unlock Jasper's cell."

The witch's eyes lit with anticipation. "You coming in, bear?"

"Yeah," he whispered, already planning to go for the jugular.

"Bear?" Logan called down the stairs. "I succeeded in finding your lieutenant. Had to go through some back channels and spend some time on the dark web, so you may need to cover me if I get caught. I've called him and have him online and will transfer to your phone. It's Duncan Vincent. Haven't found the other two guys yet."

Bear paused. If Duncan was on the ground, he could do a lot of good. Finally. He'd been trying to reach his friend for days. Figured Logan would be the one to find him. Hopefully the kid could find his other friends as well.

Bear punched a button on his phone and slapped it to his ear, moving away from the cell. "Why the fuck haven't you responded to my messages?" he snapped at one of his oldest friends and most trusted of lieutenants.

"What the fuck are you talking about?" Duncan snapped back.

Bear pinched the bridge of his nose. "Where the hell are you?"

"Still in Alaska, per your orders," Duncan snarled. "Freezing my furry ass off, in case you wondered."

"My orders?" Bear shook his head. "Are you drunk?"

Duncan barked out a laugh. "I wish. Why are you yelling at me?"

None of this was making a lick of sense. Bear tilted his head. "I've been trying to recall you for days. You can't be so far underground that you didn't know that. Why have you ignored my summons?"

Quiet ticked for the briefest of moments. "Man, you haven't called me. I've been trying to check in for days and have only received orders to lay low. There's chatter. A lot of it, and you need the facts."

Adrenaline flooded Bear's veins. A rock slammed into his gut so quickly he could barely breathe. "Duncan? Who told you to stay low?" Even as he asked the question, he already knew the answer. Turning, heat flushed down his torso as he faced Lucas, who'd pointed his laser gun at Bear's chest.

"Disengage the call," Lucas said, his eyes hard and an expression on his face that Bear had never seen before.

Bear ended the call. Everything inside him stilled. "Lucas."

"Yeah. Me." Lucas set his stance, too far away for Bear to attack without getting shot first. "I hadn't figured you'd conduct your own search for Duncan and the boys."

"Logan is the best. I figured he could backup your search." The world swirled in, rushing through Bear's head. His heartbeat pounded in his ears. "The human prospects. The kids who overdosed."

Lucas showed his teeth. "Yes."

Holy fuck. "You've been distributing Apollo through the Grizzly MC?" Bear's voice shook he was so furious. His people. Used.

Lucas lifted a broad shoulder. "You made it so easy by putting me in charge and then disappearing for three months. The distribution took a month to set up, but we've made millions since. Or I should say that I've made millions." He moved slightly to the side to take better aim.

Bear fought his body's demand to shift. The second he shimmered, Luke would shoot—not only him, but probably the men in the cells. None of this made sense. He clicked facts into order, but betrayal burned like a lit match through him and fuzzed his thoughts.

Lucas waved a hand. "Don't worry about the human prospects that dealt for me. When you kicked them out, I had them taken care of. They won't tell the DEA on me."

Bear's stomach lurched. "You had those kids killed?"

Lucas shrugged. "Why do you think the DEA hasn't been back? They can't find any witnesses."

Shit. Bear would have to deal with that guilt later. "Wait a minute." His head lifted. The hair on his nape rose. "You're the manufacturer of Apollo, too." It had to be somebody local with good connections. And a lot of money. Bear had made plenty of money for Lucas through the decades.

"Bingo," Lucas snarled. "We have a winner."

"Jesus Christ, why?" Bear snapped. "Why, Lucas?"

Lucas sighed. "You are so obtuse. They killed my parents. Left me an orphan, alone in this psychotic world."

Bear frowned. "Witches killed your parents?"

"Yeah. The Coven Nine convicted my parents of smuggling, and the sentence was death," Lucas said, his pupils contracting.

"What were they smuggling?" Bear hissed.

Boondock cleared his throat. "About a century ago?"

"Yes," Bear snapped.

"Young female witches." Boondock finally approached the bars. "I was still with the Guard, and I worked the case. They were kidnappers and slavers, not smugglers." He studied Lucas. "At the turn of the century, a group of truly evil people kidnapped female witch children to force them into servitude. Not only servitude, but sexual slavery. The kidnappers had a small but well-funded group of monsters they served."

Bear stumbled back. "What?"

Boondock nodded. "Aye. The Guard hunted them down, and the Coven Nine declared a sentence. I didn't know that any of the criminals had offspring."

"Or I'd be dead, too," Lucas muttered.

"Possibly," Boondock agreed. "At the very least, we would've watched you."

That would've been nice. Bear shook his head. "You've been planning this for decades. The entire time we've been friends."

"I almost brought you in," Lucas said, smiling. "But then you mated her. One of them. Of course, I can relate. I may have had a dalliance with a witch, too."

"Grace Sadler," Bear said slowly.

"Yes. I tracked her down, and she was more than happy to help me take down the Coven Nine. And she's been a good fuck. At least for a while. Until her sons both died during this campaign and she realized the scope of change I had planned."

Bile rose in Bear's throat, and he swallowed it down. "You tried to kill me, too."

"Yes. I moved up my timeline, and you had to go."

Bear coughed, his breath on fire. "Last night at the wolf bar. I was supposed to die."

"Yes," Lucas snapped, his face turning an ugly red. "Then that demon kid woke up and rammed the building with a truck. I had to nearly break my own head to look like I was attacked."

Rage clawed through Bear, and fur emerged on his arms. He made it recede. "Before that, you hired those wolves. You sent forces here to attack your own people."

"Oh, yeah. That witch you mated is going to die, and painfully." Lucas growled. "Along with half of the witch nation. The plan is already in motion."

Bear ducked his head, fury consuming him.

"Too late." Lucas fired three shots into Bear's neck and then aimed up. Pain exploded in Bear's head as he partially turned, taking the last bullet to the temple.

He was out cold before he hit the ground.

Chapter 32

Nessa finished adding the last red dot to the world board. "We have all Alpha Level witch members identified by location, and lockdowns are commencing." She looked at Simone. "Including you."

"Aye," Simone said, reading her screen. "I'm locked down. No need to keep me from working the campaign."

"Agreed," Nessa said, scouting the board. "The demons are moving in lower Africa?"

Nick turned to check out the screen. "Affirmative. We have seven details and will have protection in place . . . five minutes, tops."

"Thank you," Nessa said, turning toward Garrett. "You in touch with the king on the update I requested for area seven?"

"Yes. Your people are safe in Australia, and our soldiers are widening a net to find the attackers. We'll get them," Garrett said, reading a printout.

Nessa turned back to the screen. She had the entire world covered with protection and tracking forces. So much for retiring today.

Lucas loped through the secret door. "Nessa? Do you have a minute?"

She looked at him. Concern covered his face. "Is Bear all right?"

"No." Lucas looked around the room and then toward the rec room. "I just need a second."

"Go," Simone said. "We're on standby at the moment."

Nessa nodded, her temples thrumming. God, she hoped Bear wasn't hurting Jasper or Boondock. She had to believe he had good instincts and would think twice. She shut the door to keep their conversation private and followed Lucas into the rec room. "What's happening downstairs?"

Lucas turned, a stun gun in his hand. He jumped and pressed it to her neck before she could scream. Electric jolts, much higher voltage than from a human stun gun, burned through her body. The pain was excruciating. She convulsed, her legs giving way. Lucas caught her and lifted her over his shoulder.

Her hair swung down.

She couldn't move. Saliva dribbled from her mouth.

Think, damn it. There was no way he could get her out of the building. Too many guards and sharpshooters awaited outside. He turned and ran toward the dartboards. Leaning down, he smashed her head on the wood floor. "Oops," he muttered.

Pain bloomed in her skull.

Lucas rearranged loose floorboards, and the floor opened up to a long staircase. "I made a few adjustments when Bear was in Ireland for a while." Lucas stood and bounded down the stairs, jostling her until her ribs protested. The trapdoor shut quietly above them.

Dirt and earth pressed in.

Nessa opened her eyes to see a narrow dirt trail beneath Lucas's feet. She tried to struggle, but her limbs were still numb. They were under the clubhouse. Bear didn't know about the tunnel. Tears filled her eyes. Where was he?

She passed out a couple of times during the long walk, awakening briefly, confused each time. Then she'd remember, and her stomach would clench.

Finally, Lucas climbed stairs, and light flooded them. Nessa blinked her eyes against the pain and then had to shut them to keep from throwing up. Taking several deep breaths, she reopened them. She had to get away from him. The world tilted, and she found herself on the floor in what looked like a secret war room. Lucas quickly secured shackles around her wrists.

She shook her head to concentrate. A blond woman sat across from her, a collar around her throat attached to a long chain that reached outside of the room. "Grace Sadler?" Nessa croaked.

The woman nodded. Her hair was messy, her blue eyes clouded, and her neck bruised. In fact, a blue stripe marred her neck. "Aye."

Lucas moved to her and smoothed back her hair.

She tried to toss her head, but he held tight.

He sighed. "Grace and I were on the same page for so long, and then she had second thoughts." He pointed to a large screen at the end of the room that displayed green dots across the entire world. "But I'm still allowing her to watch the witch nation end."

"Let me free," Grace whispered, her voice hoarse.

"Is that a planekite collar?" Nessa asked, trying not to vomit.

Grace nodded, her eyes shooting sparks.

The poison would contain Grace's fire. And it would make her way too weak to escape.

Lucas chuckled and petted Grace's hair. "Sweet Grace was in on the plan to dismantle the Coven Nine Council. The death of the whole nation by the use of Apollo is my own pet project."

Grace snarled. "I fucking hate you more than them, now."

Lucas pulled her hair. Hard.

"It'll be okay," Nessa whispered. "Just hold on." Though the woman had more than likely committed treason, she'd obviously paid a high price already. Nessa looked around. Lucas had modeled his war room after Bear's, right down to the big screen.

Lucas released his hold on Grace and moved to a computer, punching up numbers. "I've amassed forces everywhere to take out witches. Apollo darts for everyone," he said. "It'll be a crippling blow to your nation." He turned and smiled, his expression cold and somehow blank. "My researchers are almost ready for the second attack. I'm thinking it'll take place next week."

Grace struggled against her bonds.

Nessa's body and mind flared wide awake—finally. "What is the second attack?"

Lucas looked at the world board again. "Crop dusting."

Nessa swallowed, her stomach lurching. "Excuse me?"

"We've figured out how to disperse Apollo via airplane over a wide range, and we'll hit Dublin next week. The entire city." His eyes gleamed. "It'll be like ridding a crop of bugs."

Nessa fought against the iron bands around her wrists, panic nearly choking her. "That's crazy. You'll kill both humans and witches."

He shrugged. "Dublin will be a ghost town by the end of the month." His chin firmed. "Then we'll systematically attack witches one-on-one in a ground offensive until not one of them is left standing." He looked at Grace. "Except maybe you. I might let you live." His smile returned as he focused on Nessa. "Not you, though. I've had hit squads trying to take you out ever since you arrived in town. Apparently, I have to do it myself. I'm going to kill the Guard Commissioner on live television. Tomorrow, after the first strike is over."

Grace gasped, and her eyes narrowed. "You're the commissioner?" That was definitely hate in the woman's eyes.

"Aye," Nessa said, testing the shackles. The chain held firm to the wall. She turned and looked for an exit besides the one that led underground.

Lucas followed her gaze. "Waiting for a bear to save you? How disappointing for the Commissioner of the Guard, needing a man to rescue her."

Nessa turned on him so quickly her hair flew out. "I'm absolutely fine with a fellow soldier saving my ass, you degenerate idiot. It comes with the damn job. I have no problem, whatsoever, with being nicely rescued." She huffed out air. "Part of my job is to send in rescue to help the most dangerous people on this planet." She sucked in air. "And I'm fully on board, I mean *fully on board,* with my mate coming to my rescue and ripping off your fucking head." She was yelling by the time she finished the sentence.

Grace gurgled. "You're a worthless bitch, and the Guard is an evil organization. But I would like to see you kill Lucas here. With great pain." She leaned her head back and shut her eyes. "Also, rescue would be nice."

Lucas kicked Nessa in the shin. Hard.

She winced and drew her throbbing leg up. "You are such a dick." Man, Bear had to be going nuts. Wait a minute. Her eyes widened.

"Yes," Lucas said, satisfaction lowering his voice to something way too smooth. "I shot Bear four times in the head. Even if he doesn't die, let's be honest. It'll take months for him to recuperate."

"In the head?" Nessa breathed out, her shoulders tightening.

Lucas nodded, his eyes gleaming. "Last shot was dead center through the brain. If the shot was just right, you know it could kill a shifter. But the shot would have to be perfectly aimed." He cracked his knuckles and bounced back on his heels. "Did Bear ever tell you what an expert marksman I am?"

Nessa jerked against the chains. Bear was alone beneath his war room. Jasper and Boondock were probably locked in cells and couldn't help. How long would it take for anybody to check on them? Oh God. She loved him. Everything inside her loved her predatory and sweet bear, and she'd never told him. She hadn't had the courage or taken the time to say the words to him.

Was Bear dead?

His face was cold. Pain owned his head, but Bear forced his eyes open. Voices came from far away.

"Wake the hell up, asshole," snapped an angry voice. Bear's head slid on something wet, but he turned it to see Boondock kneeling on the other side of iron bars. "Let us out. Now."

The metallic smell of blood awoke the beast inside him. Bear growled, his head feeling like it weighed three tons. He blinked and liquid squished into his eye. Blood. That was his blood. "Shouldn't I be dead?"

He flattened his hand on the wet concrete and tried to shove himself to a seated position. The world spun.

"Holy fuck." He moved to the bars and hauled himself up hand over hand until he stood, panting. "Nessa." He had to get to his mate. Bile burned his throat and he swallowed, tasting blood.

"You've been shot in the neck and temple," Boondock said, his voice echoing oddly. "Open the bars, Bear. Just one. You can do it."

Bear stretched his arm up above where the bars ended, near the ceiling, and fumbled with a large button, his bloody fingers sliding off. He made a fist and punched it.

The bars snicked open in both cells.

Jasper leaped out, already running for the stairs. "I'll find Nessa."

Boondock caught Bear as he started to fall, dropping to his knees with Bear's head in his hands. One hand covered Bear's throat and the other his temple. "Shut your eyes," Boondock ordered.

Bear's eyelids shut automatically. He had to get to Nessa. Where was she? Had Lucas gotten to her? Bear struggled, trying to control his body.

"Hold on," Boondock ordered. "Jasper will return with intel. She might be just fine in the war room. Lucas might've made a run for it."

A healing balm glided over Bear's brain, and he groaned out loud. His skull snapped back into place, and his brain started functioning again. The balm was heavier than Nessa's had been, somehow a little thicker and not as nuanced. He could actually feel it slide through the side of his brain, healing neurons.

"You're damn lucky you turned your head," Boondock muttered, his hand starting to shake. "The bullet cut through your skull and impacted your brain, but you protected the frontal lobe." He breathed out heavily. "Well."

"What?" Bear growled.

"Your skull. It's stronger than any I've ever felt. The bullet should've killed you, actually," Boondock murmured. "Lucas underestimated the dragon power in your genetics."

Bear shuddered from the pain. "I've always had a hard head."

"Aye. That's not a surprise, actually. You'll be fine. Well, as smart as you were to start with, anyway."

Bear gurgled, and blood spurted from his neck. He clamped a hand over his jugular, trying to stem the tide.

The pain receded in his head, leaving behind a dull ache.

Boondock reached for Bear's neck. "I don't have much left. Let's see what we can do here."

Bear looked up at the uncle Nessa loved. "I'm sorry," he croaked.

Boondock rolled his eyes. "Putting family members in jail cells is a typical Tuesday afternoon for my people. Now take a deep breath. This is gonna hurt."

Bear held his breath, and pain stitched through his trachea. He gasped and held on.

The balm was soothing but disappeared too quickly. Boondock drew in air and pressed harder. A balm teased and then disappeared.

Boondock sat back. "That's all I've got. Healing a brain takes everything, even a shifter brain, and I'll need an hour to recharge." He gently set Bear's head on the bloody concrete. "I'll go check on Nessa and be right back."

"No," Bear breathed, wrapping his hand around the front of his neck as tightly as he could to stem the blood. Pain shot up into his skull and down toward his chest, and he tried to ignore it. He shoved to his feet.

"Jesus," Boondock muttered, sliding a shoulder beneath Bear's arm. "I'll help you up the stairs."

Bear's throat felt like blades had cut through it repeatedly. Each step was a painful move as he tried to force healing cells to his neck.

They just kept sputtering in place. He wove back and forth but made it up the stairs and into the war room with Boondock's help. Nessa wasn't there.

Jasper ran back into the war room, his gaze panicked. "The guards are all in place, and nobody saw her leave. We're running through all of the security footage now."

Simone brought up the satellite view that showed the grounds around headquarters. "The storm is getting bad. I can't see much."

Boondock pushed Bear against the wall and dropped to his butt, his head on his knees. "I need a minute," he gasped.

Healing brains had to be tough. Bear looked around, trying to focus. Blood seeped between his fingers.

Garrett and Logan caught sight of him, jumping toward him in unison from opposite directions. Garrett's fangs slashed his own wrist, and he shoved it against Bear's mouth. "Vampire blood."

Bear drank deep, and the liquid burned harshly down his throat. Tingles exploded throughout his body, and he swayed again.

Logan shoved Garrett away and offered his own wrist. Bear took demon blood, its thickness nearly choking him. Then he shook his head, and the kids backed up.

He felt his neck stitching from within, and he bit back a growl at the incredible pain. The blood flow stopped. His skull finished repairing itself. He swallowed several times. "Thanks." The boys were damn handy to have around.

Nick Veis looked up from his computer. "I have satellite imagery for the last year downloading now. If the guards or snipers didn't see her leave, he took her under. Somehow. There's a hidden tunnel from here. We just have to find it." His gaze narrowed on Bear. "Do you need more blood? I'm game."

"No," Bear said, straightening to his full height. How was he ever going to repay these people? He'd just been saved by a witch, a demon, and a vampire. "Nick and Simone? Please find the tunnel." He turned toward the storage room and rec area. "Boys? Let's tear this place apart."

He jogged out and started punching holes in the floor, thinking about the warning he'd given Nessa about ruling with her heart, about watching her back and not trusting the people closest to her. He'd been right—just not about *her* allies.

Not once had he suspected Lucas.

What was Lucas doing to Nessa at this very minute? The shifter hated witches. Bear tried to banish the horrific thoughts, but he couldn't get her pretty face out of his mind. He'd failed to protect her again. And not once, *not once*, had he told her his feelings. The little witch owned him, and he loved her. Hell. Love wasn't a strong enough word for what he felt.

He hadn't told her. She should know. She should understand he'd be coming for her. Oh, his friend was going to die. He'd known Lucas for decades. Maybe not as well as he'd thought, but he'd known him.

The boys kicked the floor to shit around him. Bear stood and surveyed the area, running through the topography of his land. He eyed the dartboards. "Over there." He ran past broken boards and knelt, punching the floor. His hand hit concrete, and pain rippled up his arm.

He punched again and again along the wall. Finally, his hand went through into air. "Found it." Standing, he jumped as hard as he could, breaking through the trapdoor and landing on steps.

"Call for backup," he ordered the boys, turning and running down.

Chapter 33

Nessa tried to escape the cuffs, but they were well constructed. Across from her, Grace watched her carefully.

They'd have to work together to get out of this.

Lucas paced back and forth, muttering to himself. His phone rang, and he lifted it to listen. His face twisted. "Are you fucking kidding me? Where? How about Alaska? Damn it, find out." He slammed the phone down on the table.

"Campaign not going quite as expected?" Nessa drawled, hiding the terror trying to rip its way out of her chest.

"No." Lucas turned and stared at her, spittle flying from his mouth. "I can at least kill one witch to calm myself." He reached beside a keyboard and lifted a long-bladed hunting knife. The sharp edge shone in the light from the screens.

Nessa watched the glimmer, her gaze caught. Her limbs weakened. She lifted her gaze to Lucas's face, forcing her expression to show no fear. "That all you got?"

He jerked his head and huffed air, smiling. "Think I could take off your head with one swipe?"

With that blade? Definitely. "What? No foreplay?" Nessa drawled.

Grace fought against her shackles. "Be a man, asshole. At least give us a chance to fight."

Lucas licked his lips and stared at Nessa. "I've wanted to do this since the first time Bear looked at you instead of me for an answer." He crouched and pressed the flat steel of the blade against her jugular. "My best friend with a witch."

The lunatic was jealous of her relationship with Bear? "You've been lying to him for decades," she whispered, trying not to move her throat too much.

"But still. We both hated witches." Lucas watched the blade as he rubbed the knife against her skin.

"Bear never hated witches." Nessa kept perfectly still. "He's grumpy and likes to be left alone, but he's not a hater. Not like you."

Lucas nodded almost sadly. "I wish I didn't know that," he mumbled. "I disliked killing my best friend."

Chills clacked through Nessa. Bear couldn't be dead. He just couldn't be. "There's still time to stop this madness. Your plan isn't going to work. Each of your hired attack squads is being tracked right now, and they'll be stopped. My people are secure."

"You're not." Lucas dropped forward on his knees and lifted his knife high above his head.

All time stopped. Nessa took a breath, pulled her knees in, and kicked Lucas in the balls. He doubled over with a harsh groan, and she clapped his head between her knees, squeezing hard. He slashed at her, his knife hitting the floor and scraping. She opened her knees and smashed them shut again, nailing his temples.

He howled and shoved away, scrambling backward. "You bitch." He moved closer, and Grace kicked up between his legs while screaming.

He dropped to his knees, shrieking.

Grace angled toward him, kicking furiously. Nessa came from the other side, kicking him solidly in the temple.

Jumping up, he lunged, knife aimed for Nessa's throat.

The entire floor exploded.

Bear leaped through, catching Lucas around the waist before he could reach Nessa. They pummeled each other into the far wall, sending computer monitors crashing down.

Nessa ducked as ceiling tiles started dropping.

Bear and Lucas exchanged blows hard enough to topple trees. They struck and grappled, kicked and pounded. A long cut was visible along Bear's temple and skull, while his neck was a bloody mess.

Lucas punched Bear in the throat, and Bear stumbled back. He roared and leaped for his former friend, throwing them both over the table to crash on the other side.

Garrett and Logan rushed from the hidden staircase and headed for Nessa. Garrett bent and used both hands on a wrist shackle. "Logan," he muttered. Logan hustled over and grabbed the same iron band. "Now," Garrett said. The boys pulled in opposite directions, and the iron released.

Bear looked her way, his gaze running over the bruises on her face. Then he turned and lifted Lucas up and beat him against the screen of the world. The screen shattered with a deafening clash, and pieces of it rained down. Lucas dropped but reared up again, his knife shining.

"Bear," Nessa screamed, trying to move.

Garrett stopped her, he and Logan grabbing her other shackle.

The knife pierced the side of Bear's neck. He howled in pain, the sound furious.

The other shackle gave.

Nessa jumped up, and the boys both pivoted at the same time, putting her behind them. Damn it. She struggled to get between them, but they held fast. "Let me past," she hissed. "I'm the commissioner."

"Exactly," Garrett said grimly. "We'd cover the king the same way."

Fine. He had a point. She peered around Logan's body.

Bear yanked the knife out of his neck, his eyes blazing, his chin down. He threw the weapon across the room, and it struck the far wall with a loud twang.

Lucas gasped for air, his chest panting. "You mated a fucking witch. How could you?"

Bear's nostrils flared. Blood poured from beneath his jaw, and he sucked in air. The blood flow ebbed. "You lied to me and created a poison to kill people. Witches and humans."

Lucas reached behind his back and brought out another blade. "They all deserve to die."

Hurt and fury mingled in Bear's eyes. "You set me up to be killed."

"I didn't want to," Lucas said, one leg sliding back. He spit blood onto the floor. "You gave me no choice."

"I understand no choice," Bear said, also taking a fighting stance.

Nessa couldn't move. She could barely breathe. Even Grace was motionless on the floor, watching the battle.

Lucas tilted his torso, obviously preparing to strike.

Bear settled himself. "You've done a lot of wrong, Luke."

"Yeah? So what? I'm just getting started."

"But you're going to die for one reason and one reason only," Bear continued, as if Lucas hadn't spoken. "You harmed my mate."

Lucas bellowed a battle cry and struck. Bear turned at the last moment, his hand sweeping out and morphing—the paw and claws of a bear slashing through Lucas's neck. Following him down, Bear punched his claws through to the floor, and Lucas's head rolled under the table.

Bear's arm and hand returned to normal.

"Whoa," Garrett whispered to Logan. "Did you know he could do that?"

"Fuck, no," Logan said, moving to the side.

Nessa leaped for her mate.

He caught her, holding tight, pushing back her hair. "Are you okay?" he asked, his tone guttural.

"Yes," she said, gingerly touching the still-red wounds on his neck. "Are you?"

"I am now." He leaned down and gently placed a kiss on her mouth. "I love you, Nessa. Should've said so earlier."

Her heart filled along with her eyes. "I love you, too." She kissed him back, her body singing. Alive—they were both somehow alive.

The shouts of soldiers running closer brought her out of her momentary dream. Her arms felt just right wrapped around his neck. "I guess we have some work to do."

He held her tighter. "Yeah. I guess we do."

Bear watched his mate as she addressed her nation from his war room, the camera in front of her and the map of the world behind her. Her hair was up, her shoulders straight, and her face still bruised. But she stood in her Guard uniform, the buttons polished, her medals impressive.

"In conclusion, the combined forces protected all witch targets this evening and have taken multiple enemies into custody." Intelligence and determination filled her violet-blue eyes. "It has been my sincere honor to serve as your commissioner these last few decades, and I shall look forward to seeing what your next commissioner will accomplish," she said.

Simone slipped into camera range.

Nessa leaned down and signed a piece of paper. "I hereby resign from my position of Guard Commissioner," she said, standing straight again.

Simone took the paper and shook Nessa's hand. "On behalf of the Council of the Coven Nine, your resignation is accepted. Thank you from a very grateful nation." Simone's lips trembled, and she cleared her throat. "You have served with honor and great bravery."

Nessa smiled. "Thank you."

They looked at the camera. The light on top flickered from green to red. They both visibly relaxed.

"Well," Simone said. "I could use a bloody vacation."

Nessa chuckled, her gaze seeking Bear's over the camera. "Me, too."

Something dinged, and their attention swung to one of the screens. Simone waved and then moved out of range, walking by Bear and patting his arm. Her mate was waiting at the doorway, more than a little insistent that she now get some rest.

Nessa smiled. "King Kayrs. What a nice surprise."

Bear lifted his eyebrows but couldn't see the screen from his vantage point.

"Nessa, that was a lovely speech," Dage said, his voice clear.

Nessa frowned. "How did you—"

"I'm the king." Dage sighed heavily. "Have you made a decision about my job offer?"

Bear straightened away from the wall. Job offer? Weren't couples supposed to talk about that kind of stuff? He'd said he loved her, for Pete's sake.

Nessa nodded. "I have, and I'm honored, I really am. But I must decline."

Bear lifted an eyebrow.

She held her hand beneath camera range with a finger out. Fine. He could give her one minute.

Dage very loudly cleared his throat. "Nessa, you're crazy. This job is tailor-made for you, coordinating among all nations for the

Realm. I'll give you ten million a year plus bonuses. You'd write your own ticket with the job."

Bear frowned. Why the hell was she turning that down? Even from Dage's brief description, it seemed perfect for her.

Nessa sighed. "Thanks, but relocating is a deal breaker."

"Living in Idaho is nice, and you'd only be one state away from your mate," Dage said tersely.

Nessa's gaze met Bear's over the camera, and then she focused back on Dage. "That's too far. Sorry. No deal."

"Fifteen million dollars, multiple bonuses, and you draft policy. Your agenda," Dage countered.

"No." Nessa didn't even pause.

Dage was silent for a moment. "You're telling me that you're choosing Beauregard McDunphy, the most introverted shifter ever born, over the opportunity of a lifetime?"

She looked up at Bear again, her eyes clear, love in them. Yep. That was love. "Aye, King. I choose Bear."

The words nearly floored Bear. His legs wobbled. Nobody in his entire life had chosen him first. Never. He started to shake his head, to tell her to take the job. He could move to Idaho. What was the big deal? Man, he'd hate living with the Realm top brass. But for Nessa, he'd do it. He stepped forward—

"Oh, all right," Dage said. "You can live there and do the job."

Nessa breathed out sharply. Her face lit. "Are you serious?"

"Sure," Dage said.

"King," Nessa said, shaking her head, her eyes twinkling.

The interfering sonuvabitch. Bear couldn't help but smile, even though he tried really hard to keep his frown in place. Nope. He was smiling. Damn it.

Dage continued, "You're good at negotiating, Nessa. So you'll take the deal? The one caveat is that I want you here once a month for a day of meetings. It's only a five-hour drive or a thirty-minute plane ride from there."

Nessa clasped her hands together. "Twenty million a year, the right to create policy, and a plane. I'd like a plane."

Dage was quiet for two seconds. "Are you kidding?"

"No." She waited.

In that moment, Bear couldn't have been prouder. His witch was a badass negotiator.

"Deal," Dage said. The light on the panel blinked off.

Nessa looked up at Bear.

Yeah. That was definitely love in her eyes.

Chapter 34

Nessa stepped out of the river house in jeans and a sweater, her boots flat and her hands covered with gloves. Hanging up her uniform had filled her with nostalgia, but she couldn't just go around wearing it all day.

Snow drifted down again—soft and pretty. Shifters worked furiously around her, repairing the house and making it secure.

She looked across the deck to see her cranky bear barking orders left and right. Should bears bark? Humor bubbled through her, and she made her way toward him.

He lifted his head, sniffed, and then turned her way. "Go," he said to the three men he was ordering around. They moved off quickly, obviously not even thinking of hesitating or asking any questions. Relief trailed in their wake.

She smiled and reached him, running a finger along the barely closed gash in his head. "The brain wasn't the right place to attack you."

His lip quirked. In one smooth motion, he grasped her clip and tugged it free. Her hair fell around her shoulders. "That's better," he said, tangling his fingers in the mass.

She swatted him. Fire flew from her fingertips.

He yelped and patted out his wrist. "What the hell?"

She gasped, delight rushing through her. "I made fire. Bear. I made fire."

He frowned. "Wonderful."

She laughed out loud and tried again. Nothing. "I guess it'll take practice."

He looked gingerly at the burn mark on his wrist. "I feel like you should be sleeping."

"Not without you." She snuggled into him, secure in his strength. "If I stay and take that job, we'll have witches, vampires, and demons around. A lot." Aye, she probably should've discussed the job with him first.

"I've already been overrun by witches." He took her hand and led her into the trees. "There's a billion of them at Lucas's secret hideaway going through all the data there. They've found warehouses of Apollo, the distribution line, and even the hired guns all over the world. Soon, the entire operation will be a thing of the past."

She stepped carefully over a bunch of snowy branches on the ground. "That's wonderful. We should come up with a plan to hand over evidence to the DEA so they stop freezing your accounts. Something that doesn't lead back to us."

He sighed. "Sounds like subterfuge."

"It does, doesn't it?" she asked happily, already planning. By the time she was finished, the DEA would think the Grizzly MC was squeaky clean, and Bear would have his money back. Then she'd decorate his cabin for him. "Is Grace Sadler still in the cabin?"

"No. Several Guard soldiers took her to the hospital in Vancouver," Bear said, his gaze darkening. "What will happen to her after that?"

Nessa thought it out. "She'll be tried for treason."

They reached the frozen bank. The water rushed by ten feet below them. Bear looked down at her. "I'm surprised you're not in the thick of things right now, dismantling Lucas's war room."

Oh. Aye. "Jasper and my uncle can direct the job."

Bear lifted his eyebrows. "Will one of them be named commissioner?"

She tried not to smile. "Can't tell you. However, I do think that my uncle plans to stick around here for a while. Help secure the area." In fact, he was angling for a job with Dage, and that meant Nessa would get to work with her uncle again. She gave a happy hop. Jasper would make an excellent commissioner, and of course she'd be able to stay in touch with him via her new job.

"I sure hope your uncle doesn't have to leave," Bear said, trying too hard to make the words sound like truth.

The poor guy really couldn't lie. Not at all. Aye, she loved him for that. She turned and slid her hands up Bear's very nice chest. "Are you letting Garrett and Logan stick around?"

Bear sighed. "Yes. They want to stay, and I kind of owe them for saving my life. So they stay."

"That's sweet," she murmured, her heart feeling so full she barely recognized the feeling. "I'm thinking I can put them to work for me. They both have excellent connections, and I trust them. Of course, the jobs don't start until next week."

"I know," Bear said softly, brushing snow off her cheek. His honey-brown eyes mellowed. "I've been negotiating with Dage the last hour. He would like to build a command center for you that's separate from mine, considering mine is just for the shifter nations. He wants to put it next to one of the garages."

That made sense. "You said no?"

Bear grinned. "I said yes, but I'm charging him an arm and a leg for leasing the land."

Nessa threw back her head and laughed. "I like that."

A helicopter hovered above and then set down in a clearing next to the river house. "Who's here now?" she wondered.

"Who the hell knows?" Bear's exhale was heated.

The door opened, and three of the Enforcers jumped out. "Kellach, Daire, and Adam Dunne," Nessa said, her eyes widening. The brothers scouted the area and then assisted their mates out. The three women looked around, moving quickly toward the house upon seeing Simone at the door. The greetings were boisterous and full of love.

"They're probably here to finish with the intel," Bear said, his voice a low rumble.

"They're here to celebrate," Nessa said quietly. "I'm sure Moira Kayrs, the remaining Enforcer, will be here soon, too."

Bear groaned. "The Kayrs family are like rabbits. When one shows up, they all show up." He shook his head. "Why me?"

"Because I love you." She looked up and gave him everything she had.

He lost the frown, his gaze softening. "I love you more." Ducking beneath a branch and tugging her along, he grasped her hand again. "I just received a communication from my brother. Flynn and a couple of his buddies should be arriving within the hour."

Nessa's eyes widened. "Dragons are coming to Seattle?"

"The mere fact that your sentence makes sense shows how completely out of control our life has become," he sighed. "The answer to your question is yes. The dragons will land soon. For now, come on," he whispered.

She followed him, fighting a chuckle. "Where?"

He led her down a barely there trail toward the river, turning at the last second into an alcove that faced the rushing mass. A hand-carved stone bench sat inside, protected from any storm by natural rocks showing the minerals of the area. "Bear," she breathed.

He sat and tugged her onto his lap. "This is our secret place. *Only* ours. Got it?"

"Aye," she said, enchanted. "Just ours."

"Let's sit here a moment before we go back." He held her close, his lips wandering across her forehead. "I love you, Nessa. We're gonna have a good life."

She tilted her head and nuzzled beneath his hard jaw. Though she hadn't figured out how to throw fire as of yet, she would. For now, her crazy scheme of mating the big bad bear had worked. Who knew she'd end up happier than she could've ever imagined? "I love you too, Bear."

Her bear.

If you've enjoyed Rebecca Zanetti's REALM ENFORCERS,
read on for an excerpt from the first book in
Rebecca Zanetti's blazing hot romantic suspense series,
THE REQUISTION FORCE,

Hidden

*Hot alpha males band together
in a secret government agency
to combat threats to American security.*

The day he moved in next door, dark clouds covered the sky with
the promise of a powerful storm. Pippa watched from her window,
the one over the kitchen sink, partially hidden by the cheerful polka
dotted curtains. Yellow dots over a crisp white background—what
she figured happy people would use.

He moved box after box after box through the two stall garage,
all by himself, cut muscles bunching in his arms.

Angles and shadows made up his face, more shadows than angles.
He didn't smile, and although he didn't frown, his expression had
settled into harsh lines.

A guy like him, dangerously handsome, should probably have
friends helping.

Yet he didn't. His black truck, dusty yet seemingly well kept, sat
alone in the driveway containing the boxes.

She swallowed several times, instinctively knowing he wasn't a man
to cross, even if she was a person who crossed others. She was not.

For a while she tried to amuse herself with counting the boxes,
and then guessing their weight, and then just studying the man. He
appeared to be in his early thirties, maybe just a couple of years older
than she.

Thick black hair fell to his collar in unruly waves, giving him an
unkempt appearance that hinted nobody took care of him. His shoulders were tense and his body language fluid. She couldn't see his
eyes.

The damn wondering would keep her up at night.

But no way, and there was absolutely no way, would she venture
outside to appease the beast of curiosity.

The new neighbor stood well over six feet tall, his shoulders broad, his long legs encased in worn and frayed jeans. If a man could be hard all over, head to toe, even in movement, then he was.

He was very much alone as well.

A scar curved in a half-moon shape over his left eye, and some sort of tattoo, a crest of something, decorated his muscled left bicep. She tilted her head, reaching for the curtains to push them aside just a little more.

He paused, an overlarge box held easily in his arms, and turned his head, much like an animal rising to attention.

Green. Those eyes, narrow and suspicious, alert and dangerous, focused directly on her.

She gasped. Her heart thundered. She fell to the floor below the counter. Not to the side, not even in a crouch, she fell flat on her ass on the worn tile floor. Her heart ticking, she wrapped her arms around her shins and rested her chin on her knees.

She bit her lip and held her breath, shutting her eyes.

Nothing.

No sound, no hint of an approaching person, no rap on the door.

After about ten minutes of holding perfectly still, she lifted her head. Another five and she released her legs. Then she rolled up onto her knees and reached for the counter, her fingers curling over.

Taking a deep breath, she pulled herself up to stand, angling to the side of the counter.

He stood at the window, facing her, his chest taking up most of the panes.

Her heart exploded. She screamed, turned, and ran. She cleared the kitchen in three steps and plowed through the living room, smashing into an antique table that had sat in the place for more than two decades.

Pain ratcheted up her leg, and she dropped, making panicked grunting noises as she crawled past the sofa and toward her bedroom. Her hands slapped the polished wooden floor, and she sobbed out, reaching the room and slamming the door.

She scrabbled her legs up to her chest again, her back to the door, and reached up to engage the lock. She rocked back and forth just enough to not make a sound.

The doorbell rang.

Her chest tightened, and her vision fuzzed. Tremors started from her shoulders down to her waist and back up. *Not now. Not now. God, not now.* She took several deep breaths and acknowledged the oncoming panic attack much as Dr. Valentine had taught her. Sometimes letting the panic in actually abated it.

Not this time.

The attack took her full force, pricking sweat along her body. Her arms shook, and her legs went numb. Her breathing panted out, her vision fuzzed, and her heart blasted into motion.

Maybe it really was a heart attack this time.

No. It was only a panic attack.

But it could be. Maybe the doctors had missed something in her tests, and it really was a heart attack. Or maybe a stroke.

She couldn't make it to the phone to dial for help.

Her heart hurt. Her chest really ached. Glancing up at the lock, a flimsy golden thing, she inched away from the door to the bed table on her hands and knees. Jerking open the drawer, she fumbled for a Xanax.

She popped the pill beneath her tongue, letting it quickly absorb. The bitter chalkiness made her gag, but she didn't move until it had dissolved.

A hard rapping sound echoed from the living room.

Shit. He was knocking on the door. Was it locked? Of course it was locked. She always kept it locked. But would a lock, even a really good one, keep a guy like that out?

Hell, no.

She'd been watching him, and he knew it. Maybe he wasn't a guy who wanted to be watched, which was why he was moving his stuff all alone. Worse yet, had he been sent to find her? He had looked so furious. Was he angry?

If so, what could she do?

The online martial arts lessons she'd taken lately ran through her head, but once again, she wondered if one could really learn self-defense by watching videos. Something told her that all the self-defense lessons in the world wouldn't help against that guy.

Oh, why had Mrs. Melonci moved to Florida? Sure, the elderly lady wanted to be closer to her grandchildren, but Cottage Grove was a much better place to live.

The house had sold in less than a week.

Pippa had hoped to watch young children play and frolic in the large treed backyard, but this guy didn't seem to have a family.

Perhaps he'd bring one in, yet there was something chillingly solitary about him.

Of course, she hadn't set foot outside her house for nearly five years, so maybe family men had changed.

Probably not, though.

He knocked again, the sound somehow stronger and more insistent this time.

She opened the bedroom door and peered around the corner. The front door was visible above the sofa.

He knocked again. "Lady?" Deep and rich, his voice easily carried into her home.

She might have squawked.

"Listen, lady. I, ah, saw you fall and just wanna make sure you're all right. You don't have to answer the door." His tone didn't rise and remained perfectly calm.

She sucked in a deep breath and tried to answer him, but only air came out. Man, she was pathetic. She tapped her head against the doorframe in a sad attempt to self-soothe.

"Um, are you okay?" he asked, hidden by the big door. "I can call for help."

No. Oh, no. She swallowed several times. "I'm all right." Finally, her voice worked. "Honest. It's okay. Don't call for anybody." If she didn't let them in, the authorities would probably break down the door, right? She couldn't have that.

Silence came from the front porch, but no steps echoed. He remained in place.

Her heart continued to thunder against her ribs. She wiped her sweaty palms down her yoga pants. Why wasn't he leaving? "Okay?" she whispered.

"You sure you don't need help?" he called.

Her throat began to close. "I'm sure." *Go away.* Please, he had to go away.

"Okay." Heavy bootsteps clomped across her front porch, and then silence. He was gone.

Malcolm West knew the sound of terror, and he knew it well. The woman, whoever she was, had been beyond frightened at seeing him in the window. Damn it. What the hell had he been thinking to approach her house like that?

A fence enclosed their backyards together, and he'd wondered why. Had a family shared the two homes?

He grabbed another box of shit from the truck and hefted it toward the house. Maybe this had been a mistake. He'd purchased the little one story home sight unseen because of the white clapboard siding, the blue shutters, and the damn name of the town—Cottage Grove. It sounded peaceful.

He'd never truly see peace again, and he knew it.

All of the homes the real estate company had emailed him about had been sad and run down . . . until this one. It had been on the market only a few days, and the agent had insisted it wouldn't be for long. After six months of searching desperately for a place to call home, he'd jumped on the sale.

It had been so convenient as to have been fate.

If he believed in fate, which he did not.

He walked through the simple one story home and dropped the box in the kitchen, looking out at the pine trees beyond the wooden fence. The area had been subdivided into twenty-acre lots, with tons and tons of trees, so he'd figured he wouldn't see any other houses, which had suited him just fine.

Yet his house was next to another, and one fence enclosed their backyards together.

No other homes were even visible.

He sighed and started to turn for the living room when a sound caught his attention. His body automatically went on full alert, and he reached for the Sig nestled at his waist. Had they found him?

"Detective West? Don't shoot. I'm a friendly," came a deep male voice.

Malcolm pulled the gun free, the weight of it in his hand more familiar than his own voice. "Friendlies don't show up uninvited," he said calmly, eyeing the two main exits from the room in case he needed to run.

A guy strode toward him, hands loose at his sides. Probably in his thirties, he had bloodshot brown eyes, short brown hair, and graceful movements. His gaze showed he'd seen some shit, and there was a slight tremble in his right arm. Trying to kick a habit, was he?

Malcolm pointed the weapon at the guy's head. "Two seconds."

The man looked at the few boxes set around the room, not seeming to notice the gun. Even with the tremor, he moved like he could fight. "There's nowhere to sit."

"You're not staying." Malcolm could get to the vehicle hidden a mile away within minutes and then take off again. The pretty cottage was a useless dream, and he'd known it the second he'd signed the papers. "I'd hate to ruin the yellow wallpaper." It had flowers on it, and he'd planned to change it anyway.

"Then don't." The guy leaned against the wall and shook out his arm.

"What are you kicking?" Malcolm asked, his voice going low.

The guy winced. "I'm losing some friends."

"Jack, Jose, and Bud?" Mal guessed easily.

"Mainly Jack." Now he eyed the weapon. "Mind putting that down?"

Mal didn't flinch. "Who are you?"

Broad shoulders heaved in an exaggerated sigh. "My name is Angus Force, and I'm here to offer you an opportunity."

"Is that a fact? I don't need a new toaster." Mal slid the gun back into place. "Go away."

"Detective—"

"I'm not a detective any longer, asshole. Get out of my house." Mal could use a good fight, and he was about to give himself what he needed.

"Whoa." Force held up a hand. "Just hear me out. I'm part of a new unit with, ah, the federal government, and we need a guy with your skills."

Heat rushed up Mal's chest. His main skill these days was keeping himself from going ballistic on assholes, and he was about to fail in that. "I'm not interested, Force. Now get the fuck out of my house."

Force shook his head. "I understand you're struggling with the aftereffects of a difficult assignment, but you won. You got the bad guy."

Yeah, but how many people had died? In front of him? Mal's vision started to narrow. "You don't want to be here any longer, Force."

"You think you're the only one with PTSD, dickhead?" Force spat, losing his casual façade.

"No, but I ain't lookin' to bond over it." Sweat rolled down Mal's back. "How'd you find me, anyway?"

Force visibly settled himself. "It's not exactly a coincidence that you bought this house. The only one that came close to what you were looking for." He looked around the old-lady cheerful kitchen. "Though it is sweet."

Mal's fingers closed into a fist. "You set me up."

"Yeah, we did. We need you here." Force gestured around.

Mal's lungs compressed. "Why?"

"Because you're the best undercover cop we've ever seen, and we need that right now. Bad." Mal ran a shaking hand through his hair.

"Why?" Mal asked, already fearing the answer.

"The shut-in next door. She's the key to one of the biggest home-grown threats to our entire country. And here you are." Force's eyes gleamed with the hit.

Well, fuck.

Turn the page for a preview of the first novel
in the groundbreaking new series by Rebecca Zanetti!
Mercury Striking
Available now in paperback and e-book
from Zebra Books.

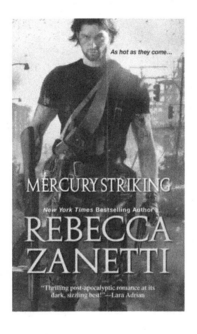

"Nothing is easy or black or white in Zanetti's grim new reality,
but hope is key, and I *hope* she writes faster!"
—*New York Times* **bestselling author Larissa Ione**

With nothing but rumors to lead her, Lynn Harmony has trekked
across a nightmare landscape to find one man—a mysterious,
damaged legend who protects the weak and leads the strong. He's
more than muscle and firepower—and in post-plague L.A., he's
her only hope. As the one woman who could cure the disease,
Lynn is the single most volatile—and vulnerable—creature in this
new and ruthless world. But face to face with Jax Mercury . . .

Danger has never looked quite so delicious . . .

Life on Earth is at the ever-increasing risk of being wiped out by a disaster, such as sudden global nuclear war, a genetically engineered virus or other dangers we have not yet thought of.—Stephen Hawking

Despair hungered in the darkness, not lingering, not languishing . . . but waiting to bite. No longer the little brother of rage, despair had taken over the night, ever present, an actor instead of an afterthought.

Lynn picked her way along the deserted twelve-lane interstate, allowing the weak light from the moon to guide her. An unnatural silence hung heavy over the empty land. Rusted carcasses of cars lined the sides, otherwise, the once vibrant 405 was dead, yet she trod carefully.

Her months of hiding had taught her stealth. Prey needed stealth, as did the hunter.

She was both.

The tennis shoes she'd stolen from an abandoned thrift store protected her feet from the cracked asphalt. A click echoed in the darkness. About time. She'd made it closer to Los Angeles, well, what used to be Los Angeles, than she'd hoped.

A strobe light hit her full on, rendering sight useless. She closed her eyes. They'd either kill her or not. Either way, no need to go blind. "I want to see Mercury."

Silence. Then several more clicks. Guns of some type.

She forced strength into her voice. "You don't want to kill me without taking me to Mercury first." Jax Mercury, to be exact. If he still existed. If not, she was screwed anyway.

"Why would we do that?" A voice from the darkness, angry and near.

She opened her eyes, allowing light to narrow her pupils. "I'm Lynn Harmony."

Gasps, low and male, echoed around her. They'd closed in silently, just as well trained as she'd heard. As she'd hoped.

"Bullshit," a voice hissed from her left.

She tilted her head toward the voice, then slowly, so slowly they wouldn't be spooked, she unbuttoned her shirt. No catcalls, no suggestive responses followed. Shrugging her shoulders, she dropped the cotton to the ground, facing the light.

She hadn't worn a bra, but she doubted the echoing exhales of shock were from her size B's. More likely the shimmering blue outline of her heart caught their attention. Yeah, she was a freak. Typhoid Mary in the body of a woman who'd made a mistake. A big one. But she might be able to save the men surrounding her. "So. Jax Mercury. Now."

One man stepped closer. Gang tattoos lined his face, inked tears showing his kills. He might have been thirty, he might have been sixty. Regardless, he was dangerous. Eyeing her chest, he quickly crossed himself. "Holy Mary, Mother of God."

"Not even close." Wearily, she reached down and grabbed her shirt, shrugging it back on. She figured the "take me to your leader" line would get her shot. "Do you want to live or not?"

He met her gaze, hope and fear twisting his scarred upper lip. "Yes."

It was the most sincere sound she'd heard in months. "We're running out of time." Time had deserted them long ago, but she needed to get a move on. "Please." The sound shocked her, the civility of it, a word she'd forgotten how to use. The slightest of hopes warmed that blue organ in her chest, reminding her of who she used to be. Who she'd lost.

Another figure stepped forward, this one big and silent. Deadly power vibrated in the shift of muscle as light illuminated him from behind, keeping his features shrouded. "I didn't tell you to put your shirt back on." No emotion, no hint of humanity echoed in the deep rumble.

The lack of emotion twittered anxiety through her abdomen. Without missing a beat, she secured each button, keeping the movements slow and sure. "I take it you're Mercury." Regardless of name, there was no doubt the guy was in charge.

"If I am?" Soft, his voice promised death.

A promise she'd make him keep. Someday. The breeze picked up, tumbling weeds across the deserted 405. She fought a shiver. Any weakness shown might get her killed. "You know who I am."

"I know who you say you are." His overwhelming form blocked out the light, reminding her of her smaller size. "Take off your shirt."

Something about the way he said it gave her pause. Before, she hadn't cared. But with him so close she could smell *male*; an awareness of her femininity brought fresh fear. Nevertheless, she unbuttoned her shirt.

This time, her hands trembled.

Straightening her spine, she squared her shoulders and left the shirt on, the worn material gaping in the front.

He waited.

She lifted her chin, trying to meet his eyes, although she couldn't see them. The men around them remained silent, yet alertness carried on the breeze. How many guns were trained on her? She wanted to tell them it would only take one. Though she'd been through hell, she'd never really learned to fight.

The wind whipped into action, lifting her long hair away from her face. Her arms tightened against her rib cage. Goose bumps rose along her skin.

Swearing softly, the man stepped in, long tapered fingers drawing her shirt apart. He shifted to the side, allowing light to blast her front. Neon blue glowed along her flesh.

"Jesus." He pressed his palm against her breastbone—directly above her heart.

Shock tightened her muscles, her eyes widening, and that heart ripping into a gallop. Her nipples pebbled from the breeze. Warmth cascaded from his hand when he spread his fingers over the odd blue of her skin. When was the last time someone had touched her gently?

And gentle, he was.

The touch had her looking down at his damaged hand. Faded white scars slashed across his knuckles, above the veins, past his wrist. The bizarre glow from her heart filtered through his long fingers. Her entire chest was aqua from within, those veins closest to her heart, which glowed neon blue, shining strong enough to be seen through her ribs and sternum.

He exhaled loudly, removing his touch.

An odd sense of loss filtered down her spine. Then surprise came as he quickly buttoned her shirt to the top.

He clasped her by the elbow. "Cut the light." His voice didn't rise, but instantly, the light was extinguished. "I'm Mercury. What do you want?"

What a question. What she wanted, nobody could provide. Yet she struggled to find the right words. Night after night, traveling under darkness to reach him, she'd planned for this moment. But the words wouldn't come. She wanted to breathe. To rest. To hide. "Help. I need your help." The truth tumbled out too fast to stop.

He stiffened and then tightened his hold on her arm. "That, darlin', you're gonna have to earn."

Jax eyed the brunette sitting in the backseat of the battered Subaru. He'd stolen the vehicle from a home in Beverly Hills after all hell had broken loose. The gardener who'd owned it no longer needed it, considering he was twelve feet under.

The luxury SUV sitting so close to the Subaru had tempted him, but the older car would last longer and use less gas, which was almost depleted, anyway. Hell, everything they had was almost depleted. From medical supplies to fuel to books to, well, hope. How the hell did he refill everybody with hope when he could barely remember the sensation?

The night raid had been a search for more gasoline from abandoned vehicles, not a search party for survivors. He'd never thought to find Lynn Harmony.

The woman had closed her eyes, her head resting against the plush leather. Soft moonlight wandered through the tinted windows to caress the sharp angles of her face. With deep green eyes and pale skin, she was much prettier than he'd expected . . . much softer. Too soft.

Though, searching him out, well now. The woman had guts.

Manny kept looking at her through the rearview mirror, and for some reason, that irritated Jax. "Watch the road."

Manny cut a glance his way. At over fifty years old, beaten and weathered, he took orders easily. "There's no one out here tonight but us."

"We hope." Jax's gut had never lied to him. Somebody was coming. If the woman had brought danger to his little place in the world, she'd pay.

Her eyes flashed open, directly meeting his gaze. The pupils contracted while her chin lifted. Devoid of expression, she just stared.

He stared back.

A light pink wandered from her chest up her face to color her high cheekbones. Fascinated, he watched the blush deepen. When was the last time he'd seen a woman blush? He certainly hadn't expected it from the woman who'd taken out most of the human race.

Around them, off-road vehicles kept pace. Some dirt bikes, a few four-wheelers, even a fancy Razor confiscated from another mansion. Tension rode the air, and some of it came from Manny.

"Say it," Jax murmured, acutely, maybe too much so, aware of the woman in the backseat.

"This is a mistake," Manny said, his hands tightening on the steering wheel. "You know who she is. What she is."

"I doubt that." He turned to glance again at the woman, his sidearm sweeping against the door. She'd turned to stare out at the night again, her shoulders hunched, her shirt hiding that odd blue glow. "Are you going to hurt me or mine?" he asked.

Slowly, she turned to meet his gaze again. "I don't know." Frowning, she leaned forward just enough to make his muscles tense in response. "How many people are yours?"

He paused, his head lifting. "All of them."

She smiled. "I'd heard that about you." Turning back to the window, she fingered the glass as if wanting to touch what was out of reach.

"Heard what?" he asked.

"Your sense of responsibility. Leadership. Absolute willingness to kill." Her tone lacked inflection, as if she just stated facts. "You are, right? Willing to kill?"

He stilled, his eyes cutting to Manny and back to the woman. "You want me to kill somebody?"

"Yes."

He kept from outwardly reacting. Not much surprised him any longer, but he hadn't been expecting a contract killing request from Lynn Harmony. "We've lost ninety-nine percent of the world's population, darlin'. Half of the survivors are useless, and the other half is just trying to survive. You'd better have a good reason for wanting someone dead."

"*Useless* isn't an accurate description," she said quietly.

"If they can't help me, if they're a hindrance, they're fucking useless." He'd turned off the switch deep down that discerned a gray area between the enemy and his people months ago, and there was no changing that. He'd become what was needed to survive and to live through desperate times. "You might want to remember that fact."

Her shoulders went back, and she rested her head, staring up at the ceiling. "I'd love to be useless."

He blinked and turned back around to the front. Her words had been soft, her tone sad, and her meaning heartbreaking. If he still had a heart. So the woman wanted to die, did she? No fucking way. The blood in her veins was more than a luxury, it might be a necessity. She didn't get to die. "Please tell me you're not the one I'm supposed to kill," he said, his heart beating faster.

Silence ticked around the dented SUV for a moment. "Not yet, no."

Great. All he needed was a depressed biological weapon in the form of a sexy brunette to mess with his already fucking fantastic daily schedule. "Lady, if you wanna eat a bullet, you should've done it before coming into my territory." Since she was there, he was making use of her, and if that meant suicide watch around the clock, he'd provide the guards to keep her breathing.

"I know." Fabric rustled, and she poked him in the neck. "When was your last injection?"

His head jerked as surprise flared his neurons to life. He grabbed her finger before turning and held tight. "Almost one month ago."

She tried to free herself and then frowned when she failed. "You're about due, then. How many vials of B do you have left?"

He tugged her closer until she was almost sitting in the front seat, his gaze near to hers. "Doesn't matter. Now I have you, don't I? If we find the cure, we won't need vitamin B." This close, under the dirt and fear, he could smell woman. Fresh and with a hint of—what was that—vanilla? No. Gardenias. Spicy and wild.

She shook her head and again tried to free herself. "You can have all the blood you want. It won't help."

"Stop the car," he said to Manny.

Manny nodded and pulled over. Jax released Lynn's finger, stepped out of the vehicle, and pressed into the backseat next to her.

Her eyes widened, and she huddled back against the other door.

He drew a hood from his back pocket. "Come here, darlin'."

"No." She scrambled away, her hands out.

With a sigh, he reached for a zip tie in his vest and way too easily secured her hands together. A second later, he pulled the hood over her head. He didn't like binding a woman, but he didn't have a choice. "In the past year, as the world has gone to hell, hasn't anybody taught you to fight?" he asked.

She kicked out, her bound hands striking for his bulletproof vest.

He lifted her onto his lap, wrapped an arm over hers and around her waist, manacling her legs with one of his. "Relax. I'm not going to hurt you, but you can't know where we're going."

"Right." She shoved back an elbow, her warm little body struggling hard.

Desire flushed through him, pounding instantly into his cock. God, she was a handful.

She paused. "Ah—"

"You're safe. Just stop wiggling." His voice was hoarse. Jesus. When was the last time he'd gotten laid? He actually couldn't remember. She was a tight little handful of energy and womanly curves, and his body reacted instantly. The more she gyrated against him, trying to fight, the more blood rushed south of his brain. He had to get her under control before he began panting like a teenager.

"No." Her voice rose, and she tried to flail around again. "You can't manhandle me like this."

If she had any clue how he'd like to handle her, she'd be screaming. He took several deep breaths and forced desire into the abyss, where it belonged. He wanted her hooded, not afraid. "If you were mine, you'd know how to fight." Where that thought came from, he'd never know.

She squirmed on his lap, fully contained. "Good thing I'm not yours, now isn't it?"

He exhaled and held her tighter until she gave up the fight and submitted against him. The light whimper of frustration echoing behind the hood sounded almost like a sigh of pleasure. When she softened, he hardened. Again.

Then he released his hold. "That's where you're wrong, Lynn Harmony. The second you crossed into my territory, the very moment you asked for my help, that's exactly what you became."

"What?" she asked, sounding breathless now.

"*Mine.*"

Dylan Patrick

New York Times and *USA Today* bestselling author REBECCA ZANETTI has worked as an art curator, Senate aide, lawyer, college professor, and a hearing examiner—only to culminate it all in stories about alpha males and the women who claim them. She writes contemporary romances, dark paranormal romances, and romantic suspense novels.

Growing up amid the glorious backdrops and winter wonderlands of the Pacific Northwest has given Rebecca fantastic scenery and adventures to weave into her stories. She resides in the wild north with her husband, children, and extended family who inspire her every day—or at the very least give her plenty of characters to write about.

Please visit Rebecca at: www.rebeccazanetti.com/
www.facebook.com/RebeccaZanetti.Author.FanPage
twitter.com/RebeccaZanetti

He remembers all
her secrets . . .

TWISTED

USA Today Bestselling Author

REBECCA
ZANETTI

"Paranormal romance at its best!"—Cynthia Eden

POWER AND PLEASURE GO HAND IN HAND . . .

SHADOWED

USA Today Bestselling Author

REBECCA ZANETTI

"If you want hot, sexy, dangerous romance… this series is for you."
— Paranormal Haven

The wildest ride yet…

USA Today Bestselling Author

REBECCA ZANETTI

TAMED

One night can change
everything...even fate.

"If you want hot, sexy, dangerous
romance...this series is for you."
—Paranormal Haven

New York Times Bestselling Author

REBECCA
ZANETTI

MARKED

REBECCA ZANETTI

WICKED
RIDE

DARK PROTECTORS

THE WITCH ENFORCERS

Printed in the United States
by Baker & Taylor Publisher Services